KT-154-619

CONTENTS

Note on Illustrations

The drawings are by Vilhelm Pedersen, with the
exception of those for the last four tales which are
by Lorenz Frølich

INTRODUCTION

THE story goes that when Andersen, in his honoured last years, was shown the plan for his projected national statue—a design which included a crowding cluster of children—he angrily protested. 'I pointed out', he wrote in his diary, 'that . . . I could not bear anyone behind me, nor had I children on my back, on my lap, or between my legs when I read; that my fairy tales were as much for older people as for children . . . The naïve was only a part of my fairy tales; humour was the real salt in them.' The children, as anyone may see who visits the King's Garden at Copenhagen, were removed. The point of Andersen's complaint, as anyone may see who goes to the stories, remains. But it is a truth that needs rediscovering.

For indeed, during his lifetime, Andersen's tremendous reputation both in Europe and America came not only from children but from the numbers of men and women who had read and savoured the tales. That at first he would have preferred to be known for his 'adult' novels and plays is neither here nor there; authors commonly have these foibles. It is true that the earliest collections—little paperback books of two, three, or four stories, thrown off between Andersen's more considered works—were published as *Fairy Tales told to the Young* (*Eventyr fortalte for Børn*). But after a few years (and 23 stories) the qualifying description was dropped. He had put it in, he declared, as a safeguard against the critics: a defence too, no doubt, against something that he unwillingly recognized in himself. The actor in Andersen—the poor boy who was finding success at last—desired to play the part of an adult in an adult world. But to write at the level of genius for the young, it is necessary *not* to be a lover of children but to have a rigid streak of childhood in oneself. This, Andersen had. It was to be throughout his life his talisman and his bane.

The first of the little story-books appeared in 1835. It contained four tales: *The Tinderbox, Little Claus and Big Claus, The Princess and the Pea,* and *Little Ida's Flowers.* The familiar first two of these were folk themes, though recast with new detail, and told in an unmistakable new voice. The third, like the others, he had heard as a child, from spinning or hop-picking women. But the fourth heralds the genuine new storymaker, in the student who entertains little Ida with paper figures and quaint stories, in the offended doll, turned out of its bed for the exhausted flowers, in the chimney-sweep toy who danced alone ('and that's no bad thing either'), and the spirited flower funeral conducted by Ida's two boy cousins, in the chattering bits and pieces. To present modern life through kitchen articles and nursery toys and yet with adult irony and wit was something new in fiction. That student, too, so apt with stories and paper toys, is our first glimpse of Andersen himself. In one guise or another, sometimes for only a fleeting moment, he may be found in almost all his tales. They are his own living story.

The second volume followed soon, in 1836, with *Thumbelina, The Naughty Boy,* and *The Travelling Companion;* the third, in 1837, with *The Little Mermaid* and *The Emperor's New Clothes.* It was the *Mermaid,* again an original tale, that really brought wide public attention to these extraordinary little volumes. Encouragement was all that Andersen wanted, and his invention flowed. Soon he had no need to go to old plots: every flower, every household article had its story to offer him. By his own reckoning—a conservative one—there were 156 tales by the end of his life.

A sparkling narrative confidence marks the stories but behind them is a strange and troubling figure. Andersen's *Autobiography* offers clues to much that he wrote—yet it seems to separate him all the more from his own achievement. 'My life', it begins with characteristic verve, 'is a beautiful fairy tale.' A fairy tale it certainly was, but one with an oddly malicious twist. Our wishes, it seems to demonstrate, are fulfilled more often than we expect, but not always in the way we desire. There is always a price to be paid. Here, to be sure, is the humble shoemaker's solitary child, dreaming, declaiming, playing with his home-made toy theatre, presenting to the village world the kind of preposterous innocence that turns away blows; here again the awkward, crazy-looking, stage-struck boy setting out at fourteen to seek his improbable fortune in the city of Copenhagen; singing, pleading, and clowning his way into the theatre and out of it, always avoiding being pinned down to his station by a trade; catching the half-hypnotized aid of patron after patron—scholars, State Councillors, ballet dancers, the King himself; sent to school at seventeen (the severest trial of all) as a State protégé, and after every kind of hardship and humiliation becoming (though not, alas, through his singing, dancing, or plays) Denmark's most illustrious son, an honoured guest in every country of Europe.

But the dark side of the story can be traced back, no less than the other, as far as the one-roomed Odense home where Andersen was born in 1805. His father, perforce a shoemaker, married in his early twenties and dead hardly a dozen years later, was a man of incipient gifts, a self-taught student, political rebel and freethinker, full of ideas, but deeply frustrated by poverty and imprisoning circumstance. It was he who built Hans Christian his toy theatre, took him on Sundays into the woods (where, under his guidance, the boy observed the creatures and grasses with a meticulous regard, each with a life of its own), and bid him in effect, rather as if telling himself, not to submit to any ordered rôle that was against his natural bent. Restlessness and poverty drove the shoemaker to volunteer as a solider in 1812; he returned a sick man, half out of his mind, and died in 1816 when his son was eleven. The mother, on the other hand, many years older than her husband, was a simple rough peasant woman, religious and superstitious. (The story *She was Good for Nothing* is a tribute to her memory.) An earlier daughter of hers, an illegitimate half-sister to Hans, received none of the devoted and sheltering affection which was the little boy's lot. Boarded out as a child and for a time a prostitute in later life, she was to haunt the easily stirred imagination of her brother, and embarrass him considerably when she did appear. The Andersen grandparents also had their part in the boy's early life. There was a dear grandmother, a kind and neat old lady who worked as gardener at the local asylum for the insane poor. But the grandfather was wandering in his wits; and when Hans Christian saw him being hooted at and pursued by boys in the Odense streets, he was filled with terror. 'I knew', he wrote, 'that I was of his flesh and blood.'

In Andersen's genius, though, these two conflicting strains were necessary. If his inventive genius and imagination came from his father, so too did his melancholy, his restlessness, and his emotional instability. If his mother passed on her superstitions, she also gave him his dogged peasant endurance, his obstinate ability to survive: certainly, too, his respect for those in high places. Well—he hadn't much use for bishops and other church dignitaries, but he dearly loved a king. In any case, without the faith and the force he could not have survived at all.

The school examinations were finally passed, and Andersen's guardians allowed him to choose his road. He chose to write. Indeed, his poems and novels gave him a fair reputation from the start. But the harsh years were to have their effect, and once the battle for recognition was over, neuroses crowded in. He suffered increasingly from fears and anxieties about money, about madness, about his half-sister, about losing his passport (remember the rat in *The Steadfast Tin Soldier*), about missing the times of coaches or, presently, railway trains. He developed a compulsive taste for travel; 'to travel', he wrote, 'is to live'. Staying in hotels or furnished rooms, or the great houses of wealthy friends, he was over sixty before he owned a bed. He was fêted and welcomed all over the world; but until his honoured final years, he never really impressed the people at home, the Danes, who knew his start.

The flaw in Andersen's personal fairy tale was the human one. The simple lad in the folk tale prospers through a kind of inspired idiocy; he does not grieve or toil, and Andersen did both. The clown's resilience of temper, the absence of offended dignity—though it did not save Andersen from bad dreams of the past when life was easier—was to protect him in the hard days of his youth. It was something that Chatterton, in similar circumstances but with a more rigid temperament, entirely lacked; unable to be the clown he had to play the tragic part. Andersen paid a different price. As a child in a world of adults, he could thrive. But this very childlike quality that opened the doors of patrons was a bar to adult relationships. Women were his kindest counsellors and friends, yet, since he failed to approach them as adult to adult, he remained through life alone. Perhaps it is best that we do not know too much when we are young about the tellers of our tales; that the scholarly brothers Grimm should remain as two troll-like figures, and Andersen not as a person but as a book.

For in the stories, all these elements in Andersen's temper have a fit and proper place. The human uncertainty is the great distinction between the tales of Andersen and the traditional tales of Grimm. In the folk narrative, everyone's path is prescribed; you cannot distinguish between witch and witch, prince and prince, goosegirl and yellow-haired goosegirl. In Andersen, not only the people have an individual human quality but the silly household objects themselves. Browning once wrote to a novelist friend: 'Even two potatoes are *unlike*—but two *men*, Isa!' No two potatoes are alike in Andersen's tales.

Once he had realized the range and power of his new invented genre, he did not have to look far for ideas. Inspiration was everywhere. 'The stories lay there like seeds', he wrote; 'all that was necessary for them to spring into bloom was a breath of air, a ray of sunshine, or a drop of wormwood.' And joys and pangs came readily enough to the mercurial creature. The stories were, of course, his own magical weapon, his personal answer to life—an answer that is usually irresistible. Pride will be humbled; the humble will have redress—this is a constant theme. *The Ugly Duckling* has long since become its classic allegory, and numerous kitchen and nursery pieces echo the moral. *The Travelling-Companion* assures us that a kindness done will bring its reward. *The Snow Queen* and *The Wild Swans* stress the power of innocence. All men, all creatures must serve the flower-like Gerda; the very toads turn into flowers at Elise's touch. Quality will out is another characteristic moral—the commonness of the princess, say, and the princeliness of the swineherd. Several tales, such as *The Steadfast Tin-Soldier*, are about endurance. But nearest of all to his own story is the theme that every wish has its price. *The Little Mermaid* (a major story marred by an unfair theological bias which the author's father would have deplored) is its most piercing version, but you can find it at a lighter level in *The Galoshes of Fortune*. Fortune sends a lady-in-waiting to do her business, but Sorrow carries out her errands herself to see that they are done properly. And when Fortune's galoshes have proved their point, Sorrow appropriates them, for they seem to be hers after all. A nice conclusion.

But the art must carry the thought: and behind the careful simplicity the art in Andersen's tales is considerable. Even in translation you can recognize his ear for dialogue; his remarkable narrative manner based on the living rhythm of speech; the gratuitous detail (a trait he shares with Dickens); the sly, flat, straightfaced comment which was so inimitably his own. The betrothed dolls received presents, 'but they had declined to accept provisions of any kind, for they intended to live on love.' 'That was a charming story', says the Queen in *The Flying Trunk*. 'You shall certainly have our daughter.' 'Yes, indeed,' adds the

King. 'You shall have her on Monday.' The broom takes some parsley from the dustbin to crown the story-telling pot 'for he knew that it would annoy the others'. Moreover, 'If I crown her today,' he thought, 'she will have to crown me tomorrow.' The Snow Queen promises Kay, if he does the task she has set, the whole world and a new pair of skates. The earth is there as well as the sky, the kitchen as well as the palace. Nothing, however marvellous, is quite beyond human touch.

It is in the tales about objects—the house or kitchen or garden pieces—that Andersen's peculiar genius is most evident: his charm, dry humour, economy, and crystal-clear, almost microscopic vision. Each kitchen, parlour, or nursery is a society in miniature; in the homely bric-à-brac, the clocks, tongs, toys, pins, and kitchen rubbish, every social and professional nuance is displayed. Consider the Darning-needle as it lies in the gutter. 'I am too fine for this world', it reflects. 'But I know my own worth, and there is always a satisfaction in that.'

One day something glittering lay close by its side, the the Needle thought it was a Diamond, though it was nothing but a Piece of Glass; but because it glittered the Needle addressed it, and introduced itself as a Breast-pin. 'You are a Diamond, I suppose?' 'Yes, I am something of that sort!' So each believed the other to be something very valuable, and they complained of the vanity of the world.

Or take this account of the toys having an evening's entertainment. The Money-pig (or Piggy-bank) looks down upon them all. 'It knew very well that what it had in its stomach would have bought all the toys, and that's what we call having self-respect.'

The moon shone through the window-frames and gave

free light. Now the fun was about to begin and all of them, even the children's Go-Cart, which certainly belonged to the coarser playthings, were invited to take part in the sport.

'Each one has his own peculiar value,' said the Go-Cart. 'We cannot all be noblemen. There must be some who do the work, as the saying is.'

The Money-pig was the only one who received a written invitation, for he was of high standing, and they were afraid he would not accept a verbal message. Indeed, he did not answer . . . nor did he come: if he was to take a part, he must do so from his own home; they were to arrange accordingly, and so they did.

. . . There was to be a tea party and a discussion for mental improvement, and with this latter part they began immediately. The Rocking Horse spoke of training and Race, and the Go-Cart of railways and steam power . . . The Clock talked politics—ticks—tocks . . . though it was whispered that he did not go correctly; the Bamboo Cane stood there, stiff and proud, for he was conceited about his brass ferule and his silver top, for being thus bound above and below; and on the sofa lay two worked Cushions, pretty and stupid . . . Each one thought of himself and of what the Money-pig might think . . .

That last sentence, like the Piece of Glass's evasive reply, is quite masterly. Another such scene may be found in the interlude-story in *The Flying Trunk*. A further outstanding example is in *The Goblin at the Provision-Dealer's*, a wonderful short story by any standards. The goblin, a simple creature, full of respect for the grocer, finds itself having to decide between the merits of poetry (the student's diet) and the grocer's delicious porridge. The reader must look to see exactly how Andersen presents these notions and the goblin's final choice.

But something else will presently strike the reader; it is that, in so many of the tales, the creative process seems to have been identical with that of poetry; like a poem, the Andersen story can be read again and again. This quality, which applies to the miniature comedies no less than the splendid pieces like the *Garden of Paradise* with its ranging landscapes, or *The Snow Queen*, or *The Wind Tells of Valdemar Daae and his Daughters*, is something quite distinct from the poetic mood which runs through the prose of these longer tales. It is worth noting that the *Valdemar Daae* story was revised many times to catch in words the exact sound of the rushing wind that tells the tale.

'I blew through the great gateway like a watchman blowing on his horn, but there was no watchman there,' said the wind, 'I turned the weathercock on the spire and it creaked and groaned as if the watchman were snoring in the turret, but there was no watchman there either: there were rats and mice: poverty laid the table, poverty sat in the wardrobe and the pantry, the door came off its hinges, cracks and crevices appeared; I went in and out,' said the wind, 'so I knew all that was going on . . . I was the only one that sang loudly in that castle . . . Whew-oo-oo! Away, away!

The Snow Queen is surely the high point of Andersen's achievement. This is not only because of the poetic construction—the crystallizing, you might say, of each episode: the dreams rushing past on the stairs, the night in the robber castle; the self-absorbed flowers telling their stories, Kay's great ride with the Queen. Nor is it only for the truly magnificent descriptions, scene after scene: summer and autumn, hut and castle, the whole vast sweep of winter—scenes which nobody who has read the story can ever really forget. But it is also one of the most effective of the tales in human terms. Take, for instance, the pretty, vain flowers, each absorbed only in its own story when Gerda seeks for help. Or the relationship of the schoolboy Kay and the Queen.

'And now you get no more kisses!' she said. 'Or else I shall kiss you to death.'

Kay looked at her: she was very beautiful; a wiser, lovelier face he could not imagine; now she no longer seemed made of ice as she had done when she sat outside the window and beckoned to him—in his eyes she was perfect. He felt no fear at all: he told her he could do mental arithmetic, even with fractions, and work out how many square miles there were in the country and how many people lived there. She smiled all the time. Then he realized that he knew very little indeed . . .

Andersen may often choose to write of toys—life, you might say, at one or two removes: but no 'adult' novelist could have improved on this.

The Snow Queen also belongs to the great line of quest-stories—a perilous journey through seasons and wonders to what seems the very end of the world. How many of us notice that it is the one great fairy tale where all the main characters (eight or more of them) are girls or women, while the victim who must be saved is a boy? Did Andersen realize this himself? By his own account, the whole long work was written at incredible speed—the pace of inspiration rather than worked-out thought. By contrast, other tales (*The Ugly Ducking*, say) took months to write.

Andersen lived at the junction of two worlds, old and new. Stage coach travel, witch-doctoring, and public executions were part of his youth; he was to welcome the railway and other scientific marvels. All new inventions extended his world of magic. He could evoke the past with a haunting insistence, the beauty and gravity of old fine things that have lived on into brisker modern days. *The Old House* (Dickens's favourite tale) is a very good instance of this. But there were evil and terrible aspects of the feudal past that he would not romanticize. *The Bishop of Børglum and his Kinsman,* a powerful story that affects one like the beating of drums, was written to stress the darkness of a cruel, priest-ruled age in Denmark's history. 'Blessed be the times we live in!' is the closing note.

The real originality of Andersen's *Eventyr*—the fairy tale form as presenter of life in miniature—can hardly be realized today. It contains whatever there was of lost dramatist, novelist, poet in the storyteller. A note in Andersen's diary runs: 'I am like water, in which everything is mirrored. Often it gives me joy and blessings, but at times it is my torment. What a strange being I am!' The thought has a curious echo of Keats, who saw the poet as the man without identity of his own but sensitive to all experiences. In what might seem his toy theatre, Andersen carries, indeed, as much of human life as you would wish to find. What he will give you, if you only put out your hand for it, is just what the Snow Queen promised Kay, no more or less: the whole world, together with a new pair of skates.

NAOMI LEWIS

TRANSLATOR'S NOTE

THE first of the fortuitous steps that led to these translations from Hans Andersen took place over sixty years ago now when I received my first school prize from Mr R. C. Keates, to whom, in 1959, the first edition of this volume was offered as a mark of my early respect and affection, and to whose still honoured memory as a warm-hearted and kindly teacher I would rededicate these tales.

The book he gave me was a copy of the *Fairy Tales*, much read and loved at the time, but later left to many years of honoured retirement on my bookshelves, until, some thirty years later, returning from a year's teaching in Denmark with a fair knowledge of the language and two or three volumes of Andersen, I searched out the old book once again to save labour with the dictionary. I had been persuaded to try my own hand at Andersen since the reading of the original text soon brought me to realize how much of Hans Andersen the English readers of that time had lost. Odd mistranslations might cause one to wince but could be dismissed as unimportant; a certain Victorian prudery, which misrepresented the parish clerk in *Little Claus and Big Claus* as the cousin of the farmer's wife and so deprived the farmer of all reasonable excuse for not being able to 'stand the sight of a parish clerk', might be smiled at and forgiven; but it was not so easy to swallow the odd twist given to the end of *The Emperor's New Clothes* and depriving the situation of its humour, and above all, it was impossible to accept the stilted and pretentious style which had throughout done so much injustice to the simplicity of the original. The pity of it was that the pomposity and elaboration of these old translations, long shrouded in a veil of anonymity, continued to appear, with few variations, Christmas after Christmas, as children's books, their publishers paying little or no heed to Andersen's text and content only to produce another picture-book.

As far as I know, this depressing series was first broken in the early 1930's when M. R. James translated forty-two of the tales almost word for word, sacrificing his English, and sometimes his sense, for the sake of complete literalness. One or two much more successful attempts, notably by Keigwin, had already been made to do Andersen justice in English at the time of my translation, and several more have appeared since, giving one grounds for hoping that the older versions of my own childhood have now disappeared from the booksellers' shelves.

In writing this translation it was my twofold object to preserve, as far as I could, the spirit of Andersen's homely style and whimsical humour, and to present him in readable and simple English. I adhered as closely as this would allow to the original and spared no pains to make my translation an accurate one. It was no easy matter to make a restricted selection from the 160 tales, much as they vary in quality: I endeavoured to include among the tales every reader would expect to see some not so well known in this country.

The illustrations are those of the original Danish editions. The earliest and best known of Andersen's illustrators was Vilhelm Pedersen, chosen by Andersen himself, and felt to be as much a part of the text as Phiz is of Dickens or E. H. Shepard of *Winnie the Pooh*.

TRANSLATOR'S NOTE

No changes have been made in the text of the 1959 edition, which preserved wherever possible Andersen's own punctuation, with its somewhat lavish use of exclamation marks, colons and semi colons, in order to suggest more clearly the colour of the original.

Grimsby
1984

SELECT BIBLIOGRAPHY

TRANSLATIONS

ANDERSEN'S first booklet of (4) tales—*Eventyr fortalte for Børn*—was published in 1835. Further small groups of tales, generally two, three, or four to a book, appeared each year for the rest of his working life: last date, 1872. The total, by Andersen's own count, was 156.

The first English translation of the tales appeared in 1846. This was Mary Howitt's (10 stories), soon followed by Caroline Peachey's (14 tales—eventually increased to 61 in later editions), Charles Boner's (12 tales), then by Mme de Chatelain's in 1852 (45 tales), Alfred Wehnert's in 1861 (42 tales), H. W. Dulcken's in 1864 (62 tales)—and others. Today all are severely criticized for inaccuracies, misreadings, bowdlerizing, and for failing to reproduce the vivid colloquial immediacy of the original. Yet these versions lived on well into our own century; indeed, long out of copyright, and almost always unacknowledged, they are still found in use today. As a result, Andersen is far too often thought of as a writer only for children, moralistic, humourless even. Moreover, the predominance of the first fifty or sixty tales (repeated again and again in the different versions) prevented any knowledge of the more adult later stories. Edmund Gosse, when visiting Andersen in 1872, was anxious to translate the unknown section, but because of the inevitable piracy in that pre-copyright period, no London publisher would take the risk. The first complete version (155 tales), published in 1914 by the Oxford University Press, was partly from

Dulcken, and completed by Mrs Craigie. It is a landmark, but has long been unavailable (and, alas, outdated).

One translator of quality stands out in the 19th century—R. Nisbet Bain, whose *Little Mermaid and Other Stories* of 1893 (27 tales) also contains a Preface discussing the previous translations. With this exception, it is fair to say that a more scrupulous attitude to translation is found mainly within the past 50 years or so of our own century. Although no standard version can be said to exist, all those listed below bring the original Andersen nearer to the reader (Leyssac, and still more Keigwin, have always been particularly valued): M. R. James (Faber, 1930)—40 stories; Paul Leyssac (Macmillan, 1937)—28 stories; R. P. Keigwin, 4 vols. (Edmund Ward, 1951, 1955, 1958, 1960)—84 stories; L. W. Kingsland (Oxford, 1959, 1961)—40 stories; Erik Christian Haugaard, *The Complete Fairy Tales and Stories*, foreword by Naomi Lewis (Gollancz, 1974); Naomi Lewis, 12 stories with Introduction and notes (Penguin, 1981). New translations by Brian Alderson of a number of Andersen's stories are in Alderson's revised Colour Fairy Books of Lang (Kestrel).

For a detailed analysis of Andersen translation into English, Brian Anderson's 48-page bibliographical commentary *Hans Christian Andersen and his Eventyr in England* (1982), a work astringent, informed, and refreshing, is essential reading (published for the International Board on Books for Young People by The Five Owls Press).

CRITICISM AND BIOGRAPHY

Though a formidable critical literature on Hans Christian Andersen exists in Denmark (some too in other European countries and America) as well as scholarly editions of his letters, journals and other documents, very little indeed has been published here, whether original work or in translation. Essays, prefaces, monographs, yes, but no full length studies, at least at the present date. Among the sources for shorter pieces (see Introductions to translations etc.) one is very well worth finding—the Andersen number of Adam International Review for 1955, Andersen's 150th anniversary year. This contains notable essays by Auden, by the great collector Dr Klein, and by the paper's editor, Miron Grindea, with other fascinating material from unexpected names.

Biography is a separate matter. Apart from two or three short books written specifically for children, we have had, in fairly recent years, two useful full-length biographical studies: *The Wild Swan* by Monica Stirling (1965), and *Hans Christian Andersen* by Elias Bredsdorff (1973). Bredsdorff, perhaps our principal link today with modern Danish work on Andersen, has made good use of this in his informative book. His bibliography too is rewarding, giving many clues to determined searchers.

Several translations exist of Andersen's autobiography (usually called *The Fairy Tale of My Life*) the latest two in 1954 and 1975. He wrote (or revised) a number of versions in his lifetime, one as early as 1832. They do not show the writer at his best, but are valuable for the anecdotal sources of many of the tales. The tales are, of course, also an autobiography in themselves.

THE TINDER-BOX

A SOLDIER came marching down the road—left, right! left, right! He had his pack upon his back and a sword by his side, for he had been to the wars and was now on his way home. On the road he met an old witch: she was so ugly her nether-lip hung right down upon her breast. 'Good evening, soldier!' she said. 'That's a fine sword you've got there, and a great pack, too—you look a proper soldier, if ever there was one! And now, if you do as I say, you shall have as much money as you like!'

'Thanks very much, old witch!' said the soldier.

'Do you see that big tree?' said the witch, as she pointed to the tree that was standing by their side. 'It's quite hollow inside. Climb up to the top of the trunk and you'll see a hole you can slip through. Then you can drop right down into the tree. I'll tie

1

a cord round your waist so that I can hoist you up again when you shout for me!'

'What have I got to do when I'm down in the tree?' asked the soldier.

'Fetch the money!' said the witch. 'When you get down to the bottom of the tree, you'll find yourself in a large passage. It's quite light, for there are more than a hundred lamps burning there. Then you'll see three doors: you can open them because the keys are in the locks. Go into the first room and you'll see in the middle of the floor a big chest with a dog sitting on it. He's got a pair of eyes as big as tea-cups—but don't let that worry you! I'll give you my blue-checked apron: you can spread it out on the floor, go boldly up to the dog, take hold of him and set him down on my apron. Then open the chest and take out as much money as you like. It's all coppers; but if you'd rather have silver, you'll have to go into the next room. The dog that sits there has a pair of eyes each as big as a millstone, but don't let that worry you—put him on my apron and help yourself to the money! If you want gold, however, you can get that, too—and as much as you can carry—when you go into the third room. But the dog that sits on the money-chest there has two eyes each as big as the Round Tower in Copenhagen. He's a real dog, you can take it from me! But don't you worry about that! Just put him down on my apron and he'll do you no harm. And then you can take as much gold as you like from the chest!'

'That doesn't sound so bad!' said the soldier. 'But what have I got to give you, old witch? I'm pretty certain you want something out of it!'

'No,' said the witch, 'not a single penny do I

2

want! All you have to do is to fetch me an old tinder-box my grandmother left behind the last time she was down there!'

'Well, let me get the cord round my waist!' said the soldier.

'Here it is!' said the witch. 'And here's my blue-checked apron!'

So the soldier climbed up the tree and dropped down the hole. There he stood, just as the witch had told him, down below in a large passage where hundreds of lamps were burning.

Then he unlocked the first door. Ooh!—There sat the dog with eyes as big as tea-cups glaring at him.

'Nice dog! Good boy!' said the soldier. He put him on the witch's apron and took as many coppers as he could carry in his pockets: then he shut the chest, put the dog back again and went into the second room. Whew!—There sat the dog with eyes as big as millstones!

'You shouldn't look at me so hard!' said the soldier. 'You might get eyestrain!' And so he put the dog on the witch's apron, but when he saw the mass of silver coins in the chest, he threw away all the coppers he had taken, and filled his pockets and his pack with nothing but silver. Then he went into the third room! Oh, it was terrible! The dog there really did have two eyes each as big as the Round Tower —and they were turning round in his head just like wheels!

'Good evening!' said the soldier and touched his cap, for he had never seen a dog like that before. But when he had looked at him a bit, he thought he had better get a move on, so he lifted him on to the floor and opened the chest. Heavens above, what masses of gold there were! With that he could buy the whole of Copenhagen, and all the sugar-pigs, tin-soldiers, whips, and rocking-horses in the world as well! That was something like money! And now the soldier threw away all the silver coins he had filled his pockets and his pack with, and took the gold instead—yes, he filled all his pockets, his pack, his cap, and his boots so that he could hardly walk! He had money enough now! He put the dog back on the chest, slammed the door to, and shouted up the tree, 'Haul me up now, old witch!'

'Have you got the tinder-box?' asked the witch.

''Strewth!' said the soldier. 'I've clean forgotten it!' Then he went and fetched it. The witch hauled him up, and so he stood upon the road once more with pockets, boots, pack, and cap all crammed full of money.

'What do you want with that tinder-box?' asked the soldier.

'That's nothing to do with you!' said the witch. 'You've got your money—now give me my tinder-box!'

'Rubbish!' said the soldier. 'Either tell me right now what you want with it, or I'll draw my sword and hack your head off!'

'No, I won't!' said the witch.

So the soldier cut her head off. And there she lay. Then he tied all his money up in her apron, heaved the bundle on to his back, put the tinder-box in his pocket, and marched straight off to the town.

It was a fine town, and he took himself into the finest inn, where he booked the very best rooms, and ordered all the things he liked best to eat, for he was rich now with all that money.

The boot-boy who took his boots to clean thought it decidedly odd that such a rich gentleman should have such an old pair. He had not yet bought himself new ones, but the next day he got new boots and fine new clothes to wear! The soldier had now become a gentleman of note, and people told him about all the fine things to be found in their town, and about their king, and what a lovely princess his daughter was.

'How can you get to see her?' asked the soldier.

'It's quite impossible to get to see her!' everybody said. 'She lives in a great castle made of copper, with ever so many walls and towers round it! No one but the king dare go in and out to her, because it's been foretold that she'll marry an ordinary common soldier, and the king doesn't like the idea at all!'

'I'd very much like to see her!' thought the soldier, but that was something he would certainly never get leave to do!

He was living a life of pleasure now, going to plays, riding in the royal gardens, and giving a great deal of money to the poor—and that was noble of him! He knew well enough from the old days how wretched it can be not to own a penny! He was rich now, he had fine clothes, and he made very many friends who all said he was a rare fellow, a proper gentleman—and that pleased the soldier greatly! But since he was spending his money every day and not getting a penny to replace it, he was left at last with no more than two shillings, and he had to move from the beautiful rooms where he had been living up to a narrow little attic right under the roof. He had to brush his own boots and mend them with a darning-needle, and none of his friends would come to visit him because there were far too many stairs to go up.

It was quite dark in the evening, and he could

not even buy himself a candle, but then he remembered that there was a little stump in the tinder-box he had taken from the hollow tree the witch had helped him to go down. He got the tinder-box and took out the candle-end, but just as he was striking a light and the sparks were flying from the flint, the door sprang open, and the dog with eyes as big as tea-cups, which he had seen down under the tree, stood before him and said, 'What are my master's commands?'

'What on earth!' said the soldier. 'This tinder-box is certainly something, if I can get what I want like this! Fetch me some money!' he said to the dog. He was off in a flash. In another flash he was back again, holding a big bag full of coppers in his mouth!

The soldier now knew what a delightful tinder-box it was! If he struck once, the dog that sat on the chest of copper coins came; if he struck twice, the one that had the silver coins came; and if he struck three times, the one with the gold came. And now the soldier moved down into his beautiful rooms again and went about in good clothes, and so all his friends recognized him immediately, and they were very fond of him. . . .

Then one day he thought, 'It's a very rum thing, though, that you can't get to see the princess! They all say how lovely she must be! But what's the good of that when she's always shut up in that great copper castle with all those towers! Can't I get to see her somehow? . . . I've got it!—Where's my tinder-box!' And so he struck a light, and in a flash there was the dog with eyes as big as tea-cups!

'I know it's the middle of the night,' said the soldier, 'but I would so love to see the princess, just for a second!'

The dog was outside the door at once, and before the soldier had time to realize it, he saw he was back again with the princess. She was sitting sound asleep on the dog's back, and she was so lovely anyone could see she was a real princess. The soldier could not stop himself—he had to kiss her, for he was a real soldier.

Then the dog ran back again with the princess, but when the morning came and the king and queen were pouring out tea, the princess said she had had such a strange dream during the night about a dog and a soldier. She had ridden on the dog, and the soldier had kissed her.

'That's a fine story, I'm sure!' said the queen.

One of the old ladies-in-waiting now had to keep watch by the princess's bed the next night to see whether it were really a dream or what else it could be.

The soldier longed terribly to see the lovely princess again, and so the dog came during the night, took her and ran off as fast as he could. But the old lady-in-waiting put her wellingtons on, and ran just as hard after him. When she saw them disappear into a large house, she thought, 'Now I know where it is!' And she drew a large cross on the gate with a piece of chalk. Then she went home and lay down, and the dog came back, too, with the princess. But when he saw that a cross had been drawn on the gate where the soldier lived, he took a piece of chalk, too, and marked crosses on all the gates throughout the whole town. And that was a clever thing to do, for now the lady-in-waiting would certainly not be able to find the right gate when there w⸱ ⸱e crosses on all of them.

Early in the morning the king and the queen,

the old lady-in-waiting, and all the officers of the court went to see where it was the princess had been to.

'There it is!' said the king when he saw the first gate with a cross on it.

'No, my dear husband, it's there!' said the queen, who was looking at the second gate with a cross on.

But there's one there—and one there!' they all cried together, and wherever they looked, there were crosses on the gates. Then they could see it was not any use trying to find it.

Now the queen was a very clever woman, who could do other things besides riding in a coach. She took her big pair of gold scissors, cut out some pieces of silk, and made a pretty little bag from them. She filled it with fine small grains of buckwheat, tied it on the princess's back, and when that was done, she clipped a little hole in the bag so that the grains would be sprinkled all the way along where the princess went.

During the night the dog came again, took the princess on his back, and ran off with her to the soldier, who was so very fond of her and wished so much he had been a prince so that he could have her for his wife.

The dog did not notice the grain sprinkled all along the road from the castle right up to the soldier's window, where he leapt up the wall with the princess. But in the morning the king and queen saw quite clearly where their daughter had been, and so they seized the soldier and threw him into prison.

And there he sat. Oh, how dark and miserable it was—and added to that they said to him, 'To-morrow you must be hanged!' That was not at all funny—and he had left his tinder-box behind at the inn. In the morning he looked between the iron bars of his little window and could see people hurrying out of town to see him hanged. He heard the drums and saw the soldiers marching by. Everybody was off to watch, and among them was a cobbler's boy wearing his leather apron and a pair of slippers. He was trotting along at such a gallop that one of his slippers flew off and landed against the wall where the soldier sat peering out between the iron bars.

'Hi, you cobbler's boy! There's no need to be in such a hurry,' the soldier said to him. 'There won't be anything doing before I get there! Just run along to where I live and fetch me my tinder-box, and I'll give you a shilling! But you must make good use of your legs!' The cobbler's boy was anxious to have his shilling and scurried off after the tinder-box. He gave it to the soldier—and now we shall hear what happened!

Outside the town a great gallows had been built, and all round it stood the soldiers and hundreds of thousands of people. The king and queen were sitting on a beautiful throne immediately opposite the judge and the whole Council.

The soldier had already mounted the ladder, but just as they were going to fasten the rope about his neck, he said that a wrong-doer was always granted a harmless request before he underwent his punishment. He would dearly love to smoke a pipe of tobacco—it would be his last pipe in this world.

Now the king could not say no to that, and so the soldier took his tinder-box and struck a light—one, two, three! And there stood all the dogs, the one with eyes as big as tea-cups, the one with eyes like millstones, and the one that had eyes as big as the Round Tower!

'Now help me, so that I shan't be hanged!' said the soldier, and so the dogs pounced upon the judge and the whole Council, took one by the legs and one by the nose, and hurled them many fathoms up in the air so that when they fell down they were smashed to pieces.

'I will not . . . !' said the king, but the biggest of the dogs seized both him and the queen, and hurled them up after the rest of them. The soldiers were terrified, and all the people cried out, 'Little soldier, you shall be our king and have our lovely princess!'

So they sat the soldier in the king's coach, and the three dogs all frisked about in front of him and shouted, 'Hurray!' And the boys whistled through their fingers, and the soldiers presented arms. The princess left the copper castle and became queen —she liked that! The wedding lasted a week, and the dogs sat with them at table, their eyes wide with astonishment.

LITTLE CLAUS AND
BIG CLAUS

THERE lived in a village two men with the same
name. Both were called Claus, but one of them
owned four horses, and the other only one. Now
to distinguish them one from the other, the one
who had four horses was called Big Claus, and the
one who had only one Little Claus. And now we
shall hear what happened to them, for this is a true
story!

The whole week through, Little Claus had to
plough for Big Claus and lend him his one horse; in
return Big Claus helped him with all four of his,
but only once a week, and that was on Sundays.
Hurray!—How Little Claus cracked his whip over
all five horses, for they were certainly as good as
his for that one day! The sun was shining beautifully, and all the bells in the church-tower were
ringing for church. As the people of the village, all

11

in their Sunday best, went by with their hymn-books under their arms, on their way to hear the parson preach his sermon, they looked at Little Claus ploughing there with five horses, and he was so delighted he cracked his whip again and again, and shouted, 'Gee-up, there, all my horses!'

'You mustn't say that!' said Big Claus. 'You know quite well only one of them is yours!'

But as soon as someone else went by on his way to church, Little Claus forgot that he mustn't say it, and shouted again, 'Gee-up, there, all my horses!'

'Now,' said Big Claus, 'I must ask you to stop it! If you say that once again, I shall strike your horse over the head. Then he'll fall dead on the spot, and that'll be the end of him!'

'I really won't say it any more!' said Little Claus, but as soon as people went past again and nodded good-day to him, he was so delighted and thought it looked so grand to have five horses to plough his field with, that he cracked his whip once more and shouted, 'Gee-up, there, all my horses!'

'I'll gee your horses up!' said Big Claus, and he took a mallet and struck Little Claus's horse over the forehead so that it fell down quite dead.

'Oh, now I've no horse at all!' said Little Claus, and started crying. Shortly afterwards he flayed his horse, took the hide and let it dry thoroughly in the wind: then he put it in a bag, slung it over his shoulders and trudged off to the town to sell his horsehide.

He had a very long way to go. He had to go through a great dark wood, and the weather had now turned frightful: he lost his way completely, and before he came upon the right road again it was evening, and it was much too far either to go on to the town or to turn back home before it was night.

Close by the roadside there lay a large farm-house. The shutters outside the windows were closed, but a light was shining out over the top of them. 'Perhaps they might let me stay the night here,' thought Little Claus. So he went up to the door and knocked.

The farmer's wife opened the door, but when she heard what he wanted she said he'd better be on his way, her husband was not at home, and she didn't let strangers in.

'Well then, I must find somewhere to lie down outside,' said Little Claus, and the farmer's wife shut the door in his face.

Close by stood a haystack, and between it and the house was built a little shed with a flat thatched roof.

'I can lie down up there!' said Little Claus, as he noticed the roof. 'That'll make a very nice bed, so long as the stork doesn't fly down and nip me in the leg.' For there was a stork standing wide-awake up on the roof, where it had its nest.

Then Little Claus climbed up on to the shed, and there he lay twisting and turning until he was comfortable. The wooden shutters in front of the windows did not meet properly at the top, and so he could see right into the living room.

There was a great table set there, with wine and a roast joint and a lovely fish. The farmer's wife and the parish-clerk were sitting at the table, and there was no one else there at all. She was pouring out for him, and he was tucking into the fish, for that was something he was very fond of.

'I'd like a bit of that, too!' said Little Claus,

13

craning his neck towards the window. My, what lovely cakes he could see down there on the table! It was a regular feast!

Then he heard someone riding along the road towards the house—it was the farmer coming home.

He was a real good-hearted man, but he had one odd weakness—he just couldn't bear to see a parish-clerk. If ever he caught sight of one, he became quite frantic. And so that was why the parish-clerk had come to say good-evening to the farmer's wife while he knew her husband was away from home, and the good woman had set before him all the nicest things she had to eat. Then when they heard her husband coming, they were so terrified that the wife told the parish-clerk to crawl into a big empty chest that stood over in the corner. And that's what he did, for he was well aware that the poor farmer couldn't stand the sight of a parish-clerk. The farmer's wife hastily hid all the lovely food and wine inside her baking-oven, for if her husband caught sight of them, he would undoubtedly ask what it was all about.

'Ah, well!' sighed Little Claus, up on the shed, as he saw all the food put away.

'Is there anyone up there?' asked the farmer, peering up at Little Claus. 'What are you lying up there for? You'd better come in with me!'

So Little Claus told him how he had lost his way, and asked if he could put him up for the night.

'Why, of course!' said the farmer. 'But we must have a bit to eat first!'

The farmer's wife seemed very pleased to see them both, spread a cloth on a long table, and gave them a large basin of porridge. The farmer was hungry and ate with a good appetite, but Little Claus couldn't stop thinking of the lovely roast joint, fish, and cakes he knew were standing inside the oven.

He had put the sack with the horsehide down by his feet under the table, for, you remember, it was to sell this in the town that he had left home that day. He didn't fancy the porridge a bit, and so he trod on the sack and the dry skin inside squeaked quite loudly.

'Sh!' said Little Claus to his sack, but at the same time he trod on it again, and it squeaked much louder than before.

'What's that you've got in your sack?' asked the farmer.

'Oh, that's a wizard!' said Little Claus. 'He says there's no need for us to eat porridge. He's conjured up a whole ovenful of roast beef, fish, and cake.'

'What!' cried the farmer, and had the oven open in a flash. There he saw all the good food his wife had hidden, but of course he believed the wizard in the sack had conjured it up for them. His wife dared not say a word. She set the food on the table at once, and they ate the fish and the roast beef and the cake. Little Claus thereupon trod on the sack again and made the hide squeak.

'What does he say now?' asked the farmer.

'He says,' said Little Claus, 'that he's also conjured up three bottles of wine for us, and they're standing in the oven, too!' And now the farmer's wife had to take out the wine she had hidden, and the farmer drank and grew quite merry: he would dearly love to own a wizard like the one Little Claus had in his sack.

'Can he conjure up the devil, too?' asked the farmer. 'I'd like to see him, for I'm feeling merry now!'

'Yes,' said Little Claus, 'my wizard can do anything I ask him. True, isn't it?' he asked, treading on the sack and making it squeak. 'Did you hear him say, "Of course!"? But the devil looks horrible. I shouldn't ask to see him if I were you!'

16

'Oh, I'm not frightened of him! What does he look like?'

'Why, he'll be the spitting image of a parish-clerk!'

'Ugh!' said the farmer. 'That'd be horrible! I'd better warn you that I just can't stand the sight of a parish-clerk! But now that I know that it's only the devil, I shan't mind so much! I've got my courage back now—but he mustn't come too near me!'

'I'll ask my wizard now,' said Little Claus, treading on his sack and bending his ear down to listen.

'What's he say?'

'He says if you go and open that chest over there in the corner, you'll see the devil skulking inside, but you must keep hold of the lid so that he can't slip out.'

'Will you help me to hold it?' asked the farmer, as he went over to the chest where his wife had hidden the real parish-clerk, who was crouching inside, much afraid.

The farmer lifted up the lid a little way and peeped under it. 'Ugh!' he shrieked, springing backwards. 'You're right! As I caught sight of him, he looked just like our parish-clerk! Oh, it was ghastly!'

They had to have a drink to recover, and then they went on drinking far into the night.

'You must sell me your wizard,' said the farmer. 'Ask whatever you like for him! Tell you what, I'll give you a bushel of money right away!'

'No, I couldn't do that!' said Little Claus. 'Just think how much my wizard can do for me!'

'Ah, I'd dearly love to have him,' said the farmer. And he went on pleading.

17

'Well,' said Little Claus at last, 'since you've been good enough to give me house-room for the night, I don't mind if I do. You shall have the wizard for a bushel of money—but the bushel must be brimfull, mind!'

'That it shall!' said the farmer. 'But you must take the chest away with you. I'll not have it in the house an hour longer—you can never tell but what he's still inside it!'

Little Claus gave the farmer the sack with the dry hide inside it, and got a bushelful of money—top measure, too—in exchange. The farmer also made him a present of a large wheelbarrow to carry away the money and the chest.

'Good-bye!' said Little Claus, as he wheeled off the money and the great chest where the parish-clerk was still crouched.

On the other side of the wood was a deep wide stream, its current running so strongly that one could hardly swim against it. A big new bridge had been built over it, and Little Claus stopped in the middle of it and said quite loudly so that the parish-clerk inside the chest could hear him:

'What on earth do I want with this damn-fool chest? It's so heavy, it might be full of stones! I'm much too tired to push it any farther, so I'll just tip it over into the stream: if it floats down to the house, well and good; if it doesn't, it's all the same to me.'

Then he took hold of the chest with one hand and lifted it a little, as if he were about to push it over into the water.

'No! No! Stop it!' cried the parish-clerk from inside the chest. 'Let me out first!'

'Ooh,' said Little Claus, pretending to be frightened, 'he's still there! I must topple it over into the stream right away and drown him!'

'Oh, no, no!' cried the parish-clerk. 'I'll give you a whole bushelful of money if you'll only stop!'

'Well, that's another matter!' said Little Claus, and opened the chest. The parish-clerk crawled out at once, kicked the empty chest into the water, and went to his house, where he gave Little Claus a whole bushelful of money. With the one he had already got from the farmer, he now had a whole wheelbarrow full!

'Well, I've been pretty well paid for my horse!' he said to himself, when he was home again in his own room, and had tipped out all the money in a great heap in the middle of the floor. 'Won't Big Claus be annoyed when he gets to know how rich I've got from my one horse—but I won't tell him right out just like that!'

Then he sent a boy over to Big Claus to borrow a bushel-measure.

'I wonder what he wants with that!' thought Big Claus, and smeared some tar on the bottom so that a little of whatever was measured in it should stick to it. And it did, too, for when he got his bushel-measure back, there were three new half-crowns sticking to it.

'What on earth!' said Big Claus, and ran straight over to Little Claus. 'Where have you got all that money from?'

'Oh, I got that for my horsehide I sold last night!'

'You got a pretty good price for it, I'll say!' said Big Claus. He ran home, took an axe and struck all four of his horses over the head with it. Then he flayed them and drove into the town with the hides.

19

'Hides! Hides! Who'll buy my hides!' he cried through the streets.

All the cobblers and tanners came running out and asked what he wanted for them.

'A bushel of money each!' said Big Claus.

'Are you mad?' they all said. 'Do you think we have money by the bushel?'

'Hides! Hides! Who'll buy my hides!' he cried again, but to everyone who asked what the hides cost he answered, 'A bushel of money!'

'He's trying to make fools of us,' they all said, and so the cobblers took their straps and the tanners their leather aprons, and they all set about Big Claus.

'Hides! Hides!' they mocked. 'We'll give you a hide all right—one that will spit red! Out of the town with him!' they cried, and Big Claus, thrashed as he had never been before, had to take to his heels for all he was worth.

'All right!' he said when he got home. 'Little Claus shall pay for this! I'll strike him dead!'

But Little Claus's grandmother lay dead in the house: true, she had always been very ill-tempered and unkind to him, but he was still quite sorry. He took the dead woman and laid her in his own warm bed to see if that would bring her back to life again. He would let her stay there all night, while he himself would sit on a chair over in the corner and go to sleep, as he had often done before.

During the night while he was sitting there, the door opened and in came Big Claus with his axe. He knew quite well where Little Claus's bed stood, and so he went straight over to it and struck the dead grandmother over the head, believing, of course, that it was Little Claus.

'There!' he said. 'Now you won't make a fool of me again!' And so he went back home.

'He's a bad wicked man!' said Little Claus. 'He wanted to strike me dead. It's a good thing the old woman was dead already, otherwise he'd have killed her!'

Then he dressed his old grandmother up in her Sunday-best, borrowed a horse from one of the neighbours, harnessed it to the cart, and sat his old grandmother up in the back seat so that she couldn't fall out when he was driving, and then they drove off through the wood. When the sun rose they were outside a large inn, where Little Claus drew up and went in to get something to eat.

The innkeeper was very, very rich: he was a very good man, too, but so quick-tempered you would have thought he was made of pepper and snuff.

'Good morning!' he said to Little Claus. 'You're up very early today in all your best clothes!'

'Yes,' said Little Claus, 'I have to go into town with my old grandmother. She's sitting outside in the cart. I can't get her inside, but would you mind taking her a glass of mead? You must speak fairly loud to her: her hearing's none too good.'

'Righto, I will!' said the innkeeper, and he poured a large glass of mead which he took out to the dead grandmother propped up in the cart.

'Here's a glass of mead from your grandson!' said the innkeeper, but the dead woman said never a word and sat quite still.

'Can't you hear!' bawled the innkeeper as loud as he could. 'Here's a glass of mead from your grandson!'

Once more he shouted the same thing, and then yet again. But as she did not make the slightest movement, he lost his temper and threw the glass right in her face so that the mead ran down her nose and she fell backwards into the cart, for she was only propped up and not fastened in any way.

'Good God!' cried Little Claus, rushing out of the door and seizing the innkeeper by his lapels. 'You've killed my grandmother! Just look at that great hole in her forehead!'

'Oh dear, oh dear, it was an accident!' wailed the innkeeper, beating his hands together. 'It's all because of my bad temper! My dear Little Claus, I'll give you a whole bushel of money and have your grandmother buried as if she were my own, if only you'll say nothing—otherwise they'll have my head off, and that'd be frightful!'

So Little Claus got a whole bushel of money, and the innkeeper buried his old grandmother as if she were his own.

Now when Little Claus got home again with all this money, he sent his lad over to Big Claus right away to ask if he might borrow a bushel-measure.

'What on earth?' said Big Claus. 'Haven't I killed him after all? I must look into this myself!' And so he took the measure over to Little Claus.

'My, where you did you get all this money from?' he asked, opening his eyes wide at the sight of all the money he had come by.

'It was my grandmother you struck dead—not me!' said Little Claus. 'I've just sold her and got a bushel of money for her!'

'That was a good price, I must say!' said Big Claus, and he hurried home, took an axe and struck his own old grandmother dead straight away. He sat her up in a cart, drove into town to where the apothecary lived and asked if he would like to buy a dead body.

'Who is it, and where have you got it from?' asked the apothecary.

'It's my grandmother!' said Big Claus. 'I hit her over the head so that I can get a bushel of money for her!'

'Heaven preserve us!' said the apothecary. 'You can't know what you're saying! For God's sake, don't say things like that or you'll lose your head!' And then he told him plainly what a terribly wicked thing he had done, and what a bad man he was, and how he ought to be punished; whereupon Big Claus was so terrified, he rushed straight out of the apothecary's shop and into his cart, whipped up the horses and made for home. But the apothecary and everybody else thought he was mad, and so they let him go wherever he would.

'You shall pay for this!' said Big Claus, when he was out on the open road. 'Yes, you shall pay for this all right, Little Claus!' And then, as soon as he got home, he took the biggest sack he could find, went over to Little Claus and said, 'Now you've made a fool of me again! First I kill my horses, and then I kill my old grandmother! And it's all your fault! But you shall never make a fool of me again!' And then he took hold of Little Claus round the waist and thrust him into the sack. He heaved him up on his shoulders and cried, 'Now I'm going out to drown you!'

It was quite a long way to go before he came to the stream, and Little Claus was not so light to carry. The road went close by the church, where the organ was playing and the congregation singing. So Big Claus put down the sack with Little

Claus inside close by the church-door. He thought it would be rather nice to go in and listen to a hymn first before he went any farther: Little Claus couldn't possibly get out, and everyone was in church: so in he went.

'Oh, dear! Oh, dear!' sighed Little Claus inside the sack: he turned and he twisted, but it was quite impossible to loosen the string. At that moment an old cattle-drover came along: he had snow-white hair and he leant upon a stout staff. He was driving a whole drove of cows and bulls in front of him, and some of them bumped against the sack where Little Claus sat huddled up, and knocked it over.

'Oh, dear!' sighed Little Claus. 'I'm so young, and I'm on my way to heaven already!'

'And poor old me!' said the cattle-drover. 'I'm so old, and I can't get there yet!'

'Open the sack!' cried Little Claus. 'If you crawl inside and take my place, you'll get to heaven right away!'

'I'd dearly love to!' said the cattle-drover, and opened the sack for Little Claus who scrambled out at once.

'Will you look after the cattle?' said the old man, as he crawled into the sack. Little Claus tied it up, and then went on his way with all the cows and bulls.

A little later Big Claus came out of the church. He heaved the sack upon his shoulders again, and thought it had become much lighter. He was quite right, for the old cattle-drover was scarcely half the weight of Little Claus. 'He feels a lot lighter now—it must be because I listened to that hymn!' So he went on to the stream that ran deep and wide, threw the sack with the old cattle-drover inside over into the water, and shouted after him—he still believed he was Little Claus, of course—'There, now you shan't make a fool of me any more!'

So he turned homewards, but when he came to the cross-roads, he met Little Claus driving his cattle along.

'What on earth!' cried Big Claus. 'Haven't I just drowned you?'

'Yes, of course you have!' said Little Claus. 'You threw me into the river not half an hour ago!'

'But where did you get all those fine cattle from?' asked Big Claus.

'They're sea-cattle!' said Little Claus. 'I must tell you the whole story—but first I must thank you for drowning me, for I'm well off now: I'm really rich, believe me!—I was very frightened when I was in that sack, and the wind whistled in my ears as you threw me over the bridge into the cold water. I sank at once to the bottom, but I didn't hurt myself, for it was covered in fine soft grass. I landed on this, and the sack was opened at once, and the loveliest young lady in a snow-white dress with a green wreath on her wet hair took me by the hand and said, "So it's you, Little Claus? First of all, here are some cattle for you! And five or six miles along the road, there's another drove waiting—and I'm going to make you a present of them, too!" Then I saw that the river was like a main road for the sea-folk: down there on the river-bed they were walking and riding all the way from the sea right up into the land where the stream comes to an end. It was lovely down there, with flowers and fresh grass and fishes swimming in the water and playing round my ears, just like birds in the sky. They were such nice-looking people there, and you should have seen the cattle walking along by the ditches and fences!'

'But why have you come up here again so soon?' asked Big Claus. 'I shouldn't have, if it was so nice down there!'

'Well,' said Little Claus, 'that's just my artfulness! You remember I told you the sea-lady said that five or six miles up the road—and by road she meant the river, of course, because she can't go anywhere else—there's another whole drove of cattle waiting for me? But you know how the river twists and turns, now this way, now that, taking you a long way out of your way. If you can do it, it's much shorter to cut across the land and join the river again higher up. I shall save about half the journey that way, and get to my sea-cattle all the more quickly!'

'What a lucky fellow you are!' said Big Claus. 'Do you think I should get some sea-cattle if I went down to the bed of the river?'

'Yes, I should think so!' said Little Claus. 'But I can't carry you in a sack all the way to the river. You're too heavy for me. But if you like to walk there by yourself and then crawl into the sack, I'll throw you into the water with the greatest pleasure!'

'Thank you very much!' said Big Claus. 'But, mind, if I don't get any sea-cattle when I get down there, I'll give you a good hiding, you trust me!'

'Oh, please, you wouldn't be so unkind!' And so they walked along to the river. As soon as the cattle, who were thirsty, saw the water, they ran as hard as they could so that they could go down and drink.

'Look at the hurry they're in!' said Little Claus. 'They're longing to get down on the river-bed again!'

'Yes, but you must help me first!' said Big Claus. 'Or else you'll get that hiding!' And so he crawled into a big sack which they had found lying across the back of one of the bulls. 'Put a stone in, else I'm afraid I shan't sink!' said Big Claus.

'You'll do that all right!' said Little Claus, but he put a big stone in the sack all the same, tied the string tight, and then gave it a good push. Splash! Over went Big Claus into the river and he sank down to the bottom at once.

'I'm afraid he won't find his sea-cattle!' said Little Claus, as he made his way home with what he had got.

THE PRINCESS AND THE PEA

THERE was once a prince who wanted to marry a
princess. But she had to be a real princess. So he
travelled all round the world to find one, but there
was always something wrong—there were plenty
of princesses, though whether they were real princesses he could never quite find out: there was
always something that was not just right. So he
came home again and was very unhappy because
he wanted so much to have a real princess.

One evening there was a dreadful storm: it thundered and lightened and the rain poured down in
torrents—it was really quite frightening! Then
there came a knock at the town-gate, and the old
king went out and opened it.

It was a princess who stood outside. But my,
what a sight she was with the rain and the storm!
Her hair and her clothes were running with water:
water was running in through the toes of her shoes

and out at the heels. But she said she was a real princess.

'Well, we shall soon find out!' thought the old queen to herself. She went into the bedroom, took all the bed-clothes off and put a pea on the bottom of the bed. Then she took twenty mattresses and laid them on top of the pea, and then twenty eiderdowns on top of the mattresses.

And there the princess had to spend the night.

In the morning they asked her how she had slept.

'Oh, terribly badly!' said the princess. 'I have hardly shut my eyes the whole night! Heaven knows what there was in the bed! I have been lying on something hard—I am black and blue all over! It's really dreadful!'

And so they could see she was a real princess, because she had felt the pea through twenty mattresses and twenty eiderdowns. No one but a real princess could possibly be so sensitive.

Then the prince married her, for he was now sure that he had found a real princess, and the pea was placed in the art museum, where it can still be seen if no one has taken it.

And that's a true story!

THUMBELINA

ONCE upon a time, there was a woman who longed for a little child of her own, but she had no idea where she could get one. So off she went to see an old witch, and she said to her, 'I'd so much like to have a little child! Won't you please tell me where I can get one from?'

'Why, yes, that's no trouble at all!' said the witch. 'You must take this grain of barley—it's not the kind that grows in the farmer's field or that hens eat, either—put it in a flower-pot, and then wait and see what happens!'

'Oh, thank you kindly!' said the woman. She gave the witch a shilling, and then went home and planted the grain of barley. A beautiful big flower sprang up at once—it looked very much like a tulip, but the petals were tightly closed as though it were still in bud.

'What a pretty flower it is!' said the woman, kissing its beautiful red and yellow petals, but just as she kissed it, the flower suddenly burst open. You could see it was a real tulip now, but right in the middle of the flower, on a green stool, sat a tiny little girl, delicate and lovely: she was not above an inch tall, and so she was called Thumbelina.

She was given a splendid lacquered walnut-shell as her cradle, blue violet-petals formed her mattress, and a rose-petal her eiderdown. There she slept at night, but during the day she played on the table where the woman had set a plate with a wreath of flowers arranged round the edge so that the stalks lay in the water. On the surface, a large tulip-petal floated, and Thumbelina could sit in it and sail from one side of the plate to the other— she had two white horsehairs to row with. It looked very pretty indeed. She could sing, too—so daintily and charmingly that no one had ever heard the like.

One night, as she lay in her beautiful bed, an ugly old toad came hopping in through the window, where there was a broken pane of glass. The toad looked very big and wet and ugly as she hopped straight down on to the table where Thumbelina lay asleep under her red rose-petal.

'She'd make a nice wife for my son!' said the toad, and so she took hold of the walnut-shell where Thumbelina was sleeping, and hopped off with her through the broken pane down into the garden.

Down at the bottom flowed a big broad stream, and close by the bank the ground was marshy and muddy: here the toad lived with her son. Ugh! he was ugly and repulsive, too, and looked exactly like his mother. 'Croak, croak, cro-ak-ak!' was all he could say when he saw the charming little girl in the walnut-shell.

'Don't talk so loud, or she'll wake!' said the old toad. 'She could still run away from us, for she's as light as swansdown! We'll put her out in the stream on one of the broad water-lily leaves—she's so light and small, it'll seem like an island to her! She won't be able to run away from there, and in the meantime we'll spring-clean the best room down under the mud, and you shall settle down and live there together!'

Out in the stream grew a mass of water-lilies with broad green leaves that looked as if they were floating on top of the water; the leaf that lay farthest out was also the biggest, and the old toad swam out to it and there she put down the walnut-shell with Thumbelina inside.

The poor little thing woke quite early in the morning, and when she saw where she was, she began to cry bitterly, for there was water all round the big green leaf, and she had no way at all of getting to land.

The old toad sat down below in the mud, decorating her room with rushes and yellow water-flowers to make it neat and pretty for her new daughter-in-law. Then she swam out with her ugly son to the leaf where Thumbelina was standing. They had come to fetch her pretty bed which they wanted to have ready in the bride's bedroom before she came. The old toad bowed deeply in the water to her and said, 'This is my son you see with me: he's going to be your husband, and the two of you shall have a very nice place to live in down below in the mud!'

But all the son could say was, 'Croak, croak! Cro-ak-ak!'

So they took her pretty little bed and swam

away with it, but Thumbelina sat quite alone on the green leaf and wept, for she had no wish to go and live with the horrid old toad, nor to have her ugly son for a husband. The little fishes, swimming down below in the water, had seen the toad and heard what she said, and so they popped their heads up to take a look at the little girl. As soon as they set eyes on her, they saw how lovely she was, and they were very upset that she had to go and live in the mud with the ugly toad. No, that should never happen! Down in the water, they swarmed round the green stalk that held the leaf she was standing on and gnawed it through with their teeth. And so the leaf floated away down the stream with Thumbelina, far away where the toad could not reach her.

Thumbelina sailed along past a great many places, and the little birds sitting in the bushes saw her and sang, 'What a charming little maiden!' The leaf floated farther and farther away with her, and so at last Thumbelina journeyed into a strange country.

A pretty little white butterfly fluttered round her for some time and at last settled on the leaf, for it had taken quite a liking to Thumbelina, and she was very happy now, for the toad could no longer reach her and everything was so lovely as she sailed along. The sun was shining upon the water and it looked like gleaming gold. Then she took her sash and tied one end of it round the butterfly and made the other end fast in the leaf so that it now sped along much more swiftly and, of course, took her with it.

Just then a great cockchafer came flying by; he caught sight of her, and in a flash fastened his claws

about her slender waist and flew up into a tree with
her. But the green leaf floated away down the

stream, and the butterfly flew with it, for it was tied
to the leaf and could not free itself.

Heavens, how terrified poor Thumbelina was
when the cockchafer flew up into the tree with her!

But she was most sorry for the beautiful white butterfly she had tied fast to the leaf: if it could not free itself, it would certainly die of hunger. But the cockchafer cared nothing for that. He sat down with her on the largest green leaf in the tree, gave her honeydew from the flowers to eat, and told her she was very pretty, although she was not at all like a cockchafer. Then all the other cockchafers that lived in the tree came to visit her. They looked at Thumbelina, and the young lady cockchafers shrugged their feelers and said, 'But she's only two legs—what a pitiful-looking thing she is!' 'She hasn't any feelers!' 'Her waist is so thin—pooh, she looks just like a human! How ugly she is!' said all the lady cockchafers—and yet Thumbelina was really very pretty! And that's what the cockchafer who had carried her off thought, too, but when all the others said she was ugly, he believed so as well in the end, and would have nothing more to do with her—she could go wherever she would. They flew down from the tree with her and set her upon a daisy; there she wept because she was so ugly that the cockchafers would have nothing to do with her, and yet she was the loveliest little thing you could imagine, as bright and dainty as the most beautiful of rose-petals.

The whole summer through, poor Thumbelina lived quite alone in the great forest. She plaited herself a bed of grasses and hung it under a large dock-leaf to keep the rain off her; she gathered the pollen from the flowers to eat, and she drank the dew that formed every morning on the leaves. And so summer and autumn passed, and winter came—a long, cold winter. All the birds that had sung so beautifully for her flew away, the trees and the flowers withered, and the large dock-leaf she had lived under curled up and nothing was left of it but a shrivelled yellow stalk. She was dreadfully cold, for her clothes were in tatters, and she herself was so delicate and small, poor Thumbelina, that she might have frozen to death. It began to snow, and every snow-flake that fell upon her felt as a whole shovelful might do if it were thrown at one of us, for we are big and she was only an inch tall. So she wrapped herself up in a withered leaf, but it did not warm her, and she shivered with cold.

Just beyond the edge of the forest which she had now come to, lay a great corn-field, but the corn had long since been carted, and now only the dry bare stubble stood up out of the frozen ground. But it was like a forest for her to go through, and oh, she shivered so much with the cold! And so she came to the field-mouse's door. It was a little hole under the stubble. There the field-mouse lived snug and comfortable with a whole store-room full of corn and a fine kitchen and dining-room. Poor Thumbelina stopped just inside the doorway like a wretched beggar-girl, and asked for a little bit of a grain of barley, for she had had nothing at all to eat for the last two days.

'You poor little thing!' said the field-mouse, for she was a good-natured old field-mouse at heart. 'Come into my warm room and have something to eat with me!'

She liked the look of Thumbelina, and so she said, 'You're welcome to stay with me for the winter, but you must keep my room nice and clean, and tell me stories, for I'm very fond of stories.' And Thumbelina did what the good old field-mouse asked of her, and lived very comfortably.

'We shall soon have a visitor!' said the field-
mouse. 'My neighbour comes to visit me every
weekday. His house is even more comfortable than
mine: he has fine large rooms, and he wears such a
lovely black velvet fur—if you could only get him
for a husband, you'd be well provided for. But he
can't see. You must tell him all the most beautiful
stories you know!'

But Thumbelina did not like that idea at all: she
had no wish to marry the neighbour, for he was a
mole. He came visiting in his black velvet fur—he
was very rich and very learned, said the field-
mouse. His house was twenty times as spacious as
the field-mouse's, and learning he had, too; but he
did not care for the sun and the beautiful flowers,
and he spoke contemptuously of them because he
had never seen them. Thumbelina had to sing for
him, and she sang both 'Ladybird, ladybird, fly
away home!' and 'The monk is walking in the
meadow'. The mole fell in love with her on account
of her beautiful voice, but he said nothing, for he
was always a very cautious man.

He had recently dug himself a long passage
through the earth from his own house to theirs, and
he gave the field-mouse and Thumbelina leave to
walk there whenever they wished. But he told them
not to be afraid of the dead bird that lay in the
passage. The bird was quite whole, with its feathers
and beak intact: it must have died quite recently
at the beginning of the winter, and it now lay buried
just where he had made his passage.

The mole took in his mouth a bit of rotten wood
which shines just like fire in the dark, and then went
in front to light the long dark passage for them.
When they came to the place where the dead bird

lay, the mole set his broad nose against the roof of
the passage and pushed the earth up, thus making
a big hole which the light could shine through. In
the middle of the floor lay a dead swallow with its
beautiful wings pressed close against its sides and
its legs and head tucked in under its feathers: the
poor bird had obviously died of cold. Thumbelina
was so sorry for it: she loved all the little birds that
had sung and twittered so beautifully for her the
whole summer through. But the mole kicked it with
his short legs and said, 'That's one that won't
whistle any more! It must be wretched to be born
a little bird! Thank heaven none of my children
will ever be one! They've nothing to say for themselves but "tweet-tweet", and in the winter they die
of hunger!'

'Yes, as a sensible man, you may well say so!'
said the field-mouse. 'What does a bird get for
all its "tweet-tweet" when winter comes? It dies
of hunger and cold—and yet it's thought so much
of!'

Thumbelina said nothing, but when the others
had turned their backs upon the bird, she bent
down, gently moved aside the feathers that lay
over its head, and kissed its closed eyes. 'Perhaps
this is the one that sang so beautifully for me during
the summer,' she thought. 'What a lot of happiness
it brought me, dear, beautiful bird!'

Then the mole stopped up the hole he had made
to let the daylight shine through, and went home
with the ladies. But that night Thumbelina could
not sleep at all: so she got out of bed and plaited
a fine large rug of hay. She carried it down and
spread it over the dead bird. She tucked some soft
cotton-wool she had found in the field-mouse's

living-room round the bird's body so that it should lie warm in the cold earth.

'Good-bye, beautiful little bird!' she said. 'Good-bye, and thank you for the lovely song you sang in the summer-time, when all the trees were green and the sun shone warmly on us!' Then she laid her head upon the bird's breast, but as she did so, she was quite startled, for it felt just as if something were knocking inside. It was the bird's heart. The bird was not dead: it lay numb with cold, and now that warmth was returning to it, it showed signs of life again.

In the autumn the swallows all fly away to warmer lands, but if one of them should be delayed, it is so overcome with cold that it falls quite lifeless to the ground. There it remains, and the cold snow covers it over.

Thumbelina had had such a fright that she was actually trembling, for she was only an inch tall and compared with her the bird was a great big creature. But she plucked up her courage, tucked the cotton-wool more closely round the poor swallow, and fetched a mint-leaf which she herself used as a bedspread and laid it over the bird's head.

The next night she crept down to the bird again. It was unmistakably alive, but so weak that it could barely open its eyes for a moment to look at Thumbelina who was standing there with a bit of rotten wood in her hand—for other light had she none.

'Thank you, thank you, pretty little child!' the sick swallow said to her. 'I'm so nice and warm now, I shall soon get my strength back and be able to fly out again into the warm sunshine!'

'Oh,' she said, 'it's so cold outside! It's snowing

and freezing! Stay in your warm bed, and I'll look after you!'

Then she brought the swallow some water in a petal, and it drank and told her how it had torn one of its wings on a thorn-bush, and so was unable to fly as fast as the other swallows, who had flown far, far away to warmer lands. At length it had fallen to the ground, but more than that it could not remember and had no idea how it came to be where it was.

The swallow stayed down there all winter, and Thumbelina was kind to it and grew very fond of it, but neither the mole nor the field-mouse was told the least thing about it, for they did not like the poor forlorn swallow.

As soon as spring came and the sun's warmth began to penetrate the earth, the swallow said good-bye to Thumbelina and opened the hole which the mole had made just above its head. It was lovely to feel the sun shining in upon them, and the swallow asked her if she would not go with it: she could sit on its back and they would fly far away into the green forest. But Thumbelina knew it would make the old field-mouse very sad if she left her like that.

'No, I can't do that!' said Thumbelina.

'Good-bye, good-bye, you kind pretty girl!' said the swallow, as it flew out into the sunshine. Thumbelina watched it go, and tears came into her eyes, for she had grown very fond of the poor swallow.

'Tweet, tweet!' sang the bird, and flew off into the green forest.

Thumbelina was very sad. She was never allowed to go out into the warm sunshine; and the corn which had been sown in the field above the field-mouse's house grew up so high that it was like a great dense forest for the poor little girl who was only an inch tall.

'Now during the summer you must get your trousseau ready!' the field-mouse said to her, for their neighbour, the tiresome mole in the black velvet fur, had now asked her to marry him. 'You must have both woollens and linens! You must have something to sit on and lie on when you're the mole's wife!'

Thumbelina had to work hard with her spindle, and the field-mouse hired four spiders to spin and weave for her night and day. Every evening the mole would pay them a visit, and his talk was always the same: when summer came to an end and the sun was no longer shining so dreadfully hot—it was baking the earth as hard as a rock—yes, when summer was over, he would marry Thumbelina. But she was very unhappy about it, for she did not like the tiresome old mole at all. Every morning when the sun rose, and every evening when it set, she would creep out-of-doors, and whenever the wind parted the corn so that she could see the blue sky, she would think how pleasant and beautiful it was outside, and she would wish so hard that she could see her dear swallow again: but it would never come back, for it had flown far away into the beautiful green forest.

When autumn came Thumbelina had the whole of her trousseau finished.

'In four weeks' time you'll be having your wedding!' the field-mouse said to her. But Thumbelina wept and said she would not have the tiresome old mole.

'Fiddle-de-dee!' said the field-mouse. 'Don't be so obstinate, or I shall bite you with my white teeth!

You're going to get a very nice husband indeed! Why, the queen herself has nothing to match his black velvet fur! And he has both a kitchen and a cellar. You should thank God for him!'

And so their wedding-day arrived. The mole had already come to take Thumbelina away; she would have to live with him deep down under the earth, and she would never be able to go out into the warm sunshine because he disliked it. The poor child was very unhappy because she had now to say good-bye to the beautiful sun, which she had still been allowed to look at from the doorway while she was living with the field-mouse.

'Good-bye, bright sun!' she said, stretching her arms up towards it, and she walked a little way from where the field-mouse lived, for the corn was now harvested and there was only the dry stubble left. 'Good-bye, good-bye!' she said, as she threw her small arms round a little red flower that was growing there. 'Give my love to the swallow if you should ever see him again!'

At that very same moment she heard, 'Tweet, tweet!' just above her: she looked up, and there was the swallow flying overhead. It caught sight of Thumbelina and was delighted to see her. She told it how she was being forced to marry the nasty old mole, and how she would then have to live right under the earth where the sun never shone. She could not help weeping at the thought of it.

'The cold winter is coming on now,' said the swallow, 'and I'm flying far away to a warmer land. Will you come with me? You can sit on my back and bind yourself fast with your sash: then we shall fly away from the nasty mole and his dark home, far away over the mountains to warm lands where the sun shines more beautifully than it does here, where there is always summer and lovely flowers. Do fly away with me, dear little Thumbelina—you saved my life when I lay frozen in the dark cellar under the earth!'

'Yes, I'll go with you,' said Thumbelina, and she seated herself upon the bird's back, with her feet resting on its outstretched wings, and tied her belt firmly to one of its strongest feathers. And so the swallow flew high up into the air, over forest and lake, high up over the great mountains where snow always lies. Thumbelina froze in the cold air, but she crept under the bird's warm feathers, and only popped her little head out to see all the beautiful scenery below her.

So they came to the warm lands where the sun shines much more brightly than it does here. The sky seemed twice as high, and along the ditches and hedges grew the loveliest green and blue grapes. Oranges and lemons hung in woods scented with myrtle and mint, and along the country lanes lovely children ran and played with great brightly coloured butterflies. But the swallow flew farther still, and everything grew more and more beautiful. Under magnificent green trees, by a blue lake, stood a palace built in ancient times of shining white marble, with vines entwined round its tall pillars. Right on top of the pillars were many swallows' nests, and in one of them lived the swallow that carried Thumbelina.

'Here's my house!' said the swallow. 'But if you will choose yourself one of those lovely flowers growing down there, I will set you down on it, and you will live as happily there as you could wish!'

'That would be lovely!' she said, clapping her little hands.

A great white marble column lay fallen on the ground: it was broken into three pieces, and between them grew the most beautiful white flowers. The swallow flew down with Thumbelina and set her upon one of the broad petals: but what a surprise she had!—there, in the middle of the flower, sat a little man, clear and transparent like glass; he had the prettiest golden crown upon his head and the loveliest bright wings on his shoulders; and he himself was no bigger than Thumbelina. He was the guardian-spirit of the flower. In every flower there lived a little man or woman just like him, but he was king over them all.

'Oh, how beautiful he is!' whispered Thumbelina to the swallow. The little prince was quite frightened of the swallow, for it was such an enormous bird by the side of this dainty little creature, but when he saw Thumbelina, he was overjoyed, for she was quite the most beautiful girl he had ever seen. And so he took the golden crown off his own head and placed it upon hers. He asked her what she was called, and he said that if she would be his wife, she should be queen over all the flowers! Well, that was a husband indeed!—quite a different matter from the toad's son and the mole with the black velvet fur! And so she said yes to the handsome prince. From every flower appeared a little lady or gentleman, so beautiful and dainty it was a joy to look at them; and every one brought Thumbelina a present, but the best of all was a pair of beautiful wings from a large white fly. They were fastened upon Thumbelina's shoulders, and then she, too, could fly from flower to flower. They were

44

all so full of joy, and the swallow sat up above in its nest and sang for them as well as it could, but it was very sad at heart, for it was so fond of Thumbelina that it wanted never to be parted from her.

'You cannot be called Thumbelina!' the flower-sprite said to her. 'It's an ugly name, and you are so beautiful. We shall call you Maia!'

'Good-bye, good-bye!' said the swallow, and flew away from the warm lands once more, far away back to Denmark. There it had a little nest by the window of the room where the man who can tell tales lives, and it sang its 'tweet, tweet!' for him, and that's how we come to know the whole story.

THE NAUGHTY BOY

THERE was once an old poet—a really kind-hearted old poet. One evening, as he was sitting at home, a dreadful storm broke: the rain poured down in torrents, but the old poet sat cosily and comfortably by the stove, where the fire was burning and apples were sizzling.

'The poor folk who are out in this weather won't have a dry stitch left on them!' he said, for he was a very kind poet.

'Oh, do open the door for me! I'm freezing cold and so wet!' cried a little child outside. He was weeping and knocking on the door, while the rain pelted down and the wind rattled all the windows.

'Poor little thing!' said the old poet, as he went and opened the door. There was a little boy standing there: he was quite naked, and his long golden hair was wringing wet. He was shaking with cold, and had he not come in he would certainly have met his death in that dreadful weather.

'You poor little thing!' the old poet said, as he

46

took him by the hand. 'Come to me and I'll soon get you warm again! You shall have some wine and a baked apple, for you're a very nice little boy!'

And he was, too. His eyes looked like two bright stars, and although his golden hair was dripping with water it was still beautifully curly. He looked like a little angel. But he had turned very pale with cold, and he was shivering all over. He had a pretty bow in his hand, but it was quite spoilt with the rain, and the wet had made all the colours on his beautiful arrows run into one another.

The old poet sat down by the stove, took the little boy on his lap, wrung the water out of his hair, warmed his hands in his own, and heated some sweet wine for him. He soon began to look better and the colour returned to his cheeks; he jumped down on to the floor and danced round the old poet.

'You're a merry little fellow!' said the old man. 'What do they call you?'

'I'm called Cupid!' he answered. 'Don't you recognize me? There's my bow over there—that's what I shoot with! Look, the weather's clearing up now; the moon's shining!'

'But your bow's spoilt!' said the old poet.

'I hope not!' said the little boy, taking it up and looking at it. 'Oh, it's dry already—it's not come to any harm! The string is quite taut! I must try it!' And so he bent the bow, fitted an arrow, took aim and shot the kind old poet right through the heart. 'There, now you can see my bow's not spoilt!' he said. He laughed loudly and ran off. Fancy shooting the old poet like that, the naughty boy, when he had let him in to his warm room and been so kind to him and given him that lovely wine and the best apple he had!

The good poet lay crying on the floor: he really was shot through the heart. 'Oh, what a naughty boy that Cupid is!' he said. 'I shall tell all good children so: then they can take care never to play with him, for if they do he'll cause them harm!'

All the good children, boys and girls alike, that he told this to certainly kept their eyes open for Cupid and his tricks, but he fooled them just the same, for he is very artful! When students are returning from their lectures, he runs along by their side with a black jacket on and a book under his arm. They have no idea who he is, and so they take him by the arm, thinking he is a student, too. And then he plants his arrows in their breasts. He goes after the girls, too, when they are on their way back from their catechism, and even when they are in church. Yes, he is after folk all the time! He sits up in the great chandelier in the theatre and burns like a bright flame, so that people think he is a lamp and take no more notice of him. He runs about in the Royal Gardens and along the Ramparts. Why, he once shot your father and mother right through the heart! You just ask them and see what they say. Oh, he's a bad boy, is Cupid, and you must never have anything to do with him! He is after everybody. Just think, he even shot an arrow at your old grandmother—but that's a long time ago now, that's over and done with: but it's something she will never forget. Shame upon him! But you have been warned about him now—you know what a naughty boy he is!

THE TRAVELLING-
COMPANION

POOR John was very sad, for his father was seriously
ill and was not expected to live. The two of them
were quite alone in their little room. The lamp on
the table was on the point of burning out, and it was
quite late in the evening.

'You've been a good son, John!' his sick father
said. 'I'm sure Our Lord will help you to get on in
the world!' He looked at him with a serious and
gentle expression in his eyes, drew a deep breath,
and died, looking just as if he were asleep. But John
cried, for now he had no one at all in the whole
world, neither father nor mother, brother nor sister.
Poor John! He leaned kneeling against the side of
the bed, kissing his dead father's hand and weeping
bitterly; but at last his eyes closed and he fell
asleep with his head on the hard wooden frame of
the bed.

Then he dreamt a strange dream: he saw the sun

and the moon bow before him, and he saw his
father lively and well again, and heard him laugh
as he always used to laugh when he was really
pleased. A lovely girl with a golden crown on her
beautiful long hair held out her hand to John, and
his father said, 'Look what a lovely bride you have!
She's the loveliest in the whole world!' Then he
woke—the beautiful dream had gone, his father
lay dead and cold in the bed, and there was no one
at all with them—poor John!

A week later the dead man was buried. John
walked close behind the coffin—he would never
again look upon the kind father who had loved him
so much. He heard the earth thrown down upon
the coffin, he saw the last corner of it before it, too,
disappeared with the next shovelful of earth thrown
in. He felt as if his heart would break in two, he was
so full of sadness. Round about him they sang a
hymn, and it sounded so beautiful that tears came
into John's eyes; he cried, and that did him good in
his sorrow. The sun was shining brightly on the
green trees as if it would say, 'You mustn't be so
sad, John! Can't you see how beautifully blue the
sky is? That's where your father is now, praying to
God that all may go well with you!'

'I will always try to be good!' said John. 'Then I
shall go to heaven, too, and be with father. How
glad we shall be to see one another again! What a
lot I shall have to tell him, and he'll be able to show
me so many things, and teach me all about the
beauty of heaven, just as he used to teach me here
on earth. Oh, what happiness that will be!'

John saw it all so clearly that he smiled at the
thought of it, even while the tears were running
down his cheeks. The little birds sitting up in the

chestnut-trees chirped, 'Tweet, tweet!', they were so joyful, for in spite of the sadness of the funeral, they were quite sure the dead man was now up in heaven with wings far greater and more beautiful than theirs, and was now happy because he had been a good man here on earth, and that filled them with joy. John watched them fly away from the green trees far into the world, and he felt a strong desire to fly away with them. But first he cut a large wooden cross to put on his father's grave, and when he brought it along in the evening he found the grave made neat with sand and decorated with flowers: their neighbours had done this, for they thought very highly of his dear father who was now dead.

Early the next morning John packed his little bundle and tucked away in his belt the whole of his inheritance—some fifty dollars and a couple of shillings—and with that he set out to make his way in the world. But first he walked over to the church-yard to his father's grave, said the Lord's Prayer, and added, 'Good-bye, dear father! I will always try to be good, so you needn't be afraid to pray to God that all may go well with me!'

As John walked along through the fields, all the flowers looked fresh and lovely in the warm sun-shine, and they nodded in the wind as if they would say, 'Welcome to the green fields! Isn't it delightful out here?' But John turned round once again to look at the old church where he had been baptized as a little child and where he had gone to church every Sunday with his old father and joined in the hymns. Then he saw the church goblin with his little red pointed hood standing high up in one of the holes in the tower and shading his face with his bent arm to keep the sun out of his eyes. John nodded good-bye to him, and the little goblin waved his red hood, put his hand upon his heart, and blew him kiss after kiss to wish him good luck and a happy journey.

John thought about all the beautiful things he was going to see in the fine wide world, and he went on and on, farther than he had ever been before. He knew neither the towns he passed through nor the people he met—he was now among strangers, far away from home.

The first night, he lay down to sleep in a hay-stack in the fields, for other bed had he none. But he thought it was just lovely—the king himself couldn't have a finer bed! The whole field, with the stream and the haystack and the blue sky over-head, was just like a beautiful bedroom. The green grass dotted with little red and white flowers was his carpet, the elderberry bushes and the hedges of wild rose his pots of flowers, and for his wash-basin he had the stream with its clear fresh water, where the rushes bowed to him and said good evening and good morning. The moon was a fine great night-light hanging high up under the blue ceiling—and it couldn't set fire to the curtains! John could sleep quite peacefully there, and he did, too. He first woke up when the sun rose and all the little birds were singing, 'Good morning, good morning! Aren't you up yet?'

It was Sunday, and the bells were ringing for church. People were passing by on their way to early morning service, and John went with them, sang a hymn and listened to the Word of God; and he felt just as if he were back in his own church where he had been christened and had sung hymns with his father.

Outside in the churchyard were a great many graves, and some of them were overgrown with tall grass. Then John thought of his father's grave: now that he was no longer there to weed it and keep it looking nice, it, too, might come to look like these. So he sat down and pulled up the grass, lifted up the wooden crosses which had fallen down, and put back again in their proper place the wreaths which the wind had torn away from the graves; and as he worked, he thought perhaps someone would do the same thing for his father's grave now that he could no longer do it himself.

Outside the churchyard gate stood an old beggar leaning on his crutch. John gave him the two odd shillings he had and then went on his way, full of happiness and joy, out into the wide world.

Towards evening a dreadful storm sprang up. John hurried along to find a roof for his head, but he was very soon overtaken by the dark. At last, however, he reached a little church which stood all alone on top of a hill. By good luck the door was on the latch, and so he slipped in: he would stay there until the storm had passed.

'I'll find a corner where I can sit down!' he said. 'I'm quite tired and I can do with a little rest!' So he sat down, clasped his hands together and said his evening prayers; and before he knew what had happened he had fallen asleep and was dreaming, while it thundered and lightened outside.

When he woke again it was the middle of the night, but the weather had cleared and the moon was shining in through the windows. In the middle of the church there stood an open coffin with a dead man inside still awaiting burial. John was not at all frightened, for he had a good conscience and he knew that the dead harm nobody—only the living cause harm. Two evil men were standing close by the dead man who had been placed there in the church before he was laid in his grave. They were intent upon doing him harm: they would not let him lie peacefully in his coffin and were about to throw his poor body outside the church door.

'Why ever do you want to do that?' asked John. 'That's bad and wicked! Let him sleep peacefully in the Name of Jesus!'

'Rubbish!' said the two bad men. 'He's swindled us! He owes us money which he couldn't pay back, and now, on top of that, he's died and we shan't get a penny! So we intend to get our own back on him —he shall lie like a dog outside the church door!'

'I've only fifty dollars,' said John. 'It's the whole of my inheritance, but I'll give it to you willingly if you'll promise me faithfully to leave the poor dead man in peace. I shall get on all right without the money; I've strong healthy limbs and Our Lord will always help me.'

'All right,' said these two loathsome fellows, 'since you're willing to pay his debts, we won't do him any harm, you can be sure of that!' So they took the money John gave them, laughed openly at his good nature, and went their way. But John set the corpse to rights again in the coffin, folded its hands over its breast, said good-bye and went contentedly upon his way through the great forest.

Round about him, wherever the moon shone through between the trees, he saw the loveliest little elves merrily at play: they were not in the least disturbed by his presence for they knew he was good and innocent, and it is only wicked folk who are not allowed to catch sight of them. Some of them were no bigger than a finger, and their long golden hair was pinned up with combs of gold. Two by two they see-sawed up and down on the great dew-drops that lay upon the leaves and the tall grasses. From time to time a dew-drop would roll off, and then they would fall down among the long grass-stalks amid the laughter and noise of the other little elves—they thought that was great fun! They sang, and John was able to pick out quite clearly all the beautiful verses he had learnt as a little boy. Great many-coloured spiders with silver crowns upon their heads were spinning long hanging bridges and palaces from one hedge to the other, and when the fine dew fell upon them, they looked like shining glass in the clear moonshine. And so it went on until sunrise, when the little elves crept into flower-buds and the wind caught their bridges and castles which drifted away in the air like large cobwebs.

John had just left the forest when a man's strong voice shouted behind him, 'Hallo, my friend! Which way does your journey take you?'

'Out into the wide world,' said John. 'I've neither father nor mother: I'm a poor lad, but Our Lord will help me!'

'I'm going out into the wide world, too!' said the stranger. 'Couldn't we be company for one another?'

'All right!' said John, and off they went together. They soon grew very fond of one another, for they were both good-hearted people. But John soon noticed that the stranger was much wiser than he was—he had been nearly all over the world, and could talk about absolutely everything.

The sun was already high when they sat down under a great tree to eat their lunch. Just at that moment an old woman came along: she was very old and quite bent; she supported herself with a stick and carried on her back a bundle of kindling which she had gathered in the forest. Her apron was tucked up and John saw three large bundles of bracken and willow-twigs sticking out of it. She was nearly up to them when her foot slipped and she fell with a loud shriek. The poor old woman had broken her leg.

John wanted to carry her home at once, but the stranger opened his bag, took out a jar, and said he had an ointment there which would make her leg quite well again right away, so that she would be able to walk home by herself just as if she had never broken her leg at all.

But in return he wanted her to make him a present of the three bundles of sticks she had in her apron.

'It's a good price to pay!' said the old woman, nodding her head rather oddly. She did not much like the idea of parting with her sticks, but it was not much fun lying there with a broken leg either: so she gave him the sticks, and as soon as he had rubbed the ointment on her leg, the old woman got up and off she walked better than ever, so great was its power—but it's not to be had from the chemist's!

'What do you want those sticks for?' John asked his travelling-companion.

'They're three fine birch-brooms!' he said. 'I've taken a fancy to them—I'm a queer sort of fellow!'

So they went on a good bit farther.

'My, look at that storm gathering!' said John, pointing straight ahead. 'Look at those dreadful thick clouds there!'

'No, they're not clouds,' said his travelling-companion. 'They're mountains, fine great mountains, where you climb right up above the clouds into clear fresh air! It's magnificent, believe me! We shall reach them tomorrow and be well on our way into the wide world!'

They were not, however, as near as they looked. It took them a whole day before they came to the mountains, where the dark forests grew right up towards the sky and where there were great masses of rock as big as whole towns. It was going to be a difficult enough journey to cross right over them, and so John and his travelling-companion went into an inn where they could have a good rest and gather strength for the next day's march.

Down in the great tap-room of the inn a large crowd of people had gathered, for there was a man there with a puppet-show. He had just set his little theatre up and people were sitting round to see his play. Right in front a stout old butcher had taken his seat, the best in the room, and his great bulldog —an ugly-looking brute it was—sat by his side staring open-eyed like the rest of them.

The play now began: it was a fine play with a king and a queen who sat on plush thrones and wore golden crowns upon their heads and robes with long trains, which, of course, they could well afford. Very charming wooden puppets with glass eyes and great moustaches stood by all the doors, and opened and shut them to let fresh air into the room. It was a really delightful play and not a bit sad, but just as the queen rose to walk across the floor the great bulldog, at a moment when the stout butcher was not holding him, gave a great bound right into the theatre, and—God knows what he was thinking of!—seized the queen by her slender waist so that it went 'Crick-crack!' It was quite terrifying!

The poor puppet-man, who, of course, was performing the whole play, was frightened out of his wits, and very upset over his queen, for she was the most charming puppet he had, and now that dreadful bulldog had bitten her head off. But afterwards, when the people had gone, the stranger who had come with John said he would very soon put her to rights again. He took out his jar and smeared the puppet with the ointment that had cured the poor old woman when she had broken her leg. As soon as the puppet was smeared with it, it was whole again at once—yes, and more than that, it could now move all its limbs by itself: there was no need at all to pull its strings—the puppet was just like a living person, with the one exception that it could not talk. The man who owned the little puppet-theatre was delighted: he would no longer have to hold the puppet now that it could dance so well by itself. And none of the others could do that!

When at last night came, and everybody in the inn had gone to bed, they heard someone sighing deeply: it was such a dreadful noise and it went on so long that they all got up to see who it could be. The man who had given the play went down to his little theatre, for that was where the sighs were coming from. All the wooden puppets lay tumbled together, the king and all his guards, and it was they who were sighing so pitifully, staring with their great glass eyes, because they did so want to be smeared with a little of the ointment like the queen so that they would be able to move by themselves, too. The queen threw herself down on her knees and held out her lovely golden crown. 'Take it,' she begged, 'but do smear my husband and my Court!' Then the poor man that owned the show and all the puppets could not help bursting into tears, for he was really so sorry for them. He immediately promised John's travelling-companion that he would give him all the money he took at the next evening's performance if he would only smear four or five of his finest puppets. But the travelling-companion said he desired nothing but the great sabre he had by his side, and when he was given it he anointed six puppets who immediately began to dance, and so charmingly that all the girls—the real live girls—who saw them joined in too. The coachman and the kitchen-maid were dancing, the waiter and the chamber-maid, all the people who were staying there, and even the coal-shovel and the fire-tongs, but these two fell over just as they did their first hop—it was a merry night indeed!

The next morning John and his travelling-companion left them all, and made their way up the high mountains and through the great forest of firs. They climbed so high that at last the church towers far down beneath them looked like small red berries dotted on the green landscape below, and they could see for miles and miles, far, far away where they had never been. Never before had John seen so much of the beauty of this lovely world at one time: the sun shone so warmly from the clear blue sky, and he heard the huntsmen, too, blowing their horns so beautifully in among the mountains, that tears of joy came into his eyes, and he could not help saying, 'Dear, kind Lord, I could kiss you for being so good to us all, and for giving us all the loveliness there is in the world!'

His companion, too, stood with folded hands and

looked out over the woods and villages in the warm sunshine. At that moment they heard a wonderfully lovely sound ring out above their heads. They looked up: a great white swan was hovering in the air; it was very beautiful and it sang as they had never before heard any bird sing. But it grew weaker and weaker, then it bowed its head and sank slowly down to their feet, where it lay dead in all its beauty.

'Two such lovely wings,' said John's companion, 'big and white like these, are worth some money! I'll take them with me. Now you see what a good thing it was I got this sabre!' And so with one stroke he cut both the wings off the dead swan and kept them.

They now travelled many, many miles onwards over the mountains, until at last they saw in front of them a great city with more than a hundred towers shining like silver in the sunshine: in the middle of the city was a magnificent marble palace roofed with red gold, and there lived the king.

John and his companion did not want to go into the city right away, and so they put up at an inn just outside where they could tidy themselves up, for they wanted to look smart when they appeared in the streets. The innkeeper told them that the king was a good sort of man who never did anybody any harm, but his daughter—God help us, there was a bad princess, if ever there was one! She was beautiful enough—no one was ever as pretty and attractive as she was—but what was the good of that? She was a bad wicked witch, and it was all through her that so many handsome princes had lost their lives. She had given everybody leave to court her: anyone could come, prince or beggar for all she

60

cared; and all he had to do was guess three things she asked him: if he could do that, she would marry him, and he would be king over the whole land when her father died; but if he could not guess the right answers she had him hanged or beheaded, so bad and wicked was she. Her father, the old king, was deeply distressed by it all, but he could not forbid her evil ways, for he had once said he would not interfere with her suitors, she was to do as she liked about them. Every prince who came and made his guesses to win the princess failed, and so he was either hanged or had his head cut off—though he had been warned in good time and could have given up the idea of wooing her. The old king was so upset by all the sorrow and misery that was caused that he spent a whole day every year upon his knees with all his soldiers praying that the princess might grow good, but she showed no sign of doing so. The old women who drank brandy coloured it black before they drank it: it was their way of showing their sorrow, and more than that they could not do.

'What a dreadful princess!' said John. 'She ought to have a good thrashing: it would do her good. If only I were the old king she'd be well and truly whipped!'

At that moment they heard the people outside shouting 'Hurray!' The princess was passing by, and she really was so lovely that everyone forgot how bad she was, and so they shouted 'Hurray!' Twelve lovely maidens, all in white silk dresses, with golden tulips in their hands, rode by her side on coal-black horses; the princess herself had a snow-white horse decked with diamonds and rubies, her riding-habit was of pure gold, and the whip she carried in her hand looked like a ray of sunlight; the golden crown upon her head glittered like small stars from heaven, and her cloak was embroidered all over with thousands of lovely butterfly wings— and yet she was far more beautiful than all her clothes put together.

When John caught sight of her he went as red in the face as a drop of blood, and he could hardly utter a word; for the princess looked exactly like the lovely girl with the golden crown he had dreamt of the night his father died. He thought she was very beautiful, and he could not help loving her deeply. It couldn't possibly be true, he thought, that she was a wicked witch who had people hanged or beheaded when they couldn't guess what she asked them. 'Everyone is free to woo her, even the poorest beggar—I must go up to the palace! I can't help it!'

They all said he shouldn't do it: he would certainly fare no better than the rest. His travelling-companion, too, advised him not to go, but John, certain all would be well, brushed his shoes and jacket, washed his hands and face, combed his beautiful fair hair, and then walked all alone into the city and up to the palace.

'Come in!' said the old king, when John knocked at the door. John opened the door, and the old king, in dressing-gown and embroidered slippers, came to meet him. He had his golden crown upon his head, his sceptre in one hand and his golden orb in the other. 'Wait a minute!' he said, tucking the orb under his arm in order to shake John by the hand. But as soon as he heard he was another suitor come to woo the princess, he burst into such a flood of tears that both sceptre and orb fell to the floor, and he had to dry his eyes on his dressing-gown, the poor old king!

'Don't do it!' he said. 'You'll come to a bad end like all the rest. Just look here!' He took John out

into the princess's pleasure-garden: what a dreadful sight it was! From every tree hung three or four king's sons who had wooed the princess but had not been able to guess the things she had asked them. Every time the wind blew all the bones rattled so that the little birds were frightened and never dared go into the garden; the flowers were all tied up to human bones, and skulls stood grinning in the flower-pots. It was a fine garden for a princess!

'Now you can see!' said the old king. 'You'll end just like all the others you see here. You'd do far better to drop the idea. You make me really unhappy—I take it all very much to heart!'

John kissed the good old king's hand and said all would be well, because he loved the beautiful princess so very much.

Just then the princess herself came riding into the palace courtyard with all her ladies, and so they went over to her and said good-day. She was lovely, there was no doubt of it, and as she gave John her hand he fell even more deeply in love with her than before—she couldn't possibly be the bad wicked witch that everybody said she was. They went up into the hall, and the little pages offered them sugared fruits and humbugs, but the old king was so upset he couldn't eat anything at all, and besides, the humbugs were too hard for him.

It was now decided that John should come up to the palace again the next morning, when the judges and the whole Court would assemble to hear whether he would succeed in guessing what the princess was thinking of. If he guessed correctly he would have to appear twice again before them; but so far no one had ever guessed right the first time, and so they had all had to lose their lives.

John was not at all worried about what would happen to him. He knew only that he was happy, and he thought of nothing but the lovely princess. He was quite certain that God would help him, though how, he neither knew nor thought about. He danced all the way down the road on his way back to the inn where his travelling-companion was waiting for him.

John could not stop telling him how charming the princess had been to him and how lovely she was. He was already longing for the next day, when he could go to the palace again and try his luck at guessing.

But his companion shook his head and was overcome with grief. 'I'm very fond of you,' he said. 'We could have spent a long time together yet, and now I must lose you already! My poor, dear John, I could cry, but I won't spoil your happiness on what is, perhaps, the last evening we shall have together. We'll be merry, really merry: tomorrow, when you are gone, I shall be free to cry!'

The news had already spread through the town that a new suitor had come to woo the princess, and there was great grief everywhere. The theatre was closed, all the women who sold cakes tied black crape round their sugar-pigs, and the king and the clergy were on their knees in church— there was such great grief because no one believed that John could do any better than all the other suitors had done.

Late in the evening John's travelling-companion made a great bowl of punch, and said they should now be really merry and drink the princess's health. But when John had drunk two glasses he became so sleepy that he could not keep his eyes open, and he could not stop himself falling asleep. His companion lifted him gently out of his chair and put him to bed. Then, when it was quite dark, he took the two great wings he had cut off the swan and bound them firmly to his shoulders; he put in his pocket the biggest of the bundles of twigs he had got from the old woman who had fallen and broken her leg; and then he opened the window and flew out over the city straight to the palace, where he settled himself in a corner high up under the window of the princess's bedroom.

The whole city was quite still, and then a quarter-to-twelve struck—the window opened, and the princess, in a large white cloak, flew with long black wings away over the city to a great mountain. But the travelling-companion made himself invisible so that she could not see him at all, and, flying behind her, thrashed the princess with his twigs so that he actually drew blood where he struck her. How swiftly they sped through the air! The wind took her cloak, spreading it out on all sides like a great sail with the moon shining through it.

'Oh, how it's hailing, how it's hailing!' said the princess with every stroke of the twigs, but she got no more than she deserved. Then at last she came to the mountain and knocked on it. There was a rolling like thunder as the mountain opened and the princess passed inside. John's travelling-companion slipped in beside her, for no one could see him since he was invisible. They went down a great long passage where the walls sparkled quite wonderfully— there were thousands of glowing spiders running up and down the walls and shining like fire. Then they entered a great hall built of silver and gold, with flowers as big as sunflowers shining red and blue from the walls: but no one could pick them, for the stalks were vile poisonous snakes and the flowers were the fire that flamed from their mouths. The whole ceiling was covered with shining glowworms and sky-blue bats beating their thin wings: it looked really wonderful. In the middle of the

floor there was a throne borne on the skeletons of
four horses with harnesses of red fire-spiders; the
throne itself was of milk-white glass, and the
cushions to sit on were small black mice biting each
other's tails. Over the top of it was a canopy of rose-
red cobweb set with the loveliest little green flies
that shone like precious stones. In the middle of the
throne sat an old troll with a crown upon his ugly
head and a sceptre in his hand. He kissed the
princess on her brow and made her sit beside him
on his costly throne. Then the music began: large
black grasshoppers played the jew's harp, and the
owl beat his belly, since he had no drum. It was a
strange concert. Tiny little goblins with will-o'-the-
wisps on their hoods danced round the hall. No one
could see John's travelling-companion: he had
placed himself just behind the throne, and heard
and saw everything. The courtiers, who now came
in, too, were very fine and distinguished-looking,
but anyone who looked at them hard could not
have failed to notice what they really were. They
were nothing but broomsticks with cabbages on top
for heads, which the troll had brought to life with
a spell and provided with finely embroidered
clothes. But it did not matter in the least—they
were only there for show.

When they had danced for some time the princess told the troll she had a new suitor, and in-
quired of him what she should think of to ask him
the next morning when he came up to the palace.

'Now, listen to me,' said the troll, 'and I'll tell
you! You must find something very easy, then he'll
never hit upon it. Think of one of your shoes. He
won't guess that. Then have his head cut off: but
don't forget, when you come and see me again

tomorrow night, to bring me his eyes—I want them to eat!'

The princess curtsied deeply and said she would not forget the eyes. Then the troll opened the mountain and she flew home again, but the travelling-companion went with her and gave her such a thrashing with the twigs that she sighed deeply over the fierce hail-storm and hastened for all she was worth to get back through her window into her bedroom again. But the travelling-companion flew back to the inn where John was still asleep, undid his wings and then lay down on the bed, too, for I've no doubt he was very tired.

It was quite early in the morning when John woke up. His companion got up, too, and told him that during the night he had dreamt a very strange dream about the princess and one of her shoes, and he begged him therefore to be sure to ask whether the princess had not been thinking of it. It was, of course, what he had heard the troll say inside the mountain, but he did not want to tell John anything about that, and so he only begged him to ask whether she had been thinking of one of her shoes.

'I might just as well say that as anything else,' said John. 'Maybe what you've dreamt is the right answer, for I've always believed Our Lord would help me! But all the same, I'll say good-bye to you, for if I should guess wrong, I shall never see you again!'

So they kissed one another and John went into the city and up to the palace. The hall was quite full of people. The judges were sitting in their arm-chairs and had soft down cushions behind their heads because they had so much to think about. The old king was standing and drying his eyes on a white handkerchief. Then the princess came in, looking even lovelier than the day before. She greeted them all very kindly, but to John she gave her hand and said, 'Good morning to you!'

And now the time had come for John to guess what she was thinking of. Lord, how friendly she seemed as she looked at him! Yet as soon as she heard him say, 'One of your shoes!' she grew deathly white in the face and trembled all over, but there was nothing she could do about it, for he had guessed right.

Hurray! How glad the old king was: he turned head over heels with excitement, and everybody clapped him, and they clapped John, too, who had now guessed the answer to the first question.

The travelling-companion beamed with joy when he learnt how well it had gone off; but John clasped his hands together and thanked God, who, he was sure, would help him again the next two times. He had to make his second guess the very next day.

The evening passed just like that of the day before. When John had fallen asleep his companion flew away after the princess to the mountain, and gave her an even harder thrashing than the previous time, for he had now taken two bundles of twigs with him. No one could see him and he heard everything that passed. The princess was to think of her glove. And he told John that as if it had been a dream. So John was able to guess right again, and there was great rejoicing in the palace. The whole Court turned head over heels, just as they had seen the king do the first time. But the princess went and lay down on the sofa, and refused to say a single word. And now everything depended upon whether John could guess right the third time. If all went well he would win the lovely princess and inherit the whole kingdom when the old king died: if he guessed wrong, he would lose his life and the troll would eat his handsome blue eyes.

That evening John went to bed early, said his prayers, and then slept quite peacefully; but his travelling-companion strapped his wings upon his back, buckled his sword by his side and took all three bundles of sticks with him, and then he flew to the palace.

It was a pitch-black night, and there was such a gale blowing that the tiles flew off the houses, and the trees in the garden where the skeletons hung swayed like reeds in the wind; lightning flashed every moment, and the thunder rolled as if there were but one single peal that lasted the whole night through. Then the window was flung open and the princess flew out; she was deathly pale, but she laughed at the storm as though she thought it was not strong enough for her, and her white cloak whirled round in the air like a great sail. The travelling-companion thrashed her so hard with his three bundles of sticks that her blood dripped upon the earth below and in the end she could hardly fly any farther. But she reached the mountain at last.

'You should see how it's hailing and blowing!' she said. 'I've never been out in such weather!'

'You can have too much even of a good thing,' said the troll. Then she told him that John had guessed right the second time as well; if he should do the same again in the morning he would have won, and she would never more be able to visit the troll in the mountain or practise witchcraft as she used to; and so she was quite downcast.

'He mustn't be able to guess!' said the troll. 'I'm sure I shall hit on something he'll never think of— or else he must be a greater wizard than I am! But now let's be merry!' And so he took the princess by both hands, and they danced round with all the little elves and will-o'-the-wisps that were in the room; the red spiders jumped up and down the walls as merrily as the rest of them, and the fire-flowers seemed to send out showers of sparks. The owl beat his drum, the crickets whistled, and the black grasshoppers blew upon their jew's harps. It was a merry ball!

Then when they had danced quite a long time, the princess had to go home for fear she might be missed at the palace. The troll said he would go with her so that they could be together a little longer.

Then they flew away into the storm, and the travelling-companion wore out his three bundles of sticks upon their backs: never had the troll been out in such a hail-storm! Outside the palace he said good-bye to the princess, at the same time whispering to her, 'Think of my head!' But the travelling-companion heard quite clearly what he said, and at the very moment when the princess slipped through the window into her bedroom and the troll was about to turn back, he caught hold of him by his long black beard, and struck his ugly troll's head right off his shoulders with his sword, so that the troll himself was not even aware of it. He threw the body out to the fish in the lake, but the head he just dipped in the water: then he tied it up in his silk handkerchief and took it home with him to the inn, where he lay down to sleep.

The next morning he gave John the handkerchief, but said he must not untie it until the princess asked him what she was thinking of.

There were so many people in the great hall of the palace that they were packed together like radishes tied in a bundle. The judges were sitting in their seats with their soft head-cushions, and the old king was wearing a new suit of clothes. The golden crown and sceptre had been polished and were looking magnificent. But the princess was quite pale, and wore a coal-black dress as if she were going to a funeral.

'What am I thinking of?' she asked John, and he immediately untied the handkerchief and was quite terrified himself when he saw that frightful troll's head. Everybody shivered, for it was gruesome to look at, but the princess sat like a statue, unable to say a single word. At last she rose and gave John her hand, for he had, of course, guessed right. She looked at no one, but sighed deeply and said, 'You are now my lord! We will be married this evening!'

'I approve of that!' said the old king. 'That's just what we'll do!' Everyone cried 'Hurray!', the Guards' band played in the streets, the bells rang, and the cake-women took the black crape off their sugar-pigs, for now there was great rejoicing. Three oxen, roasted whole and stuffed with ducks and hens, were put in the middle of the market-place, and anyone could cut himself off a slice; the finest wine gushed from the fountains; and if you bought a penny roll at the baker's, you got six big buns thrown in—and buns with raisins in, too!

In the evening the whole city was illuminated, and the soldiers let off their cannon and the boys their crackers, and there was eating and drinking, clinking of glasses and merry-making up at the palace, and all the noble gentlemen and the lovely young ladies danced together: you could hear them a long way off singing:

'Here are so many pretty maidens,
And they want to swing around

To the rhythm of the drum:
Pretty maiden, just turn round,
Let us dance and stamp our feet
Till the soles fall off our shoes!'

But the princess was still a witch, of course, and cared nothing at all for John. The travelling-companion did not forget that, and so he gave John three feathers from the wings of the swan and a little flask with some drops in it, and he told him he must have a large tub filled with water put by the bride's bed, and as the princess was climbing into bed he must give her a little push so that she would fall into the water; then he must duck her under three times after he had first thrown the feathers and the drops in, and then she would be freed from her witchcraft and grow to love him very much.

John did everything as his companion had advised him. The princess shrieked quite loudly as he ducked her under the water, and she floundered about under his hands in the form of a large coal-black swan with glinting eyes; when she came up again for the second time, she had turned to a white swan with just a single black ring round her neck. John prayed fervently to Our Lord and let the water run over the bird for the third time, and it changed back immediately into the lovely princess. She was even more beautiful than before, and she thanked him, with tears in her lovely eyes, for freeing her from the spell.

The next morning the old king came with the whole of the Royal Household, and their congratulations continued far into the day. Last of all came John's travelling-companion with his staff in his hand and his haversack on his back. John kissed him over and over again, and told him he must not go away but stay with him, since he owed him all his happiness. But his companion shook his head and said very kindly and gently, 'No, my time is up now. I have only paid my debt. Do you remember the dead man those wicked men wanted to harm? You gave all you had so that he could lie quietly in his grave. I am that dead man!'

At that very moment he was gone.

The wedding-feast lasted a whole month. John and the princess loved one another very much, and the old king lived for many a happy day, and let their little ones ride-a-cock-horse on his knee and play with his sceptre. And after his death John became king over the whole country.

THE LITTLE MERMAID

FAR out to sea the water is as blue as the petals of the loveliest cornflower, and as clear as the purest glass, but it is very deep, deeper than any anchor-chain can reach, and many church-towers would have to be put one on top of another to reach from the bottom to the surface of the water. Down there live the merfolk.

Now you must not think that there is nothing there but the bare white sandy bottom; oh no, the most wonderful trees and plants grow there, and their stems and leaves are so supple that with the least movement of the water they stir like living things. All kinds of fish, large and small, flit among the branches just as birds do in the air up here. In the very deepest place of all lies the merking's palace. Its walls are coral, and its long pointed windows the clearest amber, and its roof is made of mussel-shells that open and shut with the move-ment of the water—it looks most beautiful, for in each shell lies a shining pearl, and a single one of them would be the chief beauty in a queen's crown.

The merking down there had been a widower for many years, and his old mother kept house for him; she was a wise woman, but proud of her royal rank, and so she always went about with twelve oysters on her tail, while other high-born merfolk might have only six. Otherwise she deserved high praise, especially because she was so fond of the little merprincesses, her granddaughters. They were six lovely children, and the youngest was the most beautiful of them all—her skin was as clear and pure as a rose-petal, her eyes as blue as the deepest lake, but like all the rest, she had no feet and her body ended in a fish's tail.

All day long they could play down there in the palace, in the great halls where living flowers grew out of the walls. When the great amber windows were opened the fish would swim in to them, just as the swallows will fly in when we open our windows, but the fish would swim right up to the little princesses, eat out of their hands and let themselves be stroked.

Outside the palace there was a great garden with fiery-red and dark-blue trees, their fruit shining like gold and their flowers like burning fire, with ever-moving stems and leaves. The soil itself was the finest sand, but blue like sulphur-flames. Over everything down there lay a wonderful blue glow; you would think that, instead of being on the bottom of the sea, you were standing high up in the air with nothing but sky above and below you. In clear calm weather you could see the sun looking like a purple flower with all that light streaming out from its centre.

Each of the little princesses had her own little plot in the garden, where she could dig and plant whatever she liked. One gave her flower-bed the shape of a whale, another thought hers would look

better in the form of a little mermaid, but the youngest made hers quite round and would only have flowers that shone red like the sun. She was a strange child, quiet and thoughtful, and when the other sisters decorated their gardens with the most wonderful things they had got from wrecked ships, she would only have, apart from the rose-red flowers which looked like the sun high up above her, a beautiful marble statue, a handsome boy carved out of clear white stone and come down to the bottom of the sea with the wreck of a ship. She planted by it a rose-red weeping-willow which grew magnificently and hung its fresh branches right over the statue down to the blue sand of the ground, where its shadow showed violet and was in constant motion like its branches—its top and its roots seemed always to be playing at kissing one another.

She found her greatest delight in hearing about the world of men up above; her old grandmother had to tell her all she knew about ships and cities, men and beasts. What she thought especially wonderful and beautiful was that up on earth the flowers had a sweet scent, for that they did not have on the bottom of the sea, and the woods were green and the fish you could see there among the branches could sing so loudly and beautifully it was a joy to hear them—grandmother called the little birds fish, for otherwise they would not have been able to understand her, for they had never seen a bird.

'When you reach your fifteenth birthday,' said grandmother, 'you shall be allowed to go up out of the sea and sit in the moonshine on the rocks and watch the great ships sailing by, and you shall see woods and cities, too!'

During that year one of the sisters was fifteen, but the others—well, each was a year younger than the next, and so the youngest of them all still had five whole years to wait before she dared swim up from the bottom of the sea and see what it looks like where we live. But each one promised to tell the next what she had seen and found most lovely during her first day on earth, for their grandmother had not told them nearly enough—there was so much they wanted to know about.

None of them was so full of longing as the youngest, and she was the very one that had the longest to wait and was so quiet and thoughtful. Many a night she stood by the open window and looked up through the dark-blue water where the fish were waving their fins and tails. She could see the moon and the stars, and though they shone quite palely, they looked much larger through the water than they do to our eyes; and when it looked as if a black cloud were gliding across below them, she knew it was either a whale swimming over her or else a ship with many men on board—men who, of course, had no idea that a lovely little mermaid was standing down below and stretching her white hands up towards their keel.

And now the eldest princess was fifteen years old and could rise up above the surface of the sea.

When she came back she had hundreds of things to tell them, but the loveliest of all, she said, was to lie in the moonshine on a sandbank in the quiet of the sea, and see, close by the coast, the great city where the lights were winking like a hundred stars, hear the music and the noise and bustle of carts and people, see the towers and spires of the many churches and listen to the ringing of their bells. And just because she could not go up into the city, that was what she longed to do more than anything else.

Oh, how intently her youngest sister listened to her! And whenever, after that, she stood in the evening by the open window, looking up through the dark-blue sea, she thought of the great city with all its noise and bustle, and then she seemed to hear the church-bells ringing down to her.

The next year the second sister was allowed to rise up through the water and swim wherever she wished. She popped her head up just as the sun was going down, and that sight she found the most beautiful. The whole sky had looked like gold, she said, and the clouds—she just could not describe their loveliness! Red and violet, they had sailed away over her head, but far swifter than they, flew a flock of wild swans, like a long white ribbon, away over the water to where the sun stood; she swam off towards it, but it sank, and the rosy gleam disappeared from the surface of the sea and the clouds.

The year after, the third sister went up above— she was the most venturesome of them all, and so she swam up a broad river which flowed into the sea. She saw lovely green hills with vineyards upon them, and castles and farms peeped out from the magnificent forest. She heard all the birds singing, and the sun shone so warmly, she often had to duck under the water to cool her burning face. In a little bay she came across a crowd of little children running about quite naked and splashing in the water. She wanted to play with them, but they ran off in fright. Then a little black animal came along—it was a dog, but she had never seen a dog before. It barked at her so terrifyingly that she became alarmed and made off for the open sea, but she could never forget the magnificent forest, the green hills, and the pretty children who could swim in the water, even though they had no fish's tails.

The fourth sister was not so venturesome. She stayed out in the middle of the wild sea, and told them that was quite the loveliest place; you could see for many miles all round you, and the sky stood overhead like a huge glass bell. She had seen ships, but far away, looking like gulls; playful dolphins had turned somersaults, and great whales had spouted water up from their nostrils so that it looked as if there were hundreds of fountains round about.

Now came the turn of the fifth sister. Her birthday happened to fall in winter, and so she saw what the others, during their first visits, had not seen. The sea looked quite green, and great icebergs were swimming round about, each one looking like a pearl, she said, and yet they were far larger than the church-towers built by men. They appeared in the strangest shapes, glittering like diamonds. She had seated herself on one of the largest, and, in terror, ships sailed wide of the ice where she sat, her long hair streaming in the blast. Late in the evening the sky became overcast with cloud, and it thundered and lightened, while the dark sea lifted the great ice-floes high up and made them shine in the strong flashes of lightning. On all ships, sails were taken in, and there was alarm and fear, but she sat peacefully on her floating iceberg, and watched the blue flashes of lightning strike zig-zagging down upon the shining sea.

The first time the sisters, each in her turn, came to the surface of the sea, they were always delighted with the new and beautiful sights they saw, but now that they were grown girls and had leave to go up there whenever they wished, they were quite indifferent about it and longed for home again, and at the end of a month they said that the bottom of the sea was the most beautiful place of all, the place where they felt most comfortable and most at home.

Many an evening the five sisters would take one another by the arm and swim in a row up to the surface of the water. They had lovely voices, more beautiful than any human voice, and when the wind was blowing up to a gale and they thought ships might be lost, they would swim in front of the ships and sing so beautifully how lovely it was on the bottom of the sea and bid the sailors not to be afraid of coming down there. But the men could not understand their words: they thought it was the gale they heard. Nor did they ever see the beauty down below them, for when their ship sank the men were drowned, and only as dead men did they ever come to the merking's palace.

On those evenings when the sisters rose arm-in-arm like this high up through the sea, their little sister was left behind quite alone, gazing after them, and she looked as though she would weep, but a mermaid has no tears and so she suffers all the more.

'Oh, if only I were fifteen!' she said. 'I know that I shall really grow to love that world above the sea and all the people that live and dwell there!'

And then at last she was fifteen.

'Well, we've got you off our hands now!' said her grandmother, the old queen-dowager. 'Come along now, let me dress you up like your sisters!' And she placed a wreath of white lilies on her hair, but every petal of the flowers was half a pearl. Then the old lady fastened eight large oysters firmly on the princess's tail to show her high rank.

'But it hurts so!' said the little mermaid.

83

'We must all suffer a little to look smart!' said the old lady.

Oh, she would have loved to shake off all that finery and put down that heavy wreath! The red flowers in her garden suited her much better, but she dared not change them now. 'Good-bye!' she said, and then she rose, lightly and clearly like a bubble, up through the water.

The sun had just gone down as she raised her head up above the water, but the clouds were all still gleaming with rose and gold, and in the middle of the pale-pink sky the evening-star shone clear and lovely, the air was mild and fresh and the sea a glassy calm. A great three-masted ship lay there with only a single sail set, for there was not a breath of wind, and the sailors were sitting about in the rigging and on the spars. There was music and song, and as the evening grew darker, hundreds of coloured lights were lit—it looked as if the flags of all the countries in the world were waving in the air. The little mermaid swam right up to the cabin window, and every time she rose with the swell of the water, she could see through the crystal-clear panes where a large number of well-dressed people were standing, but the most handsome of them was the young prince with the large black eyes. He was certainly not much more than sixteen; it was his birthday, and that was why there was all this celebration. The sailors were dancing on deck, and as the young prince stepped out, over a hundred rockets shot up in the air, shining as brightly as daylight, so that the little mermaid was quite terrified and ducked under the water, but she soon popped her head up again, and it looked just as if all the stars of heaven were falling down on her.

She had never seen fireworks before. Great suns were whirling round, magnificent firefish were soaring up into the blue sky, and it was all reflected back from the clear, still sea. On the ship itself, there was so much light, you could see every little rope, let alone the people. Oh, how handsome the young prince was, shaking everyone by the hand, laughing and smiling, while the music rang out into the lovely night.

It grew late, but the little mermaid could not turn her eyes away from the ship and the handsome prince. The coloured lights were put out, no more rockets rose into the air, nor was there any more cannon-fire to be heard either, but deep down in the sea there was a murmuring and a rumbling. Meanwhile, she sat on the water, rocking up and down, so that she could look into the cabin. But the ship gathered speed as one sail was spread after another. Then the waves ran higher, great clouds closed in, and far away there were flashes of lightning. Oh, there was going to be a dreadful storm! And so the sailors took in sail. The great ship sped rolling and swaying through the wild sea, the waves rose like great black mountains about to break over the mast, but the ship dived like a swan down among the high billows and was lifted up again on the piled-up waters. To the little mermaid their speed was pleasant and amusing enough, but the sailors did not think so. The ship creaked and cracked, the stout planks bent under the heavy blows dealt by the sea, the mast snapped in the middle like a reed, and the ship heeled over on her side as the water rushed into her hold. Then the little mermaid saw that they were in danger—she herself had to look out for beams and broken ship's timbers driving on the water. At one moment it was so pitch-black that she could see nothing at all; then when the lightning flashed, it was so bright again she could make out all those on board, each man staggering about as best he could. She was searching especially for the young prince, and as the ship parted, she saw him sink down in the deep sea. For the moment she was overjoyed, for now he was coming down to her, but then she remembered that men could not live in the water, and that he could go down to her father's palace only as a dead man. No, die he must not! And so she swam off among the beams and planks driving on the sea, completely forgetting that they could have crushed her, dived deep under the water and rose again high up among the waves, and then at last she reached the young prince who could scarcely swim any farther in that stormy sea. His arms and legs were beginning to tire, his beautiful eyes had shut, and he would have been left to die had the little mermaid not come to him. She held his head up above the water and let the waves drive her with him wherever they would.

When morning came the storm had passed, but of the ship there was not a stick to be seen. The sun rose out of the water so red and bright the prince's cheeks seemed to gain life from it, but his eyes remained shut. The mermaid kissed his beautiful high forehead and stroked his wet hair back; she thought he looked like the marble statue down in her little garden; she kissed him again and wished that he might yet live.

Then she saw dry land in front of her, high blue mountains with snow shining white upon their summits as if it were swans that lay there; down by the coast were lovely green woods and before them lay a church or an abbey—she did not rightly know what, but at least a building. Oranges and lemons grew there in the garden, and in front of the gate tall palm-trees stood. The sea made a little bay there, dead still but very deep right up to the rocks where the fine white sand was washed up. She swam over to that point with the handsome prince, laid him upon the sand and took particular care that his head lay well up in the warmth of the sun.

Then the bells rang in the great white building, and many young girls came out through the garden. The little mermaid then swam farther out behind some high rocks that jutted out of the water, covered her hair and her breast in sea-foam so that no one could see her little face, and then watched to see who would come down to the poor prince.

It was not long before a young girl came down there; she seemed quite frightened, but only for a moment, and then she went and fetched some more people. And the mermaid saw the prince revive and smile at everybody round about him, but he did not turn and smile at her, for of course he did not even know that she had rescued him. She felt so sad that when he was carried into the great building, she dived sorrowfully down into the water and made her way home to her father's palace.

She had always been quiet and thoughtful, but now she became even more so. Her sisters asked her what she had seen the first time she had been above the sea, but she told them nothing.

Many an evening and morning she rose up where she had left the prince. She watched the fruit in the garden ripen and she saw it gathered in; she saw the snow melt on the high mountains, but the prince she did not see, and so, every time, she turned home even more sorrowful than before. Her one comfort was to sit in her little garden and throw her arms round the beautiful marble statue that looked so like the prince. But she no longer looked after her flowers, and they grew, as if in a wilderness, out over the paths and twisted their long stems and their leaves in among the branches of the trees until it was quite dark there.

At last she could bear it no longer, and told one of her sisters all about it, and so all the others got to know about it, too, right away, but no one else beyond them and a couple of other mermaids, who, of course, told no one, except their closest friends. One of them knew who the prince was—she, too, had seen the party on board the ship, and she knew where he was from and where his kingdom lay.

'Come, little sister!' said the other princesses, and with their arms about each others' shoulders they rose up out of the sea in a long row in front of the spot where they knew the prince's palace lay.

It was built of a gleaming pale-yellow stone, with great marble steps, some leading right down into the sea. Magnificent gilt domes rose above the roof, and between the pillars which surrounded the whole building stood marble statues that looked as if they were alive. Through the clear glass of the tall windows, you could see into the splendid halls where costly silk curtains and tapestries were hung and all the walls were adorned with great paintings that it was a real joy to look upon. In the middle of the largest hall splashed a great fountain, its jets of water mounting high up towards the glass dome in the ceiling through which the sun shone upon the water and the lovely plants that grew in the great basin.

Now she knew where he lived, and there she came to the surface of the sea many an evening and night. She would swim much closer to the shore than any of the others had ever dared to do, yes, she would go right up the narrow canal below the magnificent marble balcony which cast its long shadow out over the water. There she would sit and look at the young prince who thought he was quite alone in the clear moonlight.

She saw him many an evening sailing to music in the fine boat where the flags were flying. She would peep out from among the green rushes, and if the wind caught her long silver-white veil and anyone saw it, he thought it was a swan spreading its wings.

Many a night, when the fishermen lay with their lights upon the water, she heard them speaking so well of the young prince, and that made her glad she had saved his life when he had driven half-dead upon the waves, and she would remember how closely his head had rested upon her breast and how deeply she had kissed him—and he knew nothing at all about it, and could not even dream of her.

She came to like people more and more, more and more she wished she could go up among them; their world seemed to her far greater than her own, for they could sail away over the sea in ships and climb upon the high mountains high above the clouds, and the lands they owned stretched farther, with forests and fields, than her eye could reach. There was so much she wanted to know, but her sisters were not able to give answers to everything, and so she questioned their old grandmother, and she knew the upper world, as she very rightly called the lands above the sea, very well indeed.

'If they are not drowned, can people live for ever?' asked the little mermaid. 'Don't they die, as we do down here in the sea?'

'Yes, of course they do!' the old lady said. 'They have to die, too, and their lifetime is even shorter than ours. We can live until we are three hundred years old, but then when our life is finished here, we are only foam upon the water, we do not even have a grave down here among our dear ones. We have no immortal soul, we never again come to life, we are like the green rushes—once they are cut through, they cannot grow green again! But people on the other hand have a soul which lives for ever, which goes on living after the body has become dust; it rises up through the bright sky, up to all the shining stars! Just as we dive up out of the sea to look at the lands where people live, so they dive up to lovely unknown places that we shall never come to see.'

'Why were we not given an immortal soul?' asked the little mermaid sadly. 'I would give all the hundreds of years I have to live to be a human girl for just one day and then to receive my part in the Kingdom of Heaven!'

'You must not go thinking about such things!' said the old lady. 'We have a much happier and better time than the people up there do!'

'Then I must die and float like foam upon the sea, and not hear the music of the waves or see the lovely flowers and the red sun! Can't I do anything at all to gain an eternal soul?'

'No!' said the old lady. 'Only if a human man should fall in love with you so deeply that you would be more to him than father and mother; only if he should cling to you with all his thought and all his love, and let the priest place his right hand in yours with a vow of faith here and for all eternity: then his soul would overflow into your body, and you, too, would have your share in human fortune. He would give you a soul and yet keep his own. But that can never happen! What is especially delightful here in the sea—your fishtail —they find ugly up there on earth: they won't think any the better of you for it—there you must have two clumsy props they call legs to be thought beautiful!'

Then the little mermaid sighed and looked sadly at her fishtail.

'Let us be joyful!' said the old lady. 'We'll skip and dance through the three hundred years we have to live. It's a good long time really, and afterwards we shall be able the more contentedly to rest in our graves. We'll hold a court ball this evening!'

There was a splendour such as you would never see on earth. The walls and the ceiling of the great ballroom were of thick but clear glass. Several hundred huge mussel-shells, rose-red and grass-green, stood in rows on either side with burning blue flames in them, lighting up the whole room and shining out through the walls, so that the sea outside was quite brightly lit. You could see the countless fish, great and small, that came swimming towards the glass walls: on some shone scales of purple-red, on others they seemed to be of silver and gold. Through the middle of the hall flowed a broad running current, and on this the mermen and women danced to their own lovely singing. Such beautiful voices are not to be found among the people on earth. The little mermaid sang the most beautifully of them all, and they all applauded her. And, for the moment, she felt joy in her heart, for she knew she had the most beautiful voice of all who live upon the earth or in the sea. But she very soon found herself thinking once more of the world above her: she could not forget the handsome prince and her own sorrow at not having, like him, an immortal soul. And so she stole out of her father's palace, and while all was song and merriment inside, she sat sadly in her little garden. Then she heard the sound of a French horn ring down through the water, and she thought, 'He must be sailing up there now, him I hold dearer than father and mother, him my thoughts cling to, and into whose hands I would put my life's happiness. I would risk everything to win him and an immortal soul! While my sisters are dancing there in my father's palace, I will go and see the sea-witch— I have always been so frightened of her, but perhaps she can advise and help me!'

Then the little mermaid went out of her garden, away towards the roaring whirlpools behind which the witch dwelt. She had never been that way before. No flowers grew there, no sea-grass—only the naked grey sand of the sea-bed stretched away towards the whirlpools that whirled round like roaring mill-wheels and bore away everything that came within their grasp down with them into their depths. Right through the midst of these tremendous whirlpools she had to go to reach the sea-witch's district, and there, for a long stretch, there was no other way but over the warm bubbling mud the witch called her peat-bog. Beyond this lay her house in the middle of a lonely forest. The trees and bushes were all polyps, half beast, half plant, that looked like hundred-headed snakes growing out of the earth. All the branches were long slimy arms with fingers like supple worms, and limb by limb they were in constant motion from their roots to their topmost tips. Everything they could seize upon in the ocean they twined themselves fast about and never more let go. The little mermaid grew quite terrified as she stood just outside the forest. Her heart beat with fear and she very nearly turned back, but then she thought of the prince and the soul of man, and so she found courage. She bound her long streaming hair firmly about her head so that the polyps should not be able to seize her by it, and placed both her hands together over her breast, and in this way she flew through the water like a fish in among the grisly polyps that stretched their supple arms and fingers after her. She saw that each of them had something it had seized, and hundreds of small arms held it like strong bands of iron. Men who had perished at sea and had sunk deep down below peeped out like white skeletons from the polyps' arms. Ships' rudders and sea-chests they held in their grip, and the skeletons of land animals and a little mermaid they had seized and strangled—that almost made her more afraid than anything else.

Then she came to a great slimy opening in the forest where great fat water-snakes were frisking about and showing their ugly yellow-white bellies. In the middle of the opening, a house had been built from the bones of shipwrecked men. There the sea-witch sat letting a toad eat out of her mouth, just as people will let a little canary eat sugar. The ugly fat water-snakes she called her little chickens, and she let them roll about on her great spongy breasts.

'I know well enough what it is you want!' said the sea-witch. 'You're acting like a fool! However, you shall have your way, for it will bring you misfortune, my lovely princess! You'd like to get rid of your fishtail and have two stumps in place of it so that you can walk like a human! Then the young prince will fall in love with you, and you'll be able to get him and an immortal soul as well!' At the same time the witch laughed so loudly and unpleasantly that the toad and the snakes fell rolling on to the ground. 'You've come just at the right time,' said the witch. 'If it had been after sunrise tomorrow morning, I could not have helped you until another year had passed. I shall make you a drink: before the sun rises, you must swim to land with it, sit yourself down upon the shore, and drink it. Then your tail will divide and shrink into what men call a lovely pair of legs. But it will hurt: it will be like a sharp sword going through you. Everybody who sees you will say you are the loveliest human child they have ever seen! You will keep your gliding motion: no dancer will be able to glide along like you, but every step you take will be like treading on a sharp knife that cuts you and makes your blood flow. If you are willing to suffer all this, then I will help you.'

'Yes!' the little mermaid said in a trembling voice, and she thought of the prince and of winning an immortal soul.

'But remember,' said the witch, 'once you have taken human form, you can never become a mermaid again! You will never be able to go down through the water to see your sisters or your father's palace. And if you do not win the prince's love so that he will forget father and mother for your sake, cling to you with all his mind and let the priest place your hands in one another's so that you become man and wife, you will not get an immortal soul! The very first morning after he weds another, your heart will break, and you will become foam upon the water.'

'I am willing!' said the little mermaid, and she was as pale as death.

'But you must pay me, too!' said the witch. 'And it is no small thing I am asking for. You have the loveliest voice of all down here upon the bottom of the sea, and no doubt you think you will be able to bewitch him with it, but that voice you must give to me. The best thing you possess will I have in return for my precious drink! For I must give you my own blood in it to make the drink sharp like a two-edged sword!'

'But if you take my voice,' said the little mermaid, 'what shall I have left?'

'Your lovely figure,' said the witch, 'your gliding walk and your speaking eyes—with them you will be able to charm a man's heart, never you fear! Well, have you lost your courage? Put out your little tongue so that I can cut it off in payment, and you shall have your powerful drink!'

'It shall be done!' said the little mermaid, and the witch put her cauldron on to boil the magic potion. 'Cleanliness is a good thing!' she said, and scoured the cauldron out with the snakes which she had tied into a knot. Then she scratched herself on the breast and let her black blood drip into it. The steam formed shapes so strange and wonderful that they would have filled you with fear and dread. Every second the witch put something new into the cauldron, and when the brew was properly boiling it sounded like a crocodile weeping. At last the drink was ready—and it looked like the clearest water!

'There it is!' said the witch, and cut out the tongue of the little mermaid, who was now dumb and could neither sing nor speak.

'If the polyps should catch hold of you as you go back through my woods,' said the witch, 'you have only to throw one single drop of this potion over them and their arms and fingers will burst into a thousand pieces!' But the little mermaid had no need to do it, for the polyps drew back in fear of her when they saw the shining drink glistening in her hand like a sparkling star. And so she soon returned through the forest, the bog, and the roaring whirlpools.

She could see her father's palace: the lights were out in the great ballroom; no doubt they were all asleep in there, but yet she dared not go and look at them—she was dumb now and had made up her mind to go right away from them for ever. It seemed as if her heart would break with sorrow. She slipped into the garden, took one flower from each of her sisters' flower-beds, blew a thousand kisses towards the palace, and rose up through the dark-blue sea.

The sun had not yet risen when she saw the prince's palace and clambered on to the stately marble steps. The moon was shining lovely and clear. The little mermaid drank the sharp burning drink, and it felt as if a two-edged sword went through her delicate body. She fainted with the pain of it and lay as if she were dead. When the sun shone over the sea, she woke up and she felt a stinging pain, but right in front of her stood the

handsome young prince, his coal-black eyes fastened upon her so that she dropped her own and

saw that her fishtail had gone and that she had the
nicest little white legs any young girl could have,

but she was quite naked and so she wrapped her long thick hair about her. The prince asked who she was and how she had come there, and she looked gently yet sadly at him with her dark-blue eyes, for speak she could not. Then he took her by the hand and led her into the palace. Every step she took was, as the witch had told her it would be, like treading on pointed tools and sharp knives, but she bore it all willingly: the prince's hand on hers, she stepped as light as a bubble, and he and everyone there marvelled at her graceful gliding walk.

She was given costly clothes of silk and muslin to wear, and she was the most beautiful girl in the palace, but she was dumb and could neither sing nor talk. Beautiful slave-girls, clad in silk and gold, appeared and sang for the prince and his royal parents: one sang more beautifully than all the rest, and the prince clapped his hands and smiled at her. And then the little mermaid grew sad for she knew that she herself had sung far more beautifully. She thought, 'Oh, if only he could know that to be near him I have given my voice away for ever!'

Then the slave-girls danced graceful swaying dances to the noblest music, and the little mermaid raised her beautiful white arms, rose upon the tips of her toes and glided away over the floor, dancing as no one had ever danced before. With every movement her loveliness grew even more apparent, and her eyes spoke more deeply to the heart than the slave-girls' song.

Everyone was enraptured by it, and especially the prince, who called her his little foundling, and she danced on and on, although every time her foot touched the ground it was like treading on sharp knives. The prince said that she should remain with him always, and she was given permission to sleep outside his door on a velvet cushion.

He had a man's suit made for her so that she could go riding with him. They rode through the scented forest where the green branches brushed her shoulders and the little birds sang among the fresh leaves. She went climbing with the prince on the high mountains, and although her delicate feet bled so that all could see, she laughed at it and went with him until they saw the clouds sailing down below them like a flock of birds making their way to distant lands.

At home at the prince's palace, when the others were asleep at night, she would go out on to the broad marble steps, and standing in the cold sea-water would cool her burning feet, and then she would think of those down below in the deep.

One night her sisters came arm-in-arm, singing so sorrowfully as they swam over the water, and she waved to them and they recognized her and told her how sad she had made them all. After that they came to see her every night, and one night she saw, far out, her old grandmother, who had not been to the surface of the sea for many years, and the merking with his crown upon his head. They stretched their hands out towards her, but they dared not come as near the land as her sisters.

Day by day she grew dearer to the prince: he was fond of her as one might be fond of a dear good child, but it never occurred to him to make her his queen, and his wife she had to be, or else she would not find an immortal soul but on the morning of his wedding would become foam upon the sea.

'You are fonder of me than of all the others?' the little mermaid's eyes seemed to say when he took her in his arms and kissed her fair brow.

'Yes, of course you are dearest to me,' said the prince, 'because you have the best heart of all of them. You are the one I am most fond of, and you are like a young girl I once saw but shall never find again, no doubt. I was on board a ship which was wrecked, and the waves drove me to land near a holy temple served by several young maidens. The youngest of them found me there by the seashore and saved my life. I saw her only twice: she is the only one I could love in all the world, but you are like her—you have almost taken the place of her picture in my soul. She belongs to the holy temple, and so good fortune has sent me you—never will we part from one another!'

'Ah, he does not know that I saved his life!' thought the little mermaid. 'I bore him over the sea away to the woods where the temple stands, I hid behind the foam and watched to see if anyone would come. I saw the pretty maiden he loves more than me!' And the mermaid sighed deeply—weep she could not. 'The maiden belongs to the holy temple, he said. She will never come out into the world, they will not meet again, and I am here with him, I see him every day—I will look after him and love him and give up my life to him!'

But now everybody was saying that the prince was to marry and have the neighbouring king's lovely daughter, and it was for that purpose he was fitting out such a splendid ship. 'The prince is travelling to see the neighbouring king's land. That's what they're saying, of course, but it's really to see the neighbouring king's daughter! And he's taking a great following with him!' But the little mermaid shook her head and laughed; she knew the prince's thoughts much better than the rest of them. 'I have to make a journey,' he had told her. 'I have to go and see this lovely princess! It's my parents' wish—but they won't force me to bring her home as my bride: I cannot love her! She will not look like the lovely maiden in the temple, as you do. If I should ever choose a bride, then it would sooner be you, my dumb foundling with the speaking eyes!' And he kissed her red mouth, played with her long hair, and laid his head against her heart so that it dreamed of human happiness and an immortal soul.

'You do not seem a bit afraid of the sea, my dumb child!' he said, as they stood on the splendid ship which was to carry him to the land of the neighbouring king. And he told her of storm and calm, of rare fish in the deep and of what divers had seen. And she smiled at what he told her, for, of course, she knew more than anyone about the bottom of the sea.

In the moon-clear night when they were all asleep except the helmsman standing by the wheel, she sat by the ship's rail and gazed down through the clear water, and she thought she could see her father's palace: on the very top of it her old grandmother was standing with her silver crown upon her head, and gazing up through the swift currents towards the ship's keel. Then her sisters came up to the surface; they gazed sorrowfully at her and wrung their white hands. She waved to them and smiled and wanted to tell them that all was going well and happily with her, but the ship's boy drew near her and her sisters dived below so that he was

101

left believing that the whiteness he had seen was only foam upon the water.

The next morning the ship sailed into the harbour of the neighbouring king's fine city. All the church-bells were ringing, and trumpets blared from the high towers while the soldiers stood to attention with waving flags and glinting bayonets. Every day there was merry-making: balls and parties followed one upon another. But the princess was not there yet: she was being brought up far away in a holy temple, they said, where she was learning all the royal virtues. At last she arrived.

The little mermaid stood there eager to see her beauty, and, she had to admit it, a more graceful figure she had never seen. Her skin was so delicate and pure, and behind her long dark lashes smiled a pair of steadfast dark-blue eyes.

'It is you!' said the prince. 'You who saved me when I lay like a corpse on the shore!' And he held his blushing bride tightly in his arms. 'Oh, I am all too happy!' he said to the little mermaid. 'The best thing I could ever hope for but never dared to, has happened to me. You will be glad I am happy, for you are fonder of me than the rest of them!' And the little mermaid kissed his hand, and she thought she felt her heart breaking. His wedding morning would be her death and change her into foam upon the sea.

All the church-bells rang, the heralds rode through the streets and proclaimed the betrothal. Upon all the altars burned sweet-scented oil in precious silver lamps. The priests swung their censers, and bride and bridegroom took one another by the hand and received the bishop's blessing. The little mermaid stood in silk and gold holding the bride's train, but her ears did not hear the festive music, her eyes did not see the holy ceremony, her thoughts were upon the night of her death, upon all she had lost in this world.

That very same evening the bride and bridegroom went on board their ship. The cannon were fired and all the flags were streaming, and amidships a royal tent of gold and purple had been raised and furnished with the loveliest cushions. And there the bridal pair were to sleep in the still cool night.

The sails bellied in the wind, and the ship glided away lightly and smoothly over the clear sea.

When it grew dark many-coloured lamps were lit, and the sailors danced merry dances on deck. The little mermaid could not help thinking of the first time she had dived up to the surface of the sea and had seen the same splendour and rejoicing, and she whirled in the dance with the rest, swerving as a swallow swerves when it is pursued, and they all applauded her in admiration, for never before had she danced so brilliantly. Sharp knives seemed to cut into her delicate feet, but she did not feel it, for the pain in her heart cut yet more sharply. She knew this was the last evening she would ever see him for whom she had forsaken her kindred and her home, given up her lovely voice, and daily suffered unending torment—and he had no idea of it. This was the last night she would breathe the same air as he, or look upon the deep sea and the starry blue sky; an everlasting night without thoughts or dreams awaited her, for she had no soul and could not gain one. And all was rejoicing and merry-making on board until well gone midnight. She laughed and danced with the thought of death in her heart. The prince kissed his lovely bride, and she played with his black hair, and arm-in-arm they went to rest in the splendid tent.

The ship grew still and quiet: only the helmsman stood by the wheel. The little mermaid laid her white arms upon the rail and looked towards the east for the first red of morning—the first ray of the sun, she knew, would kill her. Then she saw her sisters rise up to the surface of the sea: they were pale like her; their beautiful long hair no longer fluttered in the breeze—it had been cut off.

'We have given it to the witch so that she would help us and you would not have to die this night! She has given us a knife—here it is! Can you see how sharp it is? Before the sun rises, you must thrust it into the prince's heart, and as his warm blood splashes on to your feet, they will grow together into a fishtail and you will be a mermaid again, and then you can come down to us in the water and live your three hundred years before you turn into the dead salt foam of the sea. Hurry! Either he or you must die before the sun rises! Our old grandmother is so overcome with sorrow that her white hair has fallen out just as ours fell before the witch's scissors. Kill the prince and come back to us! Hurry!—Do you see that red streak in the sky? In a few minutes the sun will rise, and then you must die!' And they gave a strange deep sigh and sank beneath the waves.

The little mermaid drew aside the purple hangings of the tent, and she saw the lovely bride sleeping with her head upon the prince's breast, and she bent down and kissed his fair forehead. She looked at the sky where the red of morning was shining more and more brightly; she looked at the sharp

104

knife and gazed once again upon the prince who murmured his bride's name in his dreams. She alone was in his thoughts, and the knife quivered in the mermaid's hand—but she flung it far out into the waves which shone red where it fell and looked as if drops of blood had spurted up out of the water. Once more she looked with half-glazed eyes upon the prince, threw herself from the ship down into the sea, and felt her body dissolving into foam.

Then the sun rose out of the sea and its rays fell gently and warmly on the death-cold sea-foam; and the little mermaid had no feeling of death upon her. She looked at the bright sun, and up above her floated hundreds of lovely transparent forms; through them she could see the ship's white sails and the red clouds in the sky. Their voices were music, but so ethereal were their tones that no human ear could hear them, just as no earthly eye could see them. Their own lightness bore them without wings through the air. The little mermaid noticed that she had a body like theirs that rose higher and higher out of the foam.

'To whom am I coming?' she asked, and her voice sounded like those of the other beings, so ethereal that no earthly music could echo its tones.

'To the daughters of the air!' answered the others. 'A mermaid has no immortal soul, and she can never gain one unless she wins the love of a mortal man: her immortality depends upon the power of another. The daughters of the air have no eternal soul either, but they can by good deeds create one for themselves. We are flying to the hot climates, where the warm pestilence-laden atmosphere kills people. There we waft cool breezes, we spread the sweet scent of flowers through the air and send freshness and healing. When we have striven to do what good we can for three hundred years, we gain our immortal soul and are given a share in the eternal happiness of mankind. You, poor little mermaid, have striven with your whole heart for the same thing as we strive for. You have suffered and endured, and raised yourself into the world of the spirits of the air. And now you, too, through your good deeds can create an immortal soul for yourself in three hundred years.'

And the little mermaid lifted her bright arms up towards God's sun, and for the first time she felt tears coming. On the ship there was bustle and life again: she saw the prince with his beautiful bride looking for her—they were staring sadly into the bubbling foam as if they knew she had thrown herself into the waves. Unseen, she kissed the bride's brow, smiled upon the prince, and with the other children of the air she soared up upon a rose-red cloud sailing through the air.

'In three hundred years we shall float just like this into the Kingdom of God!'

'We might come there even sooner!' whispered one. 'Unseen we float into people's homes where there are children, and for every day we find a good child that makes its parents happy and deserves their love, so God shortens our period of trial. The child does not know when we are flying through the room, and then when we smile upon it in happiness, a year is taken from our three hundred. But if we see a bad naughty child, then we must weep tears of sorrow, and every tear adds a day to the time of our trial!'

THE EMPEROR'S NEW
CLOTHES

MANY years ago there lived an Emperor who was so uncommonly fond of gay new clothes that he spent all his money on finery. He cared nothing for his soldiers; nor did he care about going to the theatre or riding in the woods, except for one thing —it gave him a chance to show off his new clothes. He had a different suit for every hour of the day, and since he spent so much time changing, instead of saying, as one does of a king, 'He is in his Council Chamber,' they said, 'The Emperor is in his Wardrobe.'

Life was very entertaining in the big city where he had his court. Strangers arrived every day, and one day there appeared two rogues who spread the

107

story that they were weavers who had mastered the art of weaving the most beautiful cloth you can imagine. Not only were the colours and patterns outstandingly lovely, but the clothes made from the cloth had the wonderful property of remaining invisible to anyone who was not fit for his job or who was particularly stupid.

'They would indeed be fine clothes to have!' thought the Emperor. 'With those on, I could find out what men in my kingdom are unfit for the jobs they have. And I should be able to tell the wise men from the fools! Yes, I must have some of that cloth made up for me at once!' And he handed over a large sum of money to the two rogues to enable them to begin the work.

So they set their two looms up and looked as if they were hard at work, but there was nothing at all on the looms. They boldly demanded the finest silk and gold thread, which they put in their haversacks, and went on pretending to work at the empty looms until far into the night.

'I should like to know how far they've got with my cloth,' thought the Emperor. But when he remembered that no one who was stupid or unfit for his job could see it, he felt somewhat hesitant about going to see for himself. Now, of course, he was quite certain that, as far as he was concerned, there were no grounds for fear, but nevertheless he felt he would rather send someone else first to see how they were getting on. Everybody in the city knew what wonderful powers the cloth had, and they were all very anxious to see how incompetent and stupid their neighbours were.

'I'll send my honest old minister to the weavers,' thought the Emperor. 'He's the best one to see how the cloth's coming on, for he's sense enough, and no one's fitter for his job than he is.'

So the good-natured old minister entered the room where the two rogues sat pretending to work at the empty looms. 'God help us!' thought the old minister, his eyes wide open, 'I can't see a thing!' But, of course, he was careful not to say so out loud.

Both rogues requested him very politely to take a step nearer, and asked him whether he didn't think the pattern beautiful and the colours charming. As they pointed to the empty loom, the poor old minister stared and stared, but he still could not see anything, for the simple reason that there was nothing to see. 'Heavens above,' he thought, 'surely I am not a stupid person! I must say such an idea has never occurred to me, and it must not occur to anyone else either! Am I really unfit for my job? No, it certainly won't do for me to say I can't see the cloth!'

'Well, you don't say anything,' said the one who was still weaving. 'Don't you like it?'

'Oh, er—it's delightful, quite the finest thing I've ever seen!' said the old minister, peering through his glasses. 'The design and the colours— oh, yes, I shall tell the Emperor they please me immensely!'

'Well, it's very kind of you to say so!' said the two weavers, and they went on to describe the colours and the unusual nature of the pattern. The old minister listened very carefully so that he could say the same thing when he returned to the Emperor. And that is just what he did.

The rogues now demanded a further supply of money, silk, and gold, which they said they must have for their work. But they put it all in their own pockets, and not a single thread ever appeared on the loom. However, they continued, as before, to weave away at the empty loom.

Soon afterwards the Emperor sent another unsuspecting official to see how the weaving was going on and whether the cloth would soon be finished. The same thing happened to him that happened to the minister: he stared and stared, but as there was nothing but the empty loom, he could not see a thing.

'Yes, it's a lovely piece of stuff, isn't it?' said the two rogues. And they showed him the cloth, and explained the charming pattern that was not there.

'Stupid I most certainly am not!' thought the official. 'Then the answer must be that I am not fit for my job, I suppose. That would be a very odd thing, and I really can't believe it. I shall have to see that no one else suspects it.' And then he praised the cloth he could not see, and assured them how happy he was with the beautiful colours and the charming pattern. 'Yes,' he told the Emperor, 'it's quite the finest thing I've ever seen!'

The story of the magnificent cloth was now on everybody's lips.

And now the Emperor wanted to see it himself while it was still on the loom.

With a large number of carefully chosen courtiers —among them the two good old men who had been there before—he paid a visit to the two crafty rogues, who were weaving away with all their might, but with neither weft nor warp.

'Isn't it really magnificent?' asked the two officials. 'Will Your Majesty be pleased to examine it? What a pattern! What colours!' And they pointed to the empty loom, fully believing that the others could undoubtedly see the cloth.

'What's this!' thought the Emperor. 'I don't see a thing! This is really awful! Am I stupid? Am I not fit to be Emperor? That would be the most shocking thing that could happen to me!—Oh, it's very beautiful,' he said aloud. 'It has my very highest approval.' He nodded in a satisfied manner, and looked at the empty loom: on no account would he tell anyone that he could not see anything. All the courtiers who had come with him stared and stared, but none of them could make out any more than the others. But they all repeated after the Emperor, 'Oh, it's very beautiful!' And they advised him to have a suit made of the wonderful new cloth so that he could wear it for the first time for the great procession that had been arranged. 'It's magnificent! Delightful, excellent!' was repeated from mouth to mouth, and they all appeared to be deeply impressed and delighted with it. The Emperor gave each of the rogues an Order of Knighthood to hang in his buttonhole and the title of Knight of the Loom.

The two rogues sat up the whole night before the morning when the procession was to take place, and they had sixteen candles burning. Everyone could see that they had a job on to get the Emperor's new clothes ready in time. They pretended to take the cloth off the loom, they cut out large pieces of air with their big tailor's scissors, they sewed away with needles that had no thread in them, and at last they said, 'Look, the clothes are ready!'

The Emperor with the most distinguished of his gentlemen came to see for himself, and the rogues both held one arm up as if they were holding something, and they said, 'Look, here are the trousers. Here's the jacket. This is the cap.' And so on and so on. 'They are as light as gossamer! You'd think you'd nothing on your body, and that, of course, is the whole point of it!'

'Yes,' said all the gentlemen, but they couldn't see anything, because there was nothing there.

'Will Your Imperial Majesty most graciously be pleased to take your clothes off?' said the rogues. 'Then we shall put the new ones on Your Majesty over here in front of the big mirror.'

The Emperor laid aside all his clothes, and the two rogues pretended to hand him his new clothes, one at a time. They put their arms round his waist, and appeared to fasten something that was obviously his train, and the Emperor turned himself round in front of the mirror.

'My, how well it suits His Majesty! What a perfect fit!' they all said. 'What a pattern! What colours! It must be worth a fortune!'

'The canopy which is to be borne over Your Majesty in the procession is waiting outside,' said the Chief Master of Ceremonies.

'Right,' said the Emperor, 'I'm quite ready. Doesn't it fit well?' And he turned round once more in front of the mirror and pretended to take a good look at his fine suit.

The Gentlemen of the Chamber, whose job it was to bear the train, fumbled on the floor with their hands as if they were picking it up, and then they held their hands up in the air. They dared not let anyone notice that they couldn't see anything.

And so the Emperor walked in the procession under his fine canopy, and everybody in the streets and at their windows said, 'My, look at the Emperor's new clothes! There's never been anything like them! Look at the beautiful train he has to his coat! Doesn't it hang marvellously!' No one would let anyone else see that he couldn't see anything, for if he did, they would have thought that he was not fit for his job, or else that he was very stupid. None of the Emperor's clothes had ever had such a success before.

'But, Daddy, he's got nothing on!' piped up a small child.

'Heavens, listen to the voice of innocence!' said his father. And what the child had said was whispered from one to another.

'He's nothing on! A little child said so. He's nothing on!'

At last, everybody who was there was shouting, 'He's nothing on!' And it gradually dawned upon the Emperor that they were probably right. But he thought to himself, 'I must carry on, or I shall ruin the procession.' And so he held himself up even more proudly than before, and the Gentlemen of the Chamber walked along carrying a train that was most definitely not there.

THE GALOSHES OF FORTUNE

1. *A Beginning*

IT happened that in Copenhagen, in one of the houses on Østergade, not far from Kongens Nytorv, there was a big party—for you must invite people to a party once in a while so that you can be invited back to theirs. Half the guests were already sitting round the card-tables, and the other half were waiting to see what would come of the hostess's remark, 'Well, let's see what we can find to do!' That's as far as they had got, and the conversation went from one thing to another. Amongst other things, the talk turned to the Middle Ages. Some regarded them as far better than our own times, and, indeed, Councillor Knap was so enthusiastically of this opinion that the hostess immediately sided with him, and they both expressed their indignation at Ørsted's article in The Almanac on old

114

and new times, in which our own age is, in everything that matters most, given first place. The
Councillor regarded the time of King Hans as the
pleasantest and happiest of all.

While they are arguing for and against—their
talk interrupted only by a glance at the newspaper
which had just come but which contained nothing
worth reading—we will go out and take a look in
the room where the overcoats, walking-sticks, umbrellas, and galoshes had been left. There were
two women sitting here, one of them young, the
other old. At first sight you might take them for
maids who had come with their mistress, an old
maiden lady, perhaps, or a widow, but if you looked
at them a little more closely, you would soon realize
that they were not ordinary servants. Their hands
were too fine for that, their bearing and all their
movements far too regal, and their clothes, too, had
quite an unusual cut of their own. They were two
fairies. The younger one was, we must confess, not
Fortune herself, but only one of the lady's maids to
one of her ladies-in-waiting who bring round the
lesser gifts of Fortune. The elder one had a thoughtful, serious look: she was Sorrow—she always goes
upon her own errands in her own high person, and
then she knows they are properly carried out.

They were telling one another where they had
been that day. The one who was lady's maid to one
of Fortune's ladies-in-waiting had so far attended
to only a few trivial errands: she had, she said,
rescued a new hat from a shower of rain, she had
got an honest man a greeting from a well-born
nonentity, and so on. But what she still had left to
do was something quite unusual.

'I must explain,' she said, 'that it's my birthday

today, and in honour of the occasion I've been entrusted with a pair of galoshes which I have to bring among men. These galoshes have strange powers: whoever puts them on will immediately find himself in whatever place or time he prefers. Every wish connected with time or place will be fulfilled at once, and so man will at last find happiness here on earth!'

'Believe what you like,' said Sorrow, 'but I assure you he will be very, very unhappy, and he'll bless the moment he's free of them again!'

'What are you talking about?' said the other. 'I shall put them down here by the door. Someone will make a mistake, and he'll be the lucky one!'

And that was their conversation.

2. *What Happened to the Councillor*

It was late: Councillor Knap, deep in the time of King Hans, wanted to go home. And now his fate directed him to put on the Galoshes of Fortune instead of his own, and out he stepped into Østergade. But owing to the magic power of the galoshes, he had stepped back into the time of King Hans, and so he put his foot right into the mire and mud of the street, for in those times there were no pavements.

'How dreadfully filthy it is here!' said the Councillor. 'The whole pavement's been taken up, and the lights are all out!'

The moon had not yet risen high enough, and there was something of a mist, so that everything round about him disappeared rapidly into the darkness. At the nearest street-corner, however, hung a lantern in front of a picture of Our Lady, but the light it shed was little better than nothing: he did not notice it until he was standing right underneath it and his eyes fell upon the painted picture of the Mother and Child.

'It must be an art-shop,' he thought, 'and they've forgotten to take their sign-board in!'

A couple of people, in the dress of the period, walked past him.

'How very odd they looked! They must have come from a fancy-dress ball!'

All at once there was a sound of drums and pipes and a strong blaze of light. The Councillor stood still and saw a most surprising procession pass by. It was led by a troop of drummers who handled their instruments right well: behind them came retainers with bows and cross-bows. The most important person in the train was a priest. The Councillor was quite astonished, and asked what it all meant and who this man was.

'It's the Bishop of Zealand!' someone answered.

'Good heavens, what on earth's come over the bishop?' The Councillor sighed and shook his head: it couldn't possibly be the bishop.

Pondering over this and without looking to left

or right, the Councillor walked along Østergade and over Højbro Place. But he could not find the bridge that led to the Palace Square. He caught a glimpse of one side of the river-bank, and at last he came across two fellows lying in a boat.

'Does your worship wish to be taken across to the Island?' they asked.

'Over to the Island?' asked the Councillor, who still had no idea what period he had wandered into. 'I want to get out to Christianshavn to Little Torvegade!'

The men looked at him.

'Just tell me where the bridge is!' he said. 'It's disgraceful—there isn't a lamp lit, and as for the filth, you might be walking through a bog!'

The longer he talked with the watermen, the more difficult he found it to understand them.

'I don't understand your Bornholm talk!' he said irritably at last, and turned his back on them. But he still could not find the bridge, nor the parapet either. 'It's a scandal! Just look at the place!' he said. Never had he found his own age a more miserable period to live in than this evening. 'I think I'll take a cab,' he thought. But where were the cabs? There wasn't one to be seen. 'I shall have to walk back to Kongens Nytorv: there are bound to be some there. I shall never get out to Christianshavn otherwise.'

And now he walked on towards Østergade, and had almost walked the length of it when the moon rose.

'Good heavens, what on earth's all that scaffolding they've put up!' he said, as he caught sight of the East Gate, which at that time was situated at the end of Østergade.

At last he found a gateway, and going through it, he came out on what is now the Nytorv, but instead of the market-place, he saw a vast stretch of meadow-land. Here and there a bush stood out, and right across the meadow ran a broad canal or stream. On the opposite bank lay a few wretched wooden huts used by the Dutch skippers after whom the place was called Holland's Ridge.

'Either it's a mirage, as they call it, or else I'm drunk!' wailed the Councillor. 'What's come over me! What's come over me!'

He turned back in the firm belief that he was ill. As he came out into the street again, he looked a little more closely at the houses—most of them were half-timbered and many had only thatched roofs.

'Oh, I'm not at all well!' he sighed. 'And I only drank a single glass of punch! It doesn't agree with me at all! It was absolutely ridiculous to give us punch and hot salmon—and I shall tell the agent's wife so, too! I wonder if I should go back again, and let them see how ill I am? But perhaps it would look rather silly!—And they may have gone to bed by now!'

He looked for the house, but it was nowhere to be found.

'This is really dreadful! I can't recognize Øster-gade—not a shop anywhere: all I can see are wretched old hovels, just as if I were in Roskilde or Ringsted! Yes, I'm ill right enough, it's no good pretending otherwise! But where in the world is the agent's apartment? This must be it, but it doesn't look a bit like itself! There's still someone up. Oh, I'm most certainly ill!'

He now gave a push to a half-open door where

the light was streaming out through the crack. It was one of the hostelries of the time, a sort of alehouse. The room had the appearance of an old-fashioned farm-house in Holstein. A number of good people—skippers, citizens of Copenhagen, and a couple of scholars—were sitting here deep in talk, their tankards beside them, and paid little attention to him as he stepped inside.

'I do beg your pardon,' said the Councillor to the hostess, as she came towards him, 'but I've been taken seriously ill! Could you possibly get me a cab to take me out to Christianshavn?'

The woman looked at him and shook her head: then she spoke to him in German. The Councillor supposed that she knew no Danish, and repeated his request in German. This, together with his dress, confirmed the woman's impression that he was a foreigner. She soon grasped the fact that he was ill, and so she gave him a tankard of water—somewhat brackish, it's true—which had been fetched from the well outside.

The Councillor propped his head on his hand, took a deep breath, and pondered over all the strange things around him.

'Is that this evening's paper?' he asked, for the sake of something to say, as he saw the woman removing a large sheet of paper.

She did not understand what he meant, but she handed him the sheet: it was a wood-cut showing strange flashes of light in the sky seen over the city of Cologne.

'It's very old!' said the Councillor, and he became quite excited at coming across such an old piece of work. 'However did you come by a rare sheet like that? It's most interesting—though it's all an old wives' tale, of course. Such flashes of light can readily be explained: they're really the Northern Lights, and they're probably caused by electricity!'

Those who sat nearest and heard what he said looked at him in wonder, and one of them got up, respectfully took his hat off, and said with the most serious expression, 'You are undoubtedly a very learned man, monsieur!'

'Oh, not at all!' replied the Councillor. 'I can talk about one or two things, but no more than most people can!'

'Modesty is a beautiful virtue!' said the man. 'For that matter, I can reply to your remark, *mihi secus videtur*—"I think otherwise"—though for the moment I will willingly suspend my *iudicium*!'

'May I not ask whom I have the pleasure of talking with?' asked the Councillor.

'I am a Bachelor of Divinity,' replied the man.

This answer satisfied the Councillor: the title matched his dress. He must be, he thought, some old village schoolmaster, the kind of eccentric fellow you can still meet with up in Jutland.

'This is hardly a *locus docendi*,' began the man, 'yet I beg you will trouble yourself to continue your discourse! You must have read widely among the Ancients!'

'Oh, yes, in a way!' answered the Councillor. 'I quite like reading old books if they contain useful information, but I'm very fond of modern ones as well—all except "Everyday Stories"—we've enough of them in real life!'

'"Everyday Stories"?' asked our Bachelor.

'Yes, I mean these new novels everyone's reading.'

'Oh,' smiled the man, 'and yet they're very ingenious, and they're much read at Court: the King is particularly fond of the Romance of Iwain and Gawain, which deals with King Arthur and the Knights of the Round Table—the one he joked about with his noblemen!'[1]

'I haven't read that one yet!' said the Councillor. 'It must be quite a new one that Heiberg's just produced!'

'No,' answered the man, 'it wasn't produced by Heiberg, but by Gottfred von Ghemen!'

'Ah, you must mean the author, not the publisher!' said the Councillor. 'That's a very old name —surely that's the name of the first printer in Denmark?'

'Oh, yes, he's our first printer!' said the man. In this way they got along quite well with one another. And now one of the good citizens began speaking of the strange pestilence which had raged a few years before—he was referring to the plague of 1484—but the Councillor took it to be the cholera they were talking of, and so the conversation continued to flow easily enough. The Pirates' War of 1490 had occurred so recently that it was bound to be mentioned. The English pirates, they said, had taken the ships lying in the roadsteads,

[1] In his *History of the Kingdom of Denmark* Holberg tells the story that one day, when he had read of King Arthur in the Romance, King Hans, jesting with the celebrated Otto Rud, of whom he was very fond, said, 'Sir Iwain and Sir Gawain, whom I find in this book, were remarkable knights: such knights are not to be found any more nowadays!' To which Otto Rud answered, 'If there were many kings like King Arthur, you would also find many knights like Sir Iwain and Sir Gawain!'

and the Councillor, whose thoughts naturally turned to the events of 1801, joined spiritedly in their abuse of the English. The rest of the conversation, however, did not go so well. Every moment they found themselves more and more out of step with one another: the good Bachelor of Divinity was altogether too ignorant, and the Councillor's simplest remarks struck him as daring and fantastic. They looked at each other, and made so little headway that the Bachelor tried speaking in Latin, thinking he might make himself better understood that way, but it wasn't any help at all.

'How are you feeling now?' asked the hostess, as she plucked him by the sleeve. And now he suddenly recollected himself, for while he had been talking he had completely forgotten all that had gone before.

'Good heavens, where am I?' he said, and his head swam as he thought of it.

'We'll have claret, mead, and German beer!' shouted one of the guests. 'And you must drink with us!'

Two girls came in, and one of them was wearing a cap of two colours. They poured out the drinks and bobbed a curtsy. The Councillor felt cold shivers running down his back. 'What on earth's all this? What is it?' he said, but they made him drink with them. They took the good man firmly but quite politely in hand. He was in despair, and when one of them said he was drunk, he didn't at all doubt the man's word, and only asked them to get him a cab—they thought he was talking Russian.[1]

---

[1] This remark has more point in the original, since Hàns Andersen uses the word *droschke* throughout for 'cab'. L. W. K.

Never had he been in such crude and simple company: it was enough to make one believe that the country had returned to heathendom. 'This is the most awful moment in my life!' he thought. But at the same time an idea occurred to him—he would slip down under the table, crawl towards the door and try to creep out. But just as he got to the doorway, the others noticed what he was up to: they grabbed him by the legs, and then, to his very good fortune, the galoshes came off—and the spell with them!

Quite clearly in front of him, the Councillor saw a bright light burning, and behind it a large building: he recognized it, and the neighbouring houses as well—it was Østergade, exactly as we all know it. He was lying with his legs stretched out towards a gateway, and right opposite sat the watchman sound asleep.

'Good grief, I've been lying here in the street and dreaming!' he said. 'Yes, it's Østergade right enough! How bright and cheerful it all is! It's terrible the way one glass of punch must have upset me!'

Two minutes later he was sitting in a cab on his way to Christianshavn. He thought of all the worry and distress he had gone through, and in his heart he considered himself very fortunate that he really lived in our own times, which, with all their defects, were nevertheless far better than those he had just been in. And that, you will agree, was very sensible of the Councillor.

3. *The Watchman's Adventures*

'Well, I never!—there's a pair of galoshes lying there!' said the watchman. 'They must belong to the lieutenant who lives up there—they're lying right in the doorway!'

The honest fellow would willingly have rung the bell and handed them in, especially as there was still a light showing, but he didn't want to wake the other people in the house, and so he decided not to.

'Must be nice and cosy with a pair of things like that on!' he said. 'What nice soft leather they're made of!' And they ended up on his feet. 'What a queer world it is! That chap up there could get into a good warm bed if he wanted to—but does he? There he goes, pacing up and down the floor! He doesn't know what a lucky chap he is. No missus, no kids! A party every evening! Wish I was him— I'd be a lucky chap then!'

125

He had no sooner put his wish into words than the galoshes he had put on got to work—the watchman changed into the lieutenant, body and soul complete. There he stood up in his room, holding between his fingers a little piece of pink paper upon which was written a poem, one of the lieutenant's own poems. For who hasn't, once in his life, been disposed to write a poem? Once you set down the thought, the verse soon comes. This is what was written:

Would I Were Rich!

'Would I were rich!' was many a time my sigh
When I was still a child but three feet high.
Would I were rich! On my lieutenant's pay,
With sword and uniform and feather gay—
The time had come: I had lieutenant's pay—
I still was never rich, unhappily.
But God helped me!

Light-hearted, young, I sat an evening through:
A little girl of seven kissed me true,
For I was rich in tales and fairy-lore,
Though, on the other hand, in silver poor.
The child cared only for her fairy-lore,
So I was rich—but not in gold, oh, no!
God knows it's so!

'Would I were rich!' is still my prayer to heaven.
And now grown-up, that little girl of seven
Is truly wise and beautiful and good.
If she my heart's own story understood;
If she, as once—if she desired my good—
But I am poor and must keep silent still.
As God it will!

Would I were rich in faith and quiet mind!—
On paper then you'd not my sorrow find.

You whom I love, if you can understand—
No, read it as a poem from Youth's hand:
For that is best, should you not understand.
I still am poor, my future dark—unless—
You may the Lord God Bless!

Yes, you write verses like that when you are in love, but a sensible man does not publish them. The lieutenant, love, and poverty formed a triangle, or, to put it differently but just as well, but one half of Fortune's dice, the other half denied him. The lieutenant felt that, too, and so he leaned his head against the window-frame and sighed deeply.

'That poor watchman out in the street is far happier than I! He doesn't know what I call want! He has a home, a wife and children who weep with his sorrow and rejoice at his happiness! I should be happier than I am, if I could change places with him, for he is happier than I!'

In that very second the watchman was the watchman again. It was through the Galoshes of Fortune that he had become the lieutenant, but as we saw, he felt less contented than ever, and would much rather be what he really was. And so the watchman was the watchman again.

'That was a bad dream!' he said. 'But a queer one, too. I thought I was the lieutenant up there, and it was no fun either! I missed the missus and the kids, always ready to smother me with kisses!'

There he sat nodding his head. The dream would not go right out of his thoughts: he still had the galoshes on his feet. A shooting-star flashed brightly across the sky.

'There it goes!' he said. 'There's enough of them left, for all that! I should rather like to see all those things a little closer, especially the moon—that doesn't slip away between your fingers. That student my wife does heavy washing for says when we die, we fly from one of them to another. That's a pack of lies, of course, but it'd be rather nice to do it all the same. If only I could give a little jump up there, my body could lie here on the steps for what I care!'

Now there are certain things in this world you have to be very careful about speaking of out loud, but you ought to be still more careful if you have the Galoshes of Fortune on your feet. Just listen to what happened to the watchman.

As far as we men are concerned, we nearly all know something of the speed of steam: we have experienced it either on the railway or sailing over the sea in a ship. But this speed is like the movement of the sloth or the march of a snail compared with the speed of light: it travels nineteen million times faster than the finest race-horse. And electricity is swifter still. Death is an electric shock we get in the heart, and on the wings of electricity the freed soul flies away. The light of the sun takes eight minutes and some few seconds on its journey of over ninety million miles. Travelling express by electricity, the soul needs even less time to make the same flight. The distance between the stars is no greater for the soul than it is for us between the houses of our friends in one and the same town, as long as they live fairly near to one another. But that electric shock in the heart will cost us the use of our body here below, unless, like the watchman here, we have the Galoshes of Fortune on.

In a few seconds the watchman had travelled the 238,000 miles to the moon, which, as we know, is created from a substance much lighter than that of our earth: it is what we should call soft, like new-fallen snow. He found himself on one of the innumerable mountain-rings, which we know from Dr. Mädler's large map of the moon—you do know it? On the inner side the mountain-ring sloped steeply down, four to five miles, into a crater. Down at the bottom lay a town which looked like the white of an egg in a glass of water, just as soft and with just the same appearance with its towers and cupolas and sail-like balconies, transparent and swaying in the thin air. Our earth hung like a great fiery-red ball overhead.

There were so many creatures, and all, I suppose, what we should call human, but they looked quite different from us. They had a language, too, but no one could possibly expect the watchman's soul to understand it—and yet it did for all that.

The watchman's soul understood moon-speech very well. They were having an argument about our earth, and wondering if it could be inhabited: the air would be too dense for any sensible moon-creature to be able to live in it. They considered the moon alone had living beings, it was the only star where the old Star People lived.

But we must pay another visit down below to Østergade, and see how the watchman's body is getting on there.

It sat lifeless on the steps. His truncheon had fallen out of his hand, and his eyes were looking up towards the moon after his honest soul which was wandering about up there.

'What's the time?' asked a passer-by. 'Hi, watchman!' But if anyone answered, it wasn't the watchman. So he flicked him gently on the nose, and he lost his balance. The body lay full-length on the ground: he was clearly dead. A great terror came over the man who had flicked his nose: the watchman was dead, and dead he remained. It was reported and talked about, and in the early morning the body was carried off to the hospital.

A fine mess the soul would be in now, if it came back and, as in all probability it would, looked for its body in Østergade and found nothing! It would most likely nip over to the police-station first, then make inquiries at the lost-property office, and finally go to the hospital. Though we can comfort ourselves with the thought that the soul is very wise when it is left to itself—it is only the body that makes a fool of it.

As I said, the watchman's body was taken to the hospital. It was brought into the cleansing-room, and the first thing they did there was, naturally, to take the galoshes off. And now the soul could get back: it made a bee-line for the body, and life immediately returned to it. The man declared it had been the most dreadful night of his life: not for two shillings would he go through it again. But now it was all over.

He was discharged the same day, but the galoshes were left in the hospital.

4. *A Heady Experience. A Recitation.*
A Very Unusual Journey

Now everyone in Copenhagen knows what the entrance to King Frederick's Hospital looks like, but as some Non-Copenhageners are likely to read this story as well, we must give a brief description of it.

The hospital is separated from the street by a rather high railing. The thick iron bars stand just far enough apart, so they say, for very thin patients to have been known to squeeze through and so make short visits outside. The most difficult part of the body to get through was the head, and here, as is so often the case in this world, the small heads were the most fortunate. This will be enough by way of introduction.

One of the young medical students, of whom it
might be said—but only in a physical sense—that
he was thick-headed, happened to be on duty
that evening. It was pouring with rain. But in spite
of both these drawbacks, he had to go out—only
for a quarter of an hour. It wasn't worth while
bothering the porter, he thought, when you could
creep through the railings. There lay the galoshes
the watchman had left behind. It never entered his
head that they were the Galoshes of Fortune. They
would be very useful in this weather: he put them
on. And now all that remained was to see whether
he could squeeze himself through—he had never
tried it before. There he now stood.

'I hope to God I can get my head through!' he
said, and straight away, although it was very thick
and big, it slipped through quite easily. The
galoshes perhaps could understand how. But now
he had to get his body out with it, and there he
still stood.

'Oh dear, I'm too fat!' he said. 'I should have
thought the head was the worst. I can't get through!'

Now he tried to jerk his head back again, but it
wouldn't go. He could move his neck easily enough,
but that was all. At first he felt himself grow angry,
and then his spirits sank right down below freezing-
point. The Galoshes of Fortune had brought him
into the most dreadful situation, and unfortunately
it did not occur to him to wish himself free. No, he
just kept on struggling and remained stuck where
he was. The rain poured down, and not a soul could
be seen in the street. He could not reach the door-
bell. How on earth could he get loose? He realized
that he might have to go on standing there until
first thing in the morning, when a smith would have

to be sent for to file the railings through. But that would take some time, and meanwhile all the boys from the Blue-Coat School just across the way would come running over, and the whole district would be there, to see him standing in the pillory. He would attract crowds of people—quite unlike the monster agave which was on show the year before. 'Ooh, the blood's mounting to my head—it might send me crazy! In fact, I'm going crazy now! Oh, if only I were free again, and it were all over!'

Now that, you see, he should have said a bit sooner: immediately, as the thought was uttered, he had his head free and rushed inside, quite upset by the fright the Galoshes of Fortune had caused him.

But we must not suppose that at this point everything was all right again—oh, no, there was even worse to come.

The night passed, and the following day as well, and no one called for the galoshes.

In the evening there was to be a performance at the Little Theatre in Kannike Street. The house was full to over-crowding. Among the numbers for recitation, a new poem was to be presented. We must hear it. The title was:

Granny's Spectacles

Of Granny's wisdom everybody's learnt:
In olden times, she'd surely have been burnt!
Of all that's happening—and more—she knows.
Her foresight pierces next year to its close,
Yea, penetrates the eighties.—So it may,
But what she sees, she's always loath to say.
I wonder what will chance this coming year?
What will there be of note? I'd love to hear

My fate, the country's, and the arts' as well—
But such things will my Granny never tell!
I plagued her then, and some success achieved.
First she was silent, then a little grieved:
But scant attention did her scolding get,
For well I knew that I was Granny's pet!

'Once in a way, I'll satisfy your pleasure,'
She now began, and handed me her treasure—
Her specs to wit—'Now go you where you will,
But choose a place there's always folk to fill,
Where you can see in comfort either sex,
And scrutinize them closely through my specs.
Now will they all resemble, by my troth,
A pack of cards spread out upon a cloth.
And by this means, you may the future spy!'
'My thanks!' I said, and hurried off to try.
I wondered now where people most assembled.
I thought of Langelinie—but I trembled:
'Twas far too cold, and I should catch a chill.
There's Østergade? No—all mud and swill!
Ah, the theatre! That idea's quite sound:
Tonight's performance suits me to the ground!
Well, here I am, presented to you now;
And Granny's specs I'll use, if you'll allow,
But only just to see—Don't run away!—
If you look like the cards you use in play!
Through these, I see Time's secrets round me press.
Your silence may I take as meaning 'Yes'?
For recompense you shall my foresight share.

We're in this all together. I'll declare
Your fate and mine, the future of the state!
Now let's see what these cards here can relate.

(And now he puts on the spectacles.)

It's right enough! No, really! I must laugh!
If you could come up here and see but half!
There's court cards everywhere, string after string,
The Queens of Hearts and Diamonds, everything!

The black ones there: yes, that's a club, a spade.
A quick inspection over all I've made!
The Queen of Spades, with great intensity,
Is thinking of the Diamond Knave, I see!
This spectacle has made me feel half tight.
There's a deal of money in the house tonight,
And many strangers from across the world.
But 'tisn't that that we should like unfurled.
Your social standing? Too far off to say,
But we shall read about it all one day:
I'll harm the Press, if I say all you wish—
I'd not take out the best bone in the dish.
The Drama then?—What news of taste or style?
But no—I can't afford to lose a smile
From the Director. Me?—But one's own part
Lies far too heavily upon the heart.
I see—I cannot say what 'tis I see:
But when it happens, then you'll know—like me!
Who is most fortunate among us here?
Most fortunate? With ease that should appear.
It is, of course—but no, he might feel shy,
And several might be hurt by my reply.
Who'll live the longest? He—or she just there?
To talk of such things would be most unfair!
Then shall I tell of—? Hardly.—Then of what?
Of—? No, I must admit I'd rather not!
I'm much embarrassed: harm's so quickly done.
To spy your thoughts out might be cleaner fun,
And to that end, I'll summon all my art!
You think?—I beg your pardon?—In your heart,
You really think there's nothing I can say?
You're all quite certain you've been led astray!
I'll say no more, good audience, do not fret!—
Your frank opinion leaves me in your debt!

The poem was superbly recited, and the per
former was a great success. In the audience was
the student from the hospital. He appeared to have
forgotten his adventure of the night before. He had

the galoshes on, because no one had come to claim them, and, as the streets were dirty, he could put them to good use.

He liked the poem.

He was much taken up with the idea: he would very much like to have a pair of spectacles like that —perhaps, if you knew how to use them properly, you could look right into people's hearts, and that, he thought, would be very much more interesting than seeing what would happen next year, for that you would do in any case, whereas you would never get to know what people were really like. 'I can just imagine, now, all those men and women there in the first row—if only you could look right into their hearts, what a revelation that would be, like looking into a kind of shop! Wouldn't my eyes just go shopping! In that woman over there, I should certainly find a large millinery department! This one's shop is empty, though it's in need of a good spring-clean; but there must be sound reliable shops as well! Ah, well!' he sighed, 'I know one where everything is sound, but there's a shop-assistant there already—that's the only thing wrong in the whole shop! Some will call out, "If you will be good enough to step inside!" Yes, if only I could step inside like a pleasant little thought going through their hearts!'

Now that was quite enough for the galoshes: the medical student vanished into a thought, and began a most unusual journey through the hearts of the first row of the audience. The first heart he entered was a woman's, but he immediately thought he was in the Orthopaedic Institute, which is what they call the place where the doctor removes growths and straightens out people's bodies. He was in the room where plaster-casts of deformed limbs hang on the wall; but there was this difference—in the Institute the casts are taken when the patients come in, but in this woman's heart they were taken and stored away after the good people had gone out. They were, in fact, casts of her friends' failings, both of body and mind, which she stored up here.

He quickly passed into the heart of another woman, but that seemed to him like a great holy church, where the white doves of Innocence fluttered above the high altar. He would willingly have fallen upon his knees, but he had to pass on into the next heart, though he still heard the organ-tones and seemed, he thought, to have become a new and better person, so that he felt not unworthy to step into the next holy place. This showed a poor attic with a sick mother, but through the open window streamed the rays of God's warm sun, lovely roses nodded from a little wooden box upon the roof, and two sky-blue birds sang of the happiness of childhood, while the sick mother called down a blessing upon her daughter.

Now he crawled upon hands and knees through an over-filled butcher's shop, where he stumbled upon flesh and flesh alone: it was the heart of a rich and respectable man, whose name you would certainly find in the directory.

Now he was in his wife's heart, an old tumble-down dove-cote: her husband's portrait was used as a weather-cock—it was connected with the doors, which opened and shut as her husband turned round.

After that he entered a room with mirrors all

round the walls, such as you have in Castle Rosenborg, but the mirrors magnified everything to an incredible size. In the middle of the floor sat, like a Dalai-Lama, the owner's insignificant self, astonished to see his own greatness.

Then he fancied himself in a narrow needle-case, full of sharp-pointed needles—this, he might well have thought, was the heart of an old maid, but that wasn't so—it was a quite young officer with several orders, a man, as they put it, of heart and spirit.

Quite bewildered, the poor student came out of the last heart in the row unable to order his thoughts: he concluded that his over-strong imagination had run away with him.

'Good heavens!' he sighed. 'It looks as if I'm going mad! And it's unforgivably hot in here! The blood's mounting to my head!' And now he called to mind what had happened the evening before, how his head had stuck fast between the iron railings in front of the hospital. 'That's what caused it!' he thought. 'I must see to it in good time. A Turkish bath might do me good. I wish I were already lying on the top shelf!'

And there he lay on the top shelf of the steam bath, but he was lying there with all his clothes on, boots and galoshes as well, and drops of hot water from the ceiling were dripping on to his face.

'Hi!' he shrieked, and jumped down to take a shower-bath. The attendant gave a loud shriek, too, when he saw a fully-dressed man in the bath.

The student, however, had enough presence of mind to whisper to him, 'I'm doing it for a bet!' But the first thing he did when he got back to his own room was to put a large plaster on the back of his neck and another on his back to draw out the madness.

The next morning his back was covered in blood, and that was all he got from the Galoshes of Fortune.

5. *The Copying-Clerk's Transformation*

Meanwhile, the watchman, whom we have certainly not forgotten, remembered the galoshes which he had found and taken with him to the hospital. He went and fetched them, but as neither the lieutenant nor anyone else in the road would own them, he handed them in at the police-station.

'They look just like my own galoshes!' said one of the copying-clerks, as he looked at the lost property and put them down beside his own. 'It would take more than a cobbler's eye to tell one from the other!'

139

A policeman, who stepped inside with some papers, called to him.

The clerk turned round and spoke to the man, but when he had done and looked at the galoshes again, he was quite bewildered and didn't know whether the ones on the left or the ones on the right belonged to him. 'Mine must be the wet ones!' he thought, but he thought wrong, for they were Fortune's—even the police must make mistakes sometimes, mustn't they? He put them on, stuffed some papers into his pocket and took some others under his arm: he would have to read them through and copy them out when he got home. But just now it was Sunday morning and the weather was fine, and a stroll to Fredericksberg, he thought, would do him good. So off he went.

No one could be more quiet and hard-working than this young man, and we wish him well of his little walk which would undoubtedly do him a great deal of good after sitting so long at his work. At first he just walked along without thinking about anything, and so the galoshes had no chance to show their magic powers.

In the avenue he met a young poet he knew, who told him he was starting off on his summer holidays the next day.

'What, are you off again?' said the clerk. 'What a lucky fellow you are to be so free! You can fly off where you will, while the rest of us are chained by the leg!'

'But you stick to the bread-fruit tree!' answered the poet. 'You don't have to trouble your head about tomorrow, and when you're old, you'll have your pension!'

'Yes, but you have the best of it!' said the clerk.

'It must be very pleasant, just sitting down and writing poetry. The whole world pays you compliments, and you are your own master as well! You ought to try sitting in court and listening to trivial cases day after day!'

The poet shook his head. The clerk shook his head, too. They both kept their own opinions, and so they parted.

'They're a race apart, these poets!' said the clerk. 'I'd like to try entering into the mind of one of them and becoming a poet myself. I'm sure I shouldn't write the slushy stuff some of them turn out! . . . It's a perfect spring day for a poet! The air is so remarkably clear, the clouds so beautiful, and the green leaves smell so sweetly! Yes, it's many years since I felt as I do at this moment.'

We notice already that he's become a poet: it didn't, of course, happen all at once, for it's a foolish idea to imagine that a poet is quite different from other men, who may have far more poetry in their natures than many a great and well-known poet has. The only difference is this, that the poet has a better imaginative memory: he can hold on to an idea or a feeling until it finds clear expression in words—and that's what the rest of us can't do. But to go from an ordinary everyday nature to a gifted one is always a great change, and this the clerk had now done.

'What a beautiful sweet smell!' he said. 'How it reminds me of the violets at Aunt Lone's! Yes, I was a small boy in those days! Dear God, it's ages since I thought about that! A good old sort, she was—she lived over there behind the Exchange. She always had a spray or a couple of green shoots in water, no matter how severe the winter might be. I remember the smell of violets when I used to press warmed pennies on the frosted window-panes to make peep-holes. It was a fine view I had. Outside on the canal the ships lay ice-bound and deserted, a screeching crow their only crew. But when the spring breezes blew, everything became busy. With songs and shouts, men sawed through the ice; ships were tarred and rigged, and left for foreign lands. And I've stayed here; here must I always stay, always sit in the police-station and watch others get their passports to travel abroad—that's my lot! Oh, well!' He sighed deeply, then suddenly stopped short. 'Good heavens, what's come over me! I've never thought or felt like this before! It must be the spring air! It's disturbing—but rather pleasant, too!'

He grasped the papers in his pocket. 'These will give me something else to think about!' he said, and let his eye wander over the first sheet. '"Mrs. Sigbrith, an Original Tragedy in Five Acts",' he read. 'What's this? It's in my own handwriting. Have I written this tragedy? "An Intrigue on the Ramparts, or The Public Holiday—A Vaudeville." But where did I get this? Someone must have put it in my pocket—here's a letter.' Yes, it was from the management of a theatre—the play had been turned down, and the letter was none too polite. 'Hm!' said the clerk, and sat down on a bench. His thoughts were very lively and his heart full of tenderness: without thinking, he picked one of the nearest flowers—it was a simple little daisy. What a botanist would take many lectures to tell us, it made clear in a minute: it told the myth of its birth, it told of the power of the sunlight which unfolded its fine petals and made them smell so sweetly.

Then he thought of the struggles of life—and they, too, awaken the feelings in our breast. Air and light were the flower's lovers, but light was its favourite: towards the light it turned, and when the light disappeared, it closed its petals together and fell asleep in the air's embrace. 'It's light that gives me beauty!' said the flower. 'But the air lets you breathe!' whispered the poet's voice.

Close by stood a boy slashing with his stick in a muddy ditch. Drops of water splashed up among the green boughs, and the clerk thought of the millions of invisible creatures hurled up in the drops to a height which was, for their size, what it would be for us to be whirled high over the clouds. As the clerk thought about this and about the change which had come over him, he smiled. 'I'm asleep and dreaming! And yet it's strange how naturally one can dream and still know that it's only a dream. If only I could remember it tomorrow when I wake! My spirits seem to be much higher than they usually are! I see everything so clearly and feel so wide awake, but I'm quite sure that if I remember anything of it tomorrow, it will seem nonsense. I've known it happen before: all the fine wise things one hears and says in dreams are like the fairy gold under the earth: when you find it, it is rich and magnificent, but seen by the light of day, it's nothing but stones and withered leaves. Ah!' he sighed sadly, and looked up at the singing birds hopping happily enough from bough to bough. 'They're much better off than I am! What a wonderful thing to be able to fly! How lucky they are to be born like that! Yes, if I should change into anything else, it would be into one of those little larks!'

Immediately, his coat-tails and sleeves grew together into wings, his clothes became feathers and the galoshes claws: he was fully aware of it, and laughed to himself. 'Well, I can see I'm dreaming now! But I've never dreamed anything so ridiculous before!' And he flew up into the green boughs and sang, but there was no poetry in his song, for he was no longer a poet. The galoshes, like anyone who does a job thoroughly, could do only one thing at a time: he wanted to be a poet, and he became one; now he wanted to be a little bird, but in becoming that he ceased to be a poet.

'This is fine!' he said. 'During the day I sit in the police-station surrounded by solid, substantial documents, and at night I can dream I'm flying like a lark in Fredericksberg Gardens.—My, you could write a whole comedy about that!'

Now he flew down into the grass, turned his head round in all directions, and with his beak struck the supple blades of grass, which, compared with his present size, seemed as big as the palm branches of North Africa.

One minute later and there was coal-black night around him: a monstrous object, as it appeared to him, had been thrown over him. It was a great cap which a boy from the neighbourhood had thrown over the bird: a hand was thrust underneath and seized the clerk by the back and wings so that he squeaked. In his first fright he cried loudly, 'You impudent puppy! I am the copying-clerk at the police-station!' But it sounded to the boy like 'Peep! Peep!' He struck the bird on the beak and wandered off.

In the avenue he met two schoolboys of the upper class—regarded, that is, from a social point of view: intellectually, they were in the lower part of the school—and they bought the bird for eight-pence. And so the clerk was taken home to Copen-hagen to a family in Gothersgade.

'It's a good thing I'm only dreaming!' said the clerk. 'Or else, by heaven, I should be angry! First I was a poet, and now I'm a lark! It must have been my poetical nature that made me turn into the little beast. And it's a miserable enough thing to be, especially when you fall into the hands of boys. I'd like to know what will come of it!'

The boys carried him into a very elegant sitting-room: a stout merry-looking woman came to meet them, but she was not at all pleased to see the common wild bird, as she called the lark, come in with them, though she would let it stay for the day and they could put it in the empty cage that stood by the window. 'Perhaps it will amuse Pollyboy!' she added and smiled at a big green parrot, who, with something of an air, was rocking himself in his ring in a fine brass cage. 'It's Pollyboy's birth-day!' she said childishly. 'So the little wild bird can congratulate him!'

Pollyboy did not answer a single word, but con-tinued, in his rather distinguished way, to rock to and fro. Meanwhile, a beautiful canary, which had been brought the summer before from the warm sweet-scented land of its birth, began to sing loudly.

'Noisy thing!' said the woman and threw a white handkerchief over the cage.

'Peep! Peep!' it sighed. 'That was a dreadful snowstorm!' And with the sigh it fell quiet.

The clerk, or, as the woman called him, the wild bird, was put into a little cage close to the canary and not far from the parrot. The only intelligible words Pollyboy could utter freely—and they often sounded very funny—were, 'Now let's be human!' The rest of its screeching was just as impossible to understand as the canary's twittering, except for the clerk, who was now a bird himself and so could understand his companions perfectly well.

'I used to fly under the green palms and the flowering almond-trees!' sang the canary. 'I would fly with my brothers and sisters over fine flowers and over the glass-clear sea where plants nodded upon its bed. I would see many lovely parrots, too, and they would tell me the funniest stories—such long ones and so many of them.'

'They were wild birds!' answered the parrot. 'They had no education. Now let's be human!— Why aren't you laughing? If the mistress and all her visitors can laugh at it, so can you! It's a great failing, not being able to appreciate what's funny. Now let's be human!'

'Oh, do you remember the beautiful girls who used to dance under the tents spread out by the flowering trees? Do you remember the sweet fruit and the cooling juice of the wild plants?'

'Oh, yes,' said the parrot, 'but I'm much better off here! I get good food and I'm treated like one of the family. I know I'm clever, and I want nothing more. Now let's be human! You have a poetic soul, as they call it; I have sound knowledge and wit: you have genius but no moderation; you go off into these rhapsodies of yours, and so they shut you up. They don't treat me like that: oh, no!—for I cost them rather more than you did! I impress them with my beak and keep up a running fire of wit— Now let's be human!'

'Oh, the warm, flower-scented land of my birth!'
sang the canary. 'I will sing of your dark-green
trees, of your peaceful bays where drooping
branches kiss the clear surface of the water, sing
of the joy of all my gleaming brothers and sisters
where the cactus grows!'

'Oh, let's have no more of your wailing!' said
the parrot. 'Tell us something to make us laugh!
Laughter is the mark of the highest level of intelligence. Look at a dog, or a horse—can they laugh?
No, they can cry, but only men have the gift of
laughter. Ha! Ha! Ha!' laughed Pollyboy, and
added his witticism, 'Now let's be human!'

'Little grey Danish bird,' said the canary, 'you're
a prisoner, too! It must be cold in your woods, but
at least there's freedom there. Fly away! They've
forgotten to shut you up, and the top window's
standing open. Fly, fly!'

And so the clerk did—in a flash he was out of his
cage. At the very same moment the half-open door
leading to the next room creaked, and stealthily,
with green shining eyes, the cat crept in and gave
chase to him. The canary fluttered in his cage, the
parrot beat his wings and cried, 'Now let's be
human!' The clerk felt a deadly terror and flew
away through the open window, over house and
street, until at last he had to rest awhile.

The house opposite had something familiar and
homelike about it: a window stood open, he flew
in, it was his own room: he perched upon the table.

'Now let's be human!' he said, imitating the
parrot, but not thinking what he was saying: and
instantly he was the clerk again, but still sitting on
the table.

'Heaven help us!' he said. 'How did I get up

here and fall asleep like this! It was a very un-comfortable dream I had—what silly nonsense it all was!'

6. *The Best Gift the Galoshes Brought*

The day after, early in the morning while the clerk still lay abed, someone knocked on his door: it was his neighbour from the same floor, a student who was reading for the Church. In he came.

'Lend me your galoshes,' he said. 'It's very wet in the garden, but the sun's shining beautifully and I'd like to go down there and smoke a pipe.'

He put the galoshes on and was soon out in the garden, which possessed one plum-tree and one pear-tree. Small as it was, it was reckoned a very magnificent garden for Copenhagen.

The student walked up and down the path: it was only six o'clock: from the street outside came the sound of a post-horn.

'Oh, to travel, to travel!' he burst out. 'That's the greatest thing in the world! That's what I'd most like to do! Then I should get rid of this restlessness I'm always feeling. But it would have to be somewhere far away! I'd like to see the magnificent scenery of Switzerland, travel in Italy and . . .'

Yes, it was a good thing the galoshes worked at once, else he would have gone on wandering far too much, both for his own sake and for ours. He was travelling. He was in the middle of Switzerland, but he was packed in, with eight other people, in the inside of a stage-coach: he had a headache, his neck was stiff, and the blood had drained into his legs, which were swollen and pinched by his boots. He hovered between dozing and waking. In his right-hand pocket he had his travellers' cheques, in his left-hand pocket his passport, and in an inside breast-pocket some gold coins sewn tightly into a little leather purse. Every time he fell into a doze he dreamed that one or other of these precious things had been lost, and so he started up feverishly, and the first movement his hand made was a triangle from right to left and up to his breast to feel if he still had them or not. Umbrellas, sticks, and hats rocked in the luggage-net overhead and rather hindered the view which was most imposing. However, he was able to glance at it sideways, while his heart sang what at least one poet we know of has sung in Switzerland but has not yet printed:

It's as beautiful here, without a doubt,
As heart could wish with Mont Blanc to see:
If only my money would last me out,
This is the place where I'd choose to be!

Nature appeared vast, grave, and dark all round

them. The forest of firs looked like heather on the high rocks, their summits hidden in a mist of cloud: now it began to snow, and a cold wind blew sharply.

'Ah!' he sighed, 'if we were on the other side of the Alps it would be summer, and I should have changed my travellers' cheques—I'm so anxious about them, I just can't enjoy Switzerland at all! Oh, I do wish I were on the other side!'

And so he was on the other side: right down in Italy he was, between Florence and Rome. Lake Trasimene lay in the evening light like flaming gold between the dark-blue mountains. Here, where Hannibal had beaten Flaminius, the vine-rows peacefully held each other by their green fingers; beautiful half-naked children watched a herd of coal-black pigs under a clump of sweet-smelling laurels by the wayside. If we could only let you see this picture as it really was, everyone would cry with delight, 'Lovely Italy!' But the student of divinity certainly didn't say that, nor did a single one of his travelling-companions in the coach.

Poisonous flies and mosquitoes flew into the coach in their thousands: vainly they flicked myrtle branches all round themselves—the flies stung all the same: there wasn't one person in the coach whose face wasn't swollen and blood-marked from their bites. The poor horses looked like carcasses, the flies had settled in such great cakes on them, and it gave them only a moment's relief when the coachman got down and scraped the beasts off. The sun was now sinking, and a brief but icy chill passed through the whole country-side—it was not at all pleasant. But all round, mountains and clouds took on a most beautiful green colour, clear and shining —go there and see for yourselves, it's better than reading a description! It was matchless! The travellers thought so, too, but—their stomachs were empty, their bodies tired, the only thing they longed for was somewhere to sleep. What sort of place would they find?—They were much more concerned with that than with the beauties of nature.

The road passed through an olive-grove, just as at home you might drive between gnarled willows, and there lay a lonely inn. Half a score of begging cripples had camped outside it, and the healthiest of them looked like 'Hunger's eldest son, who had just reached the age of discretion'. The others were either blind, or had withered legs and crawled upon their hands, or had shrunken arms and hands without fingers. It was real misery that their rags called attention to. 'Eccellenza, miserabili!' they sighed, and stretched out their sick limbs. The inn-keeper's wife, her feet bare, her hair untidy, her blouse dirty, came herself to meet her guests. The doors were tied together with string, the floors of the rooms presented a brick paving half torn up, bats flew about under the ceiling, and the stink inside . . . !

'Well, I hope she'll lay supper down in the stable!' said one of the travellers. 'At least you know what you're breathing down there!'

They opened the windows for a little fresh air to come in, but the withered arms got there first, and the endless wail of, 'Eccellenza, miserabili!' On the walls were many inscriptions—half of them against 'bella Italia'.

The meal was brought in: there was a soup made of water flavoured with pepper and rancid oil, and sure enough the same oil again on the salad; stale

151

eggs and roast cockscombs were magnificent by comparison; even the wine had an odd taste—it was a real mixture.

At night the trunks were piled up in front of the door, and one of the travellers kept guard while the rest slept: the first watch fell to the student of divinity. Oh, how close it was in the room! The heat was oppressive, the mosquitoes hummed and stung, the 'miserabili' outside moaned in their sleep.

'Travelling would be all right, I suppose,' sighed the student, 'if only one hadn't a body! If only it could rest and let the spirit fly free! Wherever I go a sense of something missing weighs upon my heart: I'm always wanting something better than the present—yes, that's it: something better, the best! But where and what is it? I know well enough at bottom what I want—I want a happy end, the happiest of all!'

And as he pronounced the words he was back home: long white curtains hung down in front of the window, and in the middle of the floor stood a black coffin—there he lay in the quiet sleep of death: his wish was fulfilled—his body was at rest, his spirit travelled free. 'Account no one happy before he is in his grave,' were the words of Solon, and here their truth was once again confirmed.

Every corpse is a sphinx guarding the secret of immortality, and neither did the sphinx that lay here in the black coffin answer for us the question the student had written down two days before:

In me, strong Death, thy silence wakens dread:
Thy tracks beyond the grave no knowledge yield—
Are then the hopes of Jacob's Ladder dead?
Shall I arise but grass in Death's vast field?

Our greatest sorrows oft will men ignore.
You who were lonely right up to the last,
In this world, weighs upon the heart much more
Than earth upon the dead man's coffin cast!

Two forms moved in the room. We know them
both: they were the fairy Sorrow and the messenger
of Fortune. They bent over the dead man.

'Do you see now,' said Sorrow, 'what kind of
happiness your galoshes brought mankind?'

'At least they've brought lasting good to him
who's sleeping here!' answered Pleasure.

'No, you are wrong,' said Sorrow. 'He left the
world of his own will: he was not called! His spirit
has not yet been given strength enough here on
earth for him to enjoy the treasures beyond death
which his destiny has prepared for him! I will do
him a truly good deed!'

And she took the galoshes off his feet: the sleep
of death ended, he returned to life and rose up.
Sorrow vanished—and the galoshes, too; clearly,
she now looked upon them as her own property.

153

THE STEADFAST TIN-SOLDIER

THERE were once five and twenty tin-soldiers:
they were all brothers, because they had all been
born from one old tin spoon. They carried rifles on
their shoulders, and they held their heads up and
looked straight in front of them. Their uniform was
red and blue and very fine indeed. The very first
thing they heard in this world, when the lid of the
box in which they lay was taken off, was the word
'Tin-soldiers!' shouted by a small boy as he clapped
his hands. He had been given them because it was
his birthday, and he now set them out on the table.
One soldier looked exactly like another—only a
single one of them was a little different: he had one
leg because he had been cast the last, and there
wasn't enough tin left. Yet he stood just as firm on
his one leg as the others did on their two, and he's
the one the story is really about.

On the table where they were set out were many

154

other toys, but the one that caught the eye most was a fine cardboard castle. Through the little windows you could see right into the rooms. Outside stood little trees round a little mirror which was meant to look like a lake. Wax swans swam on it and were reflected there. It was altogether charming, but the most charming thing about it was undoubtedly a little young lady who stood in the middle of the open castle door: she was cut out of cardboard, too, but she wore a skirt of the finest linen and a narrow blue ribbon draped round her shoulders. This was fastened in the middle by a shining spangle, as big as the whole of her face. This little lady stretched both her arms out, for she was a dancer, and raised one leg so high in the air that the tin-soldier could not find it at all, and believed that she had only one leg like himself.

'She'd be the wife for me!' he thought. 'But she's of very high birth: she lives in a castle, and I have only a box—besides, there are five and twenty of us, and there isn't room for her! But I can try to make her acquaintance!' And so he lay down full-length behind a snuff-box which stood on the table, and from there he had a good view of the fine little lady, who continued to stand on one leg without losing her balance.

When it was late in the evening, all the tin-soldiers were put in their box and the people of the house went to bed. And now the toys began to play—they played at visiting and soldiers and going to fine balls. The tin-soldiers rattled in their box, for they wanted to join in, but they couldn't get the lid off. The nut-crackers jumped head-over-heels, and the slate-pencil made a dreadful noise on the slate: there was such a row that the canary woke up and began to chat with them—in verse, too! There were only two who didn't move from their places, and they were the tin-soldier and the little dancer: she held herself so upright upon the tip of her toes, with both arms stretched out; he stood just as firmly on his one leg, and his eyes didn't leave her for one second.

Now the clock struck twelve, and with a clatter the lid sprang off the snuff-box: there was no snuff in it, no, but a little black goblin popped up—it was a sort of trick.

'Tin-soldier!' said the goblin. 'Will you keep your eyes to yourself!'

But the tin-soldier pretended he hadn't heard.

'Just you wait till tomorrow!' said the goblin.

When morning came and the children were up, the tin-soldier was put over on the window-ledge, and whether it was the goblin or a draught that did it, the window suddenly swung open and out fell the tin-soldier head-first from the third story. He fell at a dreadful pace, his leg in the air, and ended up upon his head, with his bayonet stuck between the paving-stones.

The maid and the small boy went down at once to look for him, but although they came very near to treading on him, they still couldn't see him. If the tin-soldier had shouted, 'Here I am!' they would have found him right enough, but he considered it wasn't done to cry out when he was in uniform.

Now it began to rain, and the drops fell thicker and thicker until it was a regular shower. When it was over a couple of street-urchins came by.

'Look!' said one of them. 'There's a tin-soldier! He must go for a sail!'

And so they made a boat from a newspaper, put the tin-soldier in the middle, and away he sailed down the gutter. Both the boys ran along by his side, clapping their hands. Heavens above, what waves there were in the gutter, and what a current there was! It had been a real downpour. The paper boat tossed up and down, and every now and then whirled round so quickly that the tin-soldier became quite giddy. But he remained steadfast, and without moving a muscle, he looked straight in front of him and kept his rifle on his shoulder.

All at once the boat was driven into a long stretch of gutter that was boarded over, and here it was quite as dark as it was in his box at home.

'I wonder where I shall get to now,' he thought. 'Yes, yes, it's all the goblin's fault! Ah, if only the young lady were here in the boat, it might be twice as dark for all I'd care!'

At that very moment there appeared a great water-rat that lived under the gutter-boarding.

'Have you got your passport?' asked the rat. 'This way with your passport!'

But the tin-soldier said nothing, and held his rifle even more tightly. The boat was carried along and the rat followed. Ooh, how it ground its teeth, and shouted to sticks and straws, 'Stop him! Stop him! He's not paid his toll! He's not shown his passport!'

But the current grew stronger and stronger. The tin-soldier could already catch a glimpse of daylight ahead where the boarding left off, but he also heard a roaring which was quite enough to terrify a bolder man than he: just imagine, where the boarding ended, the gutter emptied straight out into a big canal! It would be just as dangerous for him to be swept into that, as it would be for us to go sailing over a great waterfall.

He was already so close to it now that he could not stop himself. The boat swept out. The poor tin-soldier held himself as stiffly as he could—no one should say of him that he as much as blinked an eyelid. The boat spun round three or four times and filled with water right to the brim, so that nothing could stop it from sinking. The tin-soldier stood up to the neck in water, and the boat sank deeper and deeper. The paper became looser and looser, and now the water flowed over the soldier's head. Then he thought of the pretty little dancer whom he would never see again, and these words rang in the tin-soldier's ears:

> Onward, onward, warrior!
> Death's what you must suffer!

Now the paper parted, and the tin-soldier fell through—and he was at once swallowed by a big fish.

Oh, how dark it was inside! It was even worse than it was under the gutter-boarding, and it was so cramped, too! But the tin-soldier remained steadfast, and lay full-length with his rifle on his shoulder.

The fish twisted and turned about in the most frightening manner. At last it became quite still, and a flash of lightning seemed to pass right through it. Daylight shone quite brightly, and someone cried out, 'The tin-soldier!' The fish had been caught, taken to market, sold and brought up to the kitchen, where the maid had cut it open with a big knife. She picked the soldier up by the waist with two fingers and took him into the living-room, where they all wanted to see the remarkable man who had travelled about in the inside of a fish: but the tin-soldier's head was not a bit turned by their admiration. They stood him up on the table, and there—well, what wonderful things can happen in the world!—the tin-soldier was in the very same room he had been in before, he saw the very same children, and the toys were standing on the table—there was the fine castle with the lovely little dancer: she was still standing on one leg with the other raised high in the air—she, too, was steadfast. The tin-soldier was deeply moved—he was ready to weep tin tears, but that was hardly the thing to do. He looked at her and she looked at him, but they said nothing.

At that very moment one of the small boys took the tin-soldier and threw him right into the stove—he gave no reason at all for doing it: the goblin in the box must have been to blame.

The tin-soldier stood in a blaze of light and felt terribly hot, but whether it was really the heat of the fire or the heat of love, he didn't know. His bright colours had completely gone—no one could say whether this had happened on his travels or whether it was the result of his sorrow. He looked at the little dancer, and she looked at him: he felt himself melting, but he still stood steadfast with his rifle on his shoulder. A door opened and the wind caught the dancer: she flew like a sylph right into the stove to the tin-soldier, burst into flame and vanished. Then the soldier melted to a blob of tin, and the next day, when the maid cleared the ashes out, she found him in the shape of a little heart. Nothing remained of the dancer but her spangle, and that was burnt coal-black.

THE WILD SWANS

FAR away from here, where the swallows fly when
we have winter, there lived a king who had eleven
sons and one daughter, Elisa. The eleven brothers
—they were princes, of course—went to school
with stars upon their breasts and swords by their
sides: they wrote upon golden slates with diamond
slate-pencils, and said their lessons off by heart
just as well as they could read them from a book—
you could see at once that they were princes. Their
sister Elisa sat on a little stool made of looking-
glass, and had a picture-book which had cost half
a kingdom.

Oh, yes, the children had a very good time, but
it was not always to be so.

Their father, who was king over the whole land,
married a wicked queen, who was not at all kind
to the poor children. This was made clear to them
from the very first day: a great celebration was held

throughout the palace, and so the children played at visiting, but instead of getting all the cakes and baked apples that were left over, as they used to do, they were given nothing but sand in a tea-cup, and told to make believe with that.

The week after, the queen sent the little sister, Elisa, away to the country to live with a peasant family, and it was not long before she turned the king so much against the poor princes that he would have nothing more to do with them.

'Fly out into the world and shift for yourselves!' said the wicked queen. 'Fly away like great birds without voices!' She had not the power, however, to do them all the evil she would, and they became eleven beautiful wild swans. With a strange harsh cry, they flew out of the palace windows away over the park and the woods.

It was still quite early in the morning when they passed by the peasant's cottage where their sister Elisa lay asleep; they hovered over the roof, craned their long necks this way and that, and beat their wings, but no one heard them or saw them. Off they had to go again, high up towards the clouds, far away into the wide world, where they flew over a great dark forest which stretched right down to the sea-shore.

Poor little Elisa stood in the peasant's living-room and played with a green leaf—she had no other toys. She stuck a hole in the leaf, peeped through it up at the sun, and it was just as if she saw her brothers' clear eyes; and every time the warm sun-beams shone upon her cheeks, she thought of her brothers' kisses.

One day went by just like another. Whenever the wind blew through the great rose-hedge outside the cottage, it would whisper to the roses, 'Who could be more beautiful than you?' But the roses would shake their heads and say, 'Elisa!' And whenever the old woman sat in the doorway on Sundays reading her hymn-book, the wind would turn the pages over and say to the book, 'Who could be more pious than you?' 'Elisa!' the hymn-book would answer. And what the roses and the hymn-book said was the pure truth.

When she was fifteen she had to return home, and when the queen saw how beautiful she was she grew angry and spiteful. She would willingly have changed her into a wild swan like her brothers, but she dared not do that right away, because the king would want to see his daughter.

In the early morning the queen went into the bath-room, which was built of marble and decorated with soft cushions and beautiful rugs, and she took three toads with her, kissed them, and said to the first, 'When Elisa gets into the bath, sit upon her head and make her dull and lazy like you! You sit on her forehead,' she said to the second, 'and make her ugly like you, so that her father will not recognize her! Rest upon her heart,' she whispered to the third, 'and give her evil thoughts to torment her!' So she put the toads in the clear water, which immediately took on a greenish tinge, called Elisa, undressed her, and made her step into the water. As soon as she lay down, the first toad settled in her hair, the second on her forehead, and the third upon her breast, but Elisa did not seem to notice anything at all. When she stood up there were three red poppies floating on the water—if the creatures had not been poisonous and kissed by the witch, they would have

changed into red roses. They became flowers, even
so, just from resting upon her head and her heart:
she was too pious and innocent for witchcraft to
have any power over her.

When the wicked queen saw that, she rubbed
her with walnut juice so that she became quite dark
brown, she smeared her lovely face with an evil-
smelling ointment and matted her beautiful hair:
it was impossible to recognize the lovely Elisa any
longer.

And so when her father saw her he was quite
alarmed and said it was not his daughter. No one
else would own her, either, except the watch-dog
and the swallows, and they were only humble
beasts, and there was nothing they could say.

Then poor Elisa wept and thought of her eleven
brothers who were all far away. Sadly she stole out
of the palace, and all day long she wandered over
field and bog until she entered the great forest. She
had no idea where she would go, but she felt so sad
and longed so much for her brothers, who had been
driven out into the world like herself, that she made
up her mind to try to find them.

She had been in the forest only a short while
when night fell: she had left path and roadway far
behind. Then she lay down on the soft moss, said
her evening prayers, and leaned her head against
the stump of a tree. It was all so still, the air was
mild, and round about her in the grass and on the
moss hundreds of glow-worms shone like a green
fire, and when she touched one of the branches
gently with her hand, the glowing insects fell about
her like star-dust.

All night long she dreamed of her brothers: they
played again as children, they wrote with their

diamond slate-pencils upon their golden slates and they looked at that beautiful picture-book which had cost half a kingdom. But they did not, as they had done before, write nothing but noughts and straight lines upon their slates—no, they wrote of the bold deeds they had done, of all they had seen and been through: and everything in the picture-book came alive—the birds sang, and the people stepped out of the book and talked to Elisa and her brothers, but when she turned over the page, they jumped straight back again so that the pictures should not get muddled.

When she woke the sun was already high: she could not see it, of course, for the high trees spread out their branches thick and fast, but the sun-beams played upon them like a fluttering golden gauze. There was a fresh smell of green leaves, and the birds almost settled on her shoulders. She heard water splashing from many large springs which all fell into a pool with a lovely sandy bottom. True, bushes grew thickly round it, but there was one place where the deer had trodden a large opening, and through this Elisa made her way down to the water. It was so clear that if the trees and bushes had not moved with the wind, she might have thought they were painted on the bottom, so clearly was reflected every leaf, whether it caught the rays of the sun or was quite hidden in the shade.

As soon as she saw her own face she had quite a fright, it was so brown and dreadful, but when she had wetted her little hand and rubbed her eyes and forehead, the white skin shone through again. Then she put aside all her clothes and stepped into the fresh water, and there was not a lovelier king's daughter in the whole world than she was.

When she had once more dressed and plaited her long hair, she went to the gushing spring, drank from the hollow of her hand, and wandered farther into the forest without knowing where she was going. She thought upon her brothers; she thought upon the goodness of God who would surely not forsake her: He made the wild crab-apples grow to satisfy the hungry; He showed her a tree, the branches bowed with fruit, and from it she made her midday meal. She set props under its branches, and then entered the darkest part of the forest. It was so still, she heard her own footsteps, she heard every little withered leaf she trod upon. There was not a bird to be seen; not a sun-beam could penetrate the great thick branches of the trees; the tall trunks stood so close together that when she looked straight ahead, it seemed that one great trellis of timber after another shut her in. Yes, here was a loneliness she had never known before.

The night was so dark, too: not a single little glow-worm shone in the moss. Sadly she lay down to sleep: then the branches over her head seemed to part, and Our Lord looked down upon her with gentle eyes, and little angels peeped out over His head and under His arms.

When she woke in the morning she did not know whether she had dreamed it or whether it had really been so.

She had gone some steps forward when she met an old woman with berries in her basket, and the old woman gave her some of them. Elisa asked her if she had not seen eleven princes riding through the forest.

'No,' said the old woman, 'but yesterday I saw eleven swans with golden crowns upon their heads swimming down the stream close by here!'

And she led Elisa a little farther forward to a steep bank: at the bottom of the slope a stream wound its way: the trees upon its banks stretched their long leafy branches over towards each other, and where their natural growth was not sufficient for them to touch, they had torn their roots loose from the earth and leaned out over the water with their branches intertwined.

Elisa said good-bye to the old woman, and went along down the stream to where it flowed out upon the great open beach.

The beautiful sea lay open before the young girl's eyes, but not a ship appeared upon it, not a boat was to be seen, nothing to carry her farther. She looked at the countless pebbles on the shore: the water had worn them all to a round form— glass, iron, stone, everything that lay washed up on the beach had been moulded by the water, and yet it was far softer than her delicate hand. 'It goes on rolling untiringly, and so all these hard stones are made smooth and even. I will be just as tireless! Thank you for your lesson, clear, rolling waves! Some day, my heart tells me, you will bear me to my dear brothers!'

On the seaweed washed up by the tide lay eleven white swan feathers: she gathered them together like a bunch of flowers. Drops of water lay upon them, but no one could see whether they were dew or tears. It was lonely on the seashore, but she did not notice it, for the sea changed everlastingly— yes, it changed more in a few hours than fresh inland-waters in a whole year. When a great black cloud passed over it, the sea seemed to answer,

'I can look dark, too.' And then the wind would blow strong and the waves turn to white foam. But when the clouds shone brightly tinged with red and the wind slept, then the sea was like a rose-leaf. It was now green, now white, but however peacefully it rested, there was still a slight movement on the shore, the water lifting lightly like the breast of a sleeping child.

When the sun was on the point of setting, Elisa saw eleven white swans with golden crowns upon their heads flying towards the land. They came gliding one behind the other, looking like a long white ribbon. Then Elisa climbed the slope and hid behind a bush: the swans settled near her and beat their great white wings.

As the sun sank below the water, the swan-forms suddenly fell away and there stood eleven handsome princes, Elisa's brothers. She uttered a loud cry, for although they had changed much, she knew they were her brothers, she felt they must be: and she sprang into their arms, calling them by their names, and they were very, very happy when they saw and recognized their little sister who was now so grown-up and beautiful. They laughed and they cried, and they soon understood how wicked their step-mother had been to them all.

'We brothers,' said the eldest, 'fly in the likeness of wild swans as long as the sun is in the sky: when it sets we appear as men again. And so, about sunset, we always have to be careful to have a resting-place for our feet, for if we were flying high up in the clouds, we might find ourselves in human form hurtling down into the deep. We do not live here: there lies a land just as beautiful as this on the farther side of the sea; but the way is long from

167

here—we have to cross the great ocean, and there is not a single island on our way where we could spend the night, only a lonely little rock which rises steeply half-way across. It is only just big enough for us to rest upon it standing side by side: when the seas are heavy, the spray flies high over us. But yet we thank God for it. There we spend the night in our human form, and without it we could never visit the dear land of our birth, because we have to spend two of the longest days of the year on our flight here. Only once a year do we get the chance of visiting the home of our fathers and we dare not stay longer than eleven days, time enough to fly over this great forest to where we can catch a glimpse of the palace where we were born and where father still lives, and see the high tower of the church where mother is buried. Here we have the feeling that even the trees and the bushes are akin to us; here the wild horses race away over the plains just as we used to see them in our childhood; here the charcoal-burner sings the old songs we used to dance to as children—here, in short, is the land of our birth, the land that draws us back, and where we have found you, our dear little sister. We dare not stay here longer than two days now, and then we must away over the sea to a land that is beautiful but not our mother-land. How can we take you with us?—We've neither ship nor boat!'

'How can I free you from the spell?' asked their sister.

And they talked together nearly the whole night through, and dozed but a few hours.

Elisa awoke to the sound of swans' wings swishing over her. Her brothers had been transformed again, and they flew round in great circles and at

last far away, but one of them, the youngest, stayed
behind: and the swan laid its head in her lap and

she patted its white wings: they were together the
whole day. Towards evening the others came back,
and when the sun set they stood in their natural
form.

'Tomorrow we fly away from here, and we dare

not return for a whole year, but we can't leave you like this! Have you the courage to come with us? My arm is strong enough to carry you through the forest, so should not all our wings together be strong enough to fly with you over the sea?'

'Yes, take me with you!' said Elisa.

They spent the whole night plaiting a net of supple willow bark and tough rushes, and they made it big and strong: Elisa lay down in it, and when the sun rose and the brothers had changed back to wild swans, they seized the net in their beaks and flew high up towards the clouds with their dear sister who lay still sleeping. The sunbeams fell right upon her face, and so one of the swans flew above her head shading her with its broad wings.

They were far from land when Elisa woke: she thought she was still dreaming, so strange did it seem to her to be carried over the sea, high up through the sky. By her side lay a branch of lovely ripe berries and a bundle of tasty roots: the youngest of her brothers had gathered them and put them there for her, and she smiled her thanks to him, for she knew that he was the one who was flying just over her head and shading her with his wings.

They were so high up that the first ship they saw below them looked like a white sea-gull resting upon the water. A cloud lay behind them, a great mountain of a cloud, and Elisa saw her own gigantic shadow and those of the eleven swans flying on it: it was a finer picture than she had ever seen before, but as the sun rose higher and the cloud was left farther behind them, the drifting shadow-picture disappeared from view.

170

All day long they flew on like an arrow whistling through the air, but now they had their sister to carry, it was taking them longer than usual. Bad weather was blowing up and evening was drawing near: anxiously Elisa watched the sun sinking, and she was still unable to spot the lonely rock in the sea; the swans seemed to her to be beating their wings more strongly. Ah, it was her fault they were not going quickly enough: when the sun set they would change into men, fall into the sea and drown. Then she prayed earnestly in her heart to God, but she still saw no sign of the rock: the black cloud was drawing nearer, strong gusts of wind proclaimed an approaching gale, the clouds stood banked in one great threatening wave and shot forward in a solid leaden mass: lightning followed, flash upon flash.

The sun was now right upon the rim of the sea. Elisa's heart trembled: then the swans shot downwards so swiftly that she thought she would fall, but just then they straightened out again. The sun was half below the water when she first caught sight of the little rock beneath her: it looked no bigger than the head of a seal stuck up out of the water. The sun was sinking rapidly: it was now only the size of a star. As her foot touched the solid ground the sun went out like the last spark in a piece of burning paper. She saw her brothers standing round her arm in arm, but there was only just enough room for them and her. The sea beat against the rock and flung its spray like a shower of rain over the top of them. The sky was brightly lit by repeated flashes of lightning and the thunder rolled clap upon clap; but the brothers and sister held hands and sang a hymn, and that gave them comfort and courage.

At daybreak the air was clean and still, and as soon as the sun rose the swans flew away from the island with Elisa. The seas were still running high, and when she was high in the air it looked as if the white foam upon the dark-green sea were millions of swans floating on the water.

As the sun rose higher Elisa saw in front of her, half swimming in the air, a land of mountains with shining ice-masses upon the mountain-sides, and in the middle a palace stretched quite a mile in length, with one bold colonnade on top of another. In front waved woods of palm-trees and magnificent flowers as big as mill-wheels. She asked if this were the land she was bound for, but the swans shook their heads, for what she saw was the cloud-palace of Morgan le Fay, ever-changing in its loveliness, and they dared not take any human person there. As Elisa was gazing upon it, woods and palace collapsed and faded, and in their place stood twenty proud churches, all alike, with high towers and pointed windows. She thought she heard the organ play, but it was the sea she heard. Then when she was quite near the churches, they turned into a whole fleet of ships sailing down below her; she looked down, and it was only a sea-mist swirling over the water. Yes, there was an everlasting change before her eyes, and then she saw the real land she was bound for; the loveliest blue mountains rose up with forests of cedar, towns and castles. Long before the sun went down she was sitting on the hill-side in front of a great cave overgrown with delicate green creepers that looked like an embroidered carpet.

172

'Now we shall see what you'll dream here to-night!' said the youngest brother and showed her her bed-chamber.

'If only I might dream how I could set you free!' she said; and her mind was so filled with this thought, she prayed earnestly to God to help her, and even when she had fallen asleep, she went on with her prayer. Then she appeared to be flying high up in the sky to the cloud-palace of Morgan le Fay, and the fairy came to meet her, beautiful and radiant, and yet looking quite like the old woman who had given her the berries in the forest and told her of the swans with the golden crowns.

'Your brothers can be freed!' she said. 'But have you enough courage and endurance? It's true the sea is softer than your delicate hands and yet shapes hard stones, but it doesn't feel the pain your fingers will feel, and it has no heart and doesn't suffer the anxiety and torment you must endure. Do you see this stinging-nettle I am holding in my hand? Many of the same kind grow round about the cave where you are sleeping; only those and the ones that spring up from the graves in the churchyard can be used—mark that!—You must pick them—though they will sting you and raise blisters on your skin—tread the nettles with your feet and get a yarn like flax from them, and with that twist a thread and make eleven shirts like coats of mail with long sleeves. Throw these over the eleven wild swans and the spell will be broken. But you must take care to remember that from the moment you begin your task right up to the time it is finished, even though it take years, you must not speak: the first word you utter will pierce your brothers' hearts like a dagger—their lives hang upon your tongue. Remember all I have told you!'

And at the same time she touched Elisa's hand with the nettle; it was like a burning fire. Elisa woke with the pain. It was bright daylight, and close by where she had slept lay a nettle like the one she had seen in her dream. Then she fell upon her knees, thanked Our Lord, and left the cave to begin her task.

She plunged her delicate hands down among the ugly nettles that stung like fire; they burnt great blisters on her hands and arms, but she would suffer gladly if she could free her dear brothers. She trod every nettle with her naked feet, and twisted the green flax into a thread.

When the sun had set her brothers came back, and they were alarmed to find her so silent; they thought it was a new spell their wicked step-mother had put upon her. But when they saw her hands, they realized what she was doing for their sake, and the youngest brother wept, and where his tears fell she felt no more pain and the burning blisters disappeared.

She spent the night at her task, because she could not rest until she had freed her dear brothers. The whole of the following day, while the swans were away, she sat in solitude, but never had time flown so quickly. One shirt was completely finished, and she began upon the next.

Then a hunting-horn sounded through the mountains; she grew quite frightened as the sound came nearer; she heard the hounds baying, and in terror she fled into the cave, tied together in a bundle the nettles she had gathered and combed, and sat upon it.

At the same moment a great hound sprang out of the bushes, followed immediately by another and still another; they bayed loudly, retreated and sprang forward again. A few minutes later the huntsmen were all standing before the cave, and the most handsome among them was the king of the land: he stepped towards Elisa, for he had never seen a more beautiful girl.

'How do you come to be here, sweet child?' he asked. Elisa shook her head; she dared not speak, for that would cost her brothers' lives and freedom; and she hid her hands under her apron so that the king should not see what she had to suffer.

'Come with me!' he said. 'You cannot stay here! If you are as good as you are beautiful, I will clothe you in silk and velvet and put a golden crown upon your head, and you shall live in my finest castle!' And then he lifted her up upon his horse; she wept and wrung her hands, but the king said, 'I want only your happiness! One day you will thank me for this!' And so, holding her in front of him on his horse, he rode off between the mountains, and the huntsmen followed behind.

When the sun set the magnificent royal city with its churches and domes lay before them, and the king led her into the palace, where great fountains splashed in high marble halls, their walls and ceilings resplendent with paintings. But she had no eyes for it. She wept and grieved; listlessly, she let the women attire her in royal garments, plait pearls in her hair, and draw fine gloves over her blistered fingers.

When she stood there in all her finery, she was so dazzlingly beautiful that the court bowed even more deeply before her and the king chose her to be his bride, although the archbishop shook his head and whispered that the beautiful girl of the woods was undoubtedly a witch who had blinded their eyes and infatuated the king's heart.

But the king did not listen to him: he commanded the music to strike up, the richest dishes to be brought in, and the loveliest girls to dance about her. She was led through sweet-smelling gardens into magnificent halls; but not a smile passed over her lips or shone from her eyes—

sorrow stood there as her inheritance and ever-lasting possession. Then the king opened a little chamber close by, where she was to sleep: it was decorated with costly green tapestries, and looked quite like the cave where she had been found; on the floor lay the bundle of yarn she had spun from the nettles, and from the ceiling hung the shirt she had finished knitting—one of the huntsmen had brought all this along with him as something of a curiosity.

'In here you can dream you are back in your old home!' said the king. 'And here is the work you were occupied with. It will amuse you now in all your splendour to think on times gone by.'

When Elisa saw what lay so near her heart, a smile played about her mouth and the blood returned to her cheeks: she thought upon her brothers' release and kissed the king's hand, and he pressed her to his heart, and commanded all the church-bells to proclaim their wedding-feast. The beautiful dumb girl from the woods would be queen of the land.

Then the archbishop whispered evil words in the king's ear, but they made no impression upon his heart: the wedding must stand, the archbishop himself had to place the crown upon her head, and he pressed the narrow ring firmly down over her forehead with such ill will that it hurt. And yet there lay a heavier ring about her heart in her sorrow for her brothers, so that she did not feel the physical pain. Her mouth was dumb—one single word would cost her brothers their lives—but in her eyes lay a deep love for the good and handsome king, who did all he could to make her happy. Day by day she loved him more and more. Oh, if only she dare open her heart to him and tell him of her sufferings, but silent she had to be, and in silence must she complete her task. And so, at night, she would slip from his side, go to the little room that was decorated to look like the cave, and finish knitting one shirt after another. But when she began upon the seventh she ran out of yarn.

She knew that the nettles she must use grew in the churchyard, but she had to pick them herself—how could she get out to do it?

'Oh, what is the pain in my fingers to the agony my heart suffers!' she thought. 'I must risk it! Our Lord will not take his hand from me!' With fear in her heart, as if it were an evil deed she had to do, she crept down into the garden in the moon-bright night, and made her way down the long avenues, and out into the lonely streets that led to the churchyard. There she saw a coven of ugly witches sitting in a circle on one of the broadest tombstones: they took their rags off as if they were going to bathe, and then with their long skinny fingers they dug down into the fresh graves, pulled out the dead bodies, and fed upon the flesh. Elisa had to pass close by them, and they fastened their evil eyes upon her, but she said her prayers, gathered the stinging-nettles, and carried them home to the palace.

Only one single person had seen her, and that was the archbishop: he was up while the others were asleep. He was now sure he had been right in his opinion that all was not as it should be with the queen: she was a witch and had used her powers to infatuate the king and all the people.

During confession he told the king what he had seen and what he feared, and as the harsh words fell from his tongue, the carven images of the saints shook their heads as if to say, 'It is not so—Elisa is innocent!' But the archbishop took it the wrong way, and thought that they were bearing witness against her, that they were shaking their heads over her sin. Then two heavy tears rolled down the king's cheeks, and he went home with doubt in his heart. He pretended to sleep at night, but no sleep would come to close his eyes in peace: he noticed Elisa get up. Every night she did the same thing, and every time he followed her softly and watched her disappear into her little room.

Day by day his face grew darker: Elisa noticed it, but could not understand why, though it troubled her and added to the suffering she felt in her heart for her brothers. Her salt tears ran down her royal velvet and purple, and lay there like glistening diamonds; and all who saw her splendour wished they were queen too. She would soon reach the end of her task, however, for only one shirt still remained to be done, but she had no more yarn left and not a single nettle. And so once more, though this would be the last time, she would have to go to the churchyard and pick a few handfuls. She thought anxiously of the lonely walk and the frightful witches, but her will was as firm as her trust in the Lord.

And so she went, but the king and the archbishop followed her. They saw her disappear by the iron gate that led into the churchyard, and when they drew near, the witches were sitting on the grave-stones just as Elisa had seen them, and the king turned away for he imagined her among them—only that very evening had she laid her head upon his breast.

'I shall let the people judge her!' he said, and the people passed judgement that she should burn in the red flames.

She was borne away from the splendour of the royal halls into a dark damp hole where the wind whistled in through the iron bars of the window. Instead of velvet and silk, they gave her the bundle of nettles she had gathered to lay her head on, and she had to use the hard stinging shirts she had knitted as bedding and blankets. But they could have given her nothing she would sooner have— she turned to her task again, and prayed to God. Outside, the street urchins sang mocking songs about her: not a soul comforted her with a loving word.

Towards evening came the swish of a swan's wing close by the window-bars—it was the youngest of the brothers: he had found their sister. She sobbed aloud with joy, although she knew that the coming night was probably the last she had to live: but now her work was nearly finished and her brothers were there.

The archbishop came to spend her last hour with her, as he had promised the king he would, but she shook her head, and asked him with looks and gestures to go: that night she had to finish her task, or everything—pain and tears and sleepless nights —everything would have been to no purpose. The archbishop went away speaking hard words against her, but poor Elisa knew she was innocent, and went on with her work.

There were little mice running over the floor, and they dragged the nettles over to her feet, to help a little at any rate, and a thrush settled by the iron window-bars and sang the whole night through as joyfully as it could so that she should not lose heart.

It was still no more than day-break, an hour before sunrise, when the eleven brothers stood at the palace gate and demanded to be taken before the king; but they were told that could not be done —it was still night, the king was asleep and they dared not wake him. They prayed, they threatened; the guard came—yes, even the king himself stepped out to ask what it all meant; at that very moment the sun rose and the brothers were no longer there, but away over the palace flew eleven wild swans.

Everybody streamed out of the city gate to see the witch burnt. A wretched horse dragged the cart she sat in; she had been given a smock of coarse sackcloth; her lovely long hair hung loose about her beautiful head, her cheeks were deathly pale, and her lips moved softly while her fingers wove the green yarn—even on her way to death, she did not give up the task she had begun: the ten shirts lay at her feet, and she was knitting away at the eleventh, while the rabble scoffed at her.

'Look at the witch, see the way she mutters! There's no hymn-book in her hand, you bet! Look at her sitting there with her beastly witchcraft! Tear it away from her! Tear it into a thousand pieces!'

And they all pressed in upon her and would have torn it apart, when the eleven white swans came flying towards her: they settled round her on the cart and beat their great wings. The mob drew back in alarm.

'It's a sign from heaven! She must be innocent!' many whispered, but they did not risk saying so aloud.

As the executioner seized her by the hand, she hastily threw the eleven shirts over the swans, and there stood eleven handsome princes, but the youngest had a swan's wing in place of one arm because a sleeve was missing from his shirt which she had not completely finished.

'Now I can speak!' she said. 'I am innocent!'

And the people who saw what had happened bowed before her as if she were a saint, but she sank lifeless in her brothers' arms, overcome by excitement, fear, and pain.

'Yes, she is innocent!' said the eldest brother, and then he told them everything that had happened, and while he was speaking, a perfume like that of a million roses spread about them, for every stick of wood heaped about the stake had taken root and put out branches: there stood a great tall hedge fragrant with red roses. Right at the top was one flower, white and gleaming, which shone like a star; the king plucked it and placed it on Elisa's breast, and then she woke with peace and happiness in her heart.

And all the church-bells rang by themselves, and the birds came in great flocks. The way back to the palace became a wedding procession such as no king had yet seen.

THE FLYING TRUNK

THERE was once a merchant who was so rich he
could have paved the whole street with silver coins
—and have had nearly enough over for a little alley-
way as well. But that's not what he did: he had
another use for his money. Every time he laid out
a shilling, he got five shillings back. That's the sort
of merchant he was—and then he died.

All his money now went to his son, and he lived
a life of pleasure. He went to dances every night,
he made paper kites out of ten-shilling notes, and
played ducks and drakes on the lake with golden
sovereigns instead of pebbles. That was a sure way
of getting rid of his money, and get rid of it he did.
At last he had no more than five shillings left, and
all the clothes he had were a pair of slippers and an
old dressing gown. His friends no longer cared for
him now that they could not go out with him any
more, but one of them, a good-hearted young man,
sent him an old trunk, and said, 'Pack up!' Now
that was all very well, but he had nothing to pack.
And so he got into the trunk himself.

It was a queer kind of trunk; as soon as you pressed the lock, up would fly the trunk and away it would go. Now it so happened that that was just what he did, and—whoosh!—up the chimney it flew with him, high up over the clouds, farther and farther away. The bottom creaked and he was afraid it would fall to pieces, and then he would have performed a very fine somersault! At last he came to the land of the Turks. He hid the trunk in the woods under the withered leaves, and then made his way into the town. This he could do easily enough, for among the Turks everybody walked about just as he was, in dressing-gown and slippers. He met a nurse with a small child. 'Just a minute, Turkish nurse!' he called out. 'What's that great palace close by the town here with the windows so high up in the wall?'

'That's where the king's daughter lives!' she said. 'A fortune-teller once said that she would be made very unhappy over a love-affair, and so no one is allowed to visit her unless the king and queen are there!'

'Thanks!' said the merchant's son, and then he made his way back to the woods, sat down in his trunk, flew up over the roof-tops, and crept in through the window to the princess.

She was lying on the sofa asleep: she looked so lovely that the merchant's son couldn't help kissing her. She woke up and was really quite frightened, but he told her he was the Turkish god who had come down through the sky to visit her, and she thought that sounded rather nice.

So they sat down beside one another, and he told her stories about her eyes: they were the loveliest dark lakes and thoughts swam about in them like mermaids. He told her about her fore-head: it was a snow-covered mountain which had the most magnificent halls with beautiful pictures in them. And then he told her about the stork that brings sweet little babies.

Yes, indeed, they were very charming stories! Then he asked the princess to marry him, and she said, 'Yes,' right away.

'But you must come here on Saturday,' she said. 'The king and queen are coming to tea. They'll be very proud when they know I'm going to marry the Turkish god. But see that you know a really good story, for that's what my parents are especially fond of. My mother likes them to have a moral and a distinguished air about them; my father likes them jolly with something to laugh at.'

'Very well,' he said, 'I shall bring no wedding-gift but a story!' Then they parted, and the princess gave him a sword. It was set with gold coins, and those he could most certainly make use of.

He now flew away, bought himself a new dressing-gown, and then sat down in the woods to compose a story. It had to be finished by Saturday, and that wasn't so easy after all.

But at last the story was finished and Saturday came.

The king and the queen and the whole court were waiting to have tea with the princess, and they all received him in such a very pleasant way!

'Will you tell us a story?' asked the queen. 'Something instructive that one has to think about.'

'But something one can laugh at as well!' put in the king.

'Certainly!' he said, and so he began. This is the story he told, and you must listen to it carefully.

'There was once a bundle of sulphur-matches who were quite insupportably proud because of their high ancestry. Their family-tree—that is to say the great pine-tree they were all little chips of —had been a great old tree in the forest. The matches now lay upon the mantelshelf between a tinder-box and an old iron saucepan, and they were telling them about their young days. "Yes," they said, "when we were on the green bough, we were in clover right enough![1] Every morning and evening there was diamond-tea left by the dew, all day long we had sunshine, whenever the sun shone, and all the little birds would tell us stories. We couldn't help noticing how well off we were when we looked at the hardwoods, for they were clothed only in the summer-time, while our family could afford green clothing both summer and winter. But then the wood-cutters came along and caused a great social upheaval. Our family was split up: the head of the family got a job as main-mast on a fine ship which could sail wherever it wished right round the world; the other branches ended up in other places; and we have now the task of striking a light for the common herd. That's how it is that people of good family like us find themselves here in the kitchen."

'"Hm, my story's quite different from that!" said the iron saucepan that lay by the side of the matches. "Right from the very first moment I came into the world, I've been scoured and boiled time and time again! I'm all for solid respectability, I am, and, strictly speaking, I'm the most important person in the house here. My one real pleasure in

[1] In Danish the phrase 'to be on a green bough' is an idiom meaning 'to be in clover'. L. W. K.

life is to lie like this after dinner, clean and spruce upon the mantelshelf, and have a little sensible conversation with my friends. Except for the water-bucket, which goes down into the yard from time to time, it's true to say that we spend all our lives indoors. Our only newsmonger is the shopping-basket, but she's always so full of disturbing talk about the Government and the People—yes, not so long ago there was an old pot here who was so shocked by it all that he fell down and cracked himself to pieces! She's quite irresponsible, I tell you!"

'"You talk too much!" said the tinder-box, and the steel struck the flint and made the sparks fly. "Now what about a pleasant evening?"

'"Yes, let's discuss which of us is of the most consequence!" said the matches.

'"No, I don't like talking about myself," said the earthenware pot. "Let's have an evening's entertainment. I'll begin. I shall describe something everyone has experienced: that'll be something we can all enter into with pleasure, and it will be very amusing. 'Near the Baltic, by the Danish beeches—'"

'"That's a good beginning!" said all the plates together. "It's going to be the sort of story I like!"

'"Yes, I spent my youth there in a very quiet family. The furniture was polished, the floor washed, and clean curtains put up every fortnight."

'"What an interesting way you have of telling a story!" said the broom. "You can tell at once it's a woman speaking: there's a kind of theme of cleanliness running through it!"

'"Yes, I noticed that!" said the water-bucket, and gave a little hop of pleasure, so that it said, "Plonk!" on the floor.

'And the pot went on telling her story, and the end was just as good as the beginning.

'The plates all clattered with pleasure, and the broom took some green parsley from the sand-hole and made a crown for the pot, for he knew that would annoy the others. "If I crown her today," he thought, "she'll have to crown me tomorrow."

'"I'm going to dance!" said the fire-tongs, and dance she did. My, how she could stand on one leg and kick the other up in the air! The old chair-cover over there in the corner split himself just looking at her! "Can I be crowned, too?" asked the tongs. And so she was.

'"What a common lot they are!" thought the matches.

'They now called upon the tea-urn to sing, but she said she had a cold and could only sing when she was on the boil. She was, of course, standing on her dignity, and refused to sing anywhere but on the dining-room table with the master and mistress.

'Over there in the window sat an old quill-pen which the maid used to write with. There was nothing remarkable about her, except that she had been dipped far too deeply in the ink-bottle. But she was rather proud of that. "If the tea-urn doesn't want to sing," she said, "she needn't! There's a nightingale hanging in a cage outside: he can sing —though, to be sure, he never had lessons, but we won't speak harshly of him this evening!"

'"I find it most unbecoming," said the kettle, who was the prima donna of the kitchen and half-sister to the tea-urn, "that anyone should listen to such a foreign bird! I ask you, is it patriotic? I leave it to the shopping-basket to judge the matter!"

'"I'm too upset!" said the shopping-basket. "No one can imagine how deeply upset I am. Is this a proper way of passing the evening? Would it not be better to set the house to rights? Then everyone would be in his own place, and I could direct the whole thing. That would be something worth doing!"

'"Yes, let's turn the place upside-down!" they all cried together. But at that very moment the door opened. It was the maid. They stood quite still, and no one spoke a word. But there was not a pot there who did not know for certain what he could have done and how distinguished a person he was. "Yes, if I'd wanted to," they thought, "I could have made it an amusing evening all right!"

'The maid picked up the matches and struck them. My, how they spluttered and burst into flame!

'"Now," they thought, "everyone can see that we're the most important people here! What radiance we have! What enlightenment!" And then they burnt out.'

'That was a charming story!' said the queen. 'I quite felt I was in the kitchen with those sulphur-matches. Yes, you shall certainly have our daughter.'

'Yes, rather!' said the king. 'You shall have her on Monday!' And now they spoke to him like one of the family.

So the wedding was arranged, and the evening before, the whole city was illuminated; cakes and buns were thrown to the children to scramble for; the street urchins stood on their toes, cheering and whistling through their fingers; everybody had a gorgeous time.

'I must see about doing something, too,' thought

the merchant's son. And so he bought rockets and crackers and every sort of firework he could think of, put them in his trunk, and flew up in the air with them.

Whoosh, how they went! How they banged away!

The Turks were all jumping up in the air with excitement, so that their slippers were flying about their ears: they had never seen such an aerial display before. Now they fully realized that it was indeed the Turkish god himself who was going to marry their princess.

As soon as the merchant's son descended into the wood again with his trunk, he thought, 'I'll take a walk into town, and then I shall get to hear how it went off.' And it was of course quite reasonable that he should want to do so.

My, how people talked! Every single person he spoke to about it had seen it after his own particular fashion, but they all thought it beautiful.

'I saw the Turkish god himself!' said one of them. 'He had eyes like shining stars and a beard like foaming water!'

'He was flying in a cloak of fire!' said another. 'And the loveliest little cherubs were peeping out from under its folds!'

Indeed, he heard the most charming things about himself, and the next day was to be his wedding-day.

And now he made his way back to the woods to sit down and rest in his trunk—but where was it? The trunk was burnt up. A spark from the fireworks had been left behind: it had caught fire, and the trunk was in ashes. He could fly no more: no more could he come to his bride.

She stood the whole day upon the roof and waited for him. And there she is, waiting still; but he wanders round the world telling stories. But they are no longer as delightful as the one he told about the sulphur-matches.

THE ROSE-ELF

In the middle of a garden there grew a rose-tree
which was quite full of roses, and in one of these,
the loveliest of them all, dwelt an elf. He was such
a tiny little fellow that no human eye could see him.
Behind every petal in the rose he had a bedroom.
He was as well-formed and beautiful as any child
could be, and he had wings which reached from his
shoulders right down to his feet. Oh, how sweetly
perfumed his sitting-room was, and how clear and
beautiful its walls, which were, of course, the
delicate pink petals of the rose!

All day long he enjoyed himself in the warm sunshine, flying from flower to flower, dancing on the
wings of flying butterflies, and counting how many
steps he must take to cover all the by-roads and
foot-paths to be found on a single lime-tree leaf.
He took for by-roads and foot-paths what we call
the veins in the leaf, and they were, for him, roads

192

that went on for ever! Before he had been over them all the sun went down: he had been very late in starting.

It grew very cold, the dew began to fall, and a strong wind blew up: it was surely best to go home! He hurried all he could, but the rose had shut, and he could not get in. Not a single rose remained open. The poor little elf was terrified—he had never been out at night-time before, he had always slept sweetly behind his warm rose-petals. Oh, it would certainly be his death!

At the other end of the garden, he knew, was an arbour covered in a beautiful honeysuckle. Its flowers looked like great painted trumpets: he would fly down into one of these and sleep till morning.

He flew over to it. Sh!——there were two people inside, a handsome young man and a beautiful girl. They were sitting side by side, and wishing they might never, never have to part. They were very, very fond of each other, far more than the best child can possibly be of his own father and mother.

'We must part all the same!' said the young man. 'Your brother intends us no good, and that is why he is sending me on an errand so far away over the lakes and mountains! Good-bye, my sweet bride, for that's what you really are to me!'

And then they kissed one another, and the young girl wept and gave him a rose. But before she handed it to him she pressed a kiss upon it so warm and deep that the flower opened. In flew the little elf and leant his head upon the delicate scented walls. But he could clearly hear them saying, 'Good-bye! Good-bye!' and he felt the rose being placed upon the young man's breast. Oh, how his heart beat within him! The little elf found it impossible to fall asleep, it beat so hard.

The rose did not lie still upon his breast for long. The man took it out, and as he walked along, alone through the dark forest, he kissed the flower, oh, so often and so passionately, that the little elf was near to being crushed to death. He could feel the man's lips burning through the petals, and the rose itself opened as though it felt the heat of the midday sun.

Then there came another man, gloomy and angry: it was the beautiful girl's wicked brother. He took out a big, sharp knife, and while the other was kissing the rose, this wicked man stabbed him to death, cut his head off, and buried it with his body in the soft earth beneath a lime-tree.

'Now he's dead and gone, and that's the end of him!' thought the wicked brother. 'He'll never come back any more. He was going on a long journey over the lakes and mountains, where a man can easily lose his life. And that's what he's done. He'll not come back, and my sister will never dare question me about him.'

Then he scraped the withered leaves over the loose earth with his foot, and returned home through the dark night. But he did not go alone, as he thought he did. The little elf went with him, sitting in a rolled-up withered lime-leaf which had fallen upon the wicked man's hair while he was digging the grave. His hat was now placed over it, it was very dark inside, and the elf was trembling with fright and anger over the evil deed.

In the early morning the wicked man returned home. He took his hat off and went into his sister's bedroom. There the girl lay in the bloom of her beauty, dreaming of the one she loved and picturing him on his journey over the mountains and through the forests. And now her wicked brother bent over her, and laughed evilly as only a devil can laugh. Then the withered leaf fell from his hair on to the bedspread, but he didn't notice it and left her room to get a little sleep himself while it was still early. The elf slipped out of the withered leaf, crept into the sleeping girl's ear, and told her, as if in a dream, about the dreadful murder. He described to her the place where her brother had killed him and left his body, he told her of the flowering lime-tree close by, and he said, 'So that you shall know that this is not just a dream I've told you, you will find a withered leaf on your bed.' And when she woke she found it.

Oh, you wouldn't believe what salt tears she wept! And there was no one she dared trust to tell her sorrow to. Her window stood open all day long, and the little elf could easily have gone out into the garden to the roses and the other flowers, but he hadn't the heart to leave her in her grief. In the window stood a tree with Bengal roses on it: he sat down in one of the flowers and watched over the poor girl. Her brother very often came into the room. He seemed very pleased with himself but he had an evil look, and she dared not speak one word to him of the great sorrow in her heart.

As soon as it was night she stole out of the house, and going into the forest she found the place where the lime-tree stood. She scraped away the leaves from the earth, and digging down, she soon found the young man who had been stabbed to death. Oh, how she cried and prayed to Our Lord that she might soon die as well!

She wanted to carry his body home with her, but

she couldn't do it, and so she took his pale head
with its fast-shut eyes, kissed his cold mouth, and
shook the earth out of his beautiful hair. 'This I
must keep!' she said. And when she had put the
earth and the leaves back over the dead body, she
took the head home with her. She took, too, a little
branch of the jasmine which was flowering in the
forest where he was killed.

As soon as she was in her own room again, she
fetched the biggest flower-pot she could find, laid
the dead man's head in it, covered it with earth,
and then planted the slip of jasmine in the pot.

'Good-bye! Good-bye!' whispered the little elf.
He could no longer bear to see all her sorrow, and
so he flew out into the garden to his rose: but the
rose had fallen, and only a few faded petals were
left clinging to the green hip.

'Ah, dear, dear me!' sighed the elf. 'How soon
everything good and beautiful is gone!' But at last
he found another rose where he could make his
home and live in comfort behind its delicate sweet-
scented petals.

Early every morning he would fly over to the
poor girl's window, and there he would always find
her standing beside the flower-pot and weeping.
Her salt tears fell upon the jasmine, and every day,
as she grew paler and paler, the branch grew fresher
and greener. One new shoot after another sprang
from it, and as the small white buds opened into
flowers she kissed them. But her wicked brother
scolded her and asked her if she'd lost her wits. He
couldn't understand why she was always crying
over the flower-pot, and he didn't like it. Of course,
he had no idea whose eyes lay closed there, nor
whose red lips had rotted into the soil. She was

leaning her head against the flower-pot, and the little rose-elf came in and found her sleeping like it. So he climbed into her ear and told her about that evening in the arbour, and about the sweet-scented rose and the kind-hearted elves. She fell into a sweet dream, and while she was dreaming, her life slipped away: she had died a peaceful death, and she was in heaven with the one she loved.

And the jasmine flowers opened their big white bells and gave out a wonderful sweet perfume: it was the only way they knew of weeping over the dead girl.

But her wicked brother looked at the beautiful flowering tree, took it as a legacy from his sister, and put it in his own bedroom close by the bed, for it was lovely to look at and its scent was sweet and delicious. The little rose-elf went with it. He flew from flower to flower, for in each one there dwelt a spirit, and he told them about the young man who had been killed and whose head had now become part of the soil they sprang from, and about the wicked brother and his poor sister.

'We know about that!' said every spirit in the flowers. 'We know about that! Haven't we grown from the eyes and the lips of the one who was killed? We know about it! We know all about it!' And they nodded their heads strangely.

The rose-elf couldn't understand how they could be so calm about it, and he flew out to the bees who were gathering honey, and told them the story of the wicked brother. And the bees told their queen, who commanded them all to kill the murderer the very next morning.

But the night before, which was the first night

after his sister's death, the brother lay asleep in his bed beside the sweet-smelling jasmine-tree, when each flower opened its cup, and unseen but armed with poisoned spears, the flower-spirits flew out. First, they sat by his ears and told him evil dreams, and then they flew over his lips and pricked his tongue with their poisoned spears. 'Now we have avenged the dead!' they said, and made their way back again into the white bells of the jasmine flowers.

When it was morning the bedroom window was suddenly flung up, and in flew the rose-elf with the queen-bee and all her swarm to kill him.

But he was already dead. There were people standing round his bed, and they said, 'The scent of the jasmine has killed him!'

Then the rose-elf understood the revenge which the flowers had taken. He told the queen-bee about it, and with her whole swarm she buzzed round the flower-pot. The bees were not to be driven away. A man picked up the flower-pot to carry it out, and one of the bees stung him on the hand so that he let the pot fall and break in pieces.

Then they saw the white skull, and they knew that the man who lay dead in bed was a murderer. And the queen-bee flew out into the open, humming and singing of the flowers' revenge and the rose-elf, and of how there lives, behind the smallest petal, someone who can both make known an evil deed and avenge it too.

THE SWINEHERD

THERE was once a poor Prince. He had a kingdom, which was quite small, yet nevertheless quite big enough to marry on—and that's what he'd set his heart on doing.

Now it would of course be somewhat bold of him to dare to say, 'Will you have me?' to the daughter of the Emperor. But dare he did, for his name was famous far and wide, and there were hundreds of princesses who would have said, 'Yes, please!' But did the Emperor's daughter?

Let's listen to the story and see.

On the grave of the Prince's father there grew a rose-tree—oh, such a beautiful rose-tree it was!— which bloomed only once in every five years. And even then it bore only one flower, but that was a rose which smelled so sweetly that its scent would make one forget all one's sorrows and troubles. He had, too, a nightingale, which could sing as if all

199

the beautiful melodies in the world were to be found in its little throat. The Princess should have them both: and so the rose and the nightingale were placed in large silver caskets and sent to her.

The Emperor permitted them to be brought before him in the great hall where the Princess was playing 'going a-visiting' with her ladies-in-waiting, for that was all they ever did. And when she saw the large caskets with the gifts inside them, she clapped her hands with joy.

'If only it's a little pussy-cat!' she said—but there lay the beautiful rose.

'Oh, but how nicely it's made!' said all the ladies-in-waiting.

'It's more than nice!' said the Emperor. 'It's lovely!'

But when the Princess felt it she was ready to weep.

'Oh, papa!' she said. 'It's not made at all—it's real!'

'Well!' said all the ladies-in-waiting. 'It's real!'

'Now before we get angry,' said the Emperor, 'let's first see what's in the other casket!' And there was the nightingale: it sang so beautifully that for the moment they were unable to say anything bad about it.

'Superbe! Charmant!' said the ladies-in-waiting, for they all spoke French, one worse than another.

'How that bird reminds me of Her late Majesty's musical-box!' said an old courtier. 'Yes, indeed, it has just the same tone, just the same delivery!'

'Yes!' said the Emperor, sobbing like a little child.

'I'll never believe that that's real!' said the Princess.

'Indeed, it is—it's a real bird!' said those who had brought it.

'Oh,' said the Princess. 'Well, then, let it fly away.' And nothing would induce her to give the Prince permission to visit her.

But he would not let himself lose heart. He smeared his face black and brown, pushed his cap down on his head, and knocked at the door.

'Good day, Emperor!' he said. 'I couldn't get a job here in the palace, I suppose?'

'Hm, there are so many after them!' said the Emperor. 'But let me see—I do need someone who can look after the pigs, we've certainly enough of them!'

And so the Prince was engaged as Imperial Swineherd. He was given a wretched little room down by the pig-sty, and there he had to stay. All day long he sat working, and when evening came he had made a beautiful little saucepan. It had bells all round it, and as soon as the saucepan came to the boil, they rang clear and sweet, and played the old melody:

> Alas, my dearest Augustin,
> All is now lost, lost, lost!

But the most wonderful thing of all was that if you held your finger in the steam from the saucepan, you could immediately smell every dinner that was being cooked in every fire-place in the town. That was something very different from a rose!

Now the Princess was out walking with all her ladies-in-waiting, and when she heard the melody, she stood quite still and listened with a look of pleasure, for she, too, could play 'Alas, my dearest

Augustin!' In fact, it was the only thing she knew, and she played it with one finger.

'Why, that's the piece I know!' she said. 'He must be a very gifted swineherd! Listen, go in and ask him how much he wants for that instrument of his!'

And so one of the ladies-in-waiting had to run in and ask. But she put on her thick shoes first.

'What will you take for that saucepan?' said the lady-in-waiting.

'I'll take ten kisses from the Princess!' said the swineherd.

'Heaven save us!' said the lady-in-waiting.

'Yes,' said the swineherd, 'but I couldn't take less!'

'Well, what does he say?' asked the Princess.

'I really can't say it!' said the lady-in-waiting. 'It's quite dreadful!'

'Then you can whisper!' And so she whispered it.

'He's certainly very rude!' said the Princess, and immediately walked away. But when she had walked a few steps the little bells rang out again clear and sweet:

> Alas, my dearest Augustin,
> All is now lost, lost, lost!

'Listen,' said the Princess, 'ask him if he'll take ten kisses from my ladies-in-waiting!'

'No, thanks!' said the swineherd. 'Ten kisses from the Princess, or else I keep the saucepan.'

'What a tiresome fellow it is!' said the Princess. 'But you must all stand round me, so that no one can possibly see!'

And the ladies-in-waiting gathered round her and spread out their dresses; and so the swineherd got the ten kisses, and she got the saucepan.

Well, what pleasure it gave them! The whole of that evening and all the next day, the saucepan was kept boiling. There wasn't a fire-place in the whole

town, from the Court Chamberlain's to the shoe-maker's, but they knew what was cooking there. The ladies-in-waiting danced and clapped their hands.

'We know who's going to have sweet soup and pan-cakes! We know who's going to have porridge and chops! Isn't that interesting!'

'Most interesting!' said the Mistress of the Royal Household.

'Yes, but you must keep it a secret, because I'm the Emperor's daughter!'

'Heavens, of course we shall!' they all said together.

The swineherd—that's to say, the Prince; but they knew no differently, of course, and thought he was a real swineherd—didn't let the day go by without busying himself with something. And so he made a rattle: when you swung it round you could hear all the waltzes, barn-dances, and polkas that have ever been known since the creation of the world.

'But that's superb!' said the Princess as she was walking by. 'I've never heard a more beautiful piece of music! Listen, go in and ask him the price of that instrument—but I will give no more kisses!'

'He wants a hundred kisses from the Princess!' said the lady-in-waiting who had been in to ask.

'He must be mad!' said the Princess, and walked away. But when she had gone a few yards she stopped and stood still. 'We must encourage art,' she said, 'and I am the Emperor's daughter! Tell him he may have ten kisses like yesterday: he can have the rest from my ladies-in-waiting!'

'Oh, but we shouldn't like that at all!' said the ladies-in-waiting.

'What nonsense!' said the Princess. 'If I can kiss him, so can you! And remember, I provide your board and wages!' And so the lady-in-waiting had to go in and ask him again.

'A hundred kisses from the Princess,' he said, 'or we each keep our own!'

'Stand round me!!!' she said. And so all the ladies-in-waiting gathered round her, and he began to kiss her.

'What on earth can that crowd be down there by the pig-sty!' said the Emperor, as he stepped out on the balcony. He rubbed his eyes and put his glasses on. 'It's the ladies-in-waiting—up to some game, I'll be bound! I'd better go down and see!' And so he pulled his slippers up at the back—for they were really shoes which he had trodden down at the heels.

What a haste he was in, bless him!

As soon as he got down in the yard he crept up to them very quietly, and the ladies-in-waiting had so much to do with counting the kisses—so that it should be fair, and he shouldn't take too many, nor yet too few—that they were quite unaware of the Emperor. He raised himself up on his toes.

'What on earth!' he said, when he saw them kissing each other. And he struck them both over the head with his slipper just as the swineherd was taking his eighty-sixth kiss. 'Out with you!' said the Emperor, for he was really angry, and both the Princess and the swineherd were put outside his empire.

There she stood and wept, the swineherd scolded her, and the rain poured down.

'Oh, what a wretched girl I am!' said the Princess. 'If only I'd taken that lovely Prince! Oh, how unhappy I am!'

And the swineherd went behind a tree, wiped the black and brown off his face, cast aside his dirty old clothes, and stepped forth again dressed as a prince, so handsome that the Princess curtsied as she saw him.

'I've grown to despise you!' he said. 'You wouldn't have an honest prince! You couldn't appreciate the rose and the nightingale, but you could kiss the swineherd for a plaything! Now I wish you well of it!'

And so he went into his kingdom, shut the door and shot the bolt home. So there was nothing for her but to stand outside and sing:

> Alas, my dearest Augustin,
> All is now lost, lost, lost!

THE BUCKWHEAT

TIME and again, if you pass by a field of buckwheat after a thunder-storm, you will see that it has been scorched quite black, just as if a flame of fire had been over it. And then the countryman will tell you, 'It's been struck by lightning.' But why has it? I will tell you what the sparrow told me: the sparrow heard it from an old willow-tree that stood by a field of buckwheat, and stands there yet. It's a big, venerable willow, wrinkled and old, and it's split right to the middle. Grass and bramble-runners grow out of the cleft: the tree leans over and the branches hang right down to the ground just like long green hair.

In all the fields round about, corn grew—rye, barley, and oats, beautiful oats that look, when they are ripe, like a whole flight of small yellow canaries on a bough. The corn stood well blest by heaven, and the heavier it grew, the lower it bowed down in humility.

But there was also a field of buckwheat, and that field lay straight on from the old willow-tree. The buckwheat did not bow down at all, like the other corn, but held its head up proud and stiff.

'I am quite as rich in the ear as the corn,' it said, 'and I'm more beautiful as well: my flowers are as lovely as the apple-tree's. It's a joy to look at me and mine: do you know anything finer than us, old willow-tree?'

And the willow-tree nodded its head as if it would say, 'Yes, that I do—well enough!' But the buckwheat was bursting with arrogance, and said, 'Stupid tree! It's so old, grass grows in its belly!'

And now a dreadful storm was gathering: all the flowers of the field closed their petals or bowed their delicate heads while the wind swept over them; but the buckwheat stood erect in its pride.

'Bow your head like us!' said the flowers.

'I'm sure I see no need for me to do that,' said the buckwheat.

'Bow your head like us!' cried the corn. 'The Angel of the Storm is flying over us! He has wings which stretch up to the clouds and right down to the earth, and he will slash you in two before you can pray him to have mercy on you.'

'I'm sure I shan't bow down!' said the buckwheat.

'Close your flowers and bow your leaves!' said the old willow-tree. 'Don't look up at the lightning when the cloud bursts. Even men dare not do that, because when you look at the lightning you see into God's heaven. And if the mere sight of it can make men blind, what would happen to us plants of the earth—we who are far humbler—if we dared to risk it!'

'Far humbler?' said the buckwheat. 'Now I will look into God's heaven, you see if I don't!' And so, in its presumption and pride, it did. It was just as if the whole world stood bathed in a flame of fire, so fiercely the lightning flashed.

Afterwards, when the storm had passed, the flowers and the corn stood refreshed by the rain in the still, clean air. But the buckwheat was burnt coal-black by the lightning—it was now a dead useless weed in the field.

And the old willow-tree moved its branches in the wind, and great drops of water fell from its green leaves, as if the tree were weeping, and the sparrows asked, 'What are you crying for? It's all so heavenly now! Look how the sun's shining, and how the clouds are moving, and just smell the perfume of the flowers and bushes! What are you crying for, old willow-tree?'

And the willow-tree told them about the pride and arrogance of the buckwheat, and about the punishment which followed—as it always does. I, who am telling you the story, heard it from the sparrows—they told it to me one evening when I asked them for a tale.

209

THE SWEETHEARTS

THE Top and the Ball lay in a drawer together
among the other playthings, and one day the Top
said to the Ball, 'Couldn't we be sweethearts?
After all, we lie in the same drawer together, don't
we?' But the Ball, who was covered in morocco
leather, and fancied herself like any other fine
young lady, couldn't be expected to answer a
question like that.

The next day the little boy who owned the toys
came and painted the Top red and gold, and drove
a brass nail right through it: when the top spun
round, it looked really magnificent.

'Just look at me!' it said to the Ball. 'Well, what
do you say now? Don't you think we could be
sweethearts? We're really very well suited to one
another—you jump and I dance! No one could
ever be happier than we two!'

'What an idea!' said the Ball. 'You obviously
don't know that my mother and father were

morocco-leather slippers and that I've a cork inside me!'

'Yes, but I'm made of mahogany!' said the Top. 'And the mayor himself turned me—he has a lathe of his own—and it gave him a great deal of pleasure, too!'

'Do you really expect me to believe that?' said the Ball.

'May I never be whipped again if I tell a lie!' answered the Top.

'You speak very well for yourself!' said the Ball. 'But it's quite impossible—I'm as good as half engaged to a swallow. Every time I go up in the air he bobs his head out of his nest and says, "Will you? Will you?" And now I've said, "Yes!" to myself—and that's as good as half an engagement! But I promise you I shall never forget you!'

'Well, that'll be a great help!' said the Top, and after that they spoke no more to one another.

The next day the Ball was taken out. The Top watched it flying high up in the air, just like a bird, until at last it was lost to sight. It came back again every time, but it always gave a high jump as it touched the ground, and that was either because it was restless and impatient or because it had a cork inside it. The ninth time, the Ball disappeared and did not come back any more. The boy searched and searched, but there was no doubt about it—it had disappeared.

'I know well enough where it is!' sighed the Top. 'It's in the swallow's nest and it's married to the swallow!'

The more the Top thought about the Ball, the deeper in love he fell. Just because he could not have her, his passion for her grew: but the really

odd thing was that she had accepted someone else!
And the Top danced round and spun, but his
thoughts were always on the Ball, and in his fancy
she grew ever more beautiful. And so, many years
went by—and his love was a thing of the past.

The Top was no longer young. Then one day it
was gilded all over—it had never looked so handsome before. It was now a gold Top, and it jumped
about until it hummed again. Yes, that was something like! But all at once it jumped too high—
and disappeared!

They looked and looked, even down in the
cellar, but still they could not find it.

Where was it?

It had jumped into the dustbin where all sorts
of things were lying—cabbage-stalks, sweepings,
grit that had fallen down from the gutter.

'Well, this is a fine place to be in! My gilding
will soon come off here! And what sort of outcasts
have I got among?' And he looked out of the corner
of his eye at a long cabbage-stalk that had been
stripped far too closely, and at a curious round
thing that looked like an old apple—but it was no
apple, it was an old ball that had lain for many
years up in the gutter and been soaked through
with water.

'Thank heaven, here's someone of my own kind
I can talk to!' said the Ball, looking at the gilt Top.
'I'm really made of morocco-leather, stitched by a
young lady's own hands, and I have a cork inside
me, though no one would think so to look at me!
I was just going to be married to a swallow when I
fell into the gutter, and there I lay, soaking wet,
for five years! That's a long time for a young lady,
believe me!'

But the Top said nothing. He thought of his old sweetheart, and the more he heard her say, the more certain he was that this was she.

Then the maid came along to turn out the dustbin. 'Hurrah,' she said, 'here's the gold top!'

And the Top went back to the living-room and was made much of, but nothing was heard of the Ball, and the Top never mentioned his old love again. Love dies when your sweetheart has lain soaking in a gutter for five years—in fact, you take care not to recognize her again when you meet her in the dustbin.

THE UGLY DUCKLING

IT was so lovely out in the country! It was summer:
the corn stood yellow and the oats green; down in
the green meadows the hay had been stacked; and
the stork was walking about there and chattering
in Egyptian, for he had learnt that language from
his mother. Round the fields and meadows there
were vast woods, and in the midst of the woods
were deep lakes—yes, it was really lovely out in
the country! Right in the sunshine there lay an old
manor-house with deep canals round it, and great
dock-leaves grew from the wall down to the water
—they were so tall that small children could stand
upright under the biggest of them. They grew like
a wild and tangled wood. A duck was sitting on her
nest there: she was waiting for her little ducklings
to hatch out, but she was rather tired of it now
because it had lasted so long and she rarely had a
visitor—the other ducks much preferred swimming

214

round in the canals to running up and sitting under a dock-leaf to gossip with her.

At last, one after another, the eggs began to crack. 'Peep, peep!' they said—all the eggs had come alive, and the ducklings were poking their heads out.

'Quack, quack! Hurry up!' she said, and so they made as much haste as they could, and looked all round them under the green leaves, and their mother let them look as much as ever they wanted to, for green is good for the eyes.

'My, how big the world is!' said all the young ones, for they undoubtedly had much more room to move about in now than they had had inside their eggs.

'You don't think this is the whole world!' said their mother. 'Why, it stretches a long way on the other side of the garden, right into the parson's field! Though I have never been so far myself!— You're all here now, aren't you!' And so she got up. 'No, that you're not! The biggest egg is still there—however much longer is it going to be! I'm tired of it now, I can tell you!' And so she sat down again.

'Well, how is it going?' said an old duck who had come to pay her a visit.

'This one egg is taking such a long time!' said the mother-duck. 'It just won't hatch! But you must see the others now! They're the loveliest ducklings I've ever seen, all the image of their father—the wretch, he never comes to visit me!'

'Let me look at that egg that won't crack!' said the old duck. 'You can take it from me, that's a turkey's egg! I was once had, too, in the very same way, and the trouble and bother I had with the young ones! They're afraid of water, I tell you! I could not get them in! I quacked and snapped, but it was no use!—Let me see the egg! Yes, it's a turkey's egg right enough! Let it be, and teach the other children to swim!'

'No, I'll sit on it a little longer!' said the duck. 'I've been sitting so long now, I can sit until the Deer Park shuts for the winter!'

'Please yourself!' said the old duck, and off she went.

At last the big egg cracked. 'Peep, peep!' said the young one, as he tumbled out: but oh, how big and ugly he was! The duck looked at him. 'It's a terribly big duckling, that one!' she said. 'None of the others looks like that! Surely it's never a turkey-chick? Well, we shall soon find out! Into the water he shall go, even if I have to kick him in myself!'

The next day the weather was really heavenly, and the sun was shining on all the green dock-leaves. The ducklings' mother came out with all her family and went down to the canal. 'Splash!' She jumped into the water. 'Quack, quack!' she said, and, one after another, the ducklings plopped in; the water closed over their heads, but they came up again at once and floated beautifully. Their legs moved of their own accord, and there they all were, out on the water—even the ugly grey one was swimming with them.

'Well, that's no turkey!' she said. 'Look how beautifully he uses his legs and how straight he holds himself! He's my own child and no mistake! He's really quite handsome if you look at him properly! Quack, quack!—Come with me now, and I'll take you into the world and present you in the duck-yard; but mind you stay close by me all the time in case you get trodden on, and keep a sharp look-out for the cat!'

And so they went into the duck-yard. There was a frightful noise in there, for there were two families fighting over the head of an eel, and then, after all, the cat got it.

'That's the way of the world, you see!' said the ducklings' mother, licking her beak, for she would have liked the eel's head, too. 'Use your legs now!' she said. 'Hurry yourselves along, and bow your heads to that old duck over there! She is the best bred of anyone here! She has Spanish blood— that's why she's so solid-looking, and you see, she has a piece of red cloth tied round her leg! That's something very special, the greatest distinction any duck can have. It means a very great deal indeed— so much that no one will ever get rid of her, and everyone—man and beast alike—treats her with respect! Hurry up now!—Don't turn your toes in! A well-brought-up duckling walks with feet well apart, like father and mother! Now then, bow your heads and say, "Quack!"'

And so they did; but the other ducks round about looked at them and said quite loudly, 'Look at that, we shall have to have that lot as well now, as if there weren't enough of us as it is! Lord, what a queer-looking duckling that one is! We won't put up with him!' And one of the ducks immediately flew at him and pecked him in the back of the neck.

'Let him alone!' said his mother. 'He's not harming anyone!'

'Yes, but he's too big and queer-looking!' said the duck that had pecked him. 'And so he's got to be put in his place!'

'They're pretty children mother has there!' said

the old duck with the piece of red cloth round her leg. 'Every one of them pretty, except that one, and he's not turned out at all well! It's a pity she can't make him over again!'

'That can't be done, Your Grace!' said the ducklings' mother. 'He's not good-looking, but he has a very nice disposition, and he swims just as beautifully as any of the others! And what's more, I dare say he'll grow quite handsome, and in time get a little smaller! He's lain too long in the egg, and so he's spoilt his figure!' Then she pecked at the down on the back of his neck and smoothed his body. 'Besides, he's a drake,' she said, 'and so it doesn't matter so much! He'll be strong, I'm sure of it—he'll get along all right!'

'The other ducklings are beautiful!' said the old duck. 'Make yourselves at home now—you can go and see if you can find an eel's head, and then you can bring it to me!'

And so they made themselves at home.

But the poor duckling that was the last to be hatched out of the egg and was so ugly-looking, was pecked and jostled and mocked by ducks and hens alike. 'He's too big!' they all said, and the turkey-cock, who had been born with spurs on and therefore thought he was an emperor, puffed himself up like a ship in full sail, went right up to him, and gobbled until he was quite red in the face. The poor duckling did not know where to stand or where to go, he was so miserable at being so ugly and being the laughing-stock of the whole duck-yard.

And so the first day passed, and afterwards it grew worse and worse. The poor duckling was chased about by everyone; even his brothers and sisters were unkind to him, and kept on saying, 'If only the cat would get you, you ugly thing!' And his mother would say, 'I wish you were far enough!' The ducks bit him, and the hens pecked him, and the girl who fed the poultry kicked him with her foot.

Then he ran off and flew away over the hedge; the little birds in the bushes rose terrified into the air. 'That's because I'm so ugly!' thought the duckling, shutting his eyes, but he ran on all the same. Then he came out into the great marsh where the wild ducks lived. There he lay the whole night, he was so tired and unhappy.

In the morning the wild ducks flew up and took a look at their new comrade. 'What kind of a fellow are you?' they asked. The duckling turned from one to another and greeted them as well as he could.

'You're ugly all right, and no mistake!' said the wild ducks. 'But that's all the same to us, as long as you don't marry into the family!'—Poor thing, getting married had never entered his head: all he wanted was leave to lie in the rushes and drink a little of the marsh water.

There he lay for two whole days, and then there came two wild geese, or, more properly, two wild ganders, for they were cocks. It was not many hours since they had been hatched, and so they were very pert and lively.

'Listen, comrade,' they said, 'you're so ugly we've taken quite a liking to you! Will you come along with us and be a bird of passage? Close by here, in another marsh, are some lovely sweet wild geese, young ladies every one of them, and they can say, "Quack!" with the best of them. You're so ugly,

219

you're just the right fellow to try your luck with them!'

'Bang! Bang!' At that very moment there was a loud noise overhead, and both the wild ganders fell down dead in the rushes, and the water became red with blood. 'Bang! Bang!' It sounded again, and great flocks of wild geese flew up out of the rushes. Then the cracking noise was heard yet again. There was a great shoot in progress; the sportsmen lay all round the marsh, some even in the branches of the trees that stretched far out over the rushes. Blue smoke hung like clouds in among the dark trees and far out over the water. The dogs came splashing through the mud; rushes and reeds swayed on all sides. The poor duckling was terrified; just as he was ducking his head to hide it under his wing, a frightful great dog stood right in front of him, his tongue hanging right out of his mouth and his eyes shining wickedly. He thrust his muzzle right down towards the duckling and bared his sharp teeth— and then, splash! he had gone again without touching him.

'Oh, thank goodness!' sighed the duckling. 'I'm so ugly that even the dog will think twice before it bites me!'

And so he lay quite still while the duck-shot whistled in the rushes and shot after shot rang out.

It was far into the day before it was quiet again, but the poor young thing dared not move even then; he waited several hours yet before he looked round him, and then he took to his heels and left the marsh as far behind as he could; he ran over field and meadow, but the wind was blowing so sharply that he found it hard work to get along.

Towards evening he reached a poor little cottage;

it was in such a wretched state that it could not make up its mind which side to fall down, and so it remained standing. The wind howled so strongly

about the duckling that he had to sit down on his tail to withstand it; and it was growing worse and worse. Then he noticed that the door had fallen off one of its hinges and was hanging so askew that he could creep through the crack into the living-room; and that is what he did.

An old woman lived here with her cat and her hen. The cat, whom she called Sonny, could arch his back and purr; he could give out sparks, too, but he had to be stroked the wrong way first. The hen had little short legs, and so she was called Chicky Short-legs; she laid well, and the woman was as fond of her as if she had been her own child.

In the morning the strange duckling was spotted at once, and the cat began to purr and the hen to cluck.

'What's the matter?' said the woman, and looked all round her, but she could not see very well, and so she thought the duckling was a fat duck that had strayed away. 'Here's a fine catch, and no mistake!' she said. 'I can have duck-eggs now, if only it isn't a drake! Well, we shall see!'

And so the duckling was taken on trial for three weeks, but no eggs appeared. Now the cat was the master of the house and the hen was the mistress, and they always said, 'We and the world', for they considered themselves half the world, and the better half at that. The duckling thought there might be other opinions about that, but the hen would not hear of it.

'Can you lay eggs?' she asked.

'No!'

'Then you may hold your tongue!'

And the cat said, 'Can you arch your back and purr and give out sparks?'

'No!'

'Then you shouldn't express an opinion when sensible people are talking!'

And the duckling sat in the corner and felt very

depressed. Then the thought of fresh air and sunshine came into his mind, and he was seized with such a strange desire to float upon the water that at last he could not help telling the hen about it.

'What's the matter with you?' she asked. 'You've nothing to do, and that's why these odd fancies come over you! Lay an egg or purr, and you'll get over them.'

'But it's so lovely floating on the water!' said the duckling. 'So lovely ducking your head under and diving down to the bottom!'

'Yes, that must be a great pleasure!' said the hen. 'You must have lost your wits! Ask the cat—and he's the cleverest person I know—whether he likes floating on the water or diving to the bottom! I'll leave myself out of it. Ask our mistress, ask the old woman herself—there's no one in the world cleverer than she!—Do you suppose she's seized with a desire to float or duck her head under the water?'

'You don't understand!' said the duckling.

'Well, if we don't understand, then who could! It's certain you will never be cleverer than the cat and the old woman, not to mention myself! Don't show off, child! And thank your Maker for all the good things that have been done for you! Haven't you come into a warm room and found a social background you can learn something from? You talk a lot of nonsense, and your company is not at all amusing! You can believe me! I mean it for your good: I'm telling you a few home-truths about yourself, and that's how you can tell your true friends! Now just see that you lay some eggs and learn to purr or give out sparks!'

'I think I shall go out into the wide world!' said the duckling.

'Well, go on then!' said the hen.

And so the duckling went; he floated on the water and dived below the surface, but all the birds and beasts looked down on him on account of his ugliness.

Now autumn came: the leaves in the woods turned yellow and brown, the wind caught them and whirled them round in a dance; it looked cold up in the sky, the clouds hung heavy with hail and snow-flakes; and the raven, perched on the fence, screeched 'Caw! Caw!' from sheer cold—merely thinking about it was enough to make you feel regularly frozen: the poor duckling certainly did not have a very good time of it.

One evening, as the sun was setting wonderfully, a flock of lovely great birds came out of the bushes. The duckling had never seen anything so beautiful —they were shining white with long graceful necks: they were swans, and uttering a strange noise, they spread their splendid great wings and flew away from those cold parts to warmer lands and open lakes. They rose so high in the air, and the ugly little duckling felt so strange as he watched them; he turned round in the water like a wheel, craning his neck up after them and uttering a cry so loud and strange that it quite frightened him. Oh, he could not forget those lovely birds, those fortunate birds, and as soon as he lost sight of them he dived right down to the bottom, and when he came up again he seemed quite beside himself. He did not know what the birds were called nor where they were flying to, and yet he felt more deeply drawn to them than he had ever been to anything.

He did not envy them in the slightest—how could it possibly enter his mind to wish himself so beautiful!—he would have been happy if even the ducks had let him stay with them, poor ugly creature that he was!

And the winter grew so very, very cold: the duckling had to swim round and round in the water to keep it from freezing right over; but every night the hole he swam in became smaller and smaller; it froze so hard that the ice-crust creaked; the duckling had to use his legs all the time to prevent the water from icing over; at last, he was tired out; he lay quite still and froze fast in the ice.

Early in the morning a farm-labourer came by, and seeing him, went out and broke the ice up with his wooden clogs, and then carried him home to his wife. There he recovered.

The children wanted to play with him, but the duckling thought they meant to hurt him, and in his fright he flew right into the milk-pan so that the milk splashed out into the room; the woman shrieked, clapping her hands over her head, and then he flew into the tub where the butter was, and then into the barrel of flour and out again.— My, what a sight he was! The woman shrieked and struck at him with the fire-tongs, and the children, laughing and screaming, pushed one another over in their efforts to catch the duckling. It was a good thing the door stood open—he rushed out into the bushes and the new-fallen snow—and there he lay as if in a swoon.

But it would be far too sad a business to describe all the hardship and misery he had to go through during that hard winter.—He was lying among the reeds in the marsh when the sun began to shine warm again; the larks were singing, and it was a lovely spring.

Then one day he stretched his wings; they rustled more strongly than before and bore him swiftly away; and before he was fully aware of it, he was in a great garden where the apple-trees stood in bloom and the lilac hung sweet-scented on its long green boughs right down to the winding canals. Oh, it was beautiful here in the fresh spring! And right in front of him, out of the thick hanging branches, came three lovely white swans, ruffling their feathers and floating lightly on the water. The duckling recognized the magnificent birds and a strange sadness came over him.

'I will fly over to those kingly birds, and they will peck me to death for daring to come near them, I'm so ugly! But it doesn't matter—better to be killed by them than snapped at by the ducks, pecked by the hens, kicked by the girl who looks after the poultry-yard, and suffer misery throughout the winter!' Then he flew out over the water and swam towards the splendid swans. They saw him and came shooting towards him with ruffling feathers. 'Only kill me!' said the poor creature, bowing his head down towards the water and awaiting his death—but what did he see in the clear water? He saw his own reflection beneath him, but he was no longer an awkward, dark-grey bird, ugly and repulsive—he was himself a swan.

It doesn't matter about being born in a duck-yard, as long as you're hatched from a swan's egg!

He felt really glad he had suffered all that hardship and adversity: he could now appreciate his good fortune and all the loveliness that greeted him.—And the great swans swam round him and stroked him with their beaks.

Some little children came into the garden and threw bread and corn out into the water, and the youngest cried, 'There's a new one!' And the other children shouted joyfully, 'Yes, there's a new one come!' And, clapping their hands and dancing along, they ran to fetch their father and mother, and bread and cake were thrown into the water, and they all said, 'The new one is the most beautiful of them all! He is so young and lovely!' And the old swans bowed before him.

Then he felt quite shy and hid his head under his wing. He did not know what to do with himself, he was much too happy—but he was not at all proud, for a good heart is never proud. He thought of the time when he had been persecuted and despised, and now he heard them all say he was the loveliest of all those lovely birds. The lilacs bowed their branches right down to the water to him, and the sun was shining warm and fair: then he ruffled his feathers, lifted up his slender neck, and cried in the joy of his heart, 'I never dreamt I should find so much happiness when I was the ugly duckling!'

THE SNOW QUEEN

A Fairy-Tale in Seven Parts

The First Part,
which deals with the mirror and its splinters

WELL, now, let's begin—and when we come to
the end of the story we shall know more than we
do now! There was once a wicked demon—one of
the very worst—the Devil himself! One day he
was in a really good humour because he had made
a mirror which had the power of making everything good and beautiful reflected in it disappear
almost to nothing, while all that was bad and ugly
to look at showed up clearly and appeared far
worse than it really was. In this mirror the loveliest
of landscapes looked just like boiled spinach, and
even the nicest people looked hideous or else they
stood on their heads and had no bodies. Their faces

were so changed that there was no recognizing them, and if anyone had a freckle, you could be certain it would seem to spread all over his nose and mouth. It was great fun, said the Devil. If a good and holy thought passed through a person's mind, it appeared in the mirror as a grin, and then the Devil had to laugh at his own clever invention. All those who attended the School for Demons— for he ran a School for Demons—spread the news that a miracle had happened: now for the very first time, they said, you could see what the world and mankind really looked like. They ran everywhere with the mirror, until at last there was not one land or one person that had not been distorted in it. And now they wanted to fly up to Heaven itself to make fun of Our Lord and His angels. The higher they flew with the mirror, the louder it laughed, so that they could hardly keep hold of it: higher and higher they flew, nearer to God and the angels, until at last the mirror shook so violently with laughter that it sprang out of their hands and fell down to earth, where it broke into hundreds of millions, billions, and even more, pieces. For that very reason it caused much greater misfortune than before, for some of the pieces were hardly as big as grains of sand, and these flew round about the wide world, and wherever they got into people's eyes, there they stayed, and then the people saw everything distortedly, or else they had eyes only for what was bad in things, for every little splinter of glass had kept the same power that the whole mirror had. Some people even got a little bit of the mirror in their hearts, and then it was really dreadful, for their hearts became just like lumps of ice. Some pieces of the mirror were so big that they were used

as window-panes, but it did not pay to look at your
friends through them. Other pieces were used in
spectacles, and people had a bad time of it when
they put their glasses on to see properly and act
justly. The Wicked One laughed until he split his
sides, he was so highly tickled by it all. Small
splinters of glass were still flying about in the air.
So now let us hear what happened!

The Second Part.

A Little Boy and a Little Girl

In the big city where there are so many houses and
people that there is not enough room for everyone
to have a little garden, and where, therefore, most
people must content themselves with flowers in
pots, there were two poor children who had a
garden that was a little bigger than a flower-pot.

They were not brother and sister, but they were just as fond of one another as if they had been. Their parents lived right next to each other; they lived in two attics; where the roofs of the two neighbouring houses met and the gutter ran along under the eaves, two little windows faced one another, one from each house. All you need do was step over the gutter and you could get from one window to the other.

Their parents had a large wooden box outside each window, and in it grew vegetables for their use and a little rose-tree; there was one in each box, and they grew beautifully. Then their parents found that if they placed the boxes across the gutter they reached almost from one window to the other, and looked for all the world like two banks of flowers. As the boxes were very high and the children knew they must not clamber up them, they often got leave to climb out to one another and sit on their little stools under the rose-trees where they played wonderful games together.

In winter such pleasures came to an end. The windows were often completely frosted over, but then they would warm copper coins on the stove, lay hot pennies on the frozen panes and so make lovely peep-holes, perfectly round, and from behind them two sweet and gentle eyes would peep out, one from each window. It was the little boy and the little girl. He was called Kay and she was called Gerda. In summer they could be with one another in one jump; in winter they had first to climb all the way downstairs and then all the way upstairs—and outside the snow fell fast.

'That's the white bees swarming,' said the old grandmother.

'Do they have a queen-bee, too?' asked the little boy, for he knew that real bees have one.

'That they have!' said grandmother. 'There she flies, where they are swarming thickest! She is the biggest of them all, and she will never settle quietly upon the ground—up she flies again into the dark clouds. Many a winter night she flies through the streets of the town and peeps in at the windows, and then they frost over with such wonderful flower-patterns.'

'Yes, I've seen them!' said both the children, and so they knew it was true.

'Could the Snow Queen come in here?' asked the little girl.

'Just let her try!' said the boy. 'I should put her on the warm stove and then she would melt!'

But grandmother smoothed his hair and told them other tales.

In the evening when little Kay was home and half-undressed, he climbed up onto the chairs by the window and peeped out through the little hole. A few snow-flakes were falling outside, and one of them, the biggest of them all, came to rest on the edge of one of the window-boxes. The snow-flake grew bigger and bigger, until at last it turned into a lady clothed in the finest white gauze made up of millions of star-like snow-flakes. She was very beautiful and dainty, but she was of ice, dazzling, gleaming ice, all through, and yet she was alive; her eyes shone like two clear stars, but there was no rest nor quiet in them. She nodded towards the window and beckoned with her hand. The little boy was terrified and jumped down from the chair; and then it was just as if a great bird flew past the window outside.

The next day there was a clear frost—and then the thaw set in—and then came spring: the sun shone, the green shoots peeped out, the swallows built their nests, the windows were thrown up, and the little children sat once more in their tiny garden high up in the gutter above all the floors of the house.

The roses bloomed splendidly that summer. The little girl had learnt a hymn, and in it there was a line about roses, and whenever she came to it she thought about her own. She sang the hymn for the little boy, and he sang it with her:

> 'In the valley grew roses wild,
> And there we spoke with the Holy Child!'

And the little ones held each other's hands, kissed the roses, and, looking up towards God's bright sunshine, they spoke to it as though the Christ Child were there Himself. What beautiful summer days they were; how lovely it was to be outside near the fresh rose-trees that seemed as if they would never stop blooming!

Kay and Gerda sat looking at the picture-book with the animals and birds in it, and it was just at that moment—the clock was striking five in the great church-tower—that Kay said, 'Oh! There's a pricking in my heart! And now I've got something in my eye!'

The little girl put her arms about his neck; he blinked his eyes: no, there was nothing to see.

'I think it's gone!' he said; but it hadn't. It was neither more nor less than one of those splinters of glass that had sprung from the mirror, the demon-mirror we remember hearing about, the evil glass which made everything great and good reflected in it grow small and ugly, and in which all that was wicked and bad stood out clearly and every blemish became immediately noticeable. Poor Kay—he had a splinter right in his heart as well—it would soon be like a lump of ice. It did not hurt any more—but it was still there.

'What are you crying for?' he asked. 'You look so ugly like that! There's nothing at all the matter with me! Pooh!' he cried in the same breath. 'That rose over there is all worm-eaten! And look, that one's quite lopsided! They really are a disgusting lot of roses—they're just like the boxes they grow in!' And then he kicked the box hard and tore off the two roses.

'Kay, what are you doing?' cried the little girl. And when he saw how frightened she was, he pulled off another rose and sprang in at his own window away from sweet-natured little Gerda.

After that, whenever she came with the picture-book, he said it was only fit for babies; and if grandmother told her tales, he was always ready to criticize—yes, and when he got the chance, he would walk behind her, put her glasses on, and talk just like her: it was a perfect imitation and it made people laugh. He could soon mimick the speech and walk of everybody in the street. Everything that was odd or unpleasant about them Kay knew how to imitate, and so people said, 'He's certainly got a remarkable head on his shoulders, that boy!' But it was the glass he had got in his eye, the glass that had pierced his heart, and that was why he teased even little Gerda who loved him with all her soul.

His games had become quite different now from what they had been before, they were so intelligent. One winter's day when the snow was falling fast, he came with a large burning-glass, held out the corner of his jacket and let the snow-flakes fall on it.

'Now look in the glass, Gerda!' he said, and every snow-flake grew much bigger and looked like a wonderful flower or a ten-pointed star—it was lovely to look at them.

'Do you see how beautifully formed they are!' said Kay. 'They're much more interesting than real flowers! And there isn't a single blemish on them: they're quite perfect—or they would be if they didn't melt!'

Soon afterwards Kay came again, with his big gloves on and his toboggan on his back: he shouted right in Gerda's ear, 'I've got leave to take my toboggan to the big square where the others are playing!' And off he went.

Over on the square the boldest of the boys would often tie their toboggans fast to the farmers' wagons and so ride behind them for quite a long way. It was great fun. When their games were in full swing a great sledge came by: it was painted white all over, and in it sat a figure muffled in a thick white fur coat and a white fur hat. The sledge drove twice round the square, and Kay quickly managed to tie his little toboggan firmly to it. Then he rode behind it. It went faster and faster, right into the next street. The driver turned round and nodded to Kay in a very friendly fashion, just as if they knew one another. Every time Kay was about to loosen his little toboggan, the driver would nod to him again, and then Kay would remain sitting where he was. They drove right out of the city gates. Then the snow began to fall so thick and fast that the little boy could no longer see his hand in front of him as they sped along: quickly he undid the rope to free himself from the great sledge, but it was no good—his little toboggan hung on fast behind, and it went with the speed of the wind. Then he shouted as loudly as he could, but no one heard him, and the snow fell and the sledge flew on. From time to time it gave a bound as if it were flying over ditches and fences. He was completely terrified and wanted to say the Lord's Prayer, but all he could remember were his multiplication-tables.

The snow-flakes grew bigger and bigger until they looked like great white hens. All at once they swerved to one side, the great sledge pulled up, and up stood the driver with fur coat and hat made of pure snow: it was a lady, tall and proud and dazzlingly white—she was the Snow Queen.

'We've made good time,' she said. 'But are you cold? Creep under my bear-skin!' And she seated him beside her in the sledge and drew her fur coat round him—he felt as if he were sinking into a snow-drift.

'Are you still cold?' she asked him, and kissed him on the brow. Ooh, her kiss was colder than ice: it went straight to his heart, and his heart was already half-way to being a lump of ice. He felt as if he were about to die—but only for a moment, and then everything was all right again—and he no longer noticed the cold all around him.

'My toboggan! Don't forget my toboggan!' It was the first thing he thought about; it was made fast to one of the white hens, and she flew behind them with the toboggan on her back. The Snow Queen kissed Kay yet once more, and then he forgot little Gerda and grandmother and all the rest of them back home.

'And now you get no more kisses!' she said. 'Or else I shall kiss you to death!'

Kay looked at her: she was very beautiful; a wiser, lovelier face he could not imagine: now she no longer seemed made of ice as she had done when she sat outside the window and beckoned to him—in his eyes she was perfect. He felt no fear at all: he told her he could do mental arithmetic, even with fractions, and work out how many square miles there were in the country and how many people lived there. And she smiled all the time. Then he realized that he knew very little indeed. He looked up into the great vast vault of the sky, and she flew with him, high up on the dark clouds, and the stormy wind whistled and roared as though it were singing old ballads. They flew over forests and lakes, over land and sea, while below them the cold blast shrieked, the wolves howled, the snow sparkled, and over it flew the black screeching crows. But above them the moon shone large and bright, and Kay gazed upon it all through that long, long winter night. During the day he slept at the Snow Queen's feet.

The Third Part.

The Flower-Garden that belonged to the Old Woman who understood Magic

But what happened to little Gerda when Kay came back no more? Where could he be? No one knew, no one had any news of him. The boys could only say that they had seen him fasten his little sledge to another, a fine big one, that had driven out into the street and through the city gate. No one knew where he was: many tears flowed, and little Gerda wept long and sorely. Then they said he was dead, drowned in the river that ran close by the city. Oh, what long, dark winter days those were!

Then the spring came and the sun shone more warmly.

'Kay is dead and gone!' said little Gerda.

'I don't believe it!' said the sunshine.

'He's dead and gone!' she said to the swallows.

'I don't believe it!' they answered, and at last little Gerda did not believe it either.

'I will put my new red shoes on,' she said early one morning, 'the ones Kay has never seen, and then I'll go down and ask the river.'

It was quite early; she kissed her old grandmother who was still asleep, put on her red shoes, and went all alone out of the gate and down to the river.

'Is it true that you've taken my little playmate? I'll make you a present of my red shoes if you'll give him back to me!'

The waves, she thought, nodded very strangely. Then she took her red shoes, her most precious possession, and threw them both out into the river, but they fell close by the bank, and the small waves immediately carried them back to her. It was just as if the river, knowing it had not taken little Kay, would not take her most precious possession either. But Gerda now thought she had not thrown the shoes far enough out, and so she clambered into a boat that lay among the rushes, went right to the further end of it, and threw the shoes again. But the boat was not made fast, and with her movements it slipped its moorings. Seeing what had happened, she hurriedly tried to regain the bank, but before she could reach it the boat was a couple of feet out in the water and gliding away ever more swiftly.

Then little Gerda was quite terrified and began to cry, but no one heard her except the sparrows, and they could not carry her back to land. But they flew along by the bank and sang, as if to comfort her, 'Here we are! Here we are!' The boat drifted downstream; little Gerda sat quite still in her stockinged feet; her little red shoes floated after her, but they could not reach the boat, which was gathering speed.

It was very beautiful on both banks of the river: there were lovely flowers and old trees and hillsides with sheep and cattle—but not a soul to be seen anywhere.

'Perhaps the river will carry me to little Kay,' thought Gerda. With that she felt more cheerful, and standing up, she watched the beautiful green banks for hours on end. At last she came to a large cherry-orchard where there was a little cottage with odd-looking red and blue windows, a thatched roof besides, and two wooden soldiers standing outside and shouldering arms for those that sailed by.

Gerda shouted to them; she thought they were alive, but, of course, they did not answer. She came quite close to them; the river drove the boat right in towards the shore.

Gerda shouted louder still, and then there came out of the cottage an old, old woman leaning on a crooked stick. She had on a large sun-hat painted all over with the loveliest flowers.

'You poor little child!' said the old woman. 'How on earth did you come to be out on that great strong stream, driven far out into the wide world?' And the old woman waded right out into the water, caught hold of the boat firmly with her crooked stick, drew it to land, and lifted little Gerda out.

Gerda was glad to get back to dry land, though she was a little frightened of the strange old woman.

'Now come and tell me who you are and how you came here!' she said.

And Gerda told her everything; and the old woman shook her head and said, 'Hm! Hm!' And when Gerda had said all and asked her if she had not seen little Kay, the woman said that he had not passed that way yet, but he would come, sure enough, and she shouldn't be sad, but taste her cherries and see her flowers—they were more beautiful than any picture-book and every one of them could tell a whole story. Then she took Gerda by the hand, they entered the little cottage, and the old woman locked the door.

The windows were very high up, and the panes were red, blue, and yellow—the daylight shone strangely inside through all those colours. But on the table stood a dish of the loveliest cherries, and Gerda needed no encouragement to eat as many as she wanted. While she was eating them, the old

woman combed her hair with a golden comb, and
her hair curled and shone lovely and fair about her
friendly little face that was so round and like a rose.

'I've been longing for a dear little girl like you!'
the old woman said. 'You shall see now how well
we two shall get on together!' And all the time she
was combing little Gerda's hair, Gerda was forgetting her foster-brother Kay more and more—for
the old woman could cast spells, though she was
by no means a wicked witch and practised magic
only a little for her own pleasure, and now she
wanted very much indeed to keep little Gerda.
And so she now went out into the garden, stretched
out her crooked stick towards all the rose-trees,
and, blooming beautifully though they were, they
all sank down into the black earth so that you
could not even see where they had been. The old
woman was afraid that if Gerda saw the roses she
would think of her own, and then remember little
Kay and run off.

Then she took Gerda out into the flower-garden.
Oh, how fragrant and lovely it was! All the flowers
you could think of, flowers of every season of the
year, stood there in full splendour—no picture-
book could have been more gaily coloured or more
beautiful. Gerda jumped for joy and played until
the sun went down behind the tall cherry-trees.
Then she was given a lovely bed with a red silk
eiderdown stuffed with blue violets, and she slept
and dreamed as sweetly as any queen upon her
wedding-day.

The next day she was allowed to go out again
and play among the flowers in the warm sunshine
—and thus many days went by. Gerda learnt to
know every flower, yet, though there were so many

of them, one seemed to be missing, but which one she did not know. Then one day she sat looking at the old woman's sun-hat with its painted flowers, and the very loveliest of all was a rose. The old woman had forgotten to take it off her hat when she made the real ones disappear under the ground. But that's how it is when you're absent-minded! 'Why!' cried Gerda. 'Aren't there any roses here?' And she ran among the flower-beds, searching and searching. Her hot tears fell just where a rose-tree had sunk into the earth, and as her warm tears moistened the ground, the tree shot up at once, just as full of bloom as when it disappeared; and throwing her arms around it, Gerda kissed the roses and thought about the lovely roses at home—and with them, about little Kay.

'Oh, what a lot of time I've wasted!' said the little girl. 'I was going to find Kay!—Don't you know where he is?' she asked the roses. 'Do you think he's dead and gone?'

'No, he's not dead,' said the roses. 'We've been in the earth where all the dead are, but Kay wasn't there!'

'Oh, thank you, thank you!' said little Gerda, and she went over to the other flowers, and looking into their cups, she asked, 'Don't you know where little Kay is?'

The flowers stood in the sun, each dreaming its own tale: little Gerda heard many, many things from them, but none of them knew anything of Kay.

What was the tiger-lily saying?

'Can you hear the drum?—Boom, boom! There are only two notes—boom, boom! over and over again. Listen to the women's dirge! Listen to the

cry of the priests!—In her long red robe, the Hindu
woman stands on the pyre while the flames are
mounting round her and her dead husband. But the
Hindu woman is thinking of the living there among
those that encircle her, of him whose eyes burn
hotter than the flames, the fire of whose eyes
penetrates her heart more deeply than the flames
that will soon burn her body to ashes. Can the
heart's flame die in the flames of the pyre?'

'That I don't understand at all!' said little Gerda.

'That is my story!' said the tiger-lily.

What does the convolvulus say?

'High over the narrow field-path hangs an ancient
castle. Evergreen plants grow thick and close about
the old red walls, leaf upon leaf, right up round the
balcony where a lovely girl is standing. She leans
out over the parapet and looks down to the path.
No rose hanging from its stem is fresher than she,
no apple-blossom borne by the wind from the tree
is more graceful. How her fine silken gown rustles!
"Still he does not come!"'

'Is it Kay you mean?' asked little Gerda.

'I'm speaking only of my own story, my dream,'
answered the convolvulus.

What does the little snow-drop say?

'A long plank hangs by a rope between the trees
—it is a swing. Two sweet little girls sit swinging—
their dresses are as white as snow and long green
silk ribbons stream from their hats: their brother,
who is bigger than they, stands up on the swing
with his arm about the rope to keep himself steady;
he holds a little bowl in one hand and a clay pipe in
the other, and he is blowing bubbles. The swing is
in motion, and the bubbles fly away with lovely
ever-changing colours, the last still clinging to the

stem of the pipe and swaying in the breeze. The swing is still in motion. A little black dog, light as the bubbles, jumps up on his hind legs, wanting to join them on the swing. It flies out of his reach, the dog tumbles, barking furiously. They laugh at him, and the bubbles burst.—A swinging plank, a fleeting picture of foam—that is my song!'

'What you tell of may well be beautiful, but you speak of it so sadly and you don't mention little Kay at all. What do the hyacinths say?'

'There were three lovely sisters, delicate and dainty; the first was dressed in red, the second in blue, and the third in pure white. Hand in hand, they danced by the still lake in the clear moonlight. They were not fairy maidens, they were children of men. There was a strong sweet fragrance, and the girls vanished in the woods. The fragrance grew stronger—three coffins in which the lovely girls lay glided from the depth of the dense woods away over the lake. Glow-worms flew shining around them like small flickering lights. Do the dancing girls sleep, or are they dead?—the perfume of the flowers tells they are corpses: the evening bell rings out for the dead!'

'You make me quite sad,' said little Gerda. 'Your scent is so strong it makes me think of those dead girls! Ah, is little Kay really dead then? The roses have been down in the earth, and they say he's not!'

'Ding, dong!' rang the bells of the hyacinths. 'We are not ringing for little Kay—we know nothing of him! We are but singing our own song, the only one we know!'

And Gerda went over to the buttercup, gleaming from among its shiny green leaves.

'You're just like a bright little sun!' said Gerda. 'Tell me, if you can, where shall I find my play-fellow?'

The buttercup shone very prettily and looked at Gerda. What song could the buttercup sing? Not one about Kay at any rate.

'In a little courtyard God's good sun was shining warmly on the first day of spring, its rays gliding down the neighbour's white wall. Close by, the first yellow flowers were growing, gleaming gold in the warm sunbeams. Old grandmother was out-side in her chair, and her pretty granddaughter, a poor servant-girl, had come home from a short visit: she kissed her grandmother. There was gold, heart's gold, in that blessed kiss. Gold on lips, and a golden flower; gold above in the morning hour! There you are, that's my story!' said the buttercup.

'My poor old granny!' sighed Gerda. 'I know she must be longing for me—she'll be just as unhappy about me as she was about little Kay. But I shall soon be home again, and then I shall bring Kay with me.—It's no use asking the flowers: they know only their own songs; they can tell me nothing!' And so she tucked up her little frock so that she could run more quickly. But as she was jumping over it, the narcissus caught her leg. She stopped short, and looking at the tall flower, she asked, 'Perhaps you know something?' She bent right down to it. And what did it say?

'I can see myself! I can see myself!' cried the narcissus. 'Oh, how beautiful my scent is!—Up in her little attic, a little ballet-dancer is standing, half-dressed, now on one leg, now on two, and kicking her leg at the whole world—but she is only an illusion. She pours water from the tea-pot on to a piece of cloth she is holding—it is her corset:—cleanliness is a good thing! Her white dress hangs on its peg—that has been washed in the tea-pot, too, and put out to dry on the roof. She puts it on, and arranges her saffron-yellow kerchief about her neck so that the white of her dress shows brighter than ever. One leg in the air: look how well she carries herself on one stalk! I can see myself! I can see myself!'

'I don't care a bit about that!' said Gerda. 'It's not at all what I want to hear!' And so she ran to the edge of the garden.

The door was shut, but she twisted the rusty fastening until it came away and the door flew open, and then little Gerda ran barefoot out into the wide world. She looked back three times, but there was no one following her. At last she could run no more, and so she sat down on a large stone, and when she looked about her she saw that summer had gone and it was now late autumn—time had passed unnoticed in that lovely garden where there was always sunshine and flowers from every season of the year.

'Oh dear, what a time I've been!' said little Gerda. 'It's autumn already! I dare not rest any longer!' And she rose to go.

Oh, how tired and aching her little feet were! Everything round her looked cold and raw: the long willow-leaves were quite yellow, the wet mist dripped from them, one leaf fell after another. Only the sloe still bore its fruit, so sour and bitter it draws your mouth tightly together. Oh, how grey and heavy it was in the wide world!

The Fourth Part.

Prince and Princess

Gerda had to rest once more: right in front of
where she was sitting, a big crow was hopping in
the snow; he had sat looking at her and wagging
his head for a long time, and now he said, 'Caw!
Caw!—Goo' daw! Goo' daw!' He could not say
it any better, but he meant well towards the little
girl and asked where she was going to, out in the
wide world all alone. Gerda understood that word
'alone' only too well and felt how deep a meaning
it had, and so she told the crow all the story of her
life, and asked if he had seen Kay.

The crow nodded thoughtfully and said, 'It
could be—it could be!'

'What?—Do you really think you have?' cried
the little girl, kissing the crow so hard she very
nearly squeezed him to death.

'Careful! Careful!' said the crow. 'I think it may
be little Kay! But he's certainly forgotten you now
for the princess!'

'Does he live with a princess?' asked Gerda.

'Yes, listen to me!' said the crow. 'But I find it very difficult to speak your language. If you understand Crowtalk[1] I can tell you about it much better!'

'No, I'm sorry, I haven't learnt it!' said Gerda. 'But Granny used to know it, and she knew Double-Dutch as well. If only I'd learnt it, too!'

'Doesn't matter!' said the crow. 'I'll tell you as well as I can, but I shall make a bad job of it all the same.' And so he told her all he knew.

'In this very kingdom where we are now sitting, there lives a princess who's terribly clever, and on top of that, she's read all the newspapers in the whole world—and forgotten them again, she's so clever. A short while ago, as she was sitting on her throne—and that's not as pleasant as you'd think, or so I'm told—she happened to be humming a song, and what should it be but, "Oh, why should I not marry?" "You know, there's something in that!" she says, and so she decided to marry, but she wanted a husband who knew how to answer when you talked to him, not one who just stood and looked distinguished, for she'd soon grow tired of that. Then she had all her ladies-in-waiting summoned by the drum, and when they heard what was in her mind they were delighted. "Oh, what a good idea!" they said. "I was thinking the same thing, too, only the other day!"—Believe me, it's true, every word I'm telling you!' said the crow. 'I've a tame sweetheart who's free to go all over the palace, and she told me everything!'

Of course, she was a crow, too, for birds of a feather flock together, and a crow's mate is always a crow.

[1] The Danish *Kragemaal*, literally 'crow-talk', means 'gibberish', like the English 'Double-Dutch'. L. W. K.

'The newspapers came out right away with a border of hearts and the princess's monogram. Every good-looking young man, as you could read for yourself, was free to go up to the palace and talk with the princess, and the one who talked so that you could hear he felt at home there, and spoke the best, the princess would take for her husband!—Oh, yes,' said the crow, 'believe me! As sure as I'm sitting here, people just streamed in —there was such a crush and commotion! But nothing came of it, either the first day or the second. They could all talk well enough when they were out in the street, but when they came through the palace gate and saw the guard in their silver uniforms and footmen in gold all the way up the stairs and the great halls all lit up, they were dumbstruck, and when they stood before the throne where the princess was sitting, they could find nothing to say except the last word she had spoken herself, and she wasn't really interested in hearing that again. It was just as if everybody there had got snuff on the stomach and had fallen into a stupor until they came out into the street once more—they could talk all right again then. There was a line right from the city gate to the palace. I was there myself and saw it!' said the crow. 'They grew both hungry and thirsty, but they didn't get so much as a glass of luke-warm water up at the palace. Some of the most sensible, of course, had brought sandwiches with them, but they didn't share them with their neighbours, for they thought, "If only he looks hungry enough, the princess won't have him!"'

'But Kay, little Kay!' asked Gerda. 'When did he come? Was he one of the crowd?'

'Give me time! Give me time! We're coming to

him right now! It was the third day, and there came a little fellow, with neither horse nor carriage, who marched coolly up to the palace. His eyes were shining just like yours and he had lovely long hair, but his clothes were shabby!'

'That was Kay!' cried Gerda joyfully. 'Oh, so I've found him!' And she clapped her hands.

'He had a little knapsack on his back!' said the crow.

'Why, that must have been his toboggan!' said Gerda. 'He had his toboggan when he went away!'

'It might have been!' said the crow. 'I didn't look as closely as all that! But I do know from my tame sweetheart that when he came in through the palace gate and saw the Life Guards in their silver uniforms and the footmen in gold all the way up the stairs, he wasn't in the least dismayed—he nodded and said to them, "It must be very dull standing on the stairs—I'd much rather go inside!" The halls were blazing with lights; privy councillors and excellencies were walking about barefoot, carrying golden salvers: it was enough to make anyone feel awestruck! His boots squeaked dreadfully, but he wasn't at all afraid!'

'It's most certainly Kay!' said Gerda. 'I know he had new boots—I heard them squeaking in Granny's sitting-room!'

'Yes, they squeaked all right!' said the crow. 'And he went quite unconcerned straight in to the princess who was sitting on a pearl as big as a spinning-wheel; and all the ladies-in-waiting with their maids and their maids' maids, and all the gentlemen of the Court with their serving-men, their serving-men's serving-men, and their serving-men's serving-men's boys were standing drawn up

in order all round them—and the nearer they stood
to the door, the haughtier they looked. The serving-
man's serving-man's boy, who always went in
slippers, looked so haughtily in the doorway, you
hardly dare raise your eyes to him!'

'That must be terrifying!' said little Gerda. 'But
did Kay win the princess then?'

'If I hadn't been a crow, I'd have taken her myself—in spite of being engaged. He must have
talked just as well as I do when I speak Crowtalk,
or so my tame sweetheart tells me. He was confi-
dent and charming: he had no intention of coming
to woo the princess, he had come only to listen to
her wisdom, and that he found delightful—and in
return, she found him delightful, too.'

'Yes, of course it was Kay!' said Gerda. 'He was
so clever, he could do mental-arithmetic with fractions!—Oh, you will take me to the palace, won't
you?'

'That's easily said,' replied the crow, 'but how
shall we set about it? I must talk it over with my
tame sweetheart—she'll no doubt be able to advise
us, for I must tell you, a little girl like you would
never get leave to enter in the regular way!'

'Oh, yes, I should!' said Gerda. 'When Kay
knows I'm here, he'll come straight out to fetch me!'

'Wait for me by the stile there!' said the crow,
wagging his head as he flew off.

The crow did not come back again until dusk
had fallen. 'Caw! Caw!' he said. 'I'm to give you
her greetings and best wishes! And here's a little
loaf for you which she took from the kitchen—
they've bread enough there, and you must be
hungry!—It won't be possible for you to go into
the palace, not with bare feet: the guards in silver

and the footmen in gold won't allow it. But don't cry—you shall get in all the same. My sweetheart knows a little back staircase that leads to the bed-chamber, and she knows where she can get the key!'

And they made their way into the garden and along the great avenue, where the leaves were falling one after another, and when the lights went out in the palace, one by one, the crow led little Gerda over to a back-door that was standing half-open.

Oh, how Gerda's heart beat with anxiety and longing! She felt just as if she were about to do something wrong, and yet she only wanted to find out if it were little Kay: yes, it must be he—she thought so vividly about his clever eyes and his long hair that she could actually see the way he used to smile when they sat together under the roses at home. He was sure to be glad to see her, to hear what a long way she had come for his sake, and to know how sad they had all been at home when he did not come back. How frightened she felt, but how glad she was, too!

They were on the stairs now; a little lamp was burning on a cupboard; in the middle of the floor stood the tame crow, turning her head this way and that, and looking intently at Gerda who curtseyed as grandmother had taught her to.

'My young man has spoken very nicely of you, young lady,' said the tame crow. 'And your bio-graphy, as they call it, is very touching!—If you will take the lamp, I'll go in front. We're going to take the shortest way, where we shan't meet any-one!'

'I think there's someone coming right behind us

now!' said Gerda. Something swished past her, and there seemed to be shadows on the wall—horses with flowing manes and slender legs, huntsmen, lords and ladies on horseback.

'They're only dreams!' said the crow. 'They come and take their lordships' thoughts out hunting—it's a good thing, too, for they can watch them better in bed. But I hope you will let me see, if you should come to honour and dignity, that you can show a grateful heart!'

'That's hardly something we should talk about!' said the crow from the woods.

They now entered the first hall, where the walls were covered in rose-red satin and beautifully worked flowers. The dreams were already rushing past them, but they swept by so quickly that Gerda failed to see the lords and ladies. Each hall was more magnificent than the last—it was not surprising it took your breath away—and then they were in the bedchamber. Here the ceiling was like a great palm-tree with leaves of glass, costly glass, and in the middle of the floor two beds hung from a thick golden stalk; each was shaped like a lily: one was white, and in it lay the princess; the other was red, and it was there that Gerda must look for little Kay. She turned one of the red petals aside, and she saw the nape of a brown neck—Oh, it was Kay!—She cried his name aloud, holding her lamp towards him—the dreams came rushing on horseback into the room again—he woke, turned his head, and—it was not little Kay.

The prince resembled him only on the back of his neck, but he was young and handsome. And the princess peeped out of the white lily bed and asked what was the matter. Then little Gerda wept and told her whole story and everything the crows had done for her.

'You poor little thing!' said the prince and princess, and they praised the crows and said they were not at all angry with them, but nevertheless they must not do it again. Meanwhile, they should have a reward.

'Would you like to fly away free?' asked the princess. 'Or would you rather have a permanent post as Court-Crows with a right to everything that falls on to the kitchen floor?'

And both the crows bowed low and asked for the permanent post, for they thought of their old age and said, 'It would be a very good thing to have something for the old man,' as they call it.

And the prince got out of his bed and let Gerda sleep in it, and more than that he could hardly do. She folded her little hands together and thought, 'Aren't people kind—and animals, too!' And then she shut her eyes and slept peacefully. The dreams all came flying in again, and this time they looked like God's angels; they pulled a little toboggan behind them, and in it sat Kay nodding to her. But it was all nothing but a dream, and so it vanished as soon as she woke.

The next day she was clothed from top to toe in silk and velvet. She was invited to stay in the palace and enjoy herself, but the only thing she asked for was a little carriage with a horse to pull it and a little pair of boots, and then she could drive out into the wide world again and find Kay.

She was given both the boots and a muff. She was dressed beautifully, and when she was ready to go, a new carriage of pure gold drove up to the door with the prince and princess's coat-of-arms gleaming on it like a star. The coachman, the foot-men, and the postilions—there were postilions, too —sat there with golden crowns upon their heads. The prince and princess helped her into the carriage themselves and wished her good luck. The crow from the woods, who was now married, went with her for the first twelve or fifteen miles; he sat beside her, for he could not bear riding backwards. The other crow stood in the gateway flapping her wings; she did not go with them, for, ever since they got their permanent post and too much to eat, she suf-fered from headaches. The inside of the carriage was lined with sugared cakes, and on the seat were fruits and doughnuts.

'Good-bye! Good-bye!' cried prince and prin-cess, and little Gerda wept and the crow wept.— And so the first few miles went by; then the crow said good-bye, too, and that was the heaviest leave-taking of all; he flew up into a tree and flapped his black wings as long as the carriage, shining like the sun, remained in sight.

The Fifth Part.

The Little Robber-Girl

They drove through the dark forest, but the carriage shone like a flame, hurting the robbers' eyes until they could bear it no longer.

'It's gold! It's gold!' they shouted, and, rushing out, they seized the horses, struck the little postilions, the coachman, and the footmen all dead, and then dragged little Gerda out of the carriage.

'She's fat, she's a dainty little morsel, she's been fattened on nut-kernels!' said the old hag of a robber-woman with the long bristly beard and the eyebrows that hung down over her eyes. 'She's as good as a little fatted lamb! My, how tasty she'll be!' And she drew out her polished knife which gleamed most terrifyingly.

'Ow!' said the old hag at that very same moment: she had been bitten on the ear by her own little

256

daughter who was hanging on her back and was so wild and out-of-hand it was a joy to see. 'You loathsome brat!' said her mother, and she had no time to kill Gerda.

'She's going to play with me!' said the little robber-girl. 'She's going to give me her muff and her beautiful dress, and sleep in my bed with me!' And then she bit her mother again, so hard that the robber-woman jumped and turned round, and all the robbers laughed and said, 'Look at her dancing with her cub!'

'I'm going to ride in the carriage!' said the little robber-girl, and she insisted upon having her own way, for she was very spoilt and very obstinate. She and Gerda sat inside, and thus they rode over stumps and thorns deeper and deeper into the forest. The little robber-girl was the same height as Gerda, but stronger, broader in the shoulders, and dark-skinned. Her eyes were quite black and had a rather sad look. She put her arm round little Gerda's waist and said, 'They shan't kill you as long as I'm not cross with you! Are you really a princess?'

'No,' said little Gerda and told her everything that had happened to her and how fond she was of little Kay.

The robber-girl gazed at her seriously, nodding her head a little, and said, 'They shan't kill you unless I get really cross with you, and then I shall do it myself!' Then she dried Gerda's eyes, and put both her hands inside the beautiful muff that was so soft and warm.

And now the carriage stopped: they were in the middle of the courtyard of a robbers' castle; the structure was split from top to bottom, ravens and crows flew out of the gaping holes, and the great bull-dogs—every one of them looked as if it could swallow a man—sprang high in the air, but they did not bark, for that was forbidden.

In the great old sooty hall a huge fire was burning in the middle of the flagged floor; the smoke drifted about under the roof and had to find its own way out; a big cauldron of soup was on the boil, and hares and rabbits were turning on the spit.

'You shall sleep here with me tonight, where all my pets are!' said the robber-girl. They got something to eat and drink, and then went over into a corner where straw and rugs lay scattered about. Above their heads, nearly a hundred doves were roosting on laths and perches; they all seemed to be asleep, but they shifted slightly when the little girls came.

'They're all mine, every one of 'em,' said the little robber-girl, promptly seizing one of the nearest, which she held up by the legs and shook so that it beat its wings frantically. 'Kiss it!' she cried, slapping Gerda in the face with it. 'There sit the scum of the forest!' she continued, pointing behind a number of slats nailed across a hole high up in the wall. 'They're forest scum, those two! They'd fly away at once if they weren't properly locked up. And here's my old sweetheart, Bae!' And she dragged a reindeer forward by the horn. It had a bright copper ring round its neck and was tied up. 'We have to keep him under lock and key as well, else he'd run away from us. Every evening of his life I tickle his neck with my sharp knife, and he's ever so frightened of it!' The little girl pulled a long knife out of a crack in the wall and let it glide over the reindeer's neck: the poor beast struck out with its legs, and the robber-girl laughed and pulled Gerda down into the bed.

'Do you want your knife with you when you're going to sleep?' asked Gerda, looking at it somewhat apprehensively.

'I always sleep with my knife!' said the little robber-girl. 'You never know what may happen. But tell me again what you told me before about little Kay, and why you went out into the wide world.' And Gerda told the story from the beginning, and the ring-doves cooed up there in their cage, while the other doves slept. The little robber-girl put her arm round Gerda's neck, and holding her knife in the other hand, she fell asleep, as you could tell by the sound of her breathing. But Gerda was quite unable to shut her eyes; she did not know whether she was to live or die. The robbers sat round the fire, singing and drinking, and the old woman turned head over heels. It was quite terrifying for the little girl to look at.

Then the ring-doves said, 'Coo, coo! We've seen little Kay. A white hen was carrying his toboggan, and he was sitting in the Snow Queen's sledge as it swept low over the forest while we lay in our nest. She blew a cold blast on us young ones, and all died except us two. Coo! Coo!'

'What's that you're saying up there?' cried Gerda. 'Which way did the Snow Queen go? Have you any idea?'

'She was doubtless making for Lapland, for there's always snow and ice there! But you ask the reindeer tethered to that rope.'

'Yes, there's ice and snow, and everything is beautiful and good!' said the reindeer. 'There you can run about freely in the great gleaming valleys!

The Snow Queen has her summer tent there, but her stronghold lies up towards the North Pole, on the island called Spitzbergen!'

'Oh, Kay, little Kay!' sighed Gerda.

'You lie still now!' said the robber-girl. 'Or else you'll get my knife in your belly!'

In the morning Gerda told her everything the ring-doves had said, and the little robber-girl looked quite serious, but nodded her head and said, 'Never mind! Never mind!—Do you know where Lapland is?' she asked the reindeer.

'Who should know better than I?' answered the animal, his eyes shining at the thought of it. 'That's where I was born and bred and where I used to run over the snowfields.'

'Listen!' the robber-girl said to Gerda. 'You see all our menfolk are out: the old girl's still here, and here she'll stay, but later on in the morning she'll take a drink from that big bottle and then have a little nap afterwards.—Then I'll see what I can do for you!' She now sprang out of bed and jumping round her mother's neck, she pulled her beard and said, 'Good morning, my own sweet billy-goat!' Her mother flicked her under the nose and made it red and blue—but it was all done out of pure affection.

So when her mother had had a drink from her bottle and was taking a little nap, the robber-girl went over to the reindeer and said, 'I should love to go on tickling you with my sharp knife because you look so funny when I do it, but never mind, I'm going to undo your rope and help you to get away so that you can run off to Lapland, but you must put your best foot forward and take this little girl to the Snow Queen's palace where her play-mate is. I'm sure you overheard what she told me, for she talked loudly enough, and you're always eaves-dropping!'

The reindeer jumped for joy. The robber-girl lifted little Gerda up and took the precaution of tying her firmly on and giving her a little cushion to sit on as well. 'Never mind,' she said, 'you can have your fur boots, for it'll be cold; but I'm going to keep the muff—it's much too nice! However, you shan't freeze: you can have mother's big mittens—they'll reach right up to your elbows. Shove your hands in!—now they look just like my ugly old mother's!'

And Gerda wept for joy.

'I can't bear to see you snivelling!' said the little robber-girl. 'You must look pleased now! You can have these two loaves and a ham, and then you won't go hungry.' They were tied on to the rein-deer's back just behind her. The little robber-girl opened the door, shut all the big dogs up, and then, as she cut through the rope with her knife, she said to the reindeer, 'Off you run now—but see you take good care of the little girl!'

And Gerda stretched out her hands with the mittens on towards the robber-girl and said good-bye, and then the reindeer sped away as fast as he could over bushes and tree-stumps, through the great forest, and over marsh and steppe-land. The wolves were howling and the ravens were screech-ing. 'Pop! Pop!'—there was a crackling in the sky, almost as if it were sneezing blood.

'There are my dear old Northern Lights!' said the reindeer. 'Look at the way they're shining!' and with that he ran on even more swiftly, night and day. The loaves were eaten, and so was the ham, and then they found themselves in Lapland.

The Sixth Part.

The Lapland Woman and the Finland Woman

They stopped by a little cottage: it was a wretched
place with the roof reaching down to the ground
and the door so low that the family had to crawl on
their stomachs when they wanted to go in or out.
There was no one at home but an old Lapp woman
who stood grilling a fish over a whale-oil lamp. The
reindeer told her the whole of Gerda's story, but he
told his own first, for that seemed to be much more
important, and Gerda was so overcome with cold
she could not speak.

'Ah, you poor, poor things!' said the Lapp
woman. 'You've still a long way to go! You'll have
to go over four hundred miles into Finmark, for
that's where the Snow Queen is staying in the
country and burning blue lights every single evening. I'll write a few words on a dried codfish, for
paper have I none, and give it to you to take to the

Finnish woman up there—she can give you clearer directions than I can!'

And then when Gerda had warmed herself and had something to eat and drink, the Lapp woman wrote a couple of words on a dried codfish, and bidding Gerda take great care of it, she tied her firmly on to the reindeer's back once more, and off he ran. 'Pop! Pop!' came the crackling noise from up in the sky, and all night long the Northern Lights burned a beautiful blue. And then they came to Finmark and knocked on the Finnish woman's chimney-stack, for she had no door at all.

The heat inside was so overpowering that even the Finnish woman went about very nearly naked. She was short and grubby-looking. She at once loosened Gerda's clothing and took off her mittens and boots, otherwise she would have been much too hot. Then she laid a piece of ice on the reindeer's head and read what was written on the codfish. She read it three times, and then when she knew it off by heart, she put the fish into the saucepan, for it might just as well be eaten, and she never wasted anything.

Then the reindeer told his own story first and then little Gerda's, and the Finnish woman blinked her eyes wisely but said nothing.

'You're so clever,' said the reindeer, 'I know you can tie up all the winds of the world with a thread of cotton. When the skipper unties the first knot, he gets a good wind; when he unties the second, the wind blows sharp; and when he unties the third and fourth, a gale springs up and the woods come tumbling down. Won't you give the little girl a drink that will give her the strength of twelve men so that she can get the better of the Snow Queen?'

'The strength of twelve men!' said the Finnish woman. 'Yes, that should do the trick!' She went over to a shelf, took a large rolled-up skin from it and unrolled it. Strange letters were written on it, and the Finnish woman read until the sweat poured from her brow.

The reindeer again pleaded so strongly for little Gerda, and Gerda looked at the Finnish woman with such beseeching tearful eyes, that she once again began to blink her eyes and drew the reindeer over into a corner, where she put fresh ice on his head and whispered to him.

'Little Kay is with the Snow Queen right enough, and he finds everything to his liking there and thinks it's the best place on earth, but that's all because he's got a splinter of glass in his heart and a little grain of it in his eye. They must be got out first, otherwise he'll never be human again and the Snow Queen will keep her power over him!'

'But can't you give little Gerda something to take which will give her the power to put everything right?'

'I can't give her greater power than she has already! Can't you see how great that is? Can't you see how she makes man and beast serve her, and how well she's made her way in the world on her own bare feet? She mustn't know of her power from us—it comes from her heart, it comes of her being a sweet innocent child. If she can't find her way into the Snow Queen's palace and free little Kay of the glass splinters all by herself, then we can't help her! Eight or nine miles from here is the beginning of the Snow Queen's garden: you can carry the little girl there. Put her down by the big bush with the red berries which you'll see standing in the snow. Don't stand gossiping, and hurry back!' With that, the Finnish woman lifted little Gerda up on to the reindeer's back, and off he ran as fast as he could.

'Oh, I forgot to bring my boots! And I've left my mittens behind!' cried little Gerda. And she missed them in the stinging cold. But the reindeer dared not stop; he ran on till he came to the big bush with the red berries. There he put Gerda down, and as he kissed her on the lips, great glistening tears ran down the poor animal's cheeks. Then, as fast as he could, he ran back again. There stood poor Gerda, without shoes, without gloves, in the midst of the terrible icy cold of Finmark.

She ran on as well as she could, and then a whole regiment of snow-flakes came towards her; they had not fallen from the sky, for that was quite clear and bright with the Northern Lights; no, the snow-flakes were running along the ground, and the nearer they came, the bigger they grew. Gerda remembered, of course, how large and wonderfully made the snow-flakes had looked when she saw them once through a magnifying-glass. But now they were big and frightening in quite a different way—they were alive, they were the Snow Queen's outposts. They had the strangest shapes: some looked like nasty great hedgehogs, others like masses of snakes knotted together and darting their heads out, and still others like tubby little bears with bristling hair. All were gleaming white, all were living snow-flakes.

Then little Gerda said the Lord's Prayer, and the cold was so intense she could see her own breath: it rose from her lips like a column of smoke; her breath became thicker and thicker, and formed itself into

bright little angels that grew bigger and bigger as
they touched the ground. They all had helmets on
their heads and spears and shields in their hands.
There were more and more of them, and when
Gerda had finished the Lord's Prayer, there was a
whole legion of them round her. They pierced the
dreadful snow-flakes with their spears so that they
burst into hundreds of pieces, and little Gerda went
on her way safe and undismayed. The angels patted
her hands and feet, and she felt the cold less keenly
and went briskly forward towards the Snow Queen's
palace.

But we must first see how Kay is getting on. He
was certainly not thinking about little Gerda—least
of all that she was standing right outside the palace.

The Seventh Part.

What Happened in the Snow Queen's Palace, and What Happened Afterwards

The palace walls were of driven snow, the doors
and windows of cutting wind; there were over a
hundred halls, all as the drifting snow had formed
them, the largest stretching for many miles, and all
brightly lit by the strong Northern Lights. They
were vast, empty, icy-cold, and gleaming. Gaiety
never came this way, no, not so much as a little
dance for the bears, with the gale blowing up and
the polar-bears walking on their hind-legs and
showing their fine manners; never a little card-
party with slap-your-mouth and strike-your-paw;
never a little bit of fun over coffee for the young
white-fox ladies—empty, vast, and cold it was in
the Snow Queen's halls. The Northern Lights
flashed with such regularity that you could tell
when they had reached their highest point and
when they had reached the lowest. In the middle
of that empty endless hall of snow there was a
frozen lake; it had split into a thousand pieces, and
all the pieces were so exactly alike that the whole
thing looked like a trick. Whenever she was at
home the Snow Queen sat in the centre of this lake,
and then she would say she was sitting in the Mirror
of Intelligence, and that it was the best, the only,
one in the world.

Little Kay was quite blue with cold—nearly
black, in fact—but he did not notice it, for she had
kissed his shivers away, and his heart was nothing
but a lump of ice. He spent his time dragging sharp
flat pieces of ice about, arranging them in all sorts
of ways, and trying to make something out of them

—it was rather like the kind of thing we sometimes do with small flat pieces of wood when we try to make patterns from them—a Chinese puzzle they call it. Kay made patterns in the same way, most elaborate ones, a sort of intellectual ice-puzzle. In his own eyes the patterns were quite remarkable and of the utmost importance—that was what the grain of glass that was stuck in his eye did for him! He would lay out his patterns to form written words, but he could never hit upon the way to lay out the one word he wanted, the word 'eternity'. The Snow Queen had said, 'If you can work out that pattern for me, you shall be your own master, and I will present you with the whole world—and a new pair of skates.' But he could not do it.

'Now I must fly off to the warm lands!' said the Snow Queen. 'I must go and peep into the black cauldrons!'—They were the fiery mountains that we call Etna and Vesuvius.—'I must whiten them a little! It's expected of me, and it's good for the lemons and grapes!' And so the Snow Queen flew away, and Kay sat quite alone in the vast empty hall of ice, many miles in length, and gazed at the pieces of ice, thinking and thinking until his head creaked with the effort. He sat there quite stiff and still: you would have thought he was frozen to death.

It was then that little Gerda stepped into the palace through the great gale of cutting wind; but she said her evening prayers, and the cold winds dropped as if they would fall asleep. She stepped into the vast empty cold halls—then she saw Kay, she recognized him, she flung herself about his neck, held him very tight, and cried, 'Kay! Dear little Kay! So I've found you after all!'

But he sat there quite still, stiff and cold. Then little Gerda wept hot tears that fell upon his breast and penetrated to his heart. They thawed the lump of ice and destroyed the little splinter of glass inside it. He looked at her, and she sang the hymn,

'In the valley grew roses wild,
And there we spoke with the Holy Child!'

Then Kay burst into tears; he wept so desperately that the grain of glass was washed out of his eye; he recognized her and cried joyfully, 'Gerda! Dear little Gerda!—Where have you been all this time? And where have I been?' And he looked round about him. 'How cold it is here! How empty and vast it is!' And as he clung to her she laughed and cried for joy: it was a moment of such bliss that even the pieces of ice danced for joy all round them, and when they grew tired and lay down again, they formed the very letters the Snow Queen had told him he must find out if he were to be his own master and she were to give him the whole world and a new pair of skates.

Gerda kissed his cheeks and the bloom came back to them; she kissed his eyes and they shone like hers; she kissed his hands and feet and he was in perfect health. The Snow Queen could come home when she liked: his reprieve lay written there in gleaming pieces of ice.

They took one another by the hand, and as they made their way out of that vast palace they talked about grandmother and the roses on the roof; and as they walked along, the winds lay still and the sun broke through. When they reached the bush with the red berries, the reindeer was standing there and waiting for them. He had another reindeer with him, a young doe whose udders were full, and she gave the children her warm milk and kissed them on the lips. Then the reindeer carried Kay and Gerda to the Finnish woman's, where they warmed themselves in the heat of the room and were given directions for their journey home, and then to the Lapp woman who had made them new clothes and got her sledge ready.

The reindeer and the young doe ran along by their side and kept them company until they came to the boundary of that land: there the first green shoots peeped forth, and there they took their leave of the reindeer and the Lapp woman. 'Good-bye!' they all said. The first little birds began to twitter, there were green buds in the forest, and out of it came riding on a splendid horse—which Gerda recognized, for it had been harnessed to her golden coach—a young girl with a bright red cap on her head and pistols before her. It was the little robber-girl who had grown tired of being at home and had made up her mind to travel northwards first and then, if she did not like it there, in some other direction afterwards. She recognized Gerda at once, and Gerda recognized her: they were very glad to see one another.

'You're a fine sort to go wandering off like that!' she said to little Kay. 'I'd like to know whether you deserve to have someone running to the ends of the world for your sake!'

But Gerda stroked her cheek and asked after the prince and princess.

'They've gone travelling to foreign parts!' said the robber-girl.

'And the crow?' asked little Gerda.

'Oh, the crow's dead!' she answered. 'His tame

sweetheart's a widow now and goes about with
a bit of wool round her leg; she's always moan-
ing and complaining, but it's all put on!—But
tell me how you got on, and how you came across
him!'

And Gerda and Kay both told her their stories.
'And fiddle-di-fiddle-di-dee!' said the robber-girl.
She took them both by the hand, and promised that
if she ever passed through their town, she would
come up and visit them. Then she rode away out
into the wide world, but Kay and Gerda walked on
hand in hand, and as they went along the spring
was beautiful with flowers and fresh green leaves.
The church bells were ringing, and they recognized
the high towers and the great city: it was there that
they lived, and on they went till they came to
grandmother's door. They went up the stairs and
into the living-room, where everything stood in the
same place as before, and the clock said 'Tick!
Tock!' and the hands turned round. But as they
entered the door they realized that they had grown
up. The roses in the gutter were thrusting their
flowers in at the open window, and their little stools
were still standing there. Kay and Gerda sat down
in their own seats and held each other's hands.
They had forgotten like a heavy dream the cold
empty splendour of the Snow Queen's palace.
Grandmother was sitting there in God's bright sunshine and reading aloud from the Bible, 'Except ye
become as little children, ye shall not enter into
the kingdom of heaven!'

And Kay and Gerda looked into each other's
eyes, and all at once they understood the old hymn:

'In the valley grew roses wild,
And there we spoke with the Holy Child!'

There they sat together, grown up, yet children still, children at heart—and it was summer, warm and beautiful summer.

THE LITTLE MATCH-GIRL

It was so dreadfully cold! It was snowing, and the evening was beginning to darken. It was the last evening of the year, too—New Year's Eve. Through the cold and the dark, a poor little girl with bare head and naked feet was wandering along the road. She had, indeed, had a pair of slippers on when she left home: but what was the good of that! They were very big slippers—her mother had worn them last, they were so big—and the little child had lost them hurrying across the road as two carts rattled dangerously past. One slipper could not be found, and a boy ran off with the other—he said he could use it as a cradle when he had children of his own.

So the little girl wandered along with her naked little feet red and blue with cold. She was carrying a great pile of matches in an old apron and she held one bundle in her hand as she walked. No one had bought a thing from her the whole day; no one had given her a halfpenny; hungry and frozen, she went her way, looking so woe-begone, poor little thing! The snow-flakes fell upon her long fair hair that curled so prettily about the nape of her neck, but she certainly wasn't thinking of how nice she looked. Lights were shining from all the windows, and there was a lovely smell of roast goose all down the street, for it was indeed New Year's Eve—yes, and that's what she was thinking about.

Over in a corner between two houses, where one jutted a little farther out into the street than the other, she sat down and huddled together; she had drawn her little legs up under her, but she felt more frozen than ever, and she dared not go home, for she had sold no matches and hadn't got a single penny, and her father would beat her. Besides, it was cold at home, too: there was only the roof over them, and the wind whistled in, although the biggest cracks had been stopped up with straw and rags. Her little hands were almost dead with cold. Ah, a little match might do some good! If she only dared pull one out of the bundle, strike it on the wall, and warm her fingers! She drew one out— Whoosh!—How it spluttered! How it burnt! It gave a warm bright flame, just like a little candle, when she held her hand round it. It was a wonderful light: the little girl thought she was sitting in front of a great iron stove with polished brass knobs and fittings; the fire was burning so cheerfully and its warmth was so comforting—oh, what was that! The little girl had just stretched her feet out to warm them, too, when—the fire went out! The stove disappeared—and she was sitting there with the little stump of a burnt-out match in her hand.

Another match was struck; it burnt and flared, and where the light fell upon it, the wall became transparent like gauze; she could see right into the room where the table stood covered with a shining white cloth and set with fine china, and there was a roast goose, stuffed with prunes and apples, steaming deliciously—but what was more gorgeous still, the goose jumped off the dish, waddled across the floor with knife and fork in its back, and went straight over to the poor girl. Then the match went out, and there was nothing to see but the thick cold wall.

She struck yet another. And then she was sitting beneath the loveliest Christmas-tree; it was even bigger and more beautifully decorated than the one she had seen this last Christmas through the glass-doors of the wealthy grocer's shop. Thousands of candles were burning on its green branches, and gaily coloured pictures, like those that had decorated the shop-windows, were looking down at her. The little girl stretched out both her hands—and then the match went out; the multitude of Christmas-candles rose higher and higher, and now she saw they were the bright stars—one of them fell and made a long streak of fire across the sky.

'Someone's now dying!' said the little girl, for her old granny, who was the only one that had been kind to her, but who was now dead, had said that when a star falls a soul goes up to God.

Once more she struck a match on the wall. It lit up the darkness round about her, and in its radiance stood old granny, so bright and shining, so wonderfully kind.

'Granny!' cried the little girl. 'Oh, take me with you! I know you'll go away when the match goes out—you'll go away just like the warm stove and the lovely roast goose and the wonderful big Christmas-tree!'—And she hastily struck all the rest of the matches in the bundle, for she wanted to keep her granny there, and the matches shone with such brilliance that it was brighter than day-light. Granny had never before been so tall and beautiful; she lifted the little girl up on her arm, and they flew away in splendour and joy, high, high up towards heaven. And there was no more cold and no more hunger and no more fear—they were with God.

But in the corner by the house, in the cold of the early morning, the little girl sat, with red cheeks and a smile upon her lips—dead, frozen to death on the last evening of the old year. The morning of the New Year rose over the little dead body sitting there with her matches, one bundle nearly all burnt out. She wanted to keep herself warm, they said; but no one knew what beautiful things she had seen, nor in what radiance she had gone with her old granny into the joy of the New Year.

THE OLD HOUSE

Across the road there was an old, old house: it was nearly three hundred years old, as you could read for yourself on the beam where the date was carved along with tulips and hop-vines. Whole verses stood there in old-fashioned spelling, and in the beam over each window was carved a wry, mocking face. The upper story projected a long way over the lower, and just under the roof was a lead gutter with a dragon's head on it: the rain-water was supposed to run out of its jaws, but actually it ran out of its belly, for there was a hole in the guttering.

All the other houses in the street were so new

and so neat with their large window-panes and
smooth walls, that it was easy to see they did not
want to have anything to do with that old house.
No doubt they thought, 'How long is that mon-
strosity going to cumber up the street! That top-
front bay sticks out so far that no one can see
from our windows what's happening on the other
side of it! The steps are wide enough for a palace
and high enough for a church tower. The iron railing certainly looks like the gateway to an old tomb,
and it has brass knobs, too! It does look silly!'

The houses straight across the road were new
and neat as well, and they thought like the others,
but a little boy with fresh red cheeks and bright
shining eyes was sitting at the window, and he
definitely liked the old house best, both in sunshine
and moonlight. And if he looked across at the wall
where the plaster had peeled off, he could discover
the most wonderful pictures from where he sat: he
could see exactly how the street had looked long
ago, with its steps and bay-windows and steep
gables; he could see soldiers with their halberds,
and gutterings that ran along under the roofs like
dragons and serpents.—It really was a house worth
looking at! An old man lived over there: he went
about in knee-breeches, had a coat with big brass
buttons, and wore a wig which you could see was a
real one. Every morning an old fellow arrived to
tidy up for him and run errands; otherwise, the old
man in the knee-breeches was quite alone in the
old house. From time to time he would cross over
to the window and look out, and the little boy
would nod to him, and the old man would nod
back again. And so they made each other's acquaintance and became friends, although they had never

spoken to one another, not, of course, that that mattered.

One day the little boy heard his parents say, 'The old man over there is very comfortably off, but he's so dreadfully lonely!'

The next Sunday the little boy took something and wrapped it in a piece of paper, went down to the gateway, and as the old chap who ran errands came by, he said to him, 'Listen, will you take this from me to the old man across the road? I've two tin-soldiers—that's one of them: he can have it, for I know he's so dreadfully lonely.'

And the old fellow looked quite pleased, nodded, and took the tin-soldier over to the old house. Afterwards there came a message asking whether the little boy wouldn't like to come over himself and pay a visit: he got leave to go from his parents, and so he went over to the old house.

The brass knobs on the railings shone much more brightly than usual—you might have thought they had been polished in honour of his visit—and the carved trumpeters—for there were trumpeters standing in the tulips carved on the door—seemed to be blowing with all their might, their cheeks puffed out rounder than ever. Yes, they were blowing, 'Tatterata! The little boy's coming! Tatterata!' And then the door was opened. The hall was hung all over with old portraits, knights in armour and ladies in silken gowns—and the armour rattled and the silk gowns rustled. And so they came to a staircase that went a long way up and a little way down, and then led them on to a balcony which was obviously very frail with great holes and long cracks in it. But through the holes and cracks grass and green leaves grew, for the whole of the balcony outside the walls of the house was so overgrown with greenery that it looked like a garden, though it was only a balcony. Old flower-pots with faces and asses' ears stood there; and the flowers grew in wild disorder. One pot was overflowing with pinks, or rather with green shoots, one tumbling upon another and saying quite clearly, 'The air has caressed me, the sun has kissed me and promised me a little flower on Sunday, a little flower on Sunday!'

And then they entered a room with its walls covered in pig-skin tooled with gilt flowers.

> 'Though gilding fade fast,
> Yet pigskin will last!'

said the walls.

And there were arm-chairs with great high backs and carving all over them. 'Sit down! Sit down!' they said. 'Ooh, how I creak! Now I shall have rheumatism like that old cupboard! Rheumatism in the back—ooh!'

And then the little boy entered the sitting-room where the bay-window was and where the old man was sitting.

'Thank you for the tin-soldier, my little friend!' said the old man. 'And thank you for coming over to see me!'

'Thanks! Thanks!' or 'Creak! Creak!' said all the furniture; there was so much of it that the pieces very nearly got in each other's way in their efforts to see the little boy.

And in the middle of the wall hung a picture of a lovely lady, young and happy, but dressed in the fashion of days gone by with powdered hair and stiff clothes; she said neither 'Thanks' nor 'Creak', but looked at the little boy with her gentle eyes; and he at once asked the old man, 'Where did you get her?'

'Over at the second-hand shop!' said the old man. 'There are a great many pictures hanging up over there; no one knows them or cares about them, for the people are all dead. But in the old days I knew her, and now she has been dead and gone for half a century.'

Under the picture a bouquet of withered flowers hung behind glass; they must have been half a century old, too, so old did they look. And the pendulum of the great clock went to and fro, and the hand turned, and everything in the room was even older than before, though none of them noticed it.

'They say at home,' said the little boy, 'that you're dreadfully lonely!'

'Oh,' he said, 'old thoughts, and what they bring with them, come and visit me, and now you've come, too!—I've nothing to complain of!'

And then he took a picture-book down from the shelf; there were great long processions, the strangest-looking coaches such as you never see nowadays, soldiers looking like the Jack of clubs and citizens with waving banners; the tailors had on theirs a pair of scissors borne by two lions, and the shoemakers carried not a boot, but an eagle with two heads, for shoemakers have to have everything like that so that they can say, 'It's a pair!'—What a fine picture-book it was!

And the old man went into the other room to fetch sweets and apples and nuts—it was all very pleasant over in the old house.

'I can't stand it!' said the tin-soldier who was

standing on the bureau. 'It's so lonely and sad! No, when you've been used to family-life, you can't accustom yourself to this sort of thing! I can't stand it! The days are so long, and the evenings longer still! It isn't a bit like it is over at your house, with your father and mother talking so pleasantly and you and all the other sweet children making such a lovely row. My, what a lonely life the old man leads! Do you suppose anyone kisses him? Do you suppose anyone looks at him kindly or gives him a Christmas-tree? There's nothing for him but the grave!—I can't stand it!'

'You mustn't take it so badly!' said the little boy. 'I think it's lovely here, and all the old thoughts, and what they bring with them, do come visiting!'

'Well, I don't see them, and I don't know them!' said the tin-soldier. 'I can't stand it!'

'But you must!' said the little boy.

And the old man came back with the happiest face and the loveliest sweets and apples and nuts, and so the little boy thought no more about the tin-soldier.

Happy and pleased, the little boy returned home, and the days went by and the weeks went by, and nods were exchanged with the old house, and then the little boy went over there again.

And the carved trumpeters blew, 'Tatterata! It's the little boy! Tatterata!' and in the pictures of the knights sword and armour rattled and the silken dresses rustled, the pigskin spoke and the old chairs had rheumatism in the back—'Aw!'—it was exactly like the first time, for over there one day or one hour was just like another.

'I can't stand it!' said the tin-soldier. 'I've wept tears of tin! It's much too sad here! Let me go to

war and lose arms and legs—I'd much rather—
and it would be a change! I can't stand it! I know
what it is now to be visited by old thoughts and
what they bring with them! I've been visited by
mine, and, believe me, there's no pleasure in it in
the long run—in the end I came near jumping off
the bureau. I saw all of you over there in the house
as plainly as if you'd really been here. It was that
Sunday morning again—you know the one I mean!
All you children were standing in front of the table
and singing your hymn, just as you do every morning; you were standing with your hands folded
devoutly, and your father and mother were just as
solemn, and then the door opened and your little
sister Maria, who isn't two yet and who always
dances whenever she hears music or singing, no
matter what kind it is, stepped in—which she
shouldn't have done, of course—and then she
began to dance, but she couldn't pick up the time,
for the notes were so long, and so she stood first on
one foot and leant her head right over, and then on
the other foot and leant her head right over, but
still she couldn't manage it. You stood there looking very serious, all of you, though it must have
been a difficult job, but I laughed to myself and so
I came to fall off the table and get a dent which I
still have, for it wasn't right of me to laugh. But it
all goes through my mind again, together with
everything else I met with: and that must be old
thoughts and what they bring with them.—Tell
me, do you still sing on Sundays? Tell me something about little Maria! And how's my comrade
getting on—the other tin-soldier? Yes, he's a lucky
fellow, and no mistake!—I can't stand it!'

'But you've been given away as a present!' said

the little boy. 'You'll have to stay—don't you realize that?'

And the old man came back with a drawer full of many things to look at—powder-boxes, scent-sprays, and old playing-cards, much larger and more lavishly gilded than you will ever see them now. And large drawers were opened, and the spinet was opened—it had a landscape painted on the inside of the lid, and it sounded so hoarse when the old man played on it; and then he hummed a song.

'Yes, she used to sing that!' he said, as he nodded towards the portrait he had bought from the second-hand shop, and the old man's eyes were shining very bright.

'I want to go to war! I want to go to war!' shouted the tin-soldier at the top of his voice, as he tumbled down on to the floor.

Where had he got to? The old man searched, the little boy searched: he was lost, and lost he remained. 'I shall find him no doubt!' the old man said, but he never did: there were far too many gaps and holes in the floor. The tin-soldier had fallen through a crack, and there he lay in an open grave.

And that day came to an end, and the little boy went home, and the week passed by, and several more weeks, too. The windows were quite frozen over: the little boy had to sit and breathe on them to make a peep-hole for him to see over to the old house, and snow had drifted into all the carved decorations and inscriptions. It lay right up over the steps just as if there were no one at home, and there wasn't either, for the old man was dead.

In the evening a carriage stopped outside, and

he was carried down to it in his coffin; he was to be taken out into the country to lie in his grave. And so he was driven away, but no one followed, for all his friends were dead. And the little boy blew a kiss after the coffin as it drove off.

Some days later there was a sale at the old house, and from his window the little boy watched the things being taken away—the knights and the ladies of days gone by, the flower-pots with the long ears, the old chairs and the old cupboards—some went this way and some that. Her portrait, which had been found in the second-hand shop, went back to the second-hand shop, and there it remained, for no one knew her any more, and no one cared for the old picture.

In the spring the house itself was pulled down, for it was an unsightly old place, they said. From the street you could see right into the sitting-room, right to the pigskin covering of the walls, now gashed and torn. And the green plants on the balcony hung in wild disorder about the falling beams.—And so it was cleared away.

'That's better!' said the houses round about.

And a handsome house was built there with large windows and smooth white walls, and in front, where the old house had actually stood, a little garden was planted, and up against the neighbours' walls wild vines grew. In front of the garden were tall iron railings with an iron gate; it looked very fine, and people would stand still and peep inside. And the sparrows hung by the score in the vines, all chattering as hard as they could at the same time, but it was not about the old house, for that they could not remember—that had been gone for so many years that the little boy had grown up to manhood. Yes, he was a fine man who gave his parents real cause for pleasure. He had just been married, and had moved with his little wife into the house where the garden was. He stood by her side as she planted a wild flower which she found very beautiful. She planted it with her own little hand and patted the earth about it with her fingers.—Oh! What was that? She pricked herself. Something sharp and pointed was sticking right up out of the soft earth.

It was—just think!—it was the tin-soldier, the one who had been lost up in the old man's room, and had rumbled and tumbled among timbers and rubble, and finally had lain for many years in the earth.

And the young wife dried the soldier, first with a green leaf and then with her own fine handkerchief that had such a lovely perfume! And the tin-soldier felt just as if he had wakened up from a trance.

'Let me see him!' said the young man, laughing and shaking his head. 'No, he can't possibly be the same one after all this time, but he reminds me of a story about a tin-soldier I had when I was a little boy!' And so he told his wife about the old house and the old man and the tin-soldier he had sent him because he was so dreadfully lonely, and he told it in such detail, just as it had really happened, that the young wife felt tears come into her eyes over that old house and the old man who had lived there.

'But it could be the same tin-soldier!' she said. 'I shall keep it and remember all that you've told me. But you must show me the old man's grave!'

'I don't know where it is,' he said, 'and no one knows where to find it. All his friends were dead, there was no one to look after his grave, and I was only a little boy!'

'How dreadfully lonely he must have been!' she said.

'Dreadfully lonely!' said the tin-soldier. 'But it's nice not to be forgotten!'

'Nice!' cried something close by; but the tin-soldier was the only one who saw that it was a scrap of pigskin covering; it had lost all its gilding and looked like damp mould, but it still had something to say, and it said it,

'Though gilding fade fast,
Yet pigskin will last!'

But the tin-soldier refused to believe it.

THE GOBLIN AT THE
PROVISION-DEALER'S

THERE was a student—an unmistakable student—
who lived in the attic and owned nothing; there
was a provision-dealer—equally unmistakable—
who lived on the ground-floor and owned the whole
house, and he was the one the goblin attached himself to, for every Christmas Eve he gave him a dish
of porridge with a great lump of butter in it. The
provision-dealer could easily spare it, and so the
goblin stayed in the shop—and there was much to
be learnt from it.

One evening the student came in by the back
door to buy himself some candles and cheese—he
had no one to send and so he came himself. He got
what he wanted and paid for it, and the provision-
dealer and his wife nodded good evening—the wife
was a woman who could do more than nod, for she

had the gift of the gab!—and the student nodded back and then stood reading the bit of paper the cheese was wrapped in. It was a page torn out of an old book which should never have been torn up at all, an old book full of poetry.

'There's more of that lying about!' said the provision-dealer. 'I gave an old woman some coffee-beans for it. If you'd like to give me sixpence, you can have the rest.'

'Thank you,' said the student. 'You can let me have it instead of the cheese! I can make do with bread and butter. It would be sinful to tear the whole book to pieces. You're a fine man, a practical man, but you understand no more about poetry than this cask here!'

Now that was a rude thing to say, especially as far as the cask was concerned, but the provision-dealer laughed and the student laughed, for of course it was said as a kind of joke. But the goblin was annoyed that anyone dared speak like that to a provision-dealer who was the landlord of the house and sold the best butter.

That night, when the shop was shut and everyone but the student was in bed, the goblin went in and took the wife's gift of the gab—she had no use for it while she was asleep—and whatever object in the room he put it on received the power of speech and could express its thoughts and feelings just as well as she could. But only one at a time could have it, and that was a blessing, for otherwise they would all have talked at once.

And the goblin placed the gift of the gab on the cask where the old newspapers were kept. 'Is it really true,' he asked, 'that you don't know what poetry is?'

'Yes, of course I do,' said the cask. 'It's something you find at the bottom of the page in the newspaper and cut out. I should think I've more of it inside me than the student has, and I'm only a poor cask compared with the provision-dealer.'

And the goblin placed the gift of the gab on the coffee-mill—my, how it went! And he put it on the butter-tub and the till—they were all of the same opinion as the cask, and what most people are agreed upon you have to respect.

'Now I'll try it on the student!' And so the little goblin went quite quietly up the back stairs to the attic where the student lived. There was a light inside his room, and the goblin peeped through the key-hole and saw the student reading the tattered book from downstairs. But how bright it was in the room! A bright beam of light rose out of the book and grew into a trunk, a mighty tree that rose up high and spread out its broad branches over the student. Every leaf looked so fresh, and every flower was the head of a lovely girl, some with eyes so dark and shining, others with eyes so blue and strangely bright. Every fruit was a shining star, and there was a sound of wonderfully beautiful singing.

The little goblin had never even imagined anything so glorious, let alone seen and experienced it. And so he stayed there, standing tip-toe and peeping and peeping, until the light in the room went out: the student must have blown out his lamp and gone to bed, but the little goblin stayed where he was, for the song still sounded soft and lovely in his ears, a beautiful lullaby for the student who had lain down to rest.

'It's wonderful here!' said the little goblin. 'I hadn't expected anything like this!—I think I'll

stay with the student—' And he thought about it—
and thought about it very sensibly, and then he
sighed and said, 'The student hasn't any porridge!'
—and so off he went—yes, he went down again to
the provision-dealer. And it was a good thing he
did, for the cask had very nearly used up the good
lady's gift of the gab telling everybody all that was
inside it. It had already done this once from one
angle, and now it was just about to turn over so that
it could repeat it from the other angle, when the
goblin came and took the gift of the gab back to the
good lady. But from that time the whole shop, from
the till to the firewood, based its views on what the
cask said, and they held it in such high esteem and
had such confidence in it that ever after when the
provision-dealer was reading the art criticisms and
theatre notices from the evening paper, they
thought he had it all from the cask.

But the little goblin no longer sat quietly listening to all the wisdom and good sense down below:
no, as soon as the light shone from the room in the
attic, its beams were just like strong anchor-chains
dragging him upstairs, and off he had to go and
peep through the key-hole, and there he was over-
powered by a sense of greatness, such as we feel
when we stand by the rolling sea and God passes
over it in the stormy blast; and he would burst into
tears—he did not know himself why he was crying
—but there was something very blessed in those
tears.—How wonderfully delightful it would be to
sit under that tree with the student!—But that
could never be: and he was glad he had the key-
hole. He would still stand there in the cold passage
when the winds of autumn were blowing down
from the skylight and it was so very, very cold, but

the little fellow would not feel it until the light went out in the attic and the sound of music died away in the wind. Ooh! Then he would freeze and creep downstairs again into his warm corner—how cosy and comfortable it was!—And then his Christmas porridge came with its great lump of butter.—Yes, the provision-dealer was the master for him.

But in the middle of the night the goblin was awakened by a frightful banging on the window-shutters: people outside were thumping on them; the watchman was blowing his whistle; a great fire had broken out and the whole street was lit up by the flames. Was it in this house or next door? Where was it? What a panic there was! The provision-dealer's wife was so flurried that she took her gold ear-rings out of her ears and put them into her pocket so that she might at least save something; the provision-dealer ran for his bonds, and the maid for her silk mantilla—for she was well enough off to have one: everyone wanted to save what he prized most, and so, too, did the little goblin. In a couple of bounds he was up the stairs and in the attic with the student who was standing quite calmly by the open window and looking out at the fire which was in the house across the road. The little goblin seized the wonderful book from the table, put it into his red hood, and held it tight in both hands: the most precious treasure in the house had been rescued. Then off he went, right out on to the roof, right up the chimney-stack, and there he sat lit up by the flames of the burning house opposite and holding closely in both hands his red hood and the treasure that lay inside it. Then he knew where his heart lay, whom he really belonged to. But when the fire had been put out and he had become more level-headed, well—'I'll divide my time between them!' he said. 'I can't give up the provision-dealer entirely, on account of the porridge!'

And that was really quite human!—We, too, go to the provision-dealer's—for porridge.

SHE WAS GOOD FOR NOTHING

THE magistrate was standing by the open window:
he was in his dress-shirt, with a jewelled pin in his
shirt-frill, and unusually well shaved—a labour he
had performed himself; he had, however, managed
to give himself a little snick and a scrap of newspaper was stuck over the cut.

'Hey, you, little fellow!' he shouted.

The little fellow was none other than the washerwoman's son who was just passing by and respectfully took off his cap—its peak was broken to make
it fit into his pocket. In his poor but clean and very
well patched clothes, and with heavy wooden clogs
on his feet, the boy stood there as respectfully as
he would have done for the king himself.

'You're a good boy!' said the magistrate. 'You're
a well-mannered boy! I suppose your mother's
washing clothes down by the stream, and you're to
go down there with what you have in your pocket.
It's a bad habit your mother has! How much have
you got there?'

'Half a quartern!' said the boy in a scared, half-subdued voice.

'And she had the same this morning?' continued the man.

'No, that was yesterday!' answered the boy.

'Two halves make a whole!—She's good for nothing! Ah, it's a sad thing with people of that class! Tell your mother she should be ashamed of herself—and mind you never become a drunkard, though I've no doubt you will!—Poor lad!—Off you go, then!'

And the boy went on his way; he held his cap in his hand, and the wind blew his fair hair about his head in long wisps. He went down the street, into the lane, and down to the stream, where his mother was standing out in the water by her washing-stool and beating the heavy linen with her wooden bat. There was a strong current in the water because the sluices at the water-mill were open; the sheet she was beating was being dragged downstream and very nearly pulled the stool over: the washerwoman had to brace herself against it.

'I'm nearly exhausted!' she said. 'It's a good thing you've come, for I can do with a little drop to keep my strength up! It's cold out here in the water: I've been standing here for six hours. Have you got something for me?'

The boy pulled out the bottle, and his mother put it to her lips and took a gulp.

'Ah, that does you good! How warming it is! It's as good as a hot meal, and it doesn't cost as much, either! Drink some, my lad! You look so pale: you must be frozen in those thin clothes—and it's autumn, too! Ooh, the water's cold! If only I don't fall ill—but I shan't do that! Give me another sip, and drink yourself, but only a little drop, mind—you mustn't make a habit of it, poor little wretch!'

She stepped on to the plank where the boy was standing, and so on to dry land; the rush mat she had tied round her waist was wringing wet, and water streamed from her skirt.

'I slave and drudge until my fingers are nearly worn to the bone, but I don't mind, as long as I can just manage to make an honest living for you, my love!'

At that moment a somewhat older woman came along: she was poorly clad and lame in one leg, and a great big false curl hung over one eye which was meant to be hidden by it, but the curl only called all the more attention to its odd appearance. She was a friend of the washerwoman's—'Lame Maren with the curl', the neighbours called her.

'You poor thing, how you can slave away standing in that cold water! You can do with a little something to keep you warm, I'll be bound, and yet they grudge you the drop you have!'—and then the washerwoman was soon told everything the magistrate had said to the boy, for Maren had heard it all, and it had annoyed her to hear him speak like that to the child about his own mother and the drop she took, especially as he was just giving a great luncheon with wine by the bottleful. 'Fine wine, and strong wine, too! A drop too much for a great many of them! But they don't call that drinking! They're all right, but you're good for nothing!'

'So he spoke to you, lad!' said the washerwoman, her lips trembling as she spoke. 'You've a mother who's good for nothing! Perhaps he's right! But he shouldn't say so to the child! Still, I've had so much to put up with from that house!'

'You were in service there, weren't you, when the magistrate's parents were alive and living there —that's a good many years ago! Many a peck of salt has been eaten since those days, so they may well be thirsty!' And Maren laughed. 'There's a big luncheon today at the magistrate's—it should have been called off, but it was too late for them to do anything about it, the food had all been prepared. I heard about it from the farm-hand. A letter came about an hour ago to say the younger brother's dead in Copenhagen.'

'Dead!' exclaimed the washerwoman, turning deathly pale.

'Why!' said the woman. 'Does that upset you so much? Of course, you knew him from being in service in the family.'

'Is he really dead! He was one of the best, one of the kindest people! The Lord won't find many like him!' And the tears ran down her cheeks. 'Oh God, my head's going round! It's because I emptied the bottle—I've had more than I can stand! I feel so queer!'—and she supported herself against the hoarding.

'God in heaven, you're quite poorly, mother!' said the woman. 'Just take it quietly, and it may pass off!—My, you're really ill! I'd better get you home!'

'But the clothes there!'

'I'll see to them, don't you worry! Take my arm now! The boy can stay here and keep an eye on them in the mean time; then I'll come and wash the rest—there's only a little pile!'

The washerwoman was unsteady on her legs.

'I've been standing too long in the cold water! I've had neither bite nor sup since this morning, and now I'm feverish all over! Oh, Christ, help me home!—My poor child!'—and she began to cry.

The boy was soon sitting and crying by himself beside the wet clothes on the bank. The washerwoman was very unsteady, and the two women went slowly up the lane and along the street past the magistrate's house, and right outside it she collapsed on the pavement. A crowd gathered.

Lame Maren ran into the house for help. The magistrate and his guests looked out of the windows.

'It's the washerwoman!' he said. 'She's had a drop too much: she's a good-for-nothing creature! It's hard lines on that nice boy of hers. I've really taken a liking to him. But his mother's a real good-for-nothing!'

And she was brought round again and taken home to her poor room where she went to bed. Good-natured Maren went and heated a bowl of ale with butter and sugar in it—she considered that was the best medicine there was—and then she went to the stream and did the washing very badly but with the best of intentions—she really only dragged the wet clothes to land and put them into a box.

In the evening she sat in the poor room with the washerwoman. She had got from the magistrate's cook a couple of browned potatoes and a nice fat piece of ham for the sick woman, but the boy and Maren had the benefit of them—the sick woman enjoyed the smell, it was so nourishing, she said.

And the boy went to bed in the same bed as his mother, but he had his own place across the foot

299

and covered himself over with an old rug made of red and blue strips sewn together.

The washerwoman was a little better: the warm ale had strengthened her and the smell of good food had done her good.

'Thank you—you're a good soul!' she said to Maren. 'I'll tell you all about it when the boy's asleep! I think he is already! Doesn't he look sweet with his eyes shut? He doesn't know what his mother has to put up with, and I hope to God he never will!—I was in service with the Court-Councillor and his wife, the magistrate's parents, and it so happened that the youngest of their sons came home from the university. I was young and flighty in those days, but I'd swear before God there was no real harm in me!' said the washerwoman. 'The student was such good company and so sweet-natured! Every drop of blood in him was honest and good! There's never been a better man on this earth. He was a son of the family and I was only a servant, but we became sweethearts: it was all right and proper, for there's surely no harm in a kiss if you really love one another. And he told his mother about it: he thought the world of her, and she was so wise and friendly and lovable. When he went away, he put his gold ring on my finger. After he had been gone some time, the mistress called me in; she stood there and talked to me seriously, and yet so kindly, like the Lord himself: she explained to me, freely and frankly, the distance between him and me. "At the moment, he sees only your good looks, but good looks will fade! You are not educated like him; you are not each other's equals intellectually, and that's where unhappiness lies. I respect the poor," she said; "they

300

may very well gain a higher place in the sight of
God than many a rich man, but here on earth you
mustn't cross into the wrong track when you're
driving straight ahead, or else the cart will overturn—and you two will overturn! There's a good
honest man, a craftsman, who has, I know, been
courting you—Eric the glove-maker. He's a
widower, he's no children, and he's comfortably
off—think it over!" Every word she spoke went
through my heart like a knife, but the mistress was
right, and it depressed me and weighed on me.
I kissed her hand and wept bitterly; I cried even
more when I got to my room and threw myself on
the bed. It was a heavy night that followed—the
Lord knows how I struggled with myself and what
I went through. Then on the Sunday I went to com-
munion to see if I could find guidance. It seemed
just like the hand of Providence: as I was leaving
church I met Eric the glove-maker. Then there was
no longer any doubt in my mind—we were suited
to each other in station and circumstances, and he
was quite well-to-do—and so I went straight up
to him, took him by the hand and said, "Have you
still a mind to me?" "Yes, always and for ever!" he
said. "Are you willing to take a girl who honours
and respects you, but doesn't love you—though
love may come?" "It will come!" he said, and so we
gave one another our hands. I went home to my
mistress. I carried the gold ring her son had given
me in my bosom; I couldn't wear it in the day-time,
but I put it on my finger every evening when I lay
down upon my bed. I kissed the ring until my lips
bled, and then I gave it to my mistress and told her
that the banns would be read in church the next
week for me and the glove-maker. Then my mistress

took me in her arms and kissed me—she didn't say I was good for nothing, but perhaps I was better in those days, although I hadn't yet experienced so much of the troubles of the world. And so the wedding took place towards Candlemas, and the first year went well—we had a journeyman and a boy, and you were in service with us, Maren.'

'Oh, you were a good mistress!' said Maren. 'I shall never forget how kind you and your man were!'

'Those were good years when you were with us! We hadn't the child then. The student I never saw —yes, I did see him once, but he didn't see me! He had come over for his mother's funeral. I saw him standing by the grave, looking as white as a sheet and very sad, but, of course, that was on account of his mother. Afterwards when his father died, he was in foreign parts and couldn't come, and he hasn't been here since. He never married, I know— and I think he became an attorney. He didn't remember me, and if he had seen me, he would certainly not have known me again, I'd grown so plain. And a very good thing, too!'

And she spoke of the heavy days of trial, of how misfortune, as it were, swamped them. They had five hundred pounds, and there was a house in their street going for two hundred, and since it would pay them to have it pulled down and build anew, they bought the house. Builders and joiners estimated that it would cost a further thousand and twenty. Eric the glove-maker's credit was good, and he raised the money by a loan in Copenhagen, but the skipper who was to bring it was lost at sea, and the money with him.

'It was then that I gave birth to my dear boy

who's sleeping here now. His father fell seriously ill and remained so for a long time: for nine months I had to dress and undress him. We went right back: we borrowed time and time again; all our things went; and then my man died and left us.—I've slaved and drudged and worked myself to death for the sake of the child; I've washed steps and I've washed linen, coarse and fine. I shall never know anything better, for that's the way God wills it. But He will soon release me, and He'll take care of my boy.'

And so she fell asleep.

Late in the morning she felt her strength returning; she felt strong enough, as she thought, to go about her work again. She had just stepped out into the cold water when a fit of shaking seized her and she felt faint; she clutched herself convulsively, took a step towards the bank, and fell down. Her head lay on dry land, but her feet were out in the stream. Her wooden clogs, in which she had been standing on the river-bed—there was a wisp of straw in each of them—were swept away by the current. And there she was found by Maren who had come to bring her some coffee.

There had been a message at home from the magistrate who wanted her to go and see him at once as he had something to tell her. It was too late. A barber was fetched to bleed her: the washer-woman was dead.

'She's drunk herself to death!' said the magistrate.

The letter which had brought the news of his brother's death stated the contents of his will: six hundred pounds had been left to the glove-maker's widow who had once been in service with his parents. The money was to be given, in greater or smaller amounts as they thought best, to her and her child.

'There was some hanky-panky between my brother and her!' said the magistrate. 'It's a good job she's out of the way; now the boy will get the lot, and I shall find a home for him with honest folk, and then he can become a good craftsman!'— And the Lord set his blessing on those words.

The magistrate called the boy before him, promised to look after him, and told him what a good thing it was his mother was dead, for she was good for nothing!

She was carried to the churchyard and laid in a pauper's grave. Maren planted a little rose-bush over it, and the boy stood by her side.

'My dear mother!' he said, as the tears streamed down. 'Is it true she was good for nothing?'

'No, of course it isn't!' said Maren, looking up to heaven. 'I've known it isn't true for many years, and I realized it again the last night she lived. She was made of the right stuff, I tell you! And God in heaven will say so, too—let the world say she was good for nothing, as much as it likes!'

THE WIND TELLS OF
VALDEMAR DAAE AND HIS
DAUGHTERS

WHEN the wind races over it, the grass ripples like
the surface of water, and the corn breaks into waves
like a lake: that is the dance of the wind—but listen
to the tales it tells: it sings aloud, and the song that
sounds among the trees of the forest is very different from the one it sings through cracks and
crevices and holes in the wall. See how the wind
chases the clouds up there as if they were a flock
of sheep! Listen how the wind down here howls
through the open doorway like a watchman blowing his horn! It whines strangely down the chimney
and into the stove; it makes the fire flare up and
throw out a shower of sparks, shining right out into
the room, and it is so warm and cosy to sit there
and listen to it. Just let the wind tell what it will!
It knows more tales and stories than all the rest of
us put together. Listen now to what it is saying:

'Whew-oo-oo! Away, away!'—that is the refrain to the ballad.

'There lies by the Great Belt an old manor-house with thick red walls,' says the wind. 'I know every stone—I saw them all before when they formed part of Marsk Stig's castle on the ness: that had to be pulled down! The stones were raised again and built into a new wall, a new manor, in another place—it was Borreby Manor, which stands just as it was to this day.

'I have seen and known, in their changing generations, the noble men and women who dwelt there, and I shall tell you now of Valdemar Daae and his daughters!

'He carried his head so proudly—he was of royal descent! He could do more than hunt the hart and drain his tankard—that could look after itself, he used to say.

'His wife, stiff in her gown of gold brocade, stepped proudly over her polished wood-block floor; the carpets were magnificent, the furniture costly and beautifully carved. Silverware and gold she had brought to the house; it was German ale that lay in the cellar when anything lay there at all; fiery black horses whinnied in the stables: there were riches in Borreby Manor—when wealth was there.

'And children there were, too—three fine young ladies, Ide, Johanne, and Anna Dorothea: I remember their names still.

'They were rich people, people of good family, born and bred to a noble way of life! Whew-oo-oo! Away, away!' sang the wind, and then took up its tale again.

'I did not see here, as in other old manors, the high-born lady sitting in the great hall with her maids and turning her spinning-wheel; she played upon her sounding lute and sang to it—not always the old Danish songs, either, but ballads in strange tongues. There was life and hospitality here, noble guests came from near and far, and there was a noise of music and clashing goblets I was unable to drown!' said the wind. 'There was arrogance and ostentation, many a lord—but not Our Lord!

'Then just as it was May Day Eve,' said the wind, 'I came from the west: I had seen ships wrecked upon the west coast of Jutland, I had chased over the moors and the green woods of the coast, away over the Island of Funen, and now I came puffing and blowing over the Great Belt.

'Then I sank to rest on the coast of Zealand near Borreby Manor, where the woods still stood with their noble oaks.

'The young lads from the neighbourhood used to come out here and gather twigs and branches, the biggest and driest they could find. They would take them into the village, pile them up and set fire to them, and then the lads and lasses would dance and sing round the bonfire.

'I lay still,' said the wind, 'but I softly touched the branch that the most handsome of the young lads had laid there: his piece of wood blazed up and flared the highest, and so he was chosen, given the name of honour and made King of the May, and had first choice among the girls for his little May Queen. There was a joy and happiness there, greater than ever there was in the wealthy Manor of Borreby.

'On her way to the manor, the great lady came

riding past in her gilt coach with its six horses, and with her were her three daughters, so delicate and young, like three lovely flowers—rose and lily and pale hyacinth. The mother herself was like a resplendent tulip: not one of the whole crowd did she greet, as they stopped their play, bowing and scraping before her, and you might have thought her afraid of snapping in two, like the brittle stalk of the tulip itself, should she unbend so far.

'Rose and lily and pale hyacinth—yes, I saw all three of them! Whose May Queens would they be one day, I wondered: their King of the May would be some haughty knight, even a prince, perhaps!— Whew-oo-oo! Away, away, away!

'Yes, the coach carried them off, and the villagers went on dancing. Summer had ridden to town in Borreby, in Tjæreby, in all the villages round about.

'But during the night, when I rose,' said the wind, 'the high-born lady lay down never to get up again; death had come to her as it comes to everyone—there is nothing new about that. Valdemar Daae stood grave and thoughtful a little while. "The proudest tree may be bent, but it cannot be broken," he said to himself. His daughters wept, and while they all dried their eyes at the manor, Lady Daae was carried away—and I was away, too! Whew-oo-oo!' said the wind.

'I came again, I came often again, over the Island of Funen and the waters of the Belt, sinking to rest by Borreby strand, by the magnificent oak-woods where the osprey and the ring-dove built, the blue-black raven and the black stork itself. It was early in the year, and some had eggs and some had young. What a flying and a screeching there was!

The sound of an axe could be heard, blow upon blow; the wood was to be felled, for Valdemar Daae had planned to build a costly ship, a three-decker man-of-war, which the King would certainly buy, and so the wood, a landmark for sailors and a

dwelling-place for birds, was coming down. The shrike flew about in dismay, its nest destroyed; the osprey and all the birds of the wood were losing their homes, and they were flying in wild circles, screeching in fear and anger—I understood them well enough. The crow and the jackdaw cried loudly in mockery, "Off your nest! Off your nest! Off, off!"

'And in the middle of the wood, near the group of workmen, stood Valdemar Daae and his three daughters, and they all laughed at the wild screeching of the birds, but his youngest daughter, Anna

Dorothea, felt pity for them in her heart, and as the men were about to fell a half-dead tree, among the bare branches of which the black stork had built, its young poking their heads up out of the nest, she pleaded for it to be spared, pleaded for it with tears in her eyes, and so the tree was allowed to stand, and the nest of the black stork with it. It was only a small thing.

'There was much hewing and sawing—and the three-decker ship was built. The master-shipwright came of a humble brood but he had a noble bearing; his eyes and his forehead revealed how clever he was, and Valdemar Daae willingly listened to his talk, and so did little Ide, his eldest, his fifteen-year-old daughter; and while he was building the ship for her father, he was building a dream-castle for himself, where he and little Ide lived as man and wife—and it might have happened, too, if the castle had been of stone, with ramparts and moat, and woods and gardens. But with all his ability, the master-craftsman was still only a poor bird, and what kind of a figure can a sparrow cut in the dance of the cranes? Whew-oo-oo!—I sped away, and he sped away, too, for he dared not stay, and little Ide got over it, for there was nothing else she could do.

'The black horses were neighing in the stables: they were worth looking at, and they were being looked at. The admiral had been sent from the King himself to look over the new man-of-war and discuss its purchase, and he was speaking of the valuable horses with great admiration.—I heard him quite clearly,' said the wind, 'for I went through the open door with the gentlemen and strewed wisps of straw like bars of gold before their feet.

Gold was what Valdemar Daae wanted, but he failed to understand that the admiral obviously wanted the black horses since he had praised them so highly, and so the ship was not bought: it lay covered over with planks on the beach, a Noah's ark that was never launched upon the waters. Whew-oo-oo! Away, away! And a sorry sight it was!

'In the winter-time, when the fields lay under snow and the Belt was filled with drift-ice which I packed against the coast,' said the wind, 'the ravens and crows, each one blacker than the last, came in great flocks and settled on the desolate, dead and lonesome ship on the beach, and screeched hoarsely of the wood that was gone, of the many precious birds' nests laid waste, of the homeless old and the homeless young—and all for the sake of that great piece of junk, the proud vessel that would never sail out to sea.

'I whirled the snow-flakes and the snow lay like heavy seas high about it, right over it! I let it hear my voice, the voice of the howling gale: I know I did my best to give it the knowledge a ship should have. Whew-oo-oo! Away!

'And the winter passed by—winter and summer, they pass by quickly and are soon gone, as I am, too, with the drifting snow, the drifting apple-blossom, and the falling leaves; away, away, away! —and men and women with them!

'But the daughters were still young, and little Ide was still a rose, as lovely to look at as when the master-ship-builder gazed upon her. I would often catch her by her long brown hair as she stood thoughtfully by the apple-tree in the garden, not noticing the blossom I scattered on her loosened hair, and watching the red sun and the golden background of the sky between the dark trees and bushes of the garden.

'Her sister Johanne was like a lily, stiff and gleaming; she carried herself erect and proud, and looked brittle like her mother. Her pleasure lay in walking up and down the great hall where the family portraits hung. The ladies were painted in velvet and silk with tiny pearl-covered caps upon their plaited hair—and very beautiful they were! Their husbands appeared in armour or in costly squirrel-lined capes and blue ruffs, and their swords hung from the thigh and not the waist. Whereabouts upon the wall would Johanne's portrait hang one day, and what would her noble husband look like? Yes, that's what she thought about and chattered about—I heard her whenever I came whistling through the long gallery into the hall and whirled round again.

'Anna Dorothea, the pale hyacinth, a child of only fourteen, was quiet and thoughtful; her large sea-blue eyes had a pensive look, but the smile of childhood sat upon her mouth—I could not blow that away, and I had no wish to either.

'I would meet her about the garden and the sunken lanes and the fields of the manor as she gathered the herbs and flowers she knew her father could make use of for the potions and drops he distilled: Valdemar Daae was haughty and self-satisfied, but skilled and learned as well—people noticed it and whispered about it. There was a fire in his stove even in summer-time, and the door of his room was locked: he shut himself in more and more as the days and nights went by, but he spoke little of what he was doing—if one could master the powers of nature in secret, then surely one would soon discover the greatest of them all—the power to make red gold!

'And so the fumes rose from the stove, and the fire crackled and flamed. Yes, I was there!' said the wind. '"Let it alone, let it alone!" I sang through the chimney. "Nothing will come of it but smoke and embers and ashes! You will burn yourself up! Whew-oo-oo! Away, away!" But Valdemar Daae did not let it alone.

'The fine horses in the stables—what became of them? The old silver and goldware in cupboard and bower, the cows in the field, goods and manor? —They could be melted down, melted in the gold-crucibles—but still the gold did not come.

'Barn and pantry, cellar and loft were empty. Fewer folk, more mice. One window-pane cracked, one broken—I had no need to go in at the door,' said the wind. 'Where the chimney smokes, the dinner is cooking: the chimney smoked here, but it swallowed up all their meals for the sake of the red gold.

'I blew through the great gateway like a watchman blowing on his horn, but there was no watchman there,' said the wind. 'I turned the weather-cock on the spire and it creaked and groaned as if the watchman were snoring in the turret, but there was no watchman there either: there were rats and mice: poverty laid the table, poverty sat in the wardrobe and the pantry, the door came off its hinges, cracks and crevices appeared; I went in and I went out,' said the wind, 'and so I knew all that was going on.

'In smoke and ashes, in sorrow and sleepless nights, his beard and the hair about his temples grew grey, and his complexion muddy and sallow;

314

his eyes were greedy for gold, long-awaited gold.

'I puffed smoke and ashes into his face and his beard; debts came instead of gold. I sang through the cracked window-panes and the open crevices, I blew into his daughters' beds, where their clothes lay faded and torn, for they always had to make them last. It was no song to sing for children in their cradles! Their lordly way of life had grown wretched indeed! I was the only one who sang loudly in that castle!' said the wind. 'I snowed them up—that's cosy, you say, but firing had they none, for the wood they should have got it from had been felled. There was a tingling frost; I whistled through cracks and corridors, over floors and walls to keep myself in practice; there in the house, they kept to their beds because of the cold, those high-born daughters of his; and their father crept under his fur bed-cover. Nothing to eat and nothing to burn—there's a noble way of life for you! Whew-oo-oo! Let it alone!—But that is what Squire Daae could not do.

'"After the winter comes the spring," he said; "after lean times come good—but we have to wait for them, we have to wait! The estate is now mort-gaged up to the hilt! We have now reached rock-bottom—and now the gold will come! At Easter!"

'I heard him muttering into the spider's web, "Industrious little weaver! You teach me per-severance! When your web is split in two, you begin again from the beginning and complete your task! Once more it is broken, and undismayed you set to again, right from the start!—Perseverance! That is what one must learn! That is what pays in the end!"

'It was Easter Morning, the bells were ringing,

315

the sun was playing in the sky. In a fever-heat, he had kept watch, heating and cooling, mixing and distilling. I heard him sigh like a soul in despair, I heard him pray, I felt him hold his breath. The lamp had gone out, but he did not notice it; I puffed into the glowing coals, and they shone in his death-white face so that it took on a gleam of colour; his eyes were hidden in their deep sockets, but now they grew bigger and bigger, as if they would pop right out.

'Look at that alchemist's glass! There is something gleaming inside it! Something glowing, pure and heavy! He raised it with trembling hand, he cried with quavering tongue, "Gold! Gold!" With that, his head swam, and I could have blown him over,' said the wind, 'but I blew only on the glowing coals, and went with him through the door, in to where his daughters sat and froze. His coat was smothered in ash—it hung in his beard and his tangled hair. He pulled himself up to his full height, and held up his precious treasure in the fragile glass. "I've found it! I've done it!—Gold!" he cried, raising the glass which gleamed in the rays of the sun. His hand trembled, and the alchemist's glass fell to the floor and burst into a thousand splinters—and with it burst the last bubble of hope for his future happiness. Whew-oo-oo! Away, away!—And away I swept from the gold-maker's manor.

'Late in the year, in the short winter days of the north, when the mist comes with its damp cloth and wrings out wet drops on the red berries and the leafless branches, I came in a fresh breezy humour, sweeping the sky clean and cracking the rotten branches—no very hard work, but a job that has to be done. There was a clean sweep of another kind at Borreby Manor, the home of Valdemar Daae. His old enemy, Ove Ramel from Basness, was there with the mortgage he had bought on the house and the furniture. I drummed on the cracked window-panes, I slammed the delapidated doors, I whistled through rifts and cracks—whew-ee! Master Ove should have no desire to stay there. Ide and Anna Dorothea wept bitterly; Johanne stood stiff and pale, biting her thumb until it bled —a lot of help that was! Ove Ramel was prepared to let Squire Daae remain at the manor for the rest of his life, but he got no thanks for the offer. I was listening to them—I saw the landless squire pull himself up more proudly and toss his head; and I tossed a roof towards the courtyard and the old lime-trees so that the stoutest branch cracked— and it wasn't rotten either. It lay in front of the gateway like a great beesom, should anyone want to sweep the path clear—and it was swept clear: I thought it would be.

'It was a hard day, a difficult hour, but they endured it with grim courage and heads held high.

'They had nothing left but the clothes upon their backs—yes, and an alchemist's glass recently bought and filled with what had been spilt and scraped off the floor, the treasure that had been so full of promise and disappointment. Valdemar Daae put it inside his cloak, and taking his staff in his hand, the once wealthy squire and his three daughters walked out of Borreby Manor. I blew coldly on his hot cheeks, I caressed his grey beard and his long white hair, I sang as well as I could, "Whew-oo-oo! Away, away!" It was the end of their wealth and their splendour.

'Ide and Anna Dorothea walked one on either side of him; Johanne turned round in the gateway —what was the good of it? Fortune would not turn round. As she looked back at the walls with their red stone from the castle of Marsk Stig, did she think of his daughters?—

> '"The eldest took the youngest's hand;
> Wide into the world they went!"

Did she think of that song? Here were the three of them—their father with them—trudging along the road where they had so often driven in their coach. They trudged with their father like beggars to Smidstrup Mark, to the mud and wattle cottage, rented for ten marks a year, their new country seat where the rooms and the pots stood empty. Crows and jackdaws flew over their heads, screeching in mockery, "Off your nest! Off your nest! Off, off!" just as the birds had screeched in Borreby Wood when the trees were felled.

'Squire Daae and his daughters understood them well enough: I blew about their ears, for it was not worth listening to.

'And so they entered that mud-built cottage at Smidstrup Mark.—And I swept away over moor and field, through naked hedgerows and bare woods, to open seas and other lands. Whew-oo-oo! Away, away! And year after year the same!'

What happened to Valdemar Daae, what happened to his daughters? The wind will tell you.

'The last one of them I saw—and this was the last time I saw her—was Anna Dorothea, the pale hyacinth. She was old and bent then: it was half a century later. She lived the longest, she knew the whole story.

'Over on the heath, near the town of Viborg, lay the dean's grand new country house, with red brick and stepped gables, and smoke curling out of the chimney. His gentle wife and her fair daughters sat in the bay-window looking out over the box-thorn in the garden to the brown heath beyond: what were they looking at there? They were looking at the stork's nest over there on that tumble-down cottage. The thatch was overgrown with moss and house-leek—where there was any thatch left, that is, for there was little other covering than the stork's nest, and that was the only part of it in good repair —the stork looked after that.

'The cottage was all right to look at, but it wouldn't do to touch it; I had to go carefully,' said the wind. 'The cottage was allowed to stand for the sake of the stork's nest, for without it, it would have been nothing but an eyesore on the heath. The dean's family did not want to drive the stork away, and so they let the hovel remain, and the poor creature within was allowed to go on living there; and for that she could thank the bird of Egypt—or was it her reward because she once pleaded for his wild black brother's nest in Borreby Wood? Then,

319

poor thing, she was a young child, a fine pale hyacinth in a lordly garden-plot. She remembered it all, did Anna Dorothea.

'"Oh, oh!" Yes, people can sigh, even as the wind can in the reeds and rushes. "Oh!—No bells rang over your grave, Valdemar Daae! No poor school-boys sang when the former Lord of Borreby was laid to earth!—Oh, everything has an end, even misery!—Sister Ide became a peasant's wife: that was the hardest thing our father had to bear! His daughter's husband a wretched serf who could be set at his master's pleasure to ride the hard plank of the punishment horse!—He is under the earth now, isn't he? And you, too, Ide?—Yes, oh yes, it isn't over yet, poor wretched old creature that I am! Open the gates for me, in thine abundant goodness, O Christ!"

'That was Anna Dorothea's prayer in that pitiful cottage that was allowed to stand for the stork's sake.

'The most spirited of the sisters I took care of myself,' said the wind. 'She altered her clothes, and with her mind resolute, she went dressed as a poor lad and signed on with a skipper. She was sparing with her words and sullen of expression, but willing at her work; she could not climb, however,—so I blew her overboard before anyone got to know that she was a woman, and I'm sure I did the right thing,' said the wind.

'It was one Easter Morning, the day Valdemar Daae believed he had found the red gold, that I heard underneath the stork's nest a psalm being sung within those frail walls—it was Anna Dorothea's last song.

'There was no glass in the window, there was only a hole in the wall. The sunshine came and shone inside like a nugget of gold, with such a brightness! Her eyes glazed and her heart broke—they would have done anyway, even if the sun had not shone upon her that morning.

'The stork gave her a roof over her head until her dying day! I sang by her grave!' said the wind. 'I sang by her father's grave—I know where it is, and where her grave is, too, but no one else does.

'New times, other times! The old highway has given place to enclosed fields; long preserved graves are now a country road—and soon steam will come with its row of carriages and rush over the graves, as forgotten now as the names they bore. Whew-oo-oo! Away, away!

'That is the story of Valdemar Daae and his daughters. The rest of you may tell it better if you can!' said the wind as it turned round.

It was gone.

321

THE BISHOP OF BØRGLUM
AND HIS KINSMAN

WE are now up in the north of Jutland, with the wild marshes right in front of us. We can hear the sound of the North Sea; we can tell from the rolling of the breakers that it is quite near at hand. A great sand-dune rises before us; we have seen it for a long time, and we are still driving towards it, but we drive slowly in the deep sand. On top of the sand-dune lies a great old building, Børglum Abbey, its largest wing still in use as the parish church. We now come up to the top of the hill in the late evening, but the weather is clear and the nights are light; you can see far and wide all round you, down over field and marsh to Aalborg Fjord, away over moor and meadow to the dark-blue sea.

Now we are up here, we rumble in between barn and granary, and swing round into the gateway of the ancient fortress, where lime-trees stand in rows along the wall—they are sheltered from wind and weather here, and they grow so well that their branches nearly hide the windows.

We go up the stone-built winding stairs, we go down the long passage under the beamed ceiling, and the wind whistles here so strangely—outside or inside, you don't really know where—and then old tales are told. Yes, you may say a great deal, and see a great deal, when you are afraid or want to make others afraid. The old canons, they say, long since dead, glide past us into the church where they sing mass—you can hear it in the soughing of the wind. You grow so strangely attuned to it, thinking of olden times, that you really think you are back in those days.

—There is a wreck off the coast; the bishop's people are down there, and they don't spare those whom the sea has spared; the waves wash away the red blood from the cracked skulls. Shipwrecked goods are claimed by the bishop, and there are plenty of them. The tide rolls up barrels and casks full of choice wine for the abbey cellars, already filled with ale and mead. The kitchens, too, are full —with slaughtered beasts, with sausages and hams, while in the fish-ponds outside swim fat bream and delicious carp. The Bishop of Børglum is a powerful man—he has land in his possession and would gain more. Everything must give way for Oluf Glob. His wealthy kinsman lies dead in Thy, and the widow he has left behind may well learn the truth of the saying, 'Close kin is worst enemy.' Her husband was lord of all the land thereabouts, except what belongs to the Church. Her son is in foreign lands; he was sent abroad when quite a boy to learn foreign ways, for this was what he had set his mind upon. Nothing has been heard of him for years; perhaps he lies in his grave, and will never come home again to rule where his mother now rules.

'What, shall a woman rule the land?' says the bishop. He sends her a summons to appear before the Thing—but what good will that do him?.She would never yield to the law, and her position will be strong because her cause is just.

Bishop Oluf of Børglum, what mischief are you meditating? What are you writing on that smooth parchment? What does it hide under ·seal and ribbon as you give it to rider and servant, who ride away with it out of the land, a long way off, to the city of the Pope?

It is the time of falling leaves and wrecked ships; freezing winter is now coming.

Twice it came, and now at last it comes again with a welcome to rider and servant returning home from Rome with a Papal Bull, a Bull of Excommunication against the widow who dared to offend the holy bishop. 'A curse be upon her and all that is hers! Let her be expelled from Church and congregation! Let none offer her a helping hand; let friends and kinsfolk shun her like plague and leprosy!'

'What will not bend must be broken!' says the Bishop of Børglum.

They abandon her every one; but she does not abandon her faith in God—He is her shield and defence.

One single servant, an old woman, remains true to her; with her she follows the plough, and the

corn grows, although the soil lies under the curse
of Pope and bishop.

'Offspring of hell! I shall get my way yet!' says
the Bishop of Børglum. 'I'll get a writ against you,
and with the Pope's hand bring you to judgement!'

So she harnesses the last two oxen she possesses,
mounts the cart with her maid, and drives away
over the moors right out of Denmark. She comes
as a stranger to strange folk, who speak a strange
tongue and follow strange customs—far away where
the green hills rise into the mountains and the vine
grows. Merchants come travelling past them, keep-
ing an anxious eye on their heavily laden wagons,
and fearful of being attacked by men of the robber-
barons. But the two poor women have nothing to
fear as they drive their wretched cart, drawn by its
two black oxen, along the dangerous sunken roads

325

and through the thick forests. They are in Franconia. And here they meet a handsome knight with twelve mail-clad followers. He pulls up and looks at that odd conveyance; he asks the two women where they are bound for and what land they have come from. The younger of them mentions Thy in Denmark, and speaks of her sorrow and misery—but the Lord has led her to the end of her troubles, for the strange knight is her son. He stretches out his arms to her and embraces her. His mother weeps—that is something she has not been able to do for years, though she has often bitten her lips until the warm blood trickled down.

It is the fall of the leaf, the time for wrecks; the sea rolls casks of wine on to the beach for the bishop's cellar and kitchen, where game is sizzling on the spit over the flames. Now that winter is beginning to bite, it is more cosy indoors up there in the north. There is news: Jens Glob has returned home to Thy with his mother. Jens Glob serves a summons—he summonses the bishop to appear before the courts, ecclesiastical and royal.

'That'll do him a lot of good!' says the bishop. 'Let your suit proceed, Sir Jens!'

The leaves are falling the following year, it is the time of wrecks, and freezing winter comes again. The white bees are swarming, stinging the face until they melt.

'It's fresh out today!' say folk, when they have been outside. Jens Glob stands so deep in thought that he singes his loose-flowing gown—yes, and burns a hole in it.

'I'll get the better of you yet, Bishop of Børglum! The law cannot reach you hiding behind the Pope's skirts, but Jens Glob shall reach you!'

So he writes a letter to his brother-in-law, Oluf Hase in Salling, calling upon him to attend matins at Hvidberg Church on Christmas Eve. The bishop is to say mass there, and so he is travelling from Børglum to Thyland—and Jens Glob knows all about it.

Marsh and meadow lie covered in snow and ice; they bear both horse and rider, the whole train— bishop and priest and servant. They ride the shortest way among the brittle reeds and the melancholy sough of the wind.

Blow your brass trumpet, minstrel, clad in your foxskins! It sounds well in the clear air. And so they ride southwards over moor and marsh—the meadow-gardens of Morgan le Fay in the warm days of summer—for they are making their way to Hvidberg Church.

The wind blows its own trumpet more strongly, it blows a gale, a frightful storm that increases in violence. On they go to God's house in that God-forsaken weather. The house of God stands fast, but the mighty storm sweeps over field and marsh, over fjord and sea. The Bishop of Børglum reaches the church, but Oluf Hase can scarcely make it, however hard he rides. He appears with his men upon yonder side of the fjord to aid Jens Glob, and now the bishop is to be summoned before the Highest Judgement-Seat.

The house of God is the court of law, the altar the judge's bench; the candles are all lit in the massive brass candlesticks. The gale proclaims charge and judgement. The wind sweeps shrieking over marsh and moor, over the rolling waters: no ferry will set out to cross the fjord in such weather. Oluf Hase halts by Ottesund; there he dismisses his men, presents them with horse and coat-of-mail, and gives them leave to return home with greetings to his wife. Alone he will risk his life in the tumultuous waters, but his men will bear witness that it is not his fault that Jens Glob stands without aid in Hvidberg Church. His loyal followers will not desert him, however; they swim with him out into the deep water. All ten of them are washed away; Oluf Hase himself and two of his little boys reach the other shore; they still have twenty-odd miles to ride.

It is past midnight on Christmas Eve. The wind has fallen. The church is lit up; the bright gleam shines out through the windows over meadow and moor. Matins have long since ended; it is so still in the house of God that you can hear the wax drip from the candles on to the stone floor. And now comes Oluf Hase.

In the porch Jens Glob bids him good evening and says, 'I have now made a settlement with the bishop!'

'You've done what!' says Oluf. 'Then neither you nor the bishop shall leave this church alive!'

His sword is out of its sheath, and as Jens Glob slams the church door in his face, Oluf Hase strikes it and splinters the wood.

'Softly, softly, dear brother-in-law! First look upon the settlement! I've slain the bishop and all his men. They'll not say another word in this lawsuit—and neither will I about all the wrong that's befallen my mother.'

The burnt wicks of the candles upon the altar gleam red, but something redder gleams from the floor: there in his blood lies the bishop with cleft skull, and all his men lie slain about him: the Holy Night is silent and still.

In the evening three days later, the bells of Børglum Abbey ring for the dead: the murdered bishop and his slain men lie in state under a black canopy, the great candlesticks swathed in crape. In cloak of silver cloth, his crosier in his lifeless hand, lies the dead man, once a powerful lord. Incense is burning, monks are singing; there is a sound as of lamentation, as of the judgement of wrath and condemnation—it can be heard far and wide over the land, borne by the whistling wind; it does indeed sink to rest, but it never dies; it always rises again and sings its songs, it sings them still in our own days, it sings up here in the north of the Bishop of Børglum and his harsh kinsman; it is heard in the darkness of night, it is heard by the timorous peasant as he drives along the heavy sandy road past Børglum Abbey; it is heard by the sleepless who lie listening in the thick-walled rooms of Børglum, and there is a whisper in the long echoing passages leading to the church, its walled-up entrance long since closed, but not to the eyes of the superstitious—they see the door there still, and as it opens, candles are burning in the brass chandeliers, there is a smell of incense, the church is bright with the splendour of the past, the monks are singing mass over the murdered bishop lying there in his cloak of silver cloth with his bishop's staff in his lifeless hand, and on his pale proud brow gleams the bloody wound, gleaming like fire—the vanity of the world and its evil desires are being burnt out of him.

Sink into the grave, sink into night and forgetfulness, grim reminder from the days of old!

Listen to the gusts of wind, drowning the rolling of the sea! There is a gale out there that will cost men's lives! The sea has not changed its character with the new times in which we live. Tonight it is but a ravening mouth; tomorrow, perhaps, it will be a clear eye that will reflect your image—just as it was in those days of old that we have now buried. Sleep sweetly, if you can!

And now it is morning.

Our own times are shining sunnily into the room! The wind is still high. There is a report of a shipwreck, as in the olden days.

During the night, down there by the little fishing village of Løkken, whose red roofs we can see from the windows up here, a ship was stranded. It ran aground some distance from the shore, but the lifesaving rocket made fast a bridge of rope between the wreck and the firm land. All aboard were rescued; they came on shore and were put to bed; today they are the guests of Børglum Abbey. In those comfortable rooms they will find hospitality and kind looks, and be greeted in their own tongue. The piano plays tunes from their own country, and before it stops, another wire plays, soundless and yet ringing with reassurance: tidings reach the homes of the ship-wrecked men abroad announcing their safety. Then with light hearts, they can celebrate in the evening, and dance a measure in the servants' hall of Børglum. In these days of ours we shall waltz and dance old country dances; songs will be sung about Denmark, and we shall sing 'The Brave Soldier'.

Blessed be the times we live in! Ride to town, summer, on the cleansed currents of the air! Let your sun-beams shine into our hearts and thoughts! The dark legends from the hard harsh days of long ago drift past against the background of your brightness.

WHAT THE THISTLE LIVED
TO SEE

A BEAUTIFUL well-kept garden with rare trees
and flowers adjoined the wealthy manor-house:
guests at the manor exclaimed in rapture over it;
people from the country-side and market-towns
round about came on Sundays and holidays and
asked permission to see the garden; whole schools
arrived on similar visits.

Just outside the garden, up against the fence that
separated it from the field-path, stood a great thistle:
several stems sprang from its roots, and it was so
big and spread so wide that it could very well have
been called a thistle-bush. No one looked at it
except the old donkey that drew the float for the
milk-maids. He stretched out his neck towards the
thistle and said, 'You are beautiful! I could eat
you!' But the tether was not long enough for the
donkey to be able to reach it.

There was a big party at the manor with aristo-
cratic relatives from the capital and charming young
girls. Among them was a young lady from far away:
she came from Scotland, and was well-born and
richly endowed with goods and gold, a bride well
worth having, as a number of young gentlemen
remarked—and their mothers as well.

The young folk romped on the lawn and played
croquet; they walked among the flowers, and each
of the young girls picked a flower and set it in a
young gentleman's button-hole; but the young Scots
lady looked round for a long time, unable to find
what she wanted, for none of the flowers seemed to

be to her taste. Then she looked over the top of the
fence. Just outside stood the big thistle-bush with
its sturdy purple flowers. She smiled as she saw
them, and asked the son of the house to pick one
of them for her.

'It's the flower of Scotland!' she said. 'It has a place of honour in my country's coat-of-arms. Get one for me!'

And he fetched her the finest of the flowers and pricked his fingers as though it grew on the sharpest of rose-thorns.

She set the thistle flower in the young man's button-hole, and he felt highly honoured. Every one of the other young gentlemen would gladly have given his own choice bloom to have it, given, as it was, by the young Scots lady's own fair hands. And if the son of the house felt honoured, what did the thistle feel? It was as if dew and sunshine went right through it.

'There must be something more about me than I realize!' it said to itself. 'I suppose I really belong inside the fence and not outside. We find ourselves in strange situations in this world! But now I've one of my own children on the other side of the fence, and, what's more, in a button-hole, too!'

It told every bud that came out and unfolded what had happened, and before many days had gone by, the thistle-bush heard—not from people, nor from the twittering of the birds, but from the air itself that holds sound and carries it far and wide, right from the garden's most hidden walks and the rooms of the manor where windows and doors stood open—that the young gentleman who received the thistle flower at the hand of the fair young lady from Scotland, had now received her hand itself, and her heart with it. They were a fine couple, a good match.

'And I joined them together!' reflected the thistle, thinking of the flower it gave for the button-hole. Every flower that came out was told all about it.

'I'm sure to be planted inside the garden!' thought the thistle. 'Perhaps set in a pot that's too tight—and that, of course, is the greatest honour of all!'

And the thistle-bush pictured it all so vividly that it said with complete conviction, 'Yes, I shall be put in a pot!'

It promised every little thistle flower that came out that it should be put in a pot, too, perhaps in a button-hole—the very highest position it could reach. But none was put in a pot, let alone a button-hole; they drank air and light, they basked in sunshine by day and bathed in dew by night, they came into full flower and were visited by bees and flies who were looking for honey, the flowers' dowry. And the honey they took, but the flower they let stand. 'The pack of thieves!' said the thistle-bush. 'If only I could spike them!—But I can't.'

The flowers hung their heads and wilted, but new ones came in their place.

'You come as if you'd been called!' said the thistle-bush. 'Every minute I expect to find us on the other side of the fence.'

A couple of innocent daisies and plantains stood listening in deep admiration and believed everything it said.

By the side of the path the old donkey from the milk-float looked at the flowering thistle-bush out of the corner of his eye, but his tether was too short to reach it.

And the thistle thought so long about the Thistle of Scotland, reckoning it must be one of its relations, that at last it fully believed that it had itself come from Scotland and that its parents had actually grown in that kingdom's coat-of-arms. That was a great thought—but a great thistle can surely have a great thought!

'One is often of such a distinguished family that one dare not acknowledge the fact!' said the nettle that grew close by: it had some sort of idea that it could be made into nettle-cloth if it were properly handled.

And the summer went by, and the autumn went by; the leaves fell off the trees, the flowers were strong in colour and more delicately perfumed. The gardener's apprentice sang in the garden on the other side of the fence,

'Up the hill, and down the hill—
That's what life is, and will be still!'

The young fir-trees in the woods were beginning to long for Christmas, but Christmas was still a long way off.

'Here I am, still standing where I was!' said the thistle. 'It's just as if no one had given me a thought, and yet I'm the one who brought about the match: they were engaged and they had their wedding a week ago now. Well, I shall take no steps—I can't, anyway.'

Several more weeks went by. The thistle stood there with its last single flower, which had come out near the root, in full bloom. The wind blew cold over it, its colours faded and its splendour passed; its calyx, big enough for the flower of an artichoke, appeared like a silvered sunflower. Then the young couple, now man and wife, came into the garden: they walked along by the fence, and the lady looked over the top of it.

'The big thistle's still standing there!' she said. 'But it no longer has any flowers!'

'Yes, it has—there's the ghost of the last one!' he said, as he pointed to the silvery remnant of the flower, itself a flower.

'It's very lovely!' she said. 'We must have one like it carved on the frame of our picture!'

And the young man had to climb over the fence once again and break off the calyx of the thistle. It pricked his fingers—after all, he had called it 'the ghost'. And it was taken into the garden, and into the house, and then into the hall. A painting stood there—'The Young Married Couple'. In the bridegroom's button-hole a thistle was painted. They talked about it, and they talked about the calyx they had just brought in, the last flower of the thistle, now gleaming like silver, which was to be copied in the carving of the frame.

And the air carried the story outside, far and wide.

'What one can live to see!' said the thistle-bush. 'My first-born in a button-hole, my last-born in a picture-frame! What shall I come to, I wonder?'

And the donkey stood by the side of the path and looked at it out of the corner of his eye.

'Come to me, my sweet morsel! I can't come to you—my tether isn't long enough!'

But the thistle-bush did not answer: it stood there deeper and deeper in thought: it thought and it thought—right up to Christmas-time—and then its thought blossomed.

'When her children are well over the fence, a mother has to put up with being left outside!'

'That's quite a good thought!' said the sunbeam. 'But you shall have a good place, too!'

337

'In a pot or a frame?' asked the thistle.
'In a story!' said the sunbeam.
And here it is!

THE GARDENER AND THE FAMILY

Five or six miles from the capital stood an old manor house with its thick walls, towers, and stepped gables.

There lived here, but only in the summer-time, however, a rich and noble family. This manor was the finest and most beautiful of all the manors they owned: it looked brand-new outside, and it was cosy and comfortable within. The family coat-of-arms was carved in stone over the entrance, lovely roses entwined themselves about the shield and the oriel window above, and spacious lawns were spread before the house. There were red and white hawthorns, there were rare flowers—even outside the greenhouse.

The family had, too, a skilful and hard-working gardener; the flower-garden, the orchard, and the kitchen-garden were a joy to look at. Immediately beyond was still another part of the original old gardens of the manor, separated by hedges of box clipped to form crowns and pyramids. Behind these stood two old and mighty trees; they were always nearly completely leafless, and you might easily have persuaded yourself that a gale or a waterspout had bespattered them with great clumps of dung, but each clump was really a bird's nest.

Here, from time out of mind, a swarm of screeching rooks and crows had built: it was a complete bird town, and the birds were the nobility thereabouts, the owners of the property, the estate's oldest line, the real masters of the manor. They did not concern themselves with the people down below, but they tolerated those earth-bound creatures, despite the fact that, from time to time, they let off noisy guns sending shivers down the birds' spines so that they flew up in terror and screamed, 'Caw! Caw!'

The gardener often spoke to his master and mistress about having the old trees cut down—they did not look well, and if they were done away with they would most probably be free of the screeching birds who would find some other place to settle in. But the family would not hear of it: they would part with neither trees nor birds; the manor must not be deprived of them; they were something from olden times, and the past must not be entirely wiped out.

'The trees have now become the birds' heritage: let them keep it, my good Larsen!'

The gardener was called Larsen, but that's by the way and has no further significance.

'Haven't you, my dear Larsen, enough space to work in with the whole of the flower-garden, the greenhouses, the orchard, and the kitchen-garden?'

He had indeed—he tended them, looked after them and cared for them with zeal and diligence, and the family recognized it, but they did not hide from him the fact that when they went visiting they often ate fruit and saw flowers that surpassed those which they had in their own garden, and that grieved the gardener, for he wanted to produce the best and he did all he could to get it. He was a good man at heart and good at his job.

One day the master and mistress sent for him and told him in all kindness and courtesy that the day before, at the house of distinguished friends, they had had varieties of apple and pear so juicy and so delicious that they and all the other guests had exclaimed in admiration. These fruits were obviously not home-grown, but they ought to be introduced into the country and naturalized if the climate would permit it. They were known to have been bought in town at the most expensive fruiterer's: the gardener must ride over and find out where those apples and pears had come from, and then write for cuttings.

The gardener knew the fruiterer well, for he was the very man to whom he sold, on behalf of the family, the surplus fruit from the manor garden.

And the gardener went off to town and asked the fruiterer where he had got those highly praised apples and pears from:

341

'Why, they're from your own garden!' said the fruiterer, and showed him both the apples and the pears, which he recognized.

Well, what a happy man the gardener was! He hastened back to the manor and told them that both the apples and the pears were from their own garden.

That the family could not believe. 'It isn't possible, Larsen! Can you get a written assurance from the fruiterer?'

That he certainly could: he brought them a certificate in writing.

'Well, that is extraordinary!' said the family.

Large bowls of these magnificent apples and pears from their own garden were now placed every day upon the family's table; the fruit was sent by the bushel and the barrel to friends in town and out of town, yes, even abroad. It gave the family great pleasure! Though they found it necessary to add that there had been two remarkably good summers for tree-fruit, which had done well everywhere in the country.

Some time passed, and then one day the family lunched at Court. The day after, the gardener was sent for by the master and mistress. They had had melons at the royal table, such juicy, delicious ones from Their Majesties' greenhouse.

'You must go to the Court gardener, my good Larsen, and get us some of the seeds from these expensive melons!'

'But the Court gardener got his seeds from us!' replied the gardener, quite delighted.

'Then the man knew how to bring the fruit on and improve it!' answered the master. 'Every melon was excellent!'

'Well, then I've good reason to be proud of myself!' said the gardener. 'For I must tell your Lordship that the Palace gardener had no luck this year with his melons, and when he saw how well ours were growing and tasted them, he ordered three of them for the Palace!'

'Larsen, you don't imagine they were the melons from our garden!'

'I think they were!' said the gardener, and he went to the Palace gardener and got from him written evidence that the melons on the royal table had come from the manor.

It was really a great surprise for the family—and there was no secret made of the story—when the testimonial was displayed, and the melon-seeds

343

were sent far and wide, just as cuttings had been earlier.

They had news of them that they had taken, that the fruit had set and was quite outstanding, and that it had been called after the family's manor, and so, as a result, its name could be read in English, German, and French.

They had never imagined that that could happen.

'Let's hope the gardener doesn't get too big ideas about himself!' said the family.

But he took it quite differently: all his efforts were now directed towards gaining recognition as one of the best gardeners in the country; every year he endeavoured to produce something to surpass all the other garden varieties, and this he did; and yet he frequently heard them say that the very first fruit he had produced, the apples and the pears, were really his best and far exceeded his later varieties. The melons were certainly very good, but they were in a very different category; his strawberries might be considered admirable, and yet no better than other country houses produced; and then, one year, his radishes failed, and then they talked of nothing but the unlucky radishes and made no mention of his successes.

It was almost as if the family found some relief in saying, 'It wasn't a good year, my dear Larsen!' They were quite pleased to be able to say, 'It wasn't a good year!'

A couple of times a week the gardener brought fresh flowers up into the sitting-room. They were always beautifully arranged, and from the way they were grouped together, their colours stood out as though in a stronger light.

'You've taste, Larsen!' said the master. 'It's a gift which comes from God, not from yourself!'

One day the gardener came in with a great crystal bowl: a water-lily leaf lay in it, and on it was placed, with its long thick stalk down in the water, a radiant blue flower, as big as a sunflower.

'The Indian lotus!' exclaimed the family.

They had never seen such a flower: during the day it was moved into the sunshine, and in the evening set in the reflected light of a lamp. Everyone who saw it found it remarkably rare and beautiful—yes, even the most distinguished young lady of the land said so, the princess herself, wise and good-hearted.

The master made it a point of honour to present her with the flower, and it went up to the palace with the princess.

The master and mistress now went down into the garden to pick a flower of the same kind themselves, if one were still to be found, but it was not. So they called the gardener and asked him where he had got the blue lotus from.

'We've looked in vain!' they said. 'We've been in the greenhouses and all round the flower-garden!'

'No, indeed, it's not there!' said the gardener. 'It's only a common flower from the kitchen-garden! But it's beautiful, isn't it? It looks as if it were a blue cactus, and yet it's only the flower of the artichoke!'

'You should have told us so in the first place!' said the master. 'We were led to believe it was a rare exotic bloom. You've made fools of us in front of the young princess! She saw the flower when she was here and thought it very beautiful; she did not

345

know it, and she's quite good at botany, though that science takes no account of common vegetables. Whatever possessed you, my good Larsen, to put a flower like that up in the sitting-room! That's the way to make us appear ridiculous!'

. And the beautiful blue flower which had been brought from the kitchen-garden was banished from the family sitting-room where it did not belong. The master even apologized to the princess and told her that the flower was only a vegetable that the gardener had taken it into his head to display, and that he had been seriously reprimanded for it.

'That was a shame and most unjust!' said the princess. 'For he has certainly opened our eyes to a magnificent flower we had never noticed before; he has shown us beauty where we never thought to find it! As long as artichokes are in bloom, the Palace gardener shall bring me one up to my room every day!'

And it was done.

The family gave the gardener to understand that he might once more bring them a fresh artichoke flower.

'After all, it is beautiful!' they said. 'Extremely remarkable!' And the gardener was praised.

'Larsen likes that!' said the family. 'He's a spoilt child!'

In the autumn there was a dreadful gale; it sprang up late at night with such violence that many great trees on the outskirts of the woods were torn up by the roots, and to the great sorrow of the family—'sorrow' was the very word they used—but to the joy of the gardener, the two great trees with all the birds' nests were blown down. The screeching of the rooks and crows was heard above the gale, and the people in the manor said they beat the window-panes with their wings.

'Well, now you're happy, Larsen!' said the master. 'The gale has felled the trees and the birds have gone off to the woods. There's nothing to be seen of the old days now; every trace, every hint has disappeared! It's made us sad!'

The gardener said nothing, but he was thinking, as he had been doing for a long time, how he could best make use of that fine sunny patch which, until now, had been out of his control: he would make it the pride of the garden and the joy of the family.

The great trees had, in their fall, crushed and broken down the age-old box-hedges with all their carefully clipped forms. In their place he raised a thicket of wild native plants from the fields and woodlands.

What no other gardener had thought of planting, in rich abundance, in his master's garden, he set here, each plant in the kind of soil it should have, and each in shade or sunshine according to its kind. He tended them with loving care, and they grew luxuriantly.

The juniper from the moors of Jutland grew in shape and colour like an Italian cypress; the holly with its glossy prickly leaves, ever green in the cold of winter and the summer sun, stood there lovely to look at. In front of them grew ferns of many different kinds, some looking like the children of the palm-tree, and others like the parents of that lovely delicate plant we call maidenhair. Here stood the despised burdock, so beautiful in its freshness that it can appear to advantage in a bouquet. The burdock stood on dry soil, but lower down

where the ground was damper, the dockleaf grew,
another despised plant, and yet with its height and
mighty leaves so picturesque and lovely. Six feet
tall, with flower upon flower like a great many-
armed chandelier, rose the mullein transplanted
from the fields. Here were to be found woodruffs,
primroses, and lilies of the valley, the water-arum
and the delicate three-leaved wood-sorrel. It was
beautiful to see.

In front, supported on stretched wires, quite
small pear-trees from French soil grew in rows;
they had sunshine and good tending, and soon bore
large juicy fruit, as they do in the land they came
from.

In place of the two ancient leafless trees, he
raised a tall flagstaff where the flag of Denmark
fluttered, and close by yet another pole where, in
summer-time and harvest, the hop-bine with its
sweet-scented cone-like flowers twined, but where,
in winter, was hung up, after the old custom, a
sheaf of oats so that the birds of heaven might share
the joy and good cheer of Christmas.

'Our good Larsen's growing sentimental in his
old age!' said the family. 'But he's faithful and
devoted to us!'

Towards the New Year there appeared in one of
the capital's illustrated papers a picture of the old
manor; it showed the flagstaff and the oatsheaf for
the birds at Christmas-time, and the fact that an old
custom had been revived and honoured here was
remarked upon as particularly fitting for the old
manor: it was—and the paper stressed the point—
a beautiful thought.

'Everything that that Larsen does,' said the
family, is praised to high heaven. He's a lucky

man! Why, we may almost be proud that we have him!'

But they were not a bit proud of it! They were very conscious that they were the family. They could give Larsen notice, but they didn't, for they were kind people: there are very many kind people of their sort, and that is very gratifying for the Larsens of the world.

Well, that's the story of 'The Gardener and the Family'.

Now you can think it over!

GEORGE ELIOT	Daniel Deronda
	The Lifted Veil and Brother Jacob
	Middlemarch
	The Mill on the Floss
	Silas Marner
SUSAN FERRIER	Marriage
ELIZABETH GASKELL	Cranford
	The Life of Charlotte Brontë
	Mary Barton
	North and South
	Wives and Daughters
GEORGE GISSING	New Grub Street
	The Odd Woman
THOMAS HARDY	Far from the Madding Crowd
	Jude the Obscure
	The Mayor of Casterbridge
	The Return of the Native
	Tess of the d'Urbervilles
	The Woodlanders
WILLIAM HAZLITT	Selected Writings
JAMES HOGG	The Private Memoirs and Confessions of a Justified Sinner
JOHN KEATS	The Major Works
	Selected Letters
CHARLES MATURIN	Melmoth the Wanderer
WALTER SCOTT	The Antiquary
	Ivanhoe
	Rob Roy
MARY SHELLEY	Frankenstein
	The Last Man

Women's Writing 1778–1838

JAMES BOSWELL — **Life of Johnson**

FRANCES BURNEY — **Cecilia**
Evelina

JOHN CLELAND — **Memoirs of a Woman of Pleasure**

DANIEL DEFOE — **A Journal of the Plague Year**
Moll Flanders
Robinson Crusoe

HENRY FIELDING — **Joseph Andrews** and **Shamela**
Tom Jones

WILLIAM GODWIN — **Caleb Williams**

OLIVER GOLDSMITH — **The Vicar of Wakefield**

ELIZABETH INCHBALD — **A Simple Story**

SAMUEL JOHNSON — **The History of Rasselas**

ANN RADCLIFFE — **The Italian**
The Mysteries of Udolpho

SAMUEL RICHARDSON — **Pamela**

TOBIAS SMOLLETT — **The Adventures of Roderick Random**
The Expedition of Humphry Clinker

LAURENCE STERNE — **The Life and Opinions of Tristram**
Shandy, Gentleman
A Sentimental Journey

JONATHAN SWIFT — **Gulliver's Travels**
A Tale of a Tub and Other Works

HORACE WALPOLE — **The Castle of Otranto**

MARY WOLLSTONECRAFT — **Mary** and **The Wrongs of Woman**
A Vindication of the Rights of Woman

The Oxford World's Classics Website

www.worldsclassics.co.uk

- Information about new titles
- Explore the full range of Oxford World's Classics
- Links to other literary sites and the main OUP webpage
- Imaginative competitions, with bookish prizes
- Peruse the Oxford World's Classics Magazine
- Articles by editors
- Extracts from Introductions
- A forum for discussion and feedback on the series
- Special information for teachers and lecturers

www.worldsclassics.co.uk

American Literature

British and Irish Literature

Children's Literature

Classics and Ancient Literature

Colonial Literature

Eastern Literature

European Literature

History

Medieval Literature

Oxford English Drama

Poetry

Philosophy

Politics

Religion

The Oxford Shakespeare

A complete list of Oxford Paperbacks, including Oxford World's Classics, Oxford Shakespeare, Oxford Drama, and Oxford Paperback Reference, is available in the UK from the Academic Division Publicity Department, Oxford University Press, Great Clarendon Street, Oxford OX2 6DP.

In the USA, complete lists are available from the Paperbacks Marketing Manager, Oxford University Press, 198 Madison Avenue, New York, NY 10016.

Oxford Paperbacks are available from all good bookshops. In case of difficulty, customers in the UK can order direct from Oxford University Press Bookshop, Freepost, 116 High Street, Oxford OX1 4BR, enclosing full payment. Please add 10 per cent of published price for postage and packing.